THE MECHANIC

THE MECHANIC

A Novel

ALAN GOLD

YUCCA

Yucca Publishing books may be purchased in bulk at special discounts for sales promotion, corporate gifts, fund-raising, or educational purposes. Special editions can also be created to specifications. For details, contact the Special Sales Department, Yucca Publishing, 307 West 36th Street, 11th Floor, New York, NY 10018 or yucca@skyhorsepublishing.com.

Yucca Publishing® is an imprint of Skyhorse Publishing, Inc.®, a Delaware corporation.

Visit our website at www.yuccapub.com.

10 9 8 7 6 5 4 3 2 1

Library of Congress Cataloging-in-Publication Data is available on file.

Jacket design by Slobodan Cedic at KPGS
Jacket photo: PlusONE/Bigstock

Print ISBN: 978-1-63158-085-7
Ebook ISBN: 978-1-63158-092-5

Printed in the United States of America

THE MECHANIC

PROLOGUE

Cape Cod, October, 1998

THE GRAVE LINE OF mourners approached the freshly cut pit, their faces drawn and haggard through grief and wind as they followed the coffin from the church.

Newly cleft earth glistened; sods of clay wept thin brown tears while a gusty squall made the mourners unseasonably cold that October morning, with a chill that cut to their bones.

The wind blew up stronger and stronger from the Atlantic, over the Sound, gathered grit as it dusted the sand dunes on its way inland, and then eddied up and over the fence which separated the cemetery from the beach.

Gray elderly men in Homburgs, snug tailored overcoats, and black woolen scarves stood close beside dignified women wrapped in politically incorrect but protective fur coats. Whipped by the wind, the line of mourners came to a standstill and waited an interminable time as the priest made his appearance. They huddled into themselves, waiting for him to gather himself at the foot of the grave, open his prayer book against the strength of the coming gale, straighten out his cassock, and look up solemnly at the assembled company. This was his moment. His was the intercession between the soul and the deity, and though he'd never had a congregation as important as these before, they would wait upon him.

And still they stood, looking like penguins on Antarctic ice as they turned their backs away from the direction of the sea and stared into the yawning maw of the grave.

But it wasn't just the elderly who were so badly distressed by the wind. The younger men and women, whose bodies were not as easily prey to the biting Atlantic gusts, were soon affected by the wind chill. The enveloping warmth of the chapel had quickly evaporated when they stepped out into the winter air, and the younger members of the congregation regretted not wearing heavy overcoats but instead having chosen dark gray suits or dresses and black armbands.

The priest opened his mouth to read, but delayed a moment as his cassock fluttered like a noisy flag. He had been going to say something for each of the important people to remember as he walked slowly ahead of the bier proceeding to the grave. Instead, he decided to remain silent and portentous, to save his words until all were giving him their full attention. Now, as the coffin waited to be lowered into the ground, as he began his homily, because of the wind, he had to speak louder than normal so his words could be heard over the rising tempo of Nature.

He was conscious of the importance of the gathering, of the honor to him of burying such a venerable and respected member of the congregation, a leading figure in American life for the better part of the century, and his voice took on an unusually sententious ring.

A young woman, the granddaughter of the man in the coffin, exhausted from jetlag through her sudden departure from Europe, clutched the arm of her father to steady herself. She was on the verge of sobbing as the coffin settled into the bottom of the grave and the ropes and straps were pulled away. They made a hollow sound, as if there were nothing down below but an empty box. The granddaughter was utterly drained of the energy; she needed to resist the urge to cry. On the flight over, she'd thought she could cope with the formalities of the service, but she hadn't seen her grandfather for over a year and the last time she'd kissed him, she knew she'd never see him again.

The flight from Sarajevo had been long and hard. She'd thought about not rushing home to attend the funeral, because even though she loved the old man dearly, she felt guilty about leaving her colleagues to attend to the mass of details in the War Crimes Tribunal dealing with the butchers.

But Chasca Broderick had loved her grandfather. Although he had been ninety-seven when she'd last seen him, blind and confined to a wheelchair, through all her growing up he had been the most entertaining, loving, and dearest of all her relatives. His position as a Supreme Court Justice under Kennedy had been the defining reason she'd gone to Harvard to study law; and his bent for matters of social justice had convinced her not to enter some Wall Street legal practice and become a wealthy corporate lawyer, but instead to become one of the underpaid and overworked legal counsel of the United Nations War Crimes Commission.

Her father, now a retired stockbroker, hadn't followed in Grandpa Theodore's footsteps and become a lawyer. Instead, he'd taken the road to financial success, trading on Theodore's potent Broderick name, becoming rich and powerful in the boardrooms of the nation. But Chasca hated money at the best of times, and resented her father's lack of appreciation of her passion for environmental law, human rights, and anti-trust legislation. That was why, when she was adult enough to be independent of her parents, she spent less time with them, and as much as possible with old Theo. She loved her parents out of duty, but in her heart it was Grandpa Theo whom she loved with a passion. When she'd been younger, in her teens, she'd longed for school holidays so that she could go and stay with the old folk at their Cape Cod home. Her parents were concerned that she was missing out on camps and times with friends, but she reveled in the times she spent with the Theo and Detta, and came back each time a wiser and more learned person.

Her fantasies were fulfilled each and every day of her holiday . . . He even let her put on his Supreme Court Justice's robes and pretend that she was the Chief Justice of America, and he was an incoming president whom she would swear in, and then she'd advise the new president on how to run the country.

When she was a young woman, expressing serious intent about studying civil liberties law, old Theo had even let her retry a couple of the famous cases which had come before him, to see whether her determination was the same as his. As she grew older, their verdicts agreed more and more frequently.

And now he was dead. Her grandmother had died ten years earlier, and the old man had detested the succession of nurses who were installed by his children and grandchildren to look after him. And what Chasca really resented was that her parents and uncles and aunts had put the old man in some impersonal and antiseptic hospice for the last months of his life when his liver and heart were failing and diabetes was setting in, instead of allowing him to die in peace, sitting in his wheelchair, looking out over his beloved brooding Sound at the ever-challenging Atlantic Ocean. She imagined how he'd been treated by the nurses in the hospice, being called "darling" and "pop," such an indignity for a man whose entire life had been a model of dignity. Barely able to speak, he must have been mortified at being unable to castigate them for their impertinence.

But now, in his final moment, he was immersed in dignity. Surrounding the grave were two serving Supreme Court Justices, the Assistant Secretary of State representing the President of the United States, the president of Princeton University where Grandfather Broderick had served as Regent, and a double row of leaders in justice, education, and government.

His death was noticed in the obituary columns of the *New York Times*, and the *Washington Post* and the *American Jewish News* had printed special feature articles about his work as an attorney in the Nuremberg Trials. She had read them all avidly, glorying in the way her grandfather's life had been led; and now she was at his grave, imagining his frail and emaciated body, once so robust, lying cold and still, already ebbing into the past.

The priest continued his address in his theatrically somnolent voice. When he'd finished, he invited the closest relatives to throw earth and flowers into the grave, as though their going first was some privilege of rank. Despite his accomplishments, her grandfather had hated rank and privilege all his life; and he would especially have hated it now. What did rank and privilege mean when everyone, regardless of rank and privilege, ended up in a coffin?

Sods were thrown on to the coffin, and the funeral came to an end, and the important people went home, and Chasca and her parents and uncles and aunts and her brother and sister and cousins, retired to old Grandpa Theodore Broderick's house, now cold and empty and smelling musty, to contemplate what was to be done with those assets which weren't already controlled by the family trust . . . assets like his library, his papers, the furniture, and the future of the house.

While they were discussing the dissection of the old man's effects, especially whether to keep the house in the family as a holiday retreat or use the land for development for a summer apartment complex, Chasca inconspicuously slipped out and wandered about the house. It was cold now, cold because death had come to the places of her upbringing, places which she knew so fondly from her childhood, which were so much a part of her past.

She touched the dark red mahogany wood of the staircase and remembered the look of horror on her grandma Detta's face as she'd spent hour after hour sliding down the long, winding banisters; and she smiled as she remembered old Theo (he insisted on her calling him Theo because he said he wouldn't live long enough for her to say the word "grandfather") reassuring his wife that the little girl was perfectly safe in his hands; she examined the patterns in the hall runner on which she and Theo had played games of softball, much to Grandma Detta's disapproval and concern for the gifts Theo had been given as part of the offices he had held; she picked up the silver salver that had served as a letter tray in the old days when a maid used to bring in the morning post over breakfast—at Detta's insistence despite Theo's disdain—and remembered clearly her childhood hopes that one day she'd be the recipient of important letters.

Chasca smiled. All she had left were memories, reminiscences which made her feel warm and comfortable in the past, distanced from the present. But for the life of her, she couldn't remember the old man's face, nor any detail of what he looked like. But that, she knew, was the way in which Nature protected the mourner. And that, in itself, was a wonderful memorial to old Theo, to be remembered for his accomplishments, his good deeds.

But despite all the diversions which memories of her youth caused, Chasca most wanted to revisit the library the old man had loved so dearly, and in which she had spent so many enjoyable hours, discussing with him the formulation of her career decision, until law and social justice became her inevitable choice.

Chasca wasn't his only grandchild, but in her heart—though he would never, ever admit it—she knew that she was his favorite. The others visited him out of duty, but he knew that her visits were eagerly sought, a reward for doing well at school. And in her days at college, she'd write to him regularly and send him messages of regard and respect from law professors who'd found out that her Broderick name came from the same family as the great and honorable Theodore Broderick, scourge of big business and organized unions and lobby groups, a man who had introduced judgments which, by most accounts, were decades ahead of their time. And she'd make irregular but welcome visits to the Cape Cod home, always dropping in on her way to and from somewhere. Her brothers and sisters and cousins never knew; but old Theo knew.

And when it was decided that she'd study law, Theo had guided her gently yet inexorably into those legal frameworks which had been designed to protect the downtrodden, the poor, the minorities. And as he'd told her more and more about the inequities of life, he'd seared her being with a rage for justice.

Oddly, her own father and mother, who wanted her to go into the family business of stock and share broking, didn't object, rationalizing that a grounding in law could qualify her for a job in broking just as well as training in finance and commerce. It was only in her third year of Harvard, when she specialized in international law and human rights, that her parents understood the enormity of the conspiracy that Chasca and old Theo had dreamed up in her holidays in the Sound; but by then she was too old to influence, and the damage was done.

Chasca sat in old Theo's chair at his desk, and determined that, despite any potential family claims, these were the items of furniture she'd be taking for her Greenwich Village apartment when eventually she returned from the hell-hole of Bosnia. She rifled through his drawers, not feeling in the least bit guilty about breaching any privacy. There was nothing in the old man's life about which he, or she, might feel remotely ashamed. She knew every moment of his existence and was aware of every friend and associate; they'd discussed his life in intricate detail. So all she was interested in were those minutiae which might have escaped his attention in the sweeping dialogues of law and human rights which they regularly conducted, especially when she became a counsel at the Department of Justice.

She was suddenly sad. Old notes, letters dated 1978, even a dry-cleaning ticket from eight years ago, bank and check statements which were ridiculously outmoded in an era of electronic banking and e-commerce.

She opened a second drawer and found similar detritus of his life.

She opened the bottom drawer. She took out a sheaf of papers. They were old, very old. She read the cover. It was written in German. She'd studied German in Harvard as one of her majors. She undid the old red ribbon. As it came away, it left a faded mark of lightness where the rest of the paper had browned through age.

Chasca scanned the first page. Then the second. It seemed to be some sort of memoir, but when she glanced through it, it took on all the cadences of a last will and testament. It was written by somebody called Joachim Gutman. She searched in her memory, but for the life of her, couldn't ever recall her grandfather mentioning his name.

Surprised, she continued reading, suddenly feeling somewhat guilty, as though she were intruding into somebody's personal life and times.

Three hours later, Chasca asked her parents and uncles and aunts to join her in the library. She showed them the testament of the unknown Jew and asked them if they had ever heard of a German who was hanged as a war criminal in 1947, a man called Wilhelm Deutch. Nobody had heard of him. Neither her parents nor their brothers or sisters had ever heard the old man mention him, despite his constant reiteration of his most famous trials and judgments.

'Well, it appears that Grandpa Theo defended this German war criminal guy called Wilhelm Deutch, when he was acting as a defender in the Nuremberg Trials just after the Second World War; apparently this man Deutch was some sort of a mechanic in the concentration camps. He wasn't a monster like Hitler or Himmler or Göring, or anything. He was just an ordinary guy, a mechanic, but the Allied authorities wanted to show the world the guilt of the majority of Germans who had fallen in with the Nazis and just co-operated, saying they were only following orders. But according to the memoirs of this Jewish gentleman, Joachim Gutman, all this guy Deutch seems to have done was twiddle the knobs on the gas ovens. From what I can tell, this was one of the last of the Nuremberg trials. And from what Gutman says in this memoir, Deutch should never have been sent to trial at all.'

She could see her mother looking at her quizzically, wondering why she was so concerned with some ancient obscure trial of Theo's when they'd just buried the old man.

'Bear with me a moment. This is very important. It seems that justice wasn't done for this mechanic, this Wilhelm Deutch. You see, when I finished reading this memoir of the concentration camps written by Mr. Gutman, I checked into Theo's records, and it appears that despite the defense, there were no witnesses who would come forward to speak on behalf of the mechanic. I've read the remarks of the trial judge, and they were pretty damning.

'Fact is, if the judge had seen this testimony from this Jewish gentleman, Deutch not only wouldn't have hanged as a war criminal, but would have been feted as a hero.'

'So?' said her father.

Chasca looked at her father in surprise. 'Dad, a huge injustice appears to have been done. A man was hanged by the Allies who shouldn't have been. According to Gutman, Mr. Deutch was anything but a mass murderer. In fact, he wasn't even rotten and evil. He tried to save Gutman's life.'

Still, her parents and the rest of the family looked at her in silence.

The gulf between them grew into a chasm. Her father smiled and said gently, 'Chasca, darling, this all happened fifty years ago. Ancient history. We've just buried your grandfather. You're naturally upset. Why don't we just come out of this room, with all its memories, and we'll drive back to Boston and stay at a lovely hotel, and we can have a crab dinner and relax.'

She was astonished by their lack of sensitivity to the injustice she'd just uncovered. But she knew them too well to think of arguing. So she looked at them, nodded slowly, and said softly, 'Okay.'

Having flown halfway around the world, and landed in Boston and then driven straight to her grandfather's funeral, she was exhausted and didn't have the energy to fight. And Chasca knew from long experience that her parents would continue their exercise in conditioning until she gave in; and currently all she wanted to do was to sleep. So she folded the old document into two, quickly wrapped the red ribbon back over it, and put it into her pocket.

As she stood from behind Theo's desk, she made a last-ditch stand so that they didn't have things all their own way. 'One thing I am going to do, and that's to send this testimony, this diary written by Joachim Gutman to Yad VaShem, the Holocaust Museum in

Jerusalem, Israel. They'll know what to do with it. Frankly, I think I should recommend that they prepare a case to have this Wilhelm Deutch, this mechanic, rehabilitated, and even considered to be named as a Righteous Gentile Among the Nations. I reckon that would be a fitting memorial for my grandfather.'

CHAPTER ONE

Palace of Justice
Nuremberg, Allied Occupied Germany
June, 1946

Notes found in the cell of Wilhelm Deutch, prisoner

Here it begins.

Here it ends.

And in the scheme of history, what does it all matter?

Take a good look at history, if you doubt me.

Humankind has been forming societies on this earth for ... what? ... say 12,000 years.

Let's ignore the time when ancient man lived in the trees, or huddled together for protection in caves from whence he ultimately emerged after a thousand millennia, grime-covered and timorous, in order to conquer the world.

Let's only include the time in which he built huts and shelters and dwelling places and did things other than hunt and fish. Let's measure the ascent of Humankind from when he started planting seeds in time and reaping the benefit of his God-given brain.

Alright, so, in mankind's 12,000 years of civilisation, how many innocent men, women, and children have been killed in warfare? How many have been slaughtered in battles between villages or cities or countries? How many have been the casualties of skirmishes between chieftains in opposing valleys who wanted access to water or grazing fields?

How many innocents have been murdered and trampled into the mud or the sand because of the self-aggrandising words of some philosopher-king who believed that everybody should bow before himself as a deity.

How many unrecorded names disappeared from the annals of history because of the Hittites or the Akkadians or the Greeks or the Romans or the Crusaders . . . ?

Ten million? Or twenty million? Who knows, maybe a hundred million.

Nobody will ever know. Yet an American judge has just dared to call me . . . what was it? Ah yes, "the personification of evil! The mechanic who ensured that the wheels of the Nazi death machine turned efficiently and remorselessly" . . . as though he would understand the concept of evil. Was he in the concentration camps? Did he see what went on in the crematoria?

Such intemperate words. Such words of condemnation from on high. But in the scheme of things, what does it all matter. In a hundred years, who will remember my name? And who will remember the name of Adolf Hitler? And who will remember the names and the faces of six million Jews? Not today; not tomorrow; but in a hundred years, a blink in the eye of history?

And so it begins. Or is here where it all ends? Is my beginning in my ending?

Now that's something to think about . . .

If he stretched out his arms, he could almost touch opposing walls. If he stood on tiptoes, he could actually touch the spider-webbed ceiling.

But he chose not to. He made the decision not to exert himself. He chose, instead, to lie on his cot and watch the spider. It was his choice. In his cell, he made the choice. Not them. In his cell, he was the master.

He lay down because he enjoyed watching a spider lying in wait for a fly. And he liked watching the fly, which had spent the past three days circumnavigating the single electric globe. It was an eternal flame, like some obeisance to a deity, alight both during the day and all throughout the night. The Jews lit candles to remember their dead. Who would light one for him? His wife? His daughter? How would he be remembered?

The light allowed the caustic eyes of the guards to invade him through their spy hole whenever they chose. But not if he ignored them! When they shifted the metal patch which covered the hole in the door, and the single jaundiced eye filled up the gap, as though staring down the barrel of a microscope, they were able to look at him . . . They thought they controlled him, but he knew that he wasn't in their thrall. He played the game of ignoring them, and during the past eleven months, they'd spied on him less and less.

His life, now, was wholly dedicated to territory. He had been arrested while queuing for food, recognised by a man he'd never before seen, a man who was more skeleton than human, whose sunken white and pallid face seemed glued on to his skull, whose arms and legs were nothing more than bones, and who looked as if the slightest stirring of dusty wind in that cold and desolate bomb-site would blow him into his grave. Yet even though the rest of the skeleton was dead, there was life in this man's eyes, rat eyes, cunning, narrow slits which took in everything; the eyes of a camp inmate, darting around to ensure his survival; eyes which were fed on the milk of hatred, on the desire for revenge. And when this man looked at him, those eyes saw and knew and remembered!

This skeleton who walked and talked, dressed in a filthy cap and torn rags, stared at him for five minutes or more, never once taking his eyes off him. And then he screamed like a woman about to be raped, and pointed a bony finger at him, and the whole world stopped and stared. Two American MPs came running up to the skeleton and listened to the broken English of his story; then they walked over to the man and hauled him out of the queue. And the next moment he was appearing before someone called a Provost Marshal, and he hadn't been allowed to contact his family, but had been rushed to this prison where he'd spent the past eleven months.

Now his life was lived almost exclusively within four dank walls. He was a creature of the guards whom he rarely saw; he would rise when they told him to, exercise when they said, eat and drink what he was given; and use words they put in his mouth. But that was only for an hour or so a day . . . for the rest of the time, for the remaining twenty-three hours, hour after hour, day after day, he'd be alone in his cell, staring at the ceiling, contemplating his fate.

He recognised that beyond his door, beyond the spy hole, they were the masters; but in his cell, he controlled the domain. And it was his claim of territory which kept him sane. For as the indisputable master of his domain, for twenty-three of the twenty-four hours of each day, he was in command! He determined the position of his desk, his writing utensils, his chair (*he could sit by the grille of the window, or near to the door, or with his feet up on his cot, as he chose*), even the position of the plates and cutlery on which his food came to him through the slats of the door, three times a day. If he chose, he could make collection difficult by placing his empty plate and cup just out of reach of the guard. If he chose.

And he was in charge of when he stood or sat, when he rose or reclined. When he was active, writing, or passive, lying and resting. But these days, respite was a thing of the past, a faded memory. Lying on a cot in the middle of the day was his defiance of them. His act of rebellion.

But only he knew that! Only he realised that it was all an external show, an act of bravura which amounted, in the long run, to nothing. For sleep was beyond him, and without rest, his mind wandered, his thoughts were always on the edge of panic, and his stomach felt as though it were full of knotted, wriggling snakes. What did they know about him which they could use against him? Of what was he to be accused? Everyone knew of the trials of the leaders of the Third Reich, and that soon the other leaders would be put up for trial and hanged . . . the judges and the businessmen and the men who controlled the Ministries and the *Einsatzgruppen* who ran the mobile killing machines, and the doctors and the other major players who had made Germany so strong before the War, yet which now made it into such a reviled nation. They had been arrested, and many would be hanged.

Leaders . . . yes! Arrest and try the leaders by all means. Arrest the men who commanded the *Einsatzgruppen*, the fearsome squads of mass-murderers who followed the German army when it invaded a town or a village and rounded up the Jews and murdered them all. Arrest them! But why him? He was a mechanic, a knob twiddler. A nobody. An ordinary German. He was told to do a job, and he did it. He obeyed the instructions; he followed orders. And now he was to be tried and, probably, hanged, because he had followed orders. It was insane.

And that had been his life for eleven months; not preparing a defense or talking to counsel, or allowed to see the charges against him; but lying in limbo, hidden from sight, removed from the world as though he were a virus, a microbe; just like Hitler had tried to do to the Jews!

The spider sat patiently in the darkened recesses which hid the corners of the cell. The fly rested occasionally upside down on the ceiling or clinging to the black and twisted cord from which the light globe was hung. Then it would launch itself at will, and fly around the room. He followed the fly. Within his cell, the fly was free, as free as him. But like him, the fly had nowhere to hide.

He kept crusts of bread from his supper to feed the fly so it wouldn't leave his cell and disappear into the outside world. He smiled when he thought about the absurdity of his situation. Both he and the spider were spending their days trying to seduce a fly.

He listened for noises in the corridor. They were the only relief from the monotony of this part of the day, the middle part between waking and going back to sleep. A time when nothing happened. The real torture of imprisonment. Even the rack or the thumbscrew would have been a welcome relief from the aching monotony of waiting and worrying about his fate.

He lay on his bunk, trying to define distant sounds. Marching feet, orders shouted, vehicles sliding to a halt on gravel in the outside world. The hysterical revving of motorcycle couriers for whom everything made way preceded by barked instructions to move along or get out of the way. American voices oddly in place in a German world.

Whenever he heard the noise of a Jeep or a tank rumbling down a road, his heart increased in pace at the thought of what was going on outside his cell, and of the life which was passing him by. The noises of the outer world defined freedom. But the thick walls of his cell defined both his status and his place.

Most often, he would hear the sounds of movement in the prison. But as they became repetitive, the daily traffic through the corridors beyond, the sounds diminished in significance. So he waited until he heard the sound of footsteps stopping outside in the corridor. Invariably it would be accompanied by the noise of the metal eye-patch scraping against the door as it was pushed to one side. Then there would be a sudden eruption of a slanting beam of dim and dusty light, which would appear out of nowhere, illuminating a patch of his cell floor; but this beam of light would quickly be broken by the unblinking eye of a guard pinpointing his position and disposition.

More control. A statement of his entrapment made without words. Then, contemptuously sliding the eye-patch shut, the guard would walk dismissively away, as though the prisoner were a mere item, a cipher, a line in the checklist of the guard's many duties.

In the morning, he would busy himself with washing and shaving, and combing his hair. Then he would open the hatch at the bottom of his iron door, another slit with which the outside world invaded his sanctuary, and he would pull in the tin tray on which his breakfast had been placed. Always the same breakfast. Even on Sunday. Two slices of bread. Plum jam. A tin mug containing tea.

He would set aside part of his breakfast bread for the time when he returned from his exercise. He was never hungry when he awoke from the fitful rest of the night, but his hunger returned with exercise. And he never saved his drink. Water was not a scarce resource, not like real coffee and real butter in the time of the Nazis. No, there was no need for him to marshal his resources and save water, because he had a tap and a drain in his cell. And so, unlike the last days of the war when there was no water to be had except for stagnant pools in Berlin drains and gutters, he didn't need to conserve liquids.

He always savoured his tea carefully, relishing it from the first sip which burnt his upper lip to the last gulp when it was already tepid. Even the pain of being burnt held its own allure. It was part of the routine; and routine was certainty in an uncertain existence.

Always tea. Not coffee, of course. Never coffee. And after all these months of imprisonment, he was beginning to appreciate the taste of the tea. At first, at the beginning, he'd been revolted by it. It was thin and devoid of any flavor, and had an aroma of being stewed and brewed as if created by someone who hated him, by some indifferent cook who took no pride in his work; reheated from previous days, or cooked in pots which still had old and decaying tea leaves stuck to their bottoms and sides. But as time wore on, and prison food and drink destroyed his taste buds and the memory of real food, the tea began to take on a flavour of its own.

Then after breakfast he would dress in his prison uniform and follow the guards from his room as they opened his and other cell doors to let his fellow prisoners out. And they would proceed obediently behind the guards, like goslings behind a mother goose.

In the beginning, all those months ago after he and the others had first been arrested and incarcerated by the Allies, their American jailers had taunted them, jeered, and spat on them like schoolyard bullies. He and the other concentration camp employees were considered as vermin, and openly ridiculed by the young American boys, not yet old enough to shave. The immature victors emasculating the once-potent losers.

But when the evidence of the crimes of their leaders—Göring and Hess and Ribbentrop and others—was unveiled to an unsuspecting and incredulous world, things changed in the demeanour of the guards. Every day, they listened in horror to the evidence enunciated through the very Oxford tones of Sir Hartley Shawcross, or the Bostonian cadences of the American Robert Jackson, and the mood of the guards changed from ridicule to contempt, and then to outright barbarity. Not even the officers wanted to hold in check the treatment the guards meted out. As the evidence of Nazi war crimes and crimes against humanity mounted, layer upon layer of evidence given by witnesses who had been dehumanised by the concentration camp guards, the anger of the American boys towards the prisoners changed from contempt to hatred. Suddenly prisoners appeared at exercise with pronounced limps, their faces and arms and legs covered with welts and bruises. And all, it appeared, were due to clumsy accidents.

And when the United States Prosecutor began giving evidence about the death camps, the covert punishment meted out by the guards, once hidden discretely behind closed doors, became open and violent. Prisoners couldn't walk outside their cells without being kicked or punched, or threatened with the muzzle of a rifle. The unofficial though righteous indignation of the guards, young boys with the downy skin of innocence, showed in their flaring nostrils as they read their American Army newspapers, as fresh evidence of the concentration camps and the mounds of bodies became public knowledge and erupted into the minds of the victors.

But the brutality of the guards lasted only for a few months. It slowly waned and ultimately died as the novelty of the crimes of the Third Reich became timeworn, until the genocide of the Jews became history and was relegated to inside pages of the newspapers of New York and London, until the concern for justice against the war criminals was replaced by hysteria over the winner of a baseball match.

And still the guards guarded the prisoners.

Not important prisoners, of course. Not men who had strutted in the mansions of the Führer Corps, or stood proudly to accept the tributes of the NSDAP or the Wehrmacht. No! Those men, Goring and

Hess and Ribbentrop and Dönitz and Keitel and the rest now were dead or buried alive . . . tried, convicted, hanged, or imprisoned for life.

And there had been other trials in the Allies's search for retribution. The victors' trials. There was the trial of the doctors and the jurists and the I. G. Farben trial . . . and now it was his trial. He and nine other engineers and guards and workers who had kept the machinery of the state running while the Army and Air Force and Navy had waged war. He and others were being tried for following orders, for making sure that the enemies of the State were incarcerated and dealt with according to the Laws of the Führer Reich.

And for that, for doing what he was ordered to do, he was being branded a war criminal. And he would hang. Because no matter what he or his defense—his American lawyer—said, there would be no justice here. This was a place for retribution. Just as the death camps of Auschwitz and Belsen and the others had been places for settling scores with the Jews who'd conspired against Germany since the time of Martin Luther, so this court at Nuremberg was the designated killing field, the Allied camp where the Nazi prisoners were concentrated, for retribution against the men who had waged war against the rest of the world . . . and for those who had been their accomplices and helped them.

Footsteps in the corridor. His head prickled at their approach. Usually they grew louder as they grew nearer, and then he felt disappointment as they disappeared and he was shrouded again in the monotony of his cell. But this time they stopped. He raised his head above the level of the rough gray woollen blanket. The sound of a key in the lock. Then a guard opened the door. The same young American boy. Or was it? They all looked the same in their dull uniforms. He stood contemptuously in the doorway. His face and the way his body slouched betrayed his boredom.

'Up!'

A single word. Designed to demean a man old enough to be his father.

'Quick, you bastard. Up!'

'May I ask why?' he asked of the young guard.

'No, you may fucking not ask why, motherfucker. Up. Time for court. Special sitting. Maybe they're gonna stretch your fucking neck. Bastard!'

The prisoner was surprised. Yesterday, they had appeared in court for the first time, and things were said, but his American lawyer had demanded that the matter be adjourned for some time in the future. It was all beyond Deutch, but now they were suddenly called again. Why?

The guard said nothing more. He just waited for the prisoner. He held him in neither greater nor lesser disrespect than any other of the prisoners in this wing. He'd been told something of what they did. Mobile killing or gassing units or something. Anyhow, the court would take care of them. He watched and waited an additional moment for the prisoner to rouse himself from the bed, and to straighten his clothes. He was being deliberately slow. As much an act of dignity as of defiance. And so to the courtroom. But the guard didn't care. The Nazi bastard would soon hang, and that would be that. So let the mother-fucker have his moment of victory.

The guard stifled a yawn. Too much beer and poker last night. This whole thing of guarding Nazis was all so second rate. So much an afterthought. If it came to an end today, nobody would notice a thing. Even the prosecutors seemed to be anxious for the show to be over. Like a five-act Broadway play which should have finished at the end of the third act, the audience was yawning and was only interested in getting home.

The prisoner joined his co-defendants as they walked behind a squad of armed guards and climbed the stairs to file into the courtroom. They knew they were all going to their deaths, but it was a moment of change, and charge was a kind of freedom.

They were instructed to sit where Göring and Dönitz and Frank had once sat, and put on their headphones. Like the leaders of the Third Reich during their trial, he and his fellow accused wore no uni-forms. They were dressed in sober business suits, as though they were in the pews of a church, listening to a preacher. But this church was all about sin and guilt, for it was the pulpit of Savonarola, and his bony finger was pointing to their culpability.

They all stood as the tribunal of judges filtered into the court to take their seats. The high and mighty of France, Britain, and Russia were sitting with the American judge as colleagues. But although it was the American's court, all the others were still judging the cogs of the machinery of the State of Germany.

The high-pitched voice of the German interpreter invaded the silence and hurt his eardrums until he adjusted the earmuffs. The words were uttered in a monotone, all the statements made about the different participants being translated by the same man; the Germans had to strain to determine who was speaking.

'Prisoners at the bar. The court is now in session. Day Two of the deliberations of the Judicial Bench of the Control Council, American Sector of the occupied former state of Germany are now proceeding. The Honourable Justice Arthur Griegson presiding. Sitting in conjunction with his Honour are judicial observers from the Allied nations of France, Great Britain, and Russia. Yes, Mr. Prosecutor. May it please Your Honour and Your Honour's colleagues. Yesterday we heard evidence of the way in which the defendants, Matern, Haubach, Fegelein, and Deutch were responsible for increasing the capacity of the ovens of the death or extermination camps at Sobibor, Treblinka, Auschwitz-Birkenau, and Belzec to deal with increasing numbers of prisoners from April 1944 onwards. Your Honours, this court has been reconvened because the Defense counsel for the prisoner Deutch wishes to make special application. Yes, Mr. Prosecutor, we have had notification from the counsel for defense for the prisoner Deutch that he wishes to challenge certain aspects of the evidence you are about to present. Sir, I'm aware of the defense challenge, and I believe that the evidence I am about to present . . .'

And so it went on. No modulation in the translator's voice. No variation when he was translating the words of different speakers.

Each statement running into the next person's statement in the same monotones enunciated by the bored translator. Sometimes, it was impossible to determine which of the speakers the translator was translating . . . Was it their defense lawyers or one of the judges . . . ?

At the beginning of their trial, all the defendants had met together in the large holding cell below the courtroom where they ate their lunch. They agreed to complain to their defense lawyers before the court resumed, but it hadn't been an easy conversation. The lawyers made it very obvious that they were representing them because they'd been appointed by the courts, and certainly not because of any love for them. And worse, there were no German advocates who would defend them, because all the available ones to the major criminals were suddenly unavailable to these defendants, who were small fry in the scheme of things.

And so they were forced to use Americans or British or, God forbid, Russians; why couldn't they have found defense lawyers who were German? And their foreign lawyers made it absolutely clear that, even though they would use every effort to persuade the judges of their clients' collective innocence, the lawyers' every gesture, every movement, left the prisoners in no doubt that they felt dirty and disgusted they were forced to represent such beasts. And the beasts even felt diffident complaining that they couldn't properly understand the proceedings, because the translator they were forced to use to speak with their lawyers was the same translator about whom they were complaining for his incomprehensibility in the court. The verdict would be guilty and they'd all hang, so why bother complaining?

And so on this second unexpected day of their trial, events had begun. But before the court settled down to further accusations and evidence, Deutch suddenly pricked up his ears and listened intently to the translator's monotone. His lawyer was on his feet, arguing. He tried to comprehend what was going on. Words like 'unfair' and 'natural justice' were bandied around. Why couldn't they speak in German! His name was used often; it carried into his consciousness through the headphones, almost musically above the rest of the words his lawyer and the prosecutor were using. Suddenly the translator said something which he recognised had been said by the judge. 'The defendant Wilhelm Deutch will stand.'

It took a moment for him to realise that all eyes in the courtroom were on him. He glanced at his fellow defendants, who gave him quizzical looks.

'Wilhelm Deutch, do you understand the nature of the request which your counsel has put to this court?'

Wilhelm looked around to determine who was speaking. It was the only way he could make sense of the translations. He locked eyes with the central judge on the bench, the most senior of the men in robes, and realised that it was he speaking to him.

He held the earphones closer to his ear, as thought this might assist him in understanding.

'Do you understand what your defense counsel, Dr. Broderick, has asked of this court, Mr. Deutch?' repeated the judge.

Wilhelm looked at his lawyer, who stared back blankly. Wilhelm held him in utter contempt. The man was a typical patrician American, full of lofty ideals and nonsense. Through him, he'd be hanged.

He said to the judge, 'I'm sorry. Because of the inadequate translation, it is very hard for me to fully comprehend what is going on. Could you please repeat what I'm supposed to have heard.'

'Dr. Broderick, your counsel, has made a formal request that your trial be truncated at this time, and that you stand trial separately of your co-defendants. Are you in agreement with our proceeding to hear his submissions that you stand separate trial?'

Now Wilhelm remembered what his lawyer had said to him last night. He'd ignored it because it was all legal mumbo-jumbo. Something about tar and brushes. About how as an engineer in the death camps, he wasn't as complicit as the other co-defendants who had been in the *Einsatzgruppen*, truly evil men who had been seconded when their work on the construction and servicing of the mobile gassing vehicles had come to an end. Yet the American lawyer had insisted that as Wilhelm was a plumber turned engineer in Mannheim before the war, he was unfairly caught up in the machinery of evil and shouldn't be treated as though he was like the others, or some such thing. Either way, Wilhelm wasn't particular interested in a separate trial. He would hang and would rather hang with comrades.

'No. I want no separate trial. I want this over and done with.'

Theo Broderick, his lawyer, looked at him in surprise. Last night, his client had said to him that he could do whatever he wanted to do. Amazed, the lawyer quickly melted back to his seat. He returned to the role he was paid to perform, a lawyer, a ringmaster defending the beasts. By his manner, Wilhelm could tell that the American was sitting there with the other defense lawyers feeling considerable disquiet. And discomfort.

CHAPTER TWO

New York, November, 1998

CHASCA BRODERICK FOUND NEITHER incongruity nor incompatibility in upholding the majesty of the law and its handmaiden, truth, as an officer of the courts of America, and yet at the same time lying through her teeth to her parents.

Even though she was twenty-seven years old, it was only in the last couple of years that she no longer felt a deep and profound sense of shame when she told her parents a lie. She'd lied when she lost her virginity, she'd lied as a twenty-two-year-old when she told her parents that she was going on a weekend trip to Florida with her roommate, instead of admitting it was with her boyfriend, and she'd lied when she told them she couldn't come home from college for a big family function because of the pressure of study for an exam, when she'd already taken the exam and was spending the time at a rock festival.

But what Chasca found most amazing about her relationship with her parents was the fact that she had to lie. She never lied to friends, not even about the slightest thing. Indeed at Harvard, and latterly at the War Crimes Commission, she was often called '*Your Honour*' because of her uncompromising attitude to moral rectitude.

Even as a little girl, she'd been the conscience of the family, refusing to allow her mother to purchase food grown in South Africa, or anything made in Britain after the Brixton race riots. But as she grew older and saw more of injustice and immorality, she came to the understanding that when she lied to her parents, it wasn't altogether her fault, that her parents brought these little dissemblings and lies upon themselves . . . that if they were more reasonable, less controlling, more liberal, more accepting, she wouldn't have to lie to them.

And so she wasn't overwhelmed by conscience when she lied and assured her parents that she wouldn't follow through with the nonsense of that old trial Theo had been involved in, when in reality, it was just below the surface and germinating in her mind like a spring bulb. She'd taken a month's holiday from her work in the War Crimes Commission examining the behaviour of evil individuals in the genocidal armies which had fought in Croatia and Bosnia, and was thinking of spending time in California or on the snowfields of Colorado. But when the family had returned home from Cape Cod and she'd seen the people she wanted to visit, and the plays she'd wanted to see, her mind continued to wander back fifty odd years to the Nuremberg trials, and the fate of a poor, hapless, and wrongly accused man named Wilhelm Deutch.

Chasca was all too used to the prostitution of justice; she'd studied how corrupt judges had been part of the venality of regimes in wartime Germany and post-Colonial Africa and Asia and South America; but she'd never associated the abuse of justice with an American Court, even one which operated in Nuremberg and was charged with prosecuting the most evil men who had ever lived.

She went to a law library at New York University and read and studied the opening and closing statements of the Chief Prosecutor at the Nuremberg War Crimes Tribunal, the former US Attorney General Robert Jackson, whose words stood as a monument to the centrality and majesty of justice.

But somehow, in the case of this unfortunate defendant, Wilhelm Deutch, the justice system had gone horribly wrong. Her grandfather's defense had patently failed to find any answer to the prosecution's claim that Deutch was an ordinary man doing evil things, and so deserved to be hanged as a war criminal. Yet if the judges had seen the autobiography that she held in her hands, a contemporaneous diary written in the passionate words of a Jewish inmate of the concentration camps. which lauded the life-saving compassion of the defendant, the German mechanic would not only have been freed, but would have been treated like a hero.

What was he like, she mused? It was important for her to imagine the architecture of a man like Deutch; she had to picture him, so that the bleak words she'd read about the trial became flesh and blood. Was he tall and thin with a monocle, aristocratic and very proper and Germanic, clicking his heels and kissing the backs of women's hands? No, of course not . . . He was a mechanic, undereducated, but highly skilled if the testimony of this Jewish gentleman, Joachim Gutman, was to be believed.

So what did he look like? Short, stocky, heavyset, a face full of jowls, fat from sausages and beer and sauerkraut? Maybe he was one of the rollicking caricatures of the German music halls and *bierkellers*, an archetypical Herr, full of good nature and merriment and pinching little pigtailed *mädchen* on their rosy cheeks? Or was he dour and ordinary and smelling of pipe tobacco, his clothes full of the stains of oil and sludge and drudge from a lifetime of doctoring machinery? Maybe he was partially deaf from standing in noisy factories. Did he wear glasses, and if so, were they the round, old-fashioned type which you used to be able to get on the National Health Service in the United Kingdom or that the Puritans wore all those centuries ago, thin-framed spectacles with wires which you sort of threaded around the ears? Or were they horn-rimmed and very heavy, framing his face and making his eyes seem to bulge? Maybe a monocle? No, she'd already mused about monocles and dismissed them. Monocles belonged to the patrician, heel-clicking type of German, and because Deutch was a mechanic, he didn't fit into that category in her mind. She tried to stop herself musing, because she was imagining through stereotypes, and stereotypes led to racism, and she'd spent her whole life fighting racism.

But she couldn't let it go. What did he look like? How did he talk? With a lisp? Slurring his words? In clipped, Germanic cadences or in Hitlerian demonic sentences delivered at full throttle to an hysterical and adoring audience? Now she was being absurd! No, he was an ordinary man, a loving father and husband, possibly even a grandfather; he had a dog and a couple of cats; yes, okay, so he went hunting stags and wild boar in Bavaria and enjoyed killing them, but so did all other Germans before the war; no, he just hunted wild boar . . . Not stags, he didn't enjoy killing the stags.

My God, she thought, how could she ever truly imagine a man whose culture and nature were so diametrically opposite to her own? Especially such an ordinary man, caught up in the maelstrom of utter evil?

She was beginning to obsess over him and the unfairness of sending a good man to the gallows. She'd tried to put him out of her mind and enjoy her well-deserved break from the genocidal bastards of the broken-down Yugoslavia, but he was starting to dominate her life. Even when she was visiting good friends just for a social moment together and the introductory pleasantries and reminiscences were over and done with, the testament she had found in Theo's desk was the first thing she brought up. Initially it was in the form of a request for advice . . . '*What would you do if you'd found such an ancient injustice . . . ?*' But Chasca knew exactly what she was going to do, and merely wanted her friends' support.

So when she told her parents, the matter was settled in her mind! She knew exactly what she must do; indeed, she'd dismissed and already forgotten their injunction for her to put it behind her.

Chasca Broderick got a surprise when they reacted so antipathetically. 'Israel? For God's sake, why Israel? It's so dangerous over there. The Palestinian terrorists . . .'

She told them why she wanted to go, despite the upsurge in the daily horrors suffered by the Israelis. Her father reacted with characteristic techniques of management. 'Now look, young lady. I thought we'd made it perfectly clear that we don't want you chasing after some

long-dead Nazi . . . and anyway, you told us that you were going to
drop this silly notion . . .'

Her mother used the power of reason. 'What chance do you think
you have with the Israeli authorities after all these years? And the man
was a Nazi . . .'

So Chasca explained, cajoled, and in the end realised that logic had
no place in her relationship with her parents. 'Mom, Dad, I'm going to
Jerusalem. I'm going to Yad VaShem. I'm going to give this document
to them. Then it's up to them as to what they do with it. End of story.
No more discussion. That's it. Okay.'

Her mother asked pointedly, 'What's this Yad . . . whatever you
call it?'

She'd read the documentation in the New York City library, and
could answer with authority. 'Yad VaShem means 'an everlasting name,'
and it's the memorial to the six million Jews who died in the Holocaust.
It comes from a verse from the prophet Isaiah. It says, '*And to them will
I give in my house and within my walls a memorial, an everlasting name
that shall not be cut off . . .*'

Her father looked at her mother and shrugged. Then, with a final
philippic, he said, 'Look, I can save you a journey. Let me get my secretary to send it over to them by UPS and then you can spend the rest
of your holiday with us.'

Yad VaShem, Jerusalem, Israel, November, 1998

Chasca remained silent as she stood in the Hall of Remembrance in
Yad VaShem in Jerusalem. It was a vast dark hall, only dimly lit by its
permanent memorial flame burning close to the crypt which held the
ashes of some of the millions and millions who died in the Nazi atroc-
ity. On the floor, in stark relief against the blackness of the marble, were
recorded the sites of the European death camps, Majdanek, Chelmno,
Auschwitz, and many others, simple names, simple and unexceptional

towns, once unknown but now and forever infamous, names which defined the agony of millions of deaths in the name of a lunatic, in the name of a nation's hatred.

As she stood beside her guide and translator, for the first time in her life, Chasca began to realise the enormity of the devastation wrought by the Nazis. And unwillingly but inevitably, she began to compare the crimes the Nazis had perpetrated during the Holocaust against the Jews, Gypsies, homosexuals, intellectuals, and other sub-humans with the crimes and the genocide she and others were exposing today in the dilapidated state of Yugoslavia. The recent unearthing of the horrors of ethnic cleansing and the slaughters of hundreds of innocent Serbs and Bosnians and Croats by fascist and murderous armies were on the front pages of newspapers throughout the world.

Yet it wasn't until this moment, faced with the enormity of the horrors inflicted on the Jewish and other peoples by Hitler and his fanatics, that she realised how utterly evil, deliberate, and wicked the Nazis were, how incomparably mechanical and enormous were the lengths the German people went to in order to eliminate the Jews from the face of the earth.

Intellectually, she was award of the hatred felt towards Jews in Europe through the writings of men like Luther and the music of composers like Wagner; she'd read about anti-Semitism as being the longest hatred; she knew of the expulsion of the Jews from Spain, of their treatment by the Crusaders, of the horrors of the ghettos and the pogroms and Russia's Pale of Settlement; she'd known of the degradation of the Jewish religion and culture and people; she'd learned of how the Jews always rose above the venal jealousies of their Christian neighbours because of the Jewish commandment to be educated above the ignorance which surrounded them; she knew of the closeness of the Jews because of their need to find mutual protection against the regular onslaughts which assailed them; but until now, until she stood before the flames of the martyrs in the silence of comprehension; until she came to an understood of the murderous reality of anti-Semitism;

Chasca was forced to admit of her own lamentable ignorance. She had to come to terms with the fact that anti-Semitism wasn't just a philosophical evil, but that its reality was the killing of millions and millions of human beings. Until now, Chasca Broderick had not fully appreciated the end result of the hatred of Jews.

She'd been told that the Holocaust was the defining genocide for all time, but until she stood here, she never before truly understood why.

She had learned of the Holocaust at school and at Harvard; she had Jewish friends and their parents had given her personal insights; she had seen the films and read the books; yet until this moment, standing on the ground where the ashes of dead Judaism was the nexus between the horrors of the past and the hope of the future; until she read of the numbingly measureless hosts of concentration camps inmates; until she saw the pictures of skeletal humanity imprisoned behind barbed wire, saw the innocent victims of European Jewry wearing degrading striped uniforms and the infamous badges of identification, saw the crisp black uniforms of the guards and the salivating Alsatians . . . until now, Chasca Broderick realised she was just an armchair theorist, and hadn't known anything of truth of what the Holocaust meant.

And she also realised that her work in exposing the murderers of Bosnia and Croatia and Serbia had suddenly become even more vital, because even though the genocide of Yugoslavia was incomparably smaller than the Holocaust, which consumed so many of Europe's Jews, the memorial to the Jewish victims told her starkly that no murderous ruler must ever be allowed to get away with genocide, ever again . . . not Tudjman nor Milosevich nor Karadjic nor Idi Amin nor Saddam Hussein nor the Hutus nor the Tutsis nor the bastard tin-pot generals who slaughtered their own people in South America . . . nobody. Never! Ever! They must be hunted down to the ends of the earth and their evil exposed . . . if only for the sake of the memory of the victims, and the peace of the survivors.

The guide who stood beside her had experienced this reaction before. It was in part shock, in part shame, in part withdrawal.

Reactions of visitors depended on their background and why they had come; upon the past experiences of who was standing here, looking at the names of the camps, the numbers, the utter horror; if it was an elderly survivor, there were usually quiet tears at the memory of a life, once full of promise, now destroyed; if it was the member of a survivor's family, the reaction would be an upsurge in anger and a rekindling of hatred; if it was a gentile, here on a trip to Israel and a mandatory visit to Yad VaShem, the reaction would depend on the age of the visitor . . . An old person would shake his head in horror and wonder at the cruelty of the world, a young person would withdraw and feel an sense of disbelief, of incomprehension.

The guide, Smuel, noticed however that this American girl, this Chasca Broderick, was reacting differently from most other young gentile people. Indeed, one would have thought that her parents or grandparents were victims of the Nazi Holocaust; yet from what she'd told him, there was no such connection. But there was such a depth of anger and disgust in her eyes that he wondered whether she was one of the many children, especially of Americans, who had lately come to realise that their grandparents were born Jewish, but after the war had changed their identity and turned their backs on their religion because of the bestiality they had suffered in the name of a God who asked too much.

He didn't need to know and he knew not to interrupt her emotions with trite questions. When they were in a building such as this, housing the memorial to so many who had been slaughtered by such beasts, visitors only wanted to be alone with their most private thoughts. He moved away slightly to enable her to feel the protection which isolation of her horror might provide, but Chasca detected the movement and saw it for what it was, a moment of spiritual connection, of jointly sharing the intensity of emotions this place evoked.

She smiled at him, and nodded. She had seen enough. She was resolved. She had an even greater reason now to move forward.

Three days later, Chasca was back at Yad VaShem, sitting in the office of the Director of Records, Professor Eliezer Hofshee, an academic seconded from the Department of Modern Jewish History of Bar Ilan University. Having studied in Yale, his English was perfect, though heavily impregnated with an Israeli accent and the interjection *'ehrr'* between every third word.

He smiled at her broadly over his large oak desk, the document she'd given him three days earlier sitting as the only paper on its surface. After the initial pleasantries about how she was enjoying her first visit to Israel, Chasca lapsed into silence, waiting for Professor Hofshee to make his pronouncement about whether or not he'd agree to begin the process of resurrecting the reputation of this mechanic, Deutch.

He began innocuously enough. 'This is a very interesting document. It's passionately written, and I congratulate you for finding it, and for making it available to us. Right now, there's more being written about the Holocaust than at any time during the past fifty years, probably because the passage of time allows us to view the horror with a degree of dispassion. Also because it has taken survivors half a century for the memories to be sufficiently contained for them to be able to confront them. Which is why finding such an eyewitness document, written by a sufferer at the time of his experience, is so interesting.'

He picked up the document again and re-read the opening paragraphs, as though to remind himself that he was holding the memorial of a witness. Replacing the testament on the desk, he shook his head sadly. 'The silence is a tragedy . . . understandable, but a real tragedy. For nearly two generations, victims have been unable to make their grief known, have suffered in silence. When family members like children have tried to find out what happened to the parents, they were usually fobbed off with the response, *'You don't want to know.'* Yet there was a silent communication. If a child left something on his plate at mealtimes, the parent would say something like, *'Finish your food; you never know when you'll get your next meal . . .'*

'Or years after leaving the camps, the parent would be walking in a street in America or Israel or somewhere safe, and pass a dog like an Alsatian, and the parent would draw back in fear because of the unconscious or repressed memories. Or they'd recoil at chimneys belching out black smoke. And of course, the children picked up all the clues and felt guilt that their parents had suffered and they were free and safe.'

Chasca hadn't fully understood the depth of suffering of Holocaust survivors, nor the length of their continuous punishment. She recalled editorials in American newspapers or television programmes where well-meaning people told the Jews to *get over it* or to *put the past behind them* or to *forgive and forget and get on with their lives.* How little they knew.

Eliezer Hofshee continued, 'Of course, now that the grandchildren are writing school projects about the horrors of the camps and their family suffering, much is coming out. And increasingly, academic papers are now saying how it wasn't just a few madmen in the Nazi party who were responsible, but that every German was culpable. Certainly there was a shared communal guilt, but to accuse every German with the benefit of our present-day morality is somewhat frenzied, and I have little sympathy with this view. This autobiography you've found tends to support my gut instincts.'

From the way he was talking, it was obvious that the next sentence was going to begin with the word, *however* . . .

'However,' he continued, 'one document doesn't allow sufficient evidence to overthrow the verdict of the legal trial of a man hanged for war crimes; and it certainly isn't enough to elevate his memory into the status of one of the Righteous Among the Nations, which is one of the highest humanitarian honours the Israeli Government can confer on a non-Jew. People who have been honoured as the Righteous Gentiles are the sorts who worked for years in hiding Jews, saving their lives, fighting the Nazi murderers, performing individual acts of bravery, which takes them into an altogether different place in the pantheon of humanity. There are something like eight thousand such wonderful people who have been accorded this honour. These are ordinary people who, in times of unbelievable danger and difficulty, have done extraordinary things for others. Your mechanic, I'm afraid, isn't one of them. Here is the testimony of one man who tried to alleviate the conditions in a camp to make them less inhuman. A good man, yes, but not enough to have him honoured in such a way.'

'Okay,' said Chasca, 'if not an honorific, how's about we try to reverse the verdict posthumously. As a lawyer representing this man, even though he's been hanged, I'd say there's enough evidence here to examine the prospect of getting the German government to quash the findings of the judge.'

The professor nodded. 'There, I'd agree with you, bearing in mind that it was more of an American court in Germany and so I'll have to check which jurisdiction to approach. But, yes, we could certainly do something like that; however, with our relatively limited resources and with the destruction of most of the records of the Jewish community in Germany at the end of the war, it's going to be difficult, if not impossible, to find more compelling evidence to back up this single document.'

He saw her face drop in disappointment. She'd built up her hopes that she could do something in retrospect. As a war crimes prosecutor, her life in Yugoslavia was fraught with political machinations from so many sides; naively she'd hoped that this could be a relatively simple procedure. But she knew the difficulties; much evidence had been destroyed within only the previous few years in Yugoslavia, making it hard enough for her to gather documentation to use against modern war criminals. How much harder then for crimes which had been covered up for half a century and more?

Chasca looked at the man who sat opposite her. He was in his middle, perhaps late sixties, but had the virility in body and mind of a much younger man. He was the archetypal Jew, and could as easily have been a colonel in the Israel Defense Force as a rabbi; he had a face which spoke of a lifetime of study and learning, and humility was written into the lines which etched his skin. But it was his eyes which appealed to her. Intelligent, compassionate eyes in a face which was wrinkled from decades of a strong sun, yet which was a sturdy face, a fatherly face.

'I've upset you. I'm sorry, Chasca. But here we have to deal in realities. We have tens of thousands of people every year coming to Yad VaShem, trying to regain an insight into their own or their families' lives, which were stolen from them. We can help many to find the records of their early lives; our archivists and historians have done wonders, but there's only so much we can do against the coordinated and systematic destruction of evidence half a century ago.

'When the Nazis set out to wipe Jewry off the face of the earth, they meant to destroy not only people, but also an entire cultural history. Their intention was to leave only one monument to European Judaism intact, something like an exhibition in a museum to an extinct species of animal; that was the old Jewish part of Prague. Aside from that, all other memories of the Jewish connection with Europe were to be expunged from the face of the earth. We've been working to regain our heritage, and we've done an extraordinary job. But not even we can recreate millions of documents which were deliberately burned and destroyed with the Nazi's systematic efficiency.'

He looked at her fondly. She reminded him of his late daughter, killed on a border kibbutz by a Katyusha rocket fired from Syria. She had the same open and accepting expression, the same delicate smile, the same grasp on life. He suddenly felt immensely sad, sad for the senselessness of the politics of hate; it was always innocent victims like his beautiful daughter and this young man, this Yoachim Gutman, who suffered. The madmen and murderers so often escaped their rightful punishment.

Kindly, he told her, 'Maybe you, on your own, perhaps by going to Germany, would have a better chance of finding this man Gutman, if he's still alive after all these years; if not, maybe he's been fortunate enough to rebuild his life and has had children who might be able to bear witness to the decency of this German, Wilhelm Deutch. Do it for the sake of what's right, Chasca. I can see the flame of justice burning fiercely inside you. This man, this Joachim Gutman, wanted justice. Please God, he's still alive; try to find him. In that way, maybe we can examine again the evidence against this Deutch fellow, and see if we can undo the injustice of the verdict . . .'

Nuremberg Courtroom
Palace of Justice, Allied Occupied Germany
June, 1946

Wilhelm Deutch felt a sense of comradeship as he sat down again beside his colleagues, and shuffled his body on the crowded bench to regain the position he had occupied prior to being ordering to stand by the judge. He'd told the judge, through him his American lawyer, that he and his colleagues were as one, inseparable, and would face their persecutors together.

But the moment he rejoined his co-accused, he knew instinctively that by his being singled out, even though he'd redeemed himself in the eyes of all Germany, the atmosphere in the courtroom had changed. It was as though some sort of noxious odour by osmosis had somehow seeped through the German phalanx of defendants. These men had presented a united front of defiance and innocence, sitting there to defend their lives and their honour, these last remnants of the Third Reich.

But as Wilhelm Deutch sat down again and glanced sideways at the other Germans, his heart sank. He knew that from this moment onwards, he was an outsider, that the unity of the phalanx had gone forever.

Shoulders which had once touched now were separated by a hair's breadth, but enough for him to know that camaraderie was a thing of the past. Nor did he fully understand what had happened. The other day, he was sure he'd instructed his lawyer that he wished to continue standing trial with the other engineers, but obviously the translator had failed to convey his wishes. Or else Wilhelm had simply misunderstood what was expected of him. No meant yes. Yes meant no.

His co-defendants looked at him with sideways glances as he settled back on to the bench. Frowns of concern, as though they thought he was trying to be different from them . . . as though the bulwark of solidarity they had all shown when they were first asked to plead to the charges, the outward appearance of detachment and disinterest that they had agreed they would present to the judges and the prosecution, was about to be breached by him.

Wilhelm had anticipated something like this would happen when his counsel suggested that he ask for a separate trial. He'd expected to be ostracised. That's why he'd told his lawyer he would stay where he was. At the first Nuremberg trial of the leaders of the Nazis, such a separation of the defendants had been obvious to any observer. Leaders such as Dönitz and Göring and Hess had looked with disdain at lesser men like Ribbentrop and Streicher and Seyss-Inquart, the duller luminaries of Nazi brilliance.

Now Wilhelm's co-defendants were looking at him with hooded eyes, wondering what sort of a deal this . . . this plumber . . . this gasfitter . . . this tinkerer with machinery . . . was cooking up with the prosecution.

Wilhelm reacted angrily. What did they think? That this was a device engineered by him? He glared back, but their eyes were the unblinking eyes of snakes. Would they ever believe that he'd instructed his lawyer to deny him a separate trial? What was going on? And did any of it really matter?

It was during the lunchtime recess that Wilhelm found out what was going on. Hasty words, American words, were spoken between his defense lawyer Broderick and the American captain of the white-helmeted guards who stood stiffly to attention throughout the trial at the back of the defendant's dock.

While the other men were being led out of the left gate to descend into the dungeons where gruel was served, Wilhelm was led out of the right gate. His look of surprise didn't even scratch the surface of the wall of suspicion which had built itself between him and his fellow defendants during the morning.

He was ushered into a private meeting room. A table and two chairs had been set up. The American guard, a fresh-faced boy who looked as though only the previous day he'd been building a haystack on a farm in Iowa, nodded to him to sit. It wasn't a request. Guards don't make requests. Even the most minor flicker of an eyebrow was an instruction to a prisoner. Careful observation was what made life bearable for a man in Wilhelm's position . . . anticipating a command before it was made, not being screamed at for responding a fraction of a second too late.

So instead of demanding answers as to why he'd been brought there, Wilhelm simply sat. He knew the guard would act as though he was dumb . . . and even if he did speak, he would know nothing.

Ten minutes later, and his defense lawyer burst through the door with the arrogance of a German admiral. In his wake strode the translator. Wilhelm's heart sank. Without acknowledgment of Wilhelm's presence, Theodore Broderick looked at the ceiling like a man about to deliver a lecture.

'Regardless of your refusal last night and this morning, I've reapplied in camera, and have successfully been granted a separate trial,' he said. 'You have no understanding of the issues involved. The men with whom you're currently co-accused are all ex-*Einsatzgruppen* troops who, towards the end of the War, were seconded to work the gas ovens. I'm disgusted to be sitting in the same room as them. I know I've only been appointed your counsel very late in the day, but from everything I've read, and from the evidence my predecessor took, the actions of these men, the matters with which they've been charged, simply don't apply to you. You seem to be a different kettle of fish . . .' The metaphor didn't translate, but the translator, damn his hide, made no allowance, and didn't let the puzzled expression on Wilhelm's face detract from his work. 'The men upstairs in the dock are mass murderers. They followed the troops into Poland and Russia and were responsible for rounding up Jews and taking them into fields and machine-gunning them down. Hundreds at a time. And they'd round up the women and children and force them into these special trucks, and turn on the exhaust and kill them all.

'Whatever your crimes, all you did was follow orders to keep the gas ovens at Auschwitz-Birkenau in good working order. You were only a mechanic, following instructions. You're tainted with the evil of others, but I think it's up to the prosecution to prove that just by keeping things in running order, you're not deserving of the punishment which will undoubtedly be meted out to those fiends upstairs. That's why, despite your refusal, I've overruled your decision by treating you, in effect, as a hostile witness, and demanding a new trial. You'll be tried separately by a single American judge. The prosecutor in the case which is being conducted now with the beasts from the *Einsatzgruppen* has said that he'll lead the case against you, but that's okay, because he's a fair and reasonable man, and in the intervening weeks, I'm sure I'll be able to talk him into some form of judicial mitigation. Hopefully he'll take the death penalty off the table, and we'll only be talking about a custodial term at the very worst. Like I say, you'll have to wait another month or so before we get these sons of bitches out of our hair, but at least then you'll have a fair trial.'

It took the interpreter over a minute to complete the translation of what Broderick had just said. He was suddenly surprised when Wilhelm burst out laughing.

'Would you kindly ask him why he finds this funny?'

The translator listened to Deutch's response and nodded. 'He says that the concept of a fair trial is nonsense. He says you and your Allied colleagues are here to see him hanged, and this whole trial is a sham.'

The Bostonian academic lawyer frowned and shook his head. 'That's a canard. Nonsense. We're here so that the world can see we're totally different from the Nazis. Tell him that. Tell him that regardless of what the Nazis did, we will ensure that the new Germany is governed by law, and that justice is the rule rather than the exception.'

'And why should justice rule?' asked Wilhelm. 'You're victors. You have us in your power. Why not do what victors have done throughout the ages and take your revenge?'

'We might be victors, but we're not barbarians. Without the rule of law, without justice, we will become barbarians, like the Nazis. Our revenge is to see all the pestilential remnants of the Nazi regime buried in the rubble of the old Germany.'

'How little you know,' Wilhelm sneered. The translator looked at Broderick, wondering how much more the American would tolerate without walking out, but continued faithfully to record Wilhelm's disdain for the court process. 'What idea do you have of the rule of justice when a country is on its knees?'

The defender looked at his client, fighting hard to remain impassive. 'I'll tell you what I do know. Justice is the foundation for occupied Germany in 1946, unlike it was for Jews and homosexuals in the Germany of Adolf Hitler in 1936.'

Wilhelm shook his head and responded. The translator said, 'The prisoner Deutch instructs me to tell you that there's no justice in this court, and nor will there ever be while he and the others are represented by anyone other than Germans. That you and the other Allied defense lawyers are just paid hacks, doing a put-up job to make the victors look good, before hanging all the Nazis.'

Theodore Broderick bridled and flushed with anger. He didn't want to be here. He didn't want to defend one of the beasts who had plumbed the lowest depths to which humanity had ever sunk. He'd been to the concentration camps. He'd seen for himself mountains of spectacle frames and shoes and artificial limbs and bones and teeth, the white gargoyles, pushed into monstrous garbage piles of what had once been human beings. He'd smelt the damp earth, and tasted in the air the rotting flesh and bitter blood of European Jewry. Yet his sense of the fundamentals of justice, of equity, that everyone regardless of the crimes committed was entitled to the very best defense, had forced him to stay. That's why he'd agreed to defend one of the beasts upstairs; that's why he'd fought so hard for this man, Deutch, possibly the one German who could honestly and justifiably say that he was only following orders. He looked at his client. Such an ordinary man. Just a mechanic. So banal.

Broderick wanted to go home. Home, to where the air was untainted by the dust of burning humanity; home to where he'd enjoyed the pleasures of his university appointment. Where he was a respected professor of law, and a judicial ethicist, a counsel to judges and presidents on morality and standards of decency. Where he'd happily been ensconced, writing his learned commentaries on Supreme Court decisions, until one day in the *Washington Post*, he'd read of the retributive anger of Franklin D. Roosevelt's newest Supreme Court Justice Robert Houghwout Jackson, in his disgust at the effects of Nazism.

Broderick remembered vividly the opening words of Justice Jackson at the beginning of the first Nuremberg Trial a year earlier, in November 1945. '*The wrongs which we seek to condemn and punish have been so calculated, so malignant, and so devastating, that civilisation cannot tolerate their being ignored, because it cannot survive their being repeated. That four great nations, flushed with victory and stung with injury, stay the hand of vengeance and voluntarily submit their captive enemies to the judgment of the law is one of the most significant tributes that Power has ever paid to Reason.*'

Those words had burned within his breast for weeks. He'd pondered them a dozen times. What was the relationship between power and justice when a nation became anarchic? What part did reason play in a government which appropriated the judicial system to pursue its own ends? What happens when the doctrine of the separation of powers is torn up and the scraps are thrown in the face of a civil society and used to light something like Savonarola's bonfire of vanity?

That was why he had applied for special permission from his university and from the International Military Tribunal to travel to Germany to assist in the defense of the beasts. Because he had to understand how power had become so utterly corrupt, how justice had been so easily prostituted, and how reason had been so completely devalued. Nazism flew in the face of humanity. Humanity for Broderick was reason. Nazism was a denial of everything he had taught and learned. For him to continue to practice as an ethicist, as a philosopher for the judicial system, Theodore Broderick had to understand and explain Nazism.

Broderick stood. Right now, right at this very moment, he had to be away from this man. He needed to breathe clean air. His chair fell backwards on to the stone floor, but reason and self-restraint left him as he looked at Wilhelm's arrogant and smirking face.

In an unaccustomed fury, he said, 'Don't think for one minute that I either enjoy being here, or want to be representing you. I'm only interested in justice. And in America, my country, which now is the occupying force of your country, you'll abide by my laws and my system of morality. So listen up, you bastard, and understand me good and proper. You'll get a fair trial, whether you want one or not.'

Written in the remnants of Germany, occupied by the Allied Powers, 1946

From the memoirs of Joachim Gutman:

I, Joachim Gutman, am witness to unspeakable and incomprehensible acts of barbarity. Yet if I don't speak of them, who will? Who is left to act as witness? For if I don't bear witness, then they will have won, and that is something which I cannot permit. So here, I will use this opportunity while my memory is still raw and my hatred naked, to record my experiences of the Concentration Camps. This is not a last will and testament. I have survived. I am alive. But none of my family lives, so for them, voiceless but never forgotten, this will be my compact, a record of faith between the living and the dead.

Before, in the days which are coloured golden, my father and mother and brothers and sisters used to call me Yokki. As a two-year-old, I couldn't pronounce the name Joachim, and so my childhood name became my adult name.

I know that history will remember only the large picture . . . the mounds of bodies, the mountains of clothes and shoes and spectacles, the dust of what once was a proud and ancient people, the memories of five thousand years . . . but what will be forgotten in the future, as memory fades and facts become distorted, will be the small things of our lives. The individual and separate brushstrokes of what Jewish life used to be before the Nazis extinguished the light of our civilisation.

Let others paint a giant canvas; let historians and philosophers and lawyers deal with the enormity of what the Nazis did to us. Me? I'll paint a few brushstrokes here and there, a highlight, a feature, something which will tell whoever reads this, my memoir, that the Jews weren't just numbers, weren't just tattoos, weren't just lines of people queuing up to be gassed and burned, weren't just some racial memory like the Hittites or the Carthaginians, but were a people who loved and could be loved, who sang and drank and prayed and . . . and . . . were abandoned by their God.

I didn't come from an orthodox Jewish household. We were liberal intellectuals. We said blessings in Hebrew, but prayed in German. We were the finest and most carefully honed products of the enlightenment and the emancipation of the Jews from the Ghettos.

Indeed, we were more German than the Germans. Of course, despite the clothes of normality which we all wore, our neighbours didn't accept us. On social occasions, or when we dealt with Christian Germans, we always felt as though we were tolerated at best, but more usually derided behind our backs. Only on a business level were we a part of their community. My father was a lawyer in the early years of his career and in his mid-40s became a judge. But when Hitler dismissed the Jewish judges, leaving only Aryans to administer the laws of Germany, it was as though one of the eyes of justice had been put out. Yes, of course I know that Justice is blindfolded, but the law must have vision, if only to see where it has gone wrong. When my father and his fellow judges were thrown off their judicial benches like so much refuse, just because of the religion of their birth, all Germany suffered; but Aryan Germans only came to realise that when compassion disappeared as the last robed Jewish judge sadly stepped down from his chair. When Hitler's judges took over, the separation of government and justice meant that judges carried out the orders of the Nazis, and nobody was safe. Nobody. Not even good Nazis as they soon came to realise.

My father refused to accept that his career was over while he was such a young man, and immediately went to the university where he was revered for his lectures on jurisprudence, and the faculty head, also Jewish, gave him a lectureship. But that too came to an end, of course, when Hitler expunged the great Jewish thinkers from the universities and put in their places the dull minds of ordinary men who could only struggle to comprehend what their predecessors had envisioned; Germany's greatness disappeared altogether. First justice was blinded and then intellect was dulled. And these Germany thought their Hitler was a Messiah!

But I'm racing ahead. This is a problem I have. I can't wait to finish a novel I'm reading to find out what happened, and so I skip the beautiful descriptions and the development of the characters to find out who did what in the end. But these, my memoirs, are too important to me and to you, my reader, to be rushed, and so I will start from the beginning and exercise that discipline which was missing all my life . . . until I want to Auschwitz. There I learned discipline. One has to be disciplined to do the work of a Sonderkommando! The Jewish Sonderkommando had the worst job of all in the concentration camps. We were chosen because we were young and strong, and we had to . . . but I'm racing ahead. Too fast. Life is so fast these days. I must wait. So must you, until I have told you the reasons why I was a Sonderkommando. I must go on with my story.

My grandfather and grandmother came to Berlin to open up a shop in Bismarckstrasse in 1881 when the city became a separate administrative district, although its mayor still had to be personally confirmed in his position by the Kaiser. They originally came from the southeastern part of the Austro-Hungarian Empire, somewhere near the border of the Ukraine and Slovakia in the Carpathian Mountains. It was a poor and valueless life over there, and so they came west with what savings they had managed to accumulate with the intention of making a better life. Odd, now I come to think of it, that these people from a *Stetl* could ever have contemplated joining the bourgeois classes of Berlin. What they soon came to realise was that Berlin, at the end of the last century, was a large and complex city with a population approaching two million. It looked like a businessman's dream; yet despite its size, it was as exclusive as a gentleman's club. And Yiddish-speaking Jews from the East, despite the emancipation from the ghettos, were excluded.

Socially, my grandparents were at the very lowest end of the spectrum of Berlin society, which in those days was divided into a pyramid of tiers. There were some fifty rigidly structured levels of the social monolith, and unless you were at the very zenith, or you wore a uniform of a Hussar or some such, you were a nobody. And the Berlin Jews who had lived there for a generation or more were worse than the Lutherans, for they rejected those Jews who came new to the city from the East as *'dirty ostlanders.'* They were considered as inferior by the cultured and assimilated Jews of the city because of their clothes, their meagre possessions, and especially because they spoke Yiddish and not German. Yiddish is the language of Shalom Aleichem and Ahad ha Am. It's a musical language of everyday commerce, the language which gives Russian Jews the ability to talk to Polish and Ukrainian Jews. But the German Jews proudly spoke German, the language of Schiller and Heine and Beethoven. Since Moses Mendelssohn had emancipated them from the ghetto, nobody in Germany spoke Yiddish. And they treated Yiddish speakers with derision and contempt.

Did that put my grandparents off living in Berlin? Did they move on elsewhere in disgust, leaving the social climbers and elites far behind in their parochial world? No, my grandparents worked hard to throw off the shackles of being 'peasants' and instead used every means in their power to become Berliners. When their money started to accumulate from selling fabrics door to door, the first thing my grandfather did was to buy a silk top hat and tailcoat so that he could promenade along the Kurfurstendamm on a Sunday, and raise his hat and nod to the ladies and gentlemen. Of course, he had to return to his single room in the Mietskasernen district for the reality of his working week.

But as is so often the case with our people, my grandparents quickly established a place for themselves, and their fabric sales enabled them to accomplish their dream and they opened up a small haberdashery shop in the centre of town.

Riches flowed to them as maids bought ribbons and elegant ladies came in to choose something lovely for a dinner or the opera that night, and by the time my father and his brothers and sisters had been born, my grandparents and their growing family were a part of the Jewish establishment of the city. They had a large house and several servants.

Being the way of the world, my oldest uncle followed his father into the trade, my middle uncle traveled the world and became a representative for several German bullion merchants, and my own father eschewed the trade altogether and went to university, where he took law and became a first-class student.

And then the Great Patriotic War began.

By the time the madness was over in 1918, I had lost an uncle, and my grandparents were ruined. Too late, they tried to switch to making uniforms for the soldiers, but because they were Jews, the High Command excluded them from profiting from the War. So they had to struggle to stay in business. But who wants to buy laces and pretty bows when the world you used to know has collapsed at your feet and the only thing on your mind is having money to buy bread. And who would buy from a Jewish shop when all Germany was abuzz with the rumour that the only reason the old Kaiser had capitulated was because he'd been stabbed in the back by some conspiracy of the international Jewish business community.

Fortunately my father's law practice flourished in the plethora of lawsuits and injury cases when Germany began to reestablish itself, despite the crippling debt burden of the hated *Diktat*, the Treaty of Versailles. Were it not for my father, the family would have had to leave Berlin, as did so many families in the aftermath of that terrible conflict.

I was born in 1919. Although he was only twenty-four years of age, my father already had three children. Of course, I knew nothing of the deprivations which he and his family suffered, nor the Herculean stresses which were on his young narrow shoulders having to sustain not only my mother and my baby brother and sister, but also my grandparents and aunt and uncle. What did I, in my cradle, know of the Protocols of the Elders of Zion, published in Germany when I was only one? How was I to understand why the Freikorps, disaffected soldiers wandering the streets looking for warmth and shelter, picked up this pamphlet and believed that the Jews were responsible for every disaster in Europe in their manic conspiracy to control the world?

I was unaware of the four hundred political assassinations which shook the country's confidence in ever again having stable government; and how could I have know, cuddling my teddy bear, that the French-Belgian military occupation of the Ruhr in 1923 would lead to strikes and hyperinflation which ruined everybody—except those clever or rich enough to have put their money into Switzerland or America?

No, I knew none of these things. But Adolf Hitler did. When I was four, he engineered a putsch in the Munich *bierkeller*—a lamentable failure which his propaganda minister eventually turned into a moment of high drama in the ascent of Nazism. Hitler was thrown into prison, but far from being his end, it was his beginning. Martyrdom suits some people. For Adolf Hitler, it was a creed written in the blood of millions.

My growing years, my schooling and my society were made as normal as possible by my increasingly anxious parents, despite the growing anger in the streets. I was a child when Wall Street collapsed, but by the time Germany was recovering, I'd already had my Bar Mitzvah, and Adolf Hitler was about to step into the shoes of Hindenburg and become the most powerful man in Germany.

What was it like to be a thirteen-year-old Jewish boy in Berlin when the SA was beating up the parents of your friends on the streets, and when Adolf was saying that every catastrophe of Germany was the fault of your people?

Who knew? I certainly didn't. And neither did many of my friends. Because our parents shielded us. They met for dinner parties and derided the SA and the SS and the NSDAP as buffoons who would soon be thrown out of office as soon as Germany came to its senses. A second war? Nonsense. The Great Patriotic War was the war to end all wars. Everybody knew that. How could there possibly be another war when so many millions of young men had been slaughtered? When poisonous gasses had been used to blind and to maim? When monstrous and inhuman weapons like tanks had crushed bodies beneath their iron tracks and aeroplanes had flown over battlefields and dropped explosives from the sky? How could armies possibly fight armies, countries fight countries, when these weapons of evil were abroad?

How little we knew. What a fool's paradise we lived in. I still remember the derision of my lawyer father when, in the privacy of our house, or in front of our friends, he was mimicking the goosesteps of the SS as they thundered down the streets of Munich and other cities in Bavaria.

'Let them come to Berlin!' he thundered like Bismarck. 'We'll show them the contempt in which we hold bully-boys and thugs.'

Today, I weep for my father's ignorance. I despair now that I understand the enormity of his arrogance. Because of his, and the German Jews' blindness, all European Jewry is dead.

Does that sound unusually harsh? Am I defaming the memory of the dead? Am I blaming my father, and millions like him, for what happened to me?

Looking back over the mountains of rubble which is the landscape of war, it's all too easy to see the growth of Hitler's insanity. In retrospect, it isn't difficult to see where the concentration camps and the gas ovens and the *Einsatzgruppen*, the killing groups, came from.

But at the time, the evil seemed to creep over us all so slowly we accommodated to it as you slowly acclimatise to the winter, absorbed it into our daily routine, even ignored it. We got used to it as one gets used to a bad smell. We were constantly thinking that sanity would prevail, the smell would disappear as clean air blew in from beyond our borders.

And we had good grounds for so thinking. After all, at the end of June, 1934, Röhm and other top men of the SA were purged, along with most other high-profile opponents to Hitler. When we read of the purge, we all rejoiced. After all, it was Röhm and the SA who were the true evils, who organised the rallies. It was Röhm who had gathered together and controlled the vicious actions of millions and millions of unemployed men into the largest civilian army in history. And when Adolf Hitler stormed the hotel and had the leaders of the SA murdered, we thought that the Führer was reestablishing the laws of civilisation. No more beatings, no more rallies. The evil demon was dead. Germany was marshalling its resources for the Olympic Games. The loud-mouth Chancellor had come to his senses, got rid of the evil SA and now everything would be back to normal. The economy was starting to blossom. Women were again buying bows and ribbons. But this time from Aryan shopkeepers.

Prison Cells beneath the Palace of Justice
Nuremberg, Allied Occupied Germany
June, 1946

The months of isolation in the prison cell numbed his mind and made him wonder if he would ever be sane again. For over a year, he had been preparing in his mind for this denouement of his life. He was prepared for the accusations, the explanations, the verdict, the hanging. He had been a part of the machinery of death, and the moment the Reich collapsed, he had accepted that if caught, his life would be at an end. He'd been miraculously free for months before being captured by the Americans, rounded up because a concentration camp survivor had seen him queuing in the streets and informed the military. He'd even gone quietly; he'd not denied the allegations; he'd even cooperated with the Provost Marshal and filled in some of the details. Why deny it? The records were there. Denying would cause delay, and since the end of the war, he'd been waiting for a tap on the shoulder, a gun in the ribs. Yes, he'd only been a mechanic, but this was the era of allied retribution, and he was one of the operatives of the death camps, and he, like the others, would probably be brought to trial. How could he deny that he'd the mechanic who made the machinery of death work so efficiently? And when Germany lost, he was one of the guilty ones who would pay the price for Hitlermadness.

His wife knew it was coming, but his daughter, God bless her, didn't know that her father would probably never see her grow up. She would miss Daddy, and then she'd get on with her life, trying to put together the broken bricks which one day would build the foundations of a new Germany. His family would miss him, mourn the cruelty of the war, curse Hitler and the Nazis, and survive. That was all they could hope for . . . survival.

But when his trial was suddenly truncated, and he suffered the tantalising . . . the excruciating . . . agony of waiting for the trial of his former colleagues to be over so his could begin afresh, it seemed as if the torments he had willed to dormancy suddenly erupted. He was riven with anxiety, so that at times, when he lay on his bunk, he found it almost impossible to breathe. Life now was so different from when he was a defendant with all the other defendants; then, he felt he was part of a group, and the group would be found guilty. Now he was on his own and he felt totally isolated and exposed.

Only the briefings with his lawyer seemed to offer him any relief. He had started off hating the arrogant and insufferable Broderick, but during the past month, this stiff and humourless American lawyer had become his link to the outside world. Even the guards didn't talk to him anymore. They, like his former co-defendants, assumed that he had turned stool pigeon and was giving evidence to incriminate them so that he could save his neck.

Again the footsteps in the hall. Again his neck and underarms prickled at the anxiety of a guard throwing open the heavy iron door and barking out an order. It was lunchtime. He was usually called to a conference with Broderick at lunchtime, after the lawyer had spent the morning defending the others. A ten- to fifteen-minute series of barked questions about his activities during the war; evidence he'd already given to his first lawyer who'd been forced to return to America to attend his sick wife. But Broderick insisted on going through everything again. For the record. And as the days wore on, Wilhelm was forced to admit that he enjoyed their interviews. It made the day shorter.

But even though it was lunchtime, he hadn't touched the slop pushed through the slit in his door. Hunger was a memory. He was losing weight, and he didn't care. He could tell, because his trousers, once snug, were now baggy. But he had no appetite. Perhaps when he was found guilty and was hanging from the rope, he would weigh so little that it might gain him an extra couple of seconds of life . . .

'On your feet, Deutch.'

The junior guard. New York accent. *'Yer'* instead of *'your.'* A pronounced *'ai'* in the name *'Deutch'*, making it sound contemptuous. *'Daitch'*. Such anger from one so young. Did this young and innocent American Long Island boy, born and nurtured in safety and wealth, know anything about what had happened in Germany from 1923 until the advent of Adolf Hitler? What could a boy born in the wealth and security of America know of the fears of a Communist takeover, of the degradation suffered by all Germany with the imposition of the terms of the Versailles Treaty, or the enemy in the streets, or the collapse of money so that savings became worthless overnight and ruined entire families? What could a New Yorker know of the immorality of the women who prostituted themselves for silk stockings or cigarettes, or the invasion of Gypsies and homosexuals and Slavs and Jews taking up jobs and German manhood being unemployed . . . What could this rosy-cheeked guard know of any of the suffering he and his family had endured? Sure, the collapse of Wall Street had caused a depression and some stockbrokers had plunged to their deaths while a few American farmers had been kicked off their land. But they had a Messiah called Roosevelt; Germany's Messiah was called Hitler. The difference was that one was victor, the other was vanquished.

'On your fucking feet, Kraut,' the young man shouted. Wilhelm got slowly to his feet. Lack of food meant that his head began to spin with the sudden exertion. He felt giddy and teetered to one side. The guard thought he was making an escape bid and snapped his rifle into the horizontal position. 'Back away now!' the boy shouted.

Wilhelm put up both his hands to assure the guard that it was illness, not intent which had made him totter to the left, but the guard raised the rifle to his eyes and cocked the trigger. One bullet, and it would all be over. A drunken lunge at the guard, and nothingness. Was it worth it?

'Back away from the door now, Deutch, or I'll shoot. Sarge!' the frightened guard screamed suddenly. 'Prisoner trying to escape! Sarge!'

More feet. Running. Wilhelm's head was like a balloon filled with water. The events seemed to be disconnected from reality. Boots running in the hallway. Another man. Bigger, fatter. The sergeant. Revolver drawn like some Hollywood cowboy in a Western movie.

'Over to the wall, Deutch. Move! Hands in the air. Now!'

'You don't understand. I'm sick.' They didn't speak German.

No compassion.

'Move to the wall, Deutch. Right now or I'll shoot.'

Clarity. Things coming back to today, to now. Vision.

He moved to the wall and stood there like a miscreant schoolchild.

'Hands on the fucking wall. Now!'

He did as he was told.

'Higher!

He moved his hands towards the ceiling.

'Okay, son, frisk him for weapons. Move an inch, Deutch, and I'll put a bullet in your fucking Kraut skull.'

The boy felt his raised arms, his shoulders, his sides and back, his legs.

'He's clean, Sarge.'

'What the hell went on?'

'I don't know, Sarge. He came at me like he was trying to overpower me. I restrained him and called for help.'

'Good boy. Okay, Mr. German Kraut. Twenty-four hours restricted food. Punishment for an escape bid. Water only.'

Wilhelm's head was beginning to clear. He vaguely understood the punishment. Nowadays, he spoke sufficient American. And he smirked. As though increased starvation would affect his behaviour, or even alter his routine.

The three men left the cell and walked down the dank corridor before climbing the stairs to the subterranean chambers in which he would be interviewed by Broderick. It had been three days since he'd seen the light of day.

'I was born when the century was already well under way . . . in 1911, to be precise, the same year as Dr. Josef Mengele.'

Broderick looked up from his notes. He'd heard the name Mengele, but couldn't place him.

'He was the chief doctor in Auschwitz. Indeed, I met him on many occasions in the mess hall. And I also saw him when I had to do work on Bloc 10 where they conducted medical experiments.'

'I've heard of those. They were the subject of evidence of an earlier trial. Unspeakable.'

Wilhelm ignored his comments. 'Mengele cut me dead when he saw me. Dead, so to speak. He was very arrogant and distant, considering me a mere maintenance man, although I was in charge of all the functions to do with the ovens and other things in the camp. Mengele went to university and got qualifications in philosophy and medicine. I never got past gymnasium . . . what you call high school. My parents were middle-class people, and had great expectations of me; they wanted me to go into a well-paying trade or even one of the professions, but I didn't do well at school, and so reluctantly they put me into a mechanical trade.'

Broderick stood from his chair and massaged the small of his back. His testiness was increasing as the defense of the men he called beasts came to a conclusion in the courtroom above their heads, and it became increasingly obvious from the attitude of the judge that all the defendants would hang for crimes against humanity. 'Look, Deutch, let's cut to the chase.'

He paused for the translator to finish his work. He had now become used to the effect the translator had on the interview process. 'This stuff about your birth and diapers and where you went to school is all very interesting, but it can be put down on paper and my assistant can make notes from it. I want to get down to business. I want to know how you came to be an engineer at Auschwitz-Birkenau. Did you resist your assignments? Did you refuse to obey orders because you knew in your heart that what you were doing was morally reprehensible . . .'

The translator looked up at him. 'Reprehensible? I don't know the German for that, sir.'

'Try 'unacceptable.' He did. It worked.

Deutch shook his head. 'I did what I was told to do. I have a wife and a daughter. To have refused to work in the East, in Poland, towards the end of the war, when Stalingrad had been lost and the German army was in full retreat, would have been unacceptable . . .'

'But you weren't in the army.'

'We were all in the army. Even civilians. It was the great cause. Germany was stabbed in the back by the Jews and the Communists in the Great Patriotic War. For it to happen a second time was unthinkable. Even after Stalingrad our confidence in Hitler hardly wavered. Just as he did, we blamed it on the generals. The incompetents. But Göbbels made a brilliant speech, rousing us to even greater heights of patriotism. He explained why we'd lost. It was nothing to do with Hitler and the Nazis. It was the High Command which had miscalculated . . . and of course it was the Jewish financiers who had supplied the people of Stalingrad with sufficient food to hold out until the end of autumn, and just as Napoleon, the German army had been beaten by the savage Russian winter. Another Jewish conspiracy.

'When our soldiers returned, bandaged and bloodied and in tatters, I couldn't believe it. They'd marched out of cities in huge columns with tanks and armoured vehicles and whole armies of soldiers. So many soldiers we thought the columns of our men would never come to an end. How could they have lost?

'I'll tell you, when I saw them come back broken and stumbling, like the Freikorps wandered the streets after the Great Patriotic War in 1918, well, I hated the Jews so much. I could have strangled them with my bare hands. So when I was transferred from my job in maintenance at the IG Farben factory where I'd worked since I was a boy, and was told to take a troop train to work in a factory which I thought . . . which I was told . . . was in this small Polish town, I just went. I didn't even think to question my instructions. We followed orders, even those of us who didn't go to the army because we were in restricted professions in the homeland.'

'Tell me about what happened when you got to Auschwitz,' asked Broderick.

'At first, I worked in Monowitz, which was the factory complex of Auschwitz. I. G. Farben was constructing the biggest synthetic rubber plant in the world, using the unending source of slave labour which Hitler and the German Army supplied to us.

'That was only one of the factories in Auschwitz. God, how I wish I'd never heard the name. You know, we Germans call it

Auschwitz, but in Polish, it's Oswiecim. A difficult word to pronounce. We'd never heard of Auschwitz in Germany. It never came up in conversation. And we'd certainly never heard of Birkenau. It never occurred to me that Topf and Sons of Erfurt, a subsidiary of I. G. Farben, would have actually built the gas ovens on which I later worked. They were instructed to begin the building of the ovens in October, 1941, as I remember.'

Broderick looked up and frowned. He only knew the raw details, not the fine points of how Nazi Germany was organised. 'Who ordered the construction of these gas ovens and crematoria?'

'The orders came from Himmler himself. But he said they had to be built at Auschwitz. However, some time after the ovens were being manufactured, Heinz Kammler, the chief of Group C of the SS Economic-Administrative Main Office, arrived at Auschwitz on February 27, 1942 and ordered that the five-oven crematorium projected for Auschwitz be constructed at nearby Birkenau. Now you'd think that someone would be particularly brave to countermand one of Himmler's instructions, but as Kammler was one of the closest associates of Himmler, no one dared disagree . . .'

Broderick shook his head in wonder as soon as the translator had finished.

'You amaze me,' he told the German prisoner. 'You're so accurate on detail. You're so Teutonic in precision. And you applied yourself with the same meticulousness when it came to destroying an entire race of people. How do you know it was February, and October? I can't even remember my wife's birthday without writing it down, yet you can reel off names and places and dates and times as though you were a goddam adding machine.'

Deutch nodded and took no offence. Tone and contempt were untranslatable, and by the time he'd listened to the German, he'd forgotten the look of disdain, the sneer on Broderick's face, the snarl in his voice. 'Yes, we are a precise race. We keep accurate records. It used to be our strength. Now it is our undoing . . .'

'Okay, Deutch, tell me about how you first got to Auschwitz or Monowitz or wherever the hell you went. Not the train journey, but your first impressions. I need this to convince the judge that you were like a fish out of water. That you weren't a real or willing part of the horror.'

But that was only part of the reason. He needed to know for himself.

The German shook his head in bemusement. How could an American possibly understand the route which took him to Auschwitz? It was more than just a train journey, more than packing for a new job in a new town. It was a mission from up high. The Messiah had led them out of the wilderness of the great depression. Where once there'd been abject misery, now there were jobs, money, national pride, and strength. Strength through joy! Thanks to Hitler, Germany was once again a nation to be taken seriously, to which all other nations looked in awe and wonder, no longer the bruised and battered bully of the Great Patriotic War which had been taught a lesson, but a people who had risen phoenix-like from the dust and rubble of the battlefields of France and Belgium, who had recaptured their rightful place in the world of nations.

Germany's *blitzkrieg* to salvage its stolen territory, to reclaim its German-speaking people from the grasp of foreigners, had left the whole world gasping. Communities of good German *volk* beyond the nation's constrained borders were again absorbed and incorporated into Greater Germany. The French, puffed up and full of pride as they humiliated the German people with the *diktat*, were now being humiliated themselves. Arrogance and self-confidence again were swelling in the bosom of every German.

But then the country had again been stabbed in the back. Where once they'd been great military victories which would be sung about for a thousand years, suddenly Russia had brought defeat and humiliation because hidden and secretive forces had caused terrible losses in wilds of the east, and now the war in Western Europe wasn't going well.

The Führer needed his help to put the nation back on top. What? Would he have refused to go where the Führer asked? He would have shot himself if the Führer had wanted him to. So a trip to Auschwitz to maintain some rubber factory, or to help keep the gas ovens going to exterminate their enemies, or even to assist with such mundane things as kitchen equipment, was the very least he could do for his Führer and to help the lads at the Front. It was the least he could do for Adolf.

CHAPTER THREE

Allied Occupied Germany, 1946

From the memoirs of Joachim Gutman:

'Don't let the sudden arrival of Adolf Hitler amongst the pantheon of German monsters fool you. Don't think for one minute that we Jews had been honoured citizens, living in some blissful German paradise for centuries, and then this Beelzebub, this acolyte of Lucifer, suddenly erupted on the scene to the shock and horror of every decent Hans and Helga in the land. No, the Führer didn't spring up from nowhere. Like other noxious weeds, his seed had germinated in fertile ground. Hitler wasn't a new or sudden phenomenon; Hitler was of the Germans, for the Germans, and by the Germans. In retrospect, now that the War has been over for a year or so, it's possible to look back and see from which pile of dung this latest flower of German manhood grew.

'Germans and Germany have always been anti-Semitic. Even as far back as the Crusades when Jews first settled in Germany, looking for security and a better life than under the Arabs or the Spaniards or Portuguese, the good *Herrs* and *Fraus* and *Frauelines*, hearing of the approach of a Christian Army intent on freeing

Jerusalem, would round up the Jews at knifepoint and force them out of their walled cities into the oncoming path of the knights, and lock the city gates behind them, leaving them to their awful fate. These good German burghers enjoyed the naïve hope that the Knights of the Cross, impelled to personal salvation and wealth through the rantings of an anti-Semitic Papacy, would satisfy their bloodlust on the Jews and then move on, leaving the city alone. I don't know if it ever worked, but it certainly shows the utter contempt in which Jews were held by the good Christian townsfolk on the way from Europe to Jerusalem.

'There were great hopes when Martin Luther emancipated Germany from the indulgencies of Rome. He wrote his theses, held out his hand, and welcomed us as brothers. But his love of us lasted as long as it took us to reject his concept of converting the entire nation of Israel to Protestantism; he didn't take rejection very kindly, and became so infuriated that he metamorphosed from a warrior-monk indignant at the Papacy, into a ranting, anti-Semitic lunatic, Adolf Hitler's mentor and brother in arms, advocating the extermination of Jews as the vermin of the world.

'Of course, you'd think that over their hundreds of years of experience, the Jews of Germany would have learned something, wouldn't you? Yet despite all the evidence of the dangers of assimilation, despite centuries of pogroms and killings and theft and desecration, the Jews couldn't wait to leave their ghettos and mix with proper German society. When Moses Mendelssohn advocated that the Jews of Europe leave the confines of their walls and the strictures of their rabbis, and stand in the forefront of the intellectual gales ushered in by Rousseau, the German Jews were the first in line, throwing off their kaftans and prayer shawls and skull-caps and eagerly standing in the main streets in their silk hats and fur coats with their hand outstretched in the hope that some passing burgher would clasp it, hoping for the sustenance of recognition and respect.

Sceptical? Cautious? Concerned that a millennium of hatred might not end quite so easily? Not a bit of it. As the Jews emerged from the ghettos, they became intoxicated by the champagne air of the Enlightenment and made Germany their own. But Germany didn't want any part of the Jews, and their intolerance to us grew as we came out from behind our walls. Oddly, there'd been some safety when we'd been huddled together with the walls of the ghetto for protection. Sure, there were beatings and killings, but they were sporadic. So long as the Germans didn't have to see us and deal with us, but just knew we were there, they usually left us alone—given the odd blood lust or two throughout the ages. But with the emancipation, with the raising of the hopes during the Enlightenment, an increasing number of Jews were now visible in drawing rooms and trading rooms, wearing the uniform of the Good Middle-Class German; and this sudden eruption of my people from their squalid homes into the centres of the towns and cities brought confusion, then scorn, and then the traditional organisation of hatred by the Germans. We found that far from allowing us to live and breathe the free air of the cities, the wonderful Germans began organising anti-Semitic leagues and political parties with the express purpose of expunging us. And don't think that the Catholic or the Lutheran Churches came to our aid. You should read what lies about the Jews the Catholic newspapers were printing in Rome; and France was no haven for Jews, not with the scandal and lies of the trial of poor Captain Alfred Dreyfus.

'So I ask again whether the rise of Hitler in Germany a surprise to us? To those German Jews who stood back and viewed the Germany with which we were so familiar from our knowledge of our history, his coming was as predictable as that of the Messiah.

'After the ignominy of losing the Great Patriotic War, all that was needed was a rabble-rouser to blame someone else and inflame the ire of the people to boiling point. The Jews were inflamed by Rousseau; the Germans by Hitler.

'And from the rubble of reason, bound together by mortar made from the bitter ashes of emancipation, grew the foundations of Auschwitz. I didn't go to Auschwitz until April 1944. Prior to that, I had been a prisoner in Sachsenhausen Concentration Camp, twenty-five kilometres north of Berlin.

'It was there that I first met the mechanic who saved my life. He was on secondment from Auschwitz where he worked in the I. G. Farben factory making rubber. He was sent to Sachsenhausen because they couldn't fix some of the important machinery in the DAMAG works, the Deutsche Maschinenfabrik AG, close by at Falkensee. I was working there as a slave labourer, and was given to him as his assistant for the three months he was there. Sometimes he shared his lunch with me, though it was strictly forbidden. He used to see the thin watery soup we were given, and feel sorry for me, and let me eat some of his rations. And often he shared stories and good humour. But most importantly, he shared his time. He allowed me to rest. Unlike the other poor bastards who were worked, quite literally, to death.

'But I race ahead. Again, hurry, hurry. As though my memory will fade and I will fail in my duty to those who can no longer speak on their own behalf. No, what I suffered, what my people suffered, cannot be forgotten. Or forgiven! Have we forgotten our days of slavery in Egypt? Our misery under the boot of Rome? No, some in the future might want to forgive, but we can never forget. It's implanted in our racial memory for all time. And of all the evil memories which we carry with us, we will never forget Hitler and the Nazis. What frightens me, though, is that the world will forget. And what we forget today we will repeat tomorrow. And the Jews cannot survive another Hitler. I have no idea how many Jews are left in the world. American Jews are safe; but in a decade or a century, will the destruction of my fellow European Jews have led to our extermination? Will Hitler have won through the laws of nature? Are there enough of us European Jews left alive to continue our thousand-year relationship with this continent of culture?

'In Sachsenhausen, there were ten thousand of us, crammed into barrack blocks. How to describe Sachsenhausen? How do you describe hell? Dante made a valiant attempt, and frightened the wits out of his Renaissance readers, but Hitler surpassed even that Italian genius's abilities. For he actually built hell on earth. Nobody who entered Sachsenhausen could possibly forget the squalor, the filth, the stench, or the vicious salivating German shepherds clawing the ground and snarling as they strained to break out of their leashes to tear at our throats, dogs barely able to be restrained by the SS guard. Nobody could forget the pall of death which hung like a grey menacing cloud over the uniform rows of huts. And none of us who first entered the camp could possibly have imagined that there was anything worse on earth than Sachsenhausen . . . but we were so wrong, for we had never heard of Auschwitz-Birkenau!

'What I recollect most vividly when I first saw Sachsenhausen Concentration Camp, was the crowds of people ambling slowly nowhere, some of them barely moving, they were so weak. Everywhere in the degradation of the place, in the huge central compounds, were multitudes of skeletal people just standing, or shuffling about. And gliding through this forest of dying trees, of greys and deathly pallor, were the black and shining uniforms of the Nazis, a mockery of the spit and polish of the Wehrmacht. These strong young German men and women would be completely impervious to the danger of being in the middle of thousands of their sworn enemies. Yes, they carried guns, but they knew with absolute certainty that they were safe to wander in their realm. For who would dare to lift a hand to strike against them? Who had any courage or strength left? Who could summon up any will to resist, when they lived every day among the dead, and when their only willpower was devoted to the will to survive? And who could forget the way some inmates would suddenly admit their own defeat and summon up their last reserves of strength to hurl their bodies against the electrified wire in order to end the nightmare?

'In many ways, I led a charmed life at Sachsenhausen. Charmed? An interesting way to describe the manner in which I spent such important years of my youth. While young men in their early twenties in America were driving in open-top cars and going to drug stores with soda fountains and dancing at clubs and seeing movies with their girlfriends, I was being beaten and whipped and starved and forced to sleep in lice-ridden straw with three other men. It was in this bed that I learned what we came to call the night dance, constantly moving your legs and arms, even in your sleep, so that you weren't bitten by rats. And worse, I and all the others were in constant danger of being shot because I hadn't looked at a guard in the proper respectful way . . . and all for the crime of being a Jew.

'But I was young, and healthy—well! Healthy, compared to the other poor devils who died from malnutrition or disease or because they simply gave up their love of life. I was tall and had good shoulders from being a swimmer when I was in my teens, and so on selection when I first went to Sachsenhausen, I was sent to work in the slave labour camps, satellites of the internment camp, places where we Jews did our bit to support the German war effort.

'How did we arrive at Sachsenhausen? By train or by lorry. We were rounded up in Berlin in one of the daily sweeps which the Gestapo or the police made to clear out the refuse and human lice. We were forcibly evicted into the streets from out of our houses. The British bombers had made such a mess of Berlin housing, that any available house was wanted for Aryan Germans. As Jewish families were evacuated from their homes by the collection units of the SS, they were rounded up and sent to the synagogue on Levetzowstrasse, a shell of a once glorious building, still in ruins from its destruction on *Kristallnacht*. The night I and my family were rounded up was the last time I saw my mother and father and brothers and sisters. I have no idea where they are now, or if any of them are still alive. And for some reason, I don't care. For if my family were forced to live through what I lived through, death was a far better outcome than life.

'What a night that was, the night I spent in the bombed-out syn-agogue. I plumbed new depths of fear as the SS guards pushed me around with the barrels of their rifles. Despite the freezing cold, all the Jewish families were forced to remain in Levetzowstrasse for three days, exposed to the bitter elements, before being marched in procession through the city to the train station at Grunewald, where they were taken to ghettos in eastern Poland, Belorussia, Lithuania, and into Russia itself. I was fortunate. Being young and strong, I was selected for labour. Old women, children, old men . . . who knew at the time what fate had in store for them? I know now what happened to those who couldn't work, but even so, what could we have done? Their journeys on the cattle trains and the trucks across Europe must have been murderous. My journey lasted only two hours. As to my family . . .

'When we arrived at Sachsenhausen, those who were in my intake batch on arrival were divided according to the irredeemable stain of their nature . . . Jewish men to the A queue for medical examination and processing, Jewish women to the B queue, Poles and Slavs to the C queue, homosexuals to the D queue, Gypsies and other vermin to the E queue, children (regardless of race or creed) to the F queue, German and Austrian career and habitual criminals and antisocial persons to the G queue, Jehovah's Witnesses and the work-shy to the H queue. Oh, it was all so precise, so German, as though it were the first day at school.

And after processing, we were all forced to undress and run naked in a line past the guards and doctors for the medical examination. Attractive women, those with good bodies and good hair, were pulled to one side and forced to stand by the guards who would fondle their private parts. Older men and women would try to hide their shame with their hands. I looked away. I couldn't bear to see their faces, humiliated, disgraced . . . and all the while wondering whether my parents were being forced by these animals to do the same.

We were then forced to huddle, naked, in the freezing cold air waiting for the next aspect of our induction to take place, terrified of would happen to us. We tried to talk, but when one elderly and indignant man was bashed to the ground with the stock of a rifle just for asking how long we would all have to stand there, the rest of us immediately became silent. I'd seen pictures in a nature book of penguins at the South Pole, standing huddled against the fierce Antarctic winds. Was I now like some animal? Had I lost my humanity so suddenly?

Then a guard with a gun entered our midst and isolated the next group of ten, and forced us over to a troop of men dressed in filthy uniforms with vertical stripes. Even their caps had stripes. These men were the barbers. We had to kneel down as though we were going to be beheaded, and all of our hair was cut off with shears. Somebody said something about delousing, but the masses of hair were collected in sheets and I have no doubt that it would be used for making blankets or stuffing pillows. That's the Germans for you. Nothing is left to waste.

Naked both in my body and on my head, I looked around at the pathetic group of men and women who were still huddling for warmth. With their shaved heads, and their bodies emaciated from three years of the deprivations of war, it was hard to tell the difference between the groups of men and the groups of women. Nobody looked at one another. Instead we all looked at the ground, wondering how much more we would all have to suffer before the nightmare came to an end. How little we understood that it was only just the beginning.

In the air, above the howling banshee winds of winter were the merciless voices of guards, barking out orders and battering people with the butts of their rifles when they didn't respond instantly. Children were crying. Men were whimpering. But oddly, the women were stoically standing there, hiding their private parts, turning themselves inwards so that they couldn't be seen by the guards or their menfolk.

And then the Almighty descended upon us, as though from Heaven. The commandant, Obersturmbannführer Anton Kaindl, drove through the gates of the camp proper into the receiving area where we had been rounded up. He was standing—as Röhm and Hitler used to stand—in the back of his black Mercedes, stiff and formal, immaculate in his brilliant black uniform, clutching the handrail between the front and back seats, looking at the six hundred of us with utter detachment. We could have been sheep, for all our humanity.

His driver manoeuvred the car in a large circle so that it came to a halt in front of us. I remember feeling shamed that I was shaved and naked and shivering in front of a man dressed so immaculately. I felt utterly wretched. Kaindl used his automobile as a mobile podium. We weren't even worth his getting out of the car.

I'll never forget his stance. It was the arrogance, the utter confidence in his power. I remember thinking to myself, *'If this is God, then how can I be one of His chosen people?'* He remained silent for several seconds as the guards stood formally to attention and screamed at us to stand still and be quiet.

And then he spoke. At first, it was quiet and we had to strain forward to hear, but then the volume of his voice increased and his words washed over us like a cesspool let loose. *'You have been brought here to work. That is your mission, your purpose for living. Fail to work, and you will die. Work and we will reward you with food and shelter. As soon as the war is over and the Führer is in command of all of Europe and America, a special place will be made for you on an island off the coast of Africa called Madagascar. If you work hard, the rest of your lives might be enjoyable.*

'But be under no illusions. You are here because you are vermin. The worst examples of the worst peoples of the worst races which have ever walked the earth. Whether you live or not is of no consequence to me or my guards.'

And then the silence which greeted his harangue was suddenly broken when a child began to whimper. Softly at first, barely audible above the freezing winds which were turning our skins blue; but his whimper soon became a hideous cry for his mama. There was stirring in the groups of naked men and women, as though parents somewhere

70

were about to go over and comfort the child. Paternal and maternal instincts were everywhere. Mothers and fathers forgot their own misery and thought only of their children.

The noises were ominous. Obergruppenführer Kaindl stopped talking. I was close to the car, and I perceived a slight smile on his face. As if he was suddenly touched by the humanity of a terrified little child. Instinctively a guard forced his way into the group of children and hauled out the crying boy who couldn't have been a day over seven. And it was then that I realised that the benign smile on the commandant's face was merely that of an actor, pleased that he had reached a particular and favourite part in his performance. This wasn't a welcoming speech, an induction into routine; this was a morality play, an act of life and death, something which Kaindl did every time there was a new intake; a demonstration of his godhood in order to strip us of any remaining vestiges of humanity and to quell any potential and future resistance from the group. I shuddered in the absolute certainty of what was going to happen.

'Here is a boy unable to control himself,' said the commandant, looking at the now-howling child, standing alone and forlorn now, wailing in front of the group of other children. I looked at him. I have never ever seen such terror on the face of a human being. This poor boy had lost control of his bladder, he was so horrified at what was happening to him. He stood with his hands hiding his penis, trying to stop urinating, the piss running through his fingers. He was shaking his head in terror, stamping his little feet on the ground, howling in agony for his mother to come and comfort him, but not knowing what to do. All he kept screaming in his little, high-pitched voice was 'Mama, Mama.' I was close to tears. I knew I should run and hold the child in my naked arms and assure him that everything was all right, but I couldn't move. To move was impossible. Fear held me in my place.

The poor child wanted to hide, to get away from the misery. And so he started to run towards the gates, screaming, 'Mama, Mama,' all the way. The soldiers let him run. They knew what was going to happen.

They even grinned in anticipation of the fun, like an audience which knows the good bits in a play. These guards, these men, these fathers and sons and brothers and uncles, these were willing and supportive actors in the commandant's bravura performance.

'This child has no discipline,' shouted Kaindl. 'He needs to learn discipline if he is to enjoy his stay at Sachsenhausen.' He took out his pistol from his shining holster, aimed, and shot the retreating child in the back. The boy pitched forward on to the hard and unyielding ground, a hideous red stain on his shoulder. A roar of horror went up from all of us. A cry of incomprehension. And above our pain, the pain of a mother, who screamed out, 'Mein kind.'

The guards all levelled their machine guns at us as the silent child's mother struggled to get free from the women who were restraining her, for they knew that she, too, would die if she emerged from her anonymity. But she pushed her way through to the front. She ran towards her dead child, but three guards stepped forward to hold her rigidly in place, despite her struggles. And then one of the guards took out his pistol and hit the mother on the back of the head with its butt. She was stunned and stopped her screaming. She slumped down, a naked and defeated woman, held crouching by the burly guards. We looked from the boy to his mother. If her husband were in the audience, we all wondered how he would react. If it were my son and wife? What would I do? Nothing.

A sullen silence descended upon us all. Only the bitter winter winds, blowing through the nearby forest and biting into our blue skins, could be heard.

'This woman will go to the guards' recreation and enjoyment area. This is an illustration that you must keep in your minds, and remember that order and discipline are essential to your welfare all the time you are here. If you fail, then not only will your life be forfeit, but also the lives of many of those around you, who will be punished for your misdeeds. Therefore you will observe one another, and you will report troublemakers to the guards. Failure to do so will result in your death.'

The performance was over. The lesson learned. Horrified, we saw the commandant replace the gun in its holster. Without a word, the driver started the car and returned him to his villa, where he would eat his venison and *saubratten* and potatoes and drink his vintage red wine, and tell his mistresses what a hard day it had been at the office.

The woman began to moan, blood dripping from the wound in her naked scalp on to her shoulders and running down her back. I prayed that she wouldn't recover and look again upon the dead body of her son.

Three of us were forced at gunpoint to go over and pick up the boy's body and carry it to another part of the camp where, as we rounded one of the barrack blocks, we saw for the first time a mound of white and decaying skeletons which once were Jews.

It was then that I knew we were in hell. But in retrospect, how little I really knew. Two years later, I would look on Sachsenhausen as the purgatory before the hell which was Auschwitz. And who on earth would have realised that my Saviour wasn't the Messiah, but a mechanic?

Interrogation Room, Palace of Justice
Nuremberg, Allied Occupied Germany
June, 1946

'I don't understand. What were you doing at Sachsenhausen Concentration Camp? I was under the impression that you spent your entire experience of the camps and the factories at the Auschwitz complex.'

Wilhelm Deutch looked at his legal representative and gave a benign smile. Under other circumstances, would these two men willingly spend any time at all together? Deutch was German and working class, and had become elevated above his station in the new Germany because of his skill as a mechanic. He had been told that

Theodore Broderick was a high-ranking university person, apparently a top professor of law, a noted ethicist (according to one of the guards who had read a profile of him in *Stars and Stripes*), a friend of President Roosevelt and of Supreme Court judges, a humanitarian and a philanthropist. He was the backbone of Boston society. And he was here, by his own admission, because he wanted to understand what made a man into a Nazi. Would these men have spent time together under any other circumstances? Yes, if Broderick had a problem at his home and called in Deutch to come round to fix his plumbing.

But now, they were co-equals, brothers in a common fight, thrown together by the vagaries of war and peace. And for the time in which Theodore Broderick was representing him, Wilhelm Deutch would ensure that he had the patrician's full attention and respect.

'I was sent back from Poland for three months during which time I was seconded to Sachsenhausen to fix some major problems which DEMAG had with some of its machinery. The pressure from hydraulic systems kept fluctuating and failing and causing major holdups in the manufacturing process. Machinery stopped working and that ruined production schedules. The commandant was very worried. There was unbelievable pressure on him from the High Command, and those in charge of war materiel.

'The problem which he had was all to do with the steam pressure. Everything would be working well in the morning, and then suddenly everything would seize up and the boilers would be in danger of exploding and they'd have to let the steam pressure escape and that ruined the afternoon's production. They thought at first that it was the slave labour sabotaging the works, but it was soon apparent that it was not human intervention, but something mechanical. They tried to fix it themselves with engineers from Berlin, but they couldn't.

'One of the DEMAG managers had worked before the war for I. G. Farben, and knew of my expertise in hydraulics, and so they sent for me. It took me three months to work out what was wrong, and how to fix it. It was a fascinating problem, you know. And although it took me ages, months to solve it because I had to do all sorts of pressure testing, the answer, when it came, was so simple. It was all to do with the differentials in pressure between one housing and another, a slight difference in elevations of the two adjoining boilers. It wasn't so much the lie of the land, which was level, but the internal structures of the pressure tanks weren't exactly level, and so during the day, there'd be a buildup of cooler, condensed water which would begin to flow back and lower the temperature in the first boiler, and then . . .'

Broderick looked at him quizzically to see whether he was joking. He was dealing in a life and death situation, and this man was talking pressures and hydraulics. The American had no interest in the mechanics of a concentration camp boiler. He cut across him. 'In terms of slave labour, what happened at Sachsenhausen? How was it compared to Auschwitz? What was required of you? Did those with whom you were directly related participate in any crimes against humanity—any killings or torture or some such evil? Were you a participant in any of it?'

Wilhelm simply shook his head. 'I worked in a place where death happened daily. I never dealt in death. Where I worked, machinery was used to make spare parts and components.'

'But there was slave labour in your factories at Sachsenhausen! You've already admitted that.'

'Certainly! That was the reason I. G. Farben and Siemans and Volkswagen and Krupp and MAN and BMW and Leica and so many other German industrialists all supported Hitler with so much money. Without the industrialists and their money for posters and uniforms and rallies, he would never have won all those elections. And without the Wagner family, the children of the great German composer, he'd never have been introduced to the industrialists. What goes around comes around. So you could say that Richard Wagner was in part responsible both for Götterdämmerung, and for this damn war . . .'

He looked at Broderick to see his reaction, but the sarcasm went over his head. So the prisoner continued, 'These companies were convinced that if Hitler went on a limited war against countries in the east, like Poland and the Ukraine, he would be able to supply them with an endless source of free or cheap workers, which would make them super-competitive with the rest of the world. Some even built factories inside the concentration camps so that prisoners could work from six in the morning till six at night. And they didn't have to provide fancy canteens or restrooms. And it wasn't only labour from which these industrialists benefited. Once we took over the Ukraine, we had oil and factories and iron and endless supplies of all the raw materials we needed to make us into a major power overnight. We had land and a slave population and food . . . everything for expansion and space for the German people to grow beyond the confines of our crowded borders. If we'd only just taken over the East and left everyone else alone, Germany today would be the greatest and wealthiest nation on earth. No country in the West would have come to the aid of Poland or any of those Slavic countries, but once he attacked Russia . . . we could have become another America, if he hadn't attacked Russia and France.'

Again Broderick looked at him askance. He was tempted to say that America had spent two hundred hard years making itself into a major power by decency and skill, and only resorting to wars which had to be fought, but not for aggrandizement or empire or conquest. But he stopped himself, because he suddenly remembered that the South had been built on the blood and sweat of millions of black Africans, brought to America's shores in chains. Anyway, he was here as a lawyer, not a moral referee, and so he held his peace.

'Were you present at any acts of unlawful killings or torture? Slavery is a crime against humanity; but were you forced to take the slaves which were offered to you as assistants? Could you have refused to use slaves on moral grounds? Did you fight against their use with the command structure of the camp?'

Deutch hesitated for a while before answering. This, and other crucial questions would determine his fate. But his fate was already sealed by previous decisions of previous Nuremberg Trials. He knew that he was a dead man with time on his hands. 'Yes, I took the slave labour. No, I never considered turning it down. Who in their right minds would? We were at war. British bombers were killing our people in Hamburg and Berlin and Köln. Are you asking whether I had scruples about taking a gift of free labour which never went on strike, which worked when it was told to work, which ate little . . . and the supply of which was never ending. If a slave labourer dropped down dead at his machine . . . and hundreds did . . . then his body would be picked up by other labourers and carried outside. Moments later, his place would be filled by another. And when that one died, then there were a hundred thousand others to take his place. A never-ending source. If you're truly asking whether I tried to stand against the tide, then the answer is no. Not once. Never. If you ask, *'Am I ashamed?'* then, yes, now I am deeply ashamed of what I did back then. But in those days, shame never once crossed my mind. Remember we were at war. Only societies at peace have time to experience the niceties of feeling ashamed. We Germans were experiencing the needs of survival.'

He saw the look of disgust on Broderick's face. 'Tell me, Mr. Lawyer, do you ever read Nietzsche?'

Without waiting for a reply, Wilhelm continued. 'He said something which I believe applies to me, and indeed to Germany. *He who fights too long against dragons becomes a dragon himself; and if you gaze too long into the abyss, the abyss will gaze into you.*'

Broderick stared at him impassively. He'd been shown the works of Nieztche during the war by a colleague in the Department of Philosophy in an effort for the campus to understand Nazism. But outside intellectual circles, he was hardly known in America. And his appropriation by the Nazis made him unacceptable as a philosopher to be studied along with Plato and Aristotle and Erasmus.

'I see you don't follow the meaning,' said Wilhelm, almost didactically. 'War corrupts. You can fight evil as long as you like, but ultimately the evil of war makes you evil. End of story. We were fighting evil. Evil was weakening the German people. The evil of Communism, of internationalism, of the Jewish conspiracy. This is what we were told daily by Hitler and Göbbels and Himmler. We had to fight evil to survive. What I, and all Germany, did in order to fight this evil and to survive was whatever was necessary. If that included using slaves, then so be it. We were told that Jews and Slavs were subhumans. Laws were passed saying as much. When your government tells you that someone isn't a man but a subhuman, a bacterium who will infect you unless you deal with him, you tend to look at him very differently. Isn't that how the Americans in the South of your country treat Negroes? Why are we so different?

'I was applauded by my colleagues and those for whom I worked. No one told us that what we were doing was evil. Yet now, I'm forced to defend myself because a bunch of Americans who lived out the war in peace and serenity say that what I and millions of others did was evil. Very well, judge me and hang me, but when you've tightened the noose and I'm rotting in my grave, will you be any better than me? You're tainted by evil, just as I was. Is Churchill going to be prosecuted for ordering the bombing of our cities? Had Germany won the war, would we have tried and convicted Eisenhower and Patton and Montgomery?'

It took a full minute for the translator to finish, during which time Wilhelm sat with a satisfied smile on his face. Listening, Broderick became increasingly angry. When the translator had finished, Broderick snapped furiously, 'We didn't . . . wouldn't . . . have spawned concentration camps. Eisenhower and Patton wouldn't have herded millions and millions of human beings into pens to slaughter them. You and people like you mechanised death. You industrialised it. You made it into State policy. How dare you compare the Allied war effort with the greatest monsters who ever lived?'

As the words of the translator evaporated into the thinness of the air in the claustrophobic room, the two men looked at each other in disgust.

Wilhelm said quietly, 'I thought you were here to defend me.'

CHAPTER FOUR

Berlin, Germany, 1998

THE PHRASE '*NEEDLE IN a haystack*' kept going through her mind from the moment she landed in Germany. Chasca Broderick had interviewed the leaders of the remnant of the once-prodigious Berlin Jewish community, had searched the records at the Ministry of Information, the archives of the now-defunct Office for the Reconstruction of Germany, the also-defunct Office for the Welfare of Displaced Persons, the records of the Center of Historical and Cultural Studies at Humboldt University, and many more.

For two weeks, she'd scoured the landscape of what remained of the Berlin Jewish community, the synagogues, the various institutions for the reclamation of the lost culture, the societies and establishments whose function for the past half century had been to attempt to rebuild what was left after the destruction wrought by Hitler and the Nazis in their frenzy to eliminate Judaism from the memory of the world.

She'd examined the records, looked through old telephone and city books and maps, searched the census and other rolls, spoken to archivists, sought help from willing historians and librarians and document specialists who had helped her uncover the musty annuls of old Berlin. She'd walked down streets, spoken to old Jews who remained, spoken to elderly people in the legal fraternity, in the judiciary, in commerce and economics, trying to find someone who, however vaguely, remembered the Family Gutman and their connection to pre-war Berlin. But nobody remembered. And she was left wondering whether Hitler had, indeed, won his battle to eliminate the memory of European Jewry.

There were dozens of Gutmans in the directories and archives. But none which fitted the family history or the description so insubstantially written by Joachim in the early parts of his autobiography.

'Why?' she eventually asked Dorothea Elchor, a middle-aged archivist with the Council for the Records of the German Jewish Community in the Leipzigerstrasse in the Mitte District of Central Berlin. 'Why is it that a prominent Berlin Jewish family, the father a judge of all things, can suddenly have disappeared off the face of the earth? Not a single record, not a solitary document which says that the family even existed. Okay, so if Joachim's father had been a nobody, maybe that I could understand; but a lawyer, for God's sake . . . a judge. Before the war, his name would have been in newspapers or on some sort of record . . .'

Dorothea nodded in agreement. 'You'd think so, wouldn't you? But you'd be wrong. It wasn't only books the Nazis burned, or synagogues on *Kristallnacht*. They made a frantic, mechanical effort to nullify Jewish existence. Any synagogue which they found was burned, and its holy books and scrolls and records burned with it. Newspaper offices, many of which ridiculed the SA and the SS in the early days, were torched along with all their records. They put totally inferior, and often stupid and brutish, Nazi professors in charge of university departments which were once run by Jewish professors, and the Nazis made great political capital of destroying what had gone on before . . . same with the Nazi judges who replaced the Jewish judges. Chasca, you can't begin to imagine the methodical and systematic way in which Hitler and Göbbels and the rest of them made Germany *Judenfrei*.

'Does it surprise me that your search has been so unsuccessful? No. In fact, I'd have been surprised if you'd found anything.'

She could tell that Chasca, whom she'd first met a week ago as an enthusiastic and eager young American woman on a mission, was becoming burdened down by failure. Americans had such an expectation of success, their entire ethos being based upon their ability to do anything . . . just throw sufficient money or time or energy at a problem, and it'd be solved. But now Chasca was learning the reality of the thousand years of the Jewish European experience . . . that Jewish survival had been so much a matter of resilience and even good fortune; that money and time and energy were valueless against the waves of hatred which periodically swept across the troubled continent.

Jews had risen to astounding heights of influence and intellect and wealth in Europe; yet every hundred years or so, their entire edifice was knocked down by some madman who wanted to rise above the common herd. She could have named them like a litany of horrors, but where to start? At the Crusades, or Martin Luther or Richard Wagner or Friedrich Nietzche or the pogroms or the Freikorp or the rise of Nazism? And that was only Germany; Russia and Poland and the Ukraine and most other European countries had their own litanies of sustained and systematic anti-Semitism to remember.

So how could she help this lovely young American girl who was so earnestly trying to resurrect the forgotten memory of one hapless German, wrongly hanged at the end of the bloodiest and most vile war in history? She reached over the desk and grasped her hand. 'Perhaps we're starting at the wrong point, my dear. Perhaps you should be going to the family of the hanged man, Wilhelm Deutch. Maybe they might know something. It's possible that this survivor, Joachim Gutman, contacted the family Deutch after the war, and they might be able to give you his whereabouts.'

Chasca smiled and nodded in agreement.

Prison Cells beneath the Palace of Justice
Nuremberg, Allied Occupied Germany
June, 1946

Wilhelm felt himself shrinking. Physically, bodily. As though the cell in which he spent his days and nights was growing larger by the day. Odd, when he was on trial with the others, he felt bigger than his cell. He felt tall and muscular. Because he felt the security of comradeship. And as a big man, he faced his prosecutors squarely, in the unity of the oppressed; he would live and die with those who had been part of a common experience.

But that had suddenly been taken away from him. He had been cut adrift and was now alone on a strange and uncertain sea. Since his trial had been truncated, and he was to be exposed to a sole spotlight with its merciless beam illuminating him and him alone to the world, he had lost weight at an alarming rate.

His appetite had disappeared. He only touched food occasionally, and then as soon as he put some soup or some bread in his mouth, it tasted bitter, and he felt uncomfortable in his knotted stomach. He was tall and thin by nature, although in his middle years, he had begun to put on a stomach. Now his clothes were sagging on his bony frame, his face looked gaunt whenever he had the privilege of seeing himself in a mirror, and he was shocked by the way in which his hair was coming out in clumps on his comb. He had always enjoyed ruddy health; been a sportsman, enjoyed the activity of a full and often outdoor life. Even at Sachsenhausen and Auschwitz, separated from his wife and children, he'd kept up his physical fitness by regular games of soccer with the other staff. He'd even exercised his manhood with a particularly willing and adventurous Jewish girl seconded to him from the brothels. She exercised those parts of his body which soccer left untouched.

But what worried him was that he might be suffering from the growth of a cancer. He told the guards that he needed a doctor; they told him that the doctors were all busy looking after the victims of the Nazis and there were none to spare on bastards like him.

He told his lawyer that he might be suffering from a malignancy, but the lawyer at first took it for a metaphor for the party to which he had once belonged. It was only when he explained about the weight loss that the lawyer treated it seriously and called for medical attention.

The doctor had given him a thorough examination, and, in the absence of bleeding or internal pains or any other external signs, he'd said that he was probably suffering from anxiety, and that it was no wonder considering he was facing trial for his life. Wilhelm demanded a more thorough examination, an X-ray. The doctor laughed. 'Nearest X-ray machine is London. We've bombed every medical facility in this country out of existence. Anyway, it's odds on you'll follow your colleagues to the hangman's noose, so there's no point in treating you with any medicine other than that which will ensure you hear the judge's verdict.' And with that, the doctor packed up his bag and left Wilhelm to contemplate the Hippocratic Oath. Not even a bottle of tonic for the Nazis.

In the afternoon, a week before his trial was due to start, he was called to a meeting with his lawyer. He entered their interview room with what enthusiasm he could muster. In his cell, he felt weak and dissipated. Walking in the exercise yard, always on his own now that his former colleagues were being hanged, he felt as though he was ambling through a sort of intermediary state; neither of living nor of death. Was this Purgatory?

But when he entered the room, a metamorphosis seemed to take charge of his body. He was here for a meeting with his lawyer, something he'd done a number of times in the past . . . yet this time, things felt different. Possibly because he was nearing the time of his trial, possibly because a resolution was about to take place, possibly because if he was to be hanged, then his suffering would soon be over. He didn't know the reason, but as he walked into the dull prison interview room, he suddenly felt charged with life, with purpose.

In the beginning, when he'd felt betrayed by the truncation of his collective trial, he had been utterly resistant to the elegant American. He knew that this was all a sham, that he was going to be found guilty, and he would determine his own way of making peace with the World and with his maker. And the American had tried the use of reason and persuasion. All the lawyer's gestures were those of empathy, of a desire for the truth to out and an acquittal made before God or whatever spirit imbued the heart of the German. But beneath the patina of understanding, of the desire to find out what really happened, Wilhelm knew with an absolute certainty that the American lawyer loathed him, felt defiled in his presence. He tried to keep secret his utter contempt for Wilhelm and all those like him, falling back on arcane philosophies of life. But Wilhelm knew just as certainly that the American was there for some inner personal benefit, and whether Wilhelm hanged or not was a matter of total indifference.

But they had been thrown together by fate and justice, and now, as Wilhelm's story unfolded, as his confidence increased while offering explanation through narration, as his morale improved through the catharsis of being listened to if not appreciated, he began to welcome a way of defending himself. He gave Broderick glimpses into the life of one of the masters of the concentration camps. He might only have been a mechanic, but he was the chief mechanic and nothing in the camps would have worked without him. Did he use slave labour? Yes, of course. Did he like what he had done? No, not now, not then!

'I'm going through the evidence and there are things which I need to have made a great deal clearer. The prosecution will seek to condemn you as an habitual and irredeemable monster; they'll say that what happened in Auschwitz with your maintenance of the machinery was a logical extension of your willing participation in the bestiality; that you weren't just a cog in the machine of the Nazis, but you pulled many of the levers which made the machinery operate. They'll say that any moral person would have objected despite the consequences. Which means I'm going to have to find something about your earlier work for the Nazis, say at Sachsenhausen, which will disprove their contention. If they lead with the fact that you were a willing accomplice, that you accepted the slave labour you were given without remorse, without compunction, it's going to make my job difficult. I need to know whether or not you made any attempt whatsoever to alleviate the conditions in which the slaves directly worked for you.'

'Will it make any difference?'

'Of course.'

'Will the judge understand? Can he put himself in the position of a man such as me, a family man with a wife and daughter, a mechanic working happily for a large corporation who was suddenly enlisted into a huge military machine and made to twiddle knobs and participate in things which happen in the middle of a war? An ordinary man wouldn't consider killing another human being, but put him in a soldier's uniform, tell him that he's got to kill an enemy who will kill him if given the chance, and see what the reaction is. The ordinary man turns into a brute, a killer . . . a soldier.'

Deutch looked at the patrician American and felt inclined to continue without interruption now that he was explaining what had happened and the circumstances in which it had occurred.

'And the other thing you have to realise is that we were ordered . . . ordered, you understand . . . to look upon the inmates not as human beings, but as vermin, microbes, bacteria. I know that this sounds impossibly evil to a man such as you, but since the beginning of the 1930s, all we heard was Adolf Hitler screaming about the Jews and the Slavs being subhumans. He'd passed laws which took away their humanity; we were encouraged to burn their shops, make them pick up horse droppings with their bare hands; we were forbidden to befriend them, marry them, have intercourse with them. For Germans, the Jews lost their essence as people with souls, with hopes and aspirations and rights, and became the effluence which had to be expunged from society to make us safe . . .'

And then softly, so softly that the translator didn't know whether or not to translate the words, Deutch said, '. . . just like your Negroes in the American South.'

Ignoring the last remark, Broderick pinched the wings of his nose. The mechanic had found the very epicentre of the argument he intended to put before the judge; that when judging the arch-criminals such as Göring and Hess and the others, the judicial decision had been a simple one. Those men were guilty of barbarity and the invention of the machinery to commit the greatest evil ever to exist on the face of the earth. So regardless of the circumstances in which their crimes had been committed, the great criminals of Nazism ought to have the full weight of punishment brought down upon their heads. No amount of reflection, no consideration of the environment in which the crimes were committed, could mitigate for the wickedness. It was the wickedness which was punished, not the reasons for it!

But in the case of the mechanic, he'd been swept up into a sea of evil, and from what Theodore could ascertain, he'd reacted in the way that most people would react in that environment. When all around are sustained by the food of hatred, it's difficult not to sup from the same vessel. And so the mechanic, by his own account just an ordinary man, had done what was expected of him . . . He'd made the machinery of evil run smoothly; he'd used those workers who had been given to him, without enquiring whether they were free men or slaves; he'd hit them when his masters demanded they be hit, worked them for the hours which his masters determined that slaves should work.

All that Theodore hoped was that the judge could put himself into the position of judging the accused man within the environment he was forced to work, rather than viewing the accused as a free agent with the right to determine the working conditions of those in his employ.

Breathing deeply, he said to Wilhelm, 'I know that brutal things are done in war. What we have to convince the judge of is that there was a spark of humanity in you while the slaves worked for you. That you had no part in the organisation of the slave labour. That you were merely a worker. Now, without putting words into your mouth, what happened in Sachsenhausen?'

Deutch smiled. 'If I tell you I was a humanitarian who risked his own life to save those around me, who will believe a word of it? Who will come forward to speak on my behalf? If I did any good deeds, Professor, I'm afraid that they're destined to be buried along with the mounds of corpses which are rotting in the concentration camps.'

Allied Occupied Germany, 1946

From the memoirs of Joachim Gutman:

I think that the first three months in Sachsenhausen were the most murderous times for me in the entire war. For it was my first intro-duction to true barbarity. As a Jew growing up in Nazi Germany, I'd known brutality and evil and cruelty; I'd known prejudice and hard-ship and deprivation. But not barbarity. The Germans were always so proper when they were stabbing you in the back.

How does that accord with what happened in the streets, with the SA and then the SS and the leather-coated Gestapo pulling people out of buildings and into cars which sped off and you never saw the people again? Or with the Brownshirts and the Blackshirts attacking Jews in shops or on footpaths and beating them? Or making Jews clean up horse droppings with their bare hands and put them into their pockets?

At the time, I thought it was the ultimate in evil. To see my people denigrated and abused, with ordinary Germans, neighbours, looking on and approving . . . even nodding in agreement . . . even laughing. Even joining the Brownshirts and participating!

But then the rumours about the camps 'in the east' began to circu-late through Berlin. Killing camps. Mass extermination camps. Camps where human beings–Jews, Slavs, homosexuals, Communists–were rounded up and herded as though they were cattle being readied for the slaughter. Of course we didn't believe them. Who would? How, we asked sceptically, could a people who had produced Schiller and Bach and Mozart (yes, we included Mozart after the Anschluss) possibly have conceived of factory killings of human beings as though they were pigs or hens? The Nazis were talking about the mass emigration of the Jews from Europe. They were Zionists. They wanted us to go to Palestine, or Uganda or Madagascar or Zanzibar. They just wanted to see us go and leave Europe Jew-free, not to kill us.

So my first three months in Sachsenhausen were more than just a time when I tried to survive. They were also a time for me to learn. To learn of the depths to which a people can fall when unchecked, to learn what it means to be deprived of dignity, to learn of the two natures of a single race. And learn I did. Had I not learned, I would have died. But I was young and strong and I quickly adapted to my new conditions. And because of my strength and resolve, I was quickly put into the gangs of slave labourers who were roused at five in the morning by the barracks captain, someone appointed by one of the kapos. The kapos? These were evil specimens of humankind, as bad as the Nazis. They were usually German criminals or Poles, or worse, Jews who had been sent to the camps, but who immediately collaborated with the Nazis to get special privileges. They made sure that we left the barracks on time. We quickly learned that it was in our interests to rouse ourselves from that shallow state which mimicked sleep and run quickly to the barracks door.

Sleep? How can you sleep when there's no air in a room, or where the stench of two hundred men makes you want to vomit, or where you sleep three to a wooden bunk filled with straw, or where rats take chunks of flesh from your arms or legs, or where the lice get into your nose and your ears and make your body crawl? Sleep? Well, the moment we heard the doors opening, we painfully struggled down to the freezing cold ground and made for the door. If we delayed, or we were late getting out of the barracks, we were beaten so severely that some of us died.

Outside in the dim light of dawn—in winter in the freezing cold and blackness which comes before daytime—we were forced to stand in long lines outside our barracks. The kapos stood rigidly to attention, as though they were soldiers on parade. When the Camp Adjutant came to our row, the kapo walked up and down and counted the numbers. If they didn't tally, the kapo had to explain the difference.

'*Three died in the night,*' he would shout.

'*I killed two this morning for being late. Beat the fuckers to death,*' he would boast.

'*One man short. Starved to death. Never mind, more food for the rest of us.*'

And always there'd be that grin of superiority in his voice, audible and visible, despite his back being turned from us.

The Adjutant would tick off the figures, nod, and move on to the next barracks. Death was merely a statistic to him, an accountant from hell doing the rounds of a factory where human beings were both the machinery and the product.

After five thirty, we walked across the compound to the food truck, where large vats of what passed for food had been prepared by other prisoners. We always carried our tin mugs with us, our tin plates and our tin spoons. We would line up, our stomachs complaining bitterly. There was rarely any smell from the food in the cold morning air. It was all so squalid. Eventually, I would find myself at the front of the queue, and would be handed two slices of what they called bread (it actually was a type of bread but the flour had been mixed with sawdust to save cost), some margarine if we were lucky, some marmalade, and what the cooks called coffee. I never became used to the taste of the coffee in Sachsenhausen. It was only later that I was told it wasn't coffee at all, but ground up toasted acorns mixed with chicory.

We wandered back to our barracks, ate this muck hungrily and then paraded outside for collection by the work detail to be sent to the factories. Every day we looked for familiar faces. Sadness no longer overcame us when someone with whom we'd been working for two or three months suddenly wasn't there any more. At first, in the beginning, we were distressed beyond belief. But as death became the routine rather than the exception amongst us, we viewed a friend's death as a blessed way out, a holiday from further work. A Sabbath.

The work I did in the DEMAG factory was for a mechanic, a maintenance man. No, that's not a fair description. He was an expert at hydraulics. He was doing something on pressure levels in boilers or something, and he needed a couple of strong men to help him lift and carry and push things from one side of the boiler to another.

At first, when I was assigned to him and when we began working together, he was cold and distant. He commanded me to do things. *'Pick this up. Put it there. Don't do that.'* I just obeyed. He was the master, I the slave. I viewed him as a typical Nazi, a Christian German who hated me and viewed me as the others in the camp hierarchy viewed me, a piece of filth, mere vermin.

And that's what I thought for the first week or two. He worked me hard in difficult circumstances. Every night, I would cry in my bed as my muscles and bones ached from the exhaustion of work I wasn't used to doing. But my exhaustion was different from the other poor souls who worked in the factories. They came back to our barracks as though the very life force had been drained out of them. I saw them working from my vantage points, walking around the boilers with Deutch—that was his name—or going outside to examine the pressure levels at various points in the pipes.

I had led a lazy and indulgent life before being sent to the camp. Most of my exercise had been in sport. So doing this mechanical work, carrying heavy and unwieldy loads, working without a break, was exhausting. I thought I'd drop down dead every night. But compared to the others in my barracks . . . well, they suffered from true, real exhaustion. They returned grey with tiredness. They stripped off their clothes supporting themselves on their bunks, and their legs were blue with numbness. They had been standing all day without a break. Working at their machines, or fetching and carrying loads which in another life would have been the job of mules or oxen. Their hands were red raw and bloodied; their faces sweat-stained; their hair matted to their scalps. And when they'd managed to pull off their stripped uniforms with that last reserve of energy before falling on to their beds, they sank to their knees and clambered into their bunks, just for the joy of lying instead of standing.

As I need to point out, my work was completely different from the way the others worked. They were at lathes or machinery from six in the morning till six at night, with only the shortest break imaginable for a thin soup of potatoes and beets. Guards with whips and German shepherds walked amongst them, and if they weren't working at top speed, they would be beaten.

But the work I did was paced according to the routine of this man, Deutch, and while certainly not lazy, he didn't exactly work himself into a frenzy. Indeed, he took frequent breaks in order to sit on top of a boiler where the pressure monitors and dials had been placed, and work out what was going wrong. It required a lot of thinking, and there was little we could do while he was pondering the problem. So we would sit at his feet and watch him think. In the beginning, he made us stand to attention while he was pondering some aspect of what was going wrong with the machinery. And he tried to keep that up for some weeks. 'Do this . . .' 'Do that . . .'

But he wasn't the type. So after the first couple of weeks, he'd ignore us while he was fiddling and turning dials and putting in new pressure monitoring equipment. And we would hang around underneath the boilers out of his sight.

That only lasted as long as it took for one of the Work Group Commanders to make an inspection and find me and my co-slave, Henny, sitting underneath the boiler, talking. The Work Group Commander yelled at Deutch to come down from on top of the boiler immediately. The commander was furious and shouted at Deutch that slaves had to be worked day in, day out, and if Deutch didn't have sufficient work for us, then we would be taken from him and redeployed. Deutch screamed at us to fetch the pails of water he told us to fetch ten minutes ago and apologised to the Commander for not keeping a better eye on these Jew scum. Deutch promised that we would be beaten severely for our laziness. But the Work Group Commander obliged and beat us horribly with a truncheon.

When we returned with pails of water, we could tell immediately that Deutch felt guilty that his lies had got us battered. From then on, he kept me close to him all the while and would somehow sense when he was being viewed by a guard, or when one was on the prowl, making an inspection. He couldn't keep his eyes on both of us, so he reassigned poor Henny to another job. That left just the German mechanic, Deutch, and me working on the huge boilers.

When I was working with him he would make me lay down on top of the boiler so I wasn't visible to the guards on the ground down below. Sometimes, I would see a twinkle in his eye as a guard walked passed and gave him a friendly wave. He would respond, and then would look at me as though I were a naughty schoolboy who had tricked a teacher.

But best of all was the lunchtime. He obviously didn't like the commander, and so used me to get back at him. He always demanded that I sit with him on the top of a boiler (I would lie flat and out of sight, while he sat up), and he would open his leather attaché case. Then he would take out his lunch, which he'd had the kitchen staff make up for him in the morning. After the first month of working together, we would regularly play a game, he and I. He would first take out the bread, then the pickles, then the slices of ham and sausage and cheeses, then the pickled herrings, then the pickled cabbage and onions. And finally, joy of joys, he'd take out a bottle of milk and a single cup. And as my eyes grew wider, he would reach in to the very bottom of the attache case, and he would dig around, and then . . . miracle of miracles . . . he would find another cup which he would pass across the top of the boiler towards me. Never had food tasted so divine. Never, ever, had I properly understood the joy of not feeling hungry.

Did I feel guilty? Of course. How could I not feel guilty when I returned to the barracks with a still-glowing feeling of all those tastes and flavours coursing through my body, with a full stomach and the delicious afterglow of cheese and milk and pickles still clinging to my mouth? How could I look my fellow prisoners in their hollow eyes and emaciated faces when I was so hale and full?

And then I reached a compromise, with myself and with those who were around me. Instead of eating everything, I 'stole' from myself, secreting slices of cheese and sausage into my pocket, which I then shared out with those with whom I shared my bunk. I was like a god to them, and the food I gave them was Manna from heaven. Where had I come across such nectar, they asked. I stole it from the guards, I told them. Be careful, they pleaded, though I knew that they were less concerned for my life than for their continuing supply.

And so it was for three months, until Wilhelm Deutch was finished. He found the source of the problem. The DEMAG factory had been built on level land, but the inside of one of the boilers had been built slightly sloping, and no allowance for this had been made when siting the boilers. But after months of painstaking measurements, the mechanic made the exact and proper allowance by putting the feet of the front boiler on slightly elevated leggings. What this did was to correct the problem of the unequal pressure which built up in the interior tubings of the boiler, which meant that although the outside was level with the floor, the insides were not level with each other . . . hence the pressure difference when some of the water condensed. The differential was only a matter of a couple of centimetres over the ten metres of the two boilers, but sufficient to make the steam vapour ebb backwards, condense on the colder part of the top of the boiler, and create a partial vacuum.

There was a consequential runoff of water, which migrated into the tubes which linked the two boilers and hence back pressure from the front boiler to the back caused the back boiler to become dangerously overstressed. Had they not shut it down each time, it would eventually have blown. A simple equalising exhaust tube was placed in the top of the second boiler, attached to a one-way pressure valve, and the problem was fixed.

Even though he deliberately delayed many days, eventually he had to bow to the pressure of the DEMAG management and fix the problem. Yes, he actually delayed unveiling the solution because he knew that when the thing was fixed, I'd have to return to the old job, the old rations, and my life would quickly end. We had built a rapport, a friendship, perhaps even a mutual respect. I will never forget the feeling as he said good-bye to me. To him, I was a new and valued colleague, albeit a Jew and a subhuman; to me, he was my Messiah, my saviour, my health, and my welfare.

He walked off quite jauntily, handing me back to a guard. But I knew that his jauntiness was *bravura*, a performance to show that he, like every good German, couldn't give a damn about the life of a subhuman Jew. But in his heart, I knew that he was upset, maybe even concerned for me.

The guard's German shepherd snarled and salivated. I was put on to a lathe and told to work quicker than I had ever worked before. My days of Paradise had ended; now I entered the halls of hell. Above the portal leading into Dante's hell were the words, *'Abandon hope all ye who enter here.'* No such words needed to be written above the door of our factory . . . We were told that work makes us free.

Within a day, I had abandoned all hope of living beyond the next week.

Interrogation Room, The Palace of Justice
Nuremberg, Allied Occupied Germany
June, 1946

'Tell me about the slave labourers that worked for you.'

Broderick suddenly realised with a flush of shame that he'd used the impersonal pronoun 'that' instead of 'who.' Odd, not something he would have done in an article he might have written for a learned journal, or allowed to pass in an essay from one of his students. Yet because he was dealing with a man who valued human life as of lesser worth than that of the machinery he maintained, Broderick found himself caught up in the language of impurity; he himself was now objectifying men and women.

Wilhelm, by now garrulous in his definition of his role in the war machine, was reflective. As the days of gathering evidence mounted and the trial date neared, he was painting a portrait of himself as a man caught up in a massive machine, a minuscule object squashed by an irresistible force. The American lawyer was waiting patiently for the next phase of his client's justification. Deutch had yet to claim to have used slave labour unwillingly, and neither did he pretend that he had attempted to resist the organisation which spawned it. But the moment when he claimed innocence was drawing closer, and Broderick anticipated the self-justification in a state of perplexity, wondering how he would deal with the plea.

'I dealt with them as I had to,' Deutch said softly.

'Meaning?'

'Meaning that the work had to be done; the hours were set by the camp commandant; the working conditions were laid down; the food rations already determined; the living conditions in place. What more can I say? What employer today would go into an employee's home and judge the way in which he was living, or the size of his bank account, or the exhaustion he felt after a day's work? I was an employer. It was my job to fix a problem. I used what resources were given to me.'

Broderick felt the *frisson* of anger. Resources! Was this a way to refer to human beings? But then the defense lawyer in him took over and he felt relief. So far, his client hadn't claimed to be an innocent. 'But didn't you feel any need to ease the burden of those who worked for you? Just in order to prolong their lives . . . or at least make their lives somehow more bearable?'

Wilhelm breathed deeply for a moment and stared at the ceiling of the interview room. Broderick noticed a sudden change, as though the German was remembering back to times when he was the master of his world, not a prisoner of the victorious Americans, living in an alien environment. Was it sadness in his eyes that this had come to pass?

'What do you want to hear?' asked Deutch.

'The truth.'

A wry smile. 'Truth is an odd word from the mouth of a lawyer.'

Broderick let the insult pass and remained silent.

'What is truth? A child is drowning in a river, and I am standing by the bank, doing nothing. An observer far away accuses me of total indifference, of participating in the child's death. That, for him, is the truth. Yet I cannot swim. If I plunge into the water, we will both drown. That for me is the truth. Which truth is the real truth?'

Broderick made some doodles on the page in front of him. It was a simple exercise in philosophy. A naïve conundrum. A first year ethics student could have worked out the parameters. Should he introduce Deutch to the thoughts of Saint Augustine or tell him that Aristotle held that we use reason to determine the best way to achieve the highest moral good? No, this was not the place, and certainly not the time. He remained silent. Yet in his silence, the opening words of Augustine's City of God echoed in his mind . . .

'I have undertaken its defense against those who prefer their own gods to the Founder of this city—a city surpassingly glorious, whether we view it as it still lives by faith in this fleeting course of time, and sojourns as a stranger in the midst of the ungodly, or as it shall dwell in the fixed stability of its eternal seat, which it now with patience waits for, expecting until 'righteousness shall return unto judgment,' and it obtain, by virtue of its excellence, final victory and perfect peace. A great work this, and an arduous; but God is my helper . . .'

For a moment, Broderick found it hard to breathe. His whole life had been spent in the pursuit of justice and understanding. Now he was in the presence of true and unalloyed evil, and he found it in such conflict with anything he had previously understood of life, that logic and reason were nowhere to be found. And neither was truth . . .

'Truth!' the German repeated contemptuously. 'If I told you the truth, you would never believe me. Oh, you and your fellow Americans would believe the truth of the barbarity; you've seen the concentration camps for yourself; you've seen the films they took. No, I'm talking about the islands of sanity in the years of war, the food I shared with starving prisoners, the extended rest periods from work which I allowed them at my own risk, the privileges I ensured they enjoyed, despite the dangers to myself. If I told you about these things, you'd just assume I was lying to save my own skin. And who would be there to support me? We Germans got rid of most of the evidence. As the Allies and the Russians were closing in, we burnt and buried and killed all who could testify against us. And that's why I'm going to hang, like those I was being tried with last month. Because in our collective guilt, in our mania to hide what we'd done, we inadvertently killed those few who could testify on our behalf. Do you think we were all monsters? We were a nation of tens of millions. Were we all barbarians? It's convenient for you to label us all as evil. But in every society there is good and bad. By lumping us all together and pointing your finger and screaming 'guilty,' you're just as bad as us. As we accused all Jews of being evil, so now you're accusing all Germans of being evil. Are you any better than us?'

Theodore Broderick pondered the reality of Deutch's defense, now exposed and bare, as raw as the damning evidence against him. He closed his notebook slowly. Wordlessly, he stood and left the room.

Allied Occupied Germany, 1946

From the memoirs of Joachim Gutman:

'I remember very little about that year which I spent in Sachsenhausen. All I remember is the numbness which overcame me. From being fed and protected, a special person, I became one of the gray and dying trees I had first noticed when I entered the camp, dead trunks which shuffled around the parade ground, men and women just hobbling along in an effort to keep warm. And in days, I joined them going from one side of the compound to the other, aimlessly. Sometimes a man would slowly amble over and begin a conversation, but talking was hard. Any effort given to that which didn't immediately keep us alive was effort wasted. And conversation was of little value. Why say anything when the only thing of importance was keeping alive?

What was of value was newspapers. Not for that they said! No, we had no willingness to waste a precious newspaper on the words printed on it. What we used newspapers for was to stuff into the wooden clogs they gave us to wear. It softened the hardness of the wood, it insulated our feet from the icy cold; it made us feel in some way like human beings.

Of course, shuffling around the camps was an activity I did only for a few hours a day. I worked from six in the morning till six at night on starvation rations. Then I walked in the long line of slaves back to the barracks, where I struggled to lay down on my bed to rest. My legs were the worst. The wooden clogs which they forced us to wear made walking near impossible, and made standing an agony which spread from the feet to the ankles to the calves to the legs and buttocks, and quickly turned my whole body into a torture chamber.

The cramps and numbness in my legs were what gave me the most trouble. Twelve hours of standing. At least my hands and arms and body were moving as I operated the lathe, or carried heavy timbers or iron girders. But my legs were immobile for most of the day, and after about ten in the morning, I failed to feel anything in them which wasn't pain. I was terrified that they would collapse on me, and I would fall down at the lathe. And if that happened, a guard would happily set a German shepherd on me, and the vicious dog would take great delight in tearing at my throat. It did happen. It is not my imagination. I'd seen a dog attack on the slaves before, many times. Fear of it happening to me was what kept me going. Two lathes away from me, a man had suddenly sat on the floor, feeling faint. He tried to stand because he knew he was courting death. But a dog was let loose by a guard on the other side of the factory, and like a meteor, it wove its way through the machinery and pounced on the Jew. He didn't even try to defend himself. He had no strength. He just screamed for a brief moment, and then his throat and voice box were torn from his neck. He twitched a couple of time as blood poured out of him. He was carried, still twitching, from the lathe, and within an hour another man was turning the same machinery. And so life continued.

I'd seen many dog attacks in my year in the DEMAG factory. Men who were too slow, or who answered a guard back, or who didn't look right, were the ones earmarked for attack. The guard would smile his evil smile—they were often ignorant Bavarians or Ukrainian collaborators—and would release the dog, urging him on by shouting in the dog's ear. The dog would then bound over to the man and jump on him, pushing him to the ground. The victim's screaming would impel the dog and drive him to even higher frenzies of attack. He'd tear at the man's throat or face or arms. The man would be weak and puny and starved and little more than a skeleton. What match, then, against a dog whose rations were ten times what the man was given to eat?

So to prevent my legs from collapsing, at the occasional breaks we were allowed, I would force myself to go to the benches to eat something—potato soup, a couple of slices of bread . . . if there was something solid in the soup, we'd go fishing for it with our spoons, but it was usually just thin, watery muck—and then I'd walk to exercise my legs.

They starved us because they knew that we would work till we dropped, and then we'd be replaced by other slaves. There were a hundred million slave labourers Hitler could bring in from the East, from Poland and Hungary and the Ukraine and the Czech lands. Why waste food and effort on men and women workers? Get the most out of them, and when they dropped, throw them on the rubbish heap, and put a dozen more in their place.

Normally we lasted for only three months before malnutrition and disease and infection carried us off. Why did I last a year? Maybe because of those three months in which I had been well fed. Maybe I'd built up reserves of energy and fat. Maybe it was Deutch who save my life. But saved it for what?

But for whatever reason, survive I did.

Until I was sent to Auschwitz.

CHAPTER FIVE

The Subsidiary Courtroom of the Palace of Justice
Nuremberg, Allied Occupied Germany
June, 1946

COURTROOM SEVEN

The trial of an alleged War Criminal W. A. Deutch, before the International Military Tribunal. 11/14/1946. Occupied Territory, United States Jurisdiction.

Accession Number: AX-00452-C1947

Defendant: (No Military Title) **WILHELM AUGUSTUS DEUTCH**

Charge and Indictment:

That the defendant Wilhelm Augustus Deutch, adult German citizen, along with other person or persons unknown and uniden-tified at this time, during a period of years preceding 5/8/1945,

participated as organiser, instigator, and accomplice in the execu-
tion of a Common Plan or Conspiracy to commit Crimes against
Humanity, as defined in the Charter of this Tribunal, and, in accor-
dance with the provisions of the Charter, is individually respon-
sible for his own act or acts. The Common Plan or Conspiracy of
the former Government of Germany, embraced the commission of
Crimes against Humanity, in that the defendant committed such
crimes concerning the enforcement and slavery of captured and
unlawfully imprisoned persons, such deprivations as which were in
violation of international treaties, agreements, or assurances and
in contravention of the rights ascribed to humanity by the general
consent of Nations.

Assistant United States Prosecutor **William Sherman**, Allied Nations (US Jurisdiction), Advocate for the International Military Tribunal.

Professor **Theodore Broderick**, Advocate for the Defendant.

Presiding Judge: **Justice Jonathan Parker**, Alternative United States Justice.

'Yes, Mr. Prosecutor.'

'May it please Your Honour. This court has been called to a special hearing of the charges laid against the defendant Deutch, whose previous trial was aborted after two days at the request of his defense counsel, Professor Broderick.

'Dr. Broderick believed that the evidence which was to be laid against Deutch would become confused in the judicial mind with the evidence of the other defendants whom, I might remind Your Honour, have recently been sentenced to death by your brother judges for their part in the commission of Crimes against Humanity.

'It was Professor Broderick's contention that the evidence against Deutch and the crimes he was alleged to have committed were of a far lesser nature than those laid against his former co-defendants, and as a result, in the interests of justice, the Prosecutor's Office agreed to allow him the unique distinction of a separate trial.

'Upon opening the prosecution's case against Wilhelm Deutch, may I remind your honour of the words of the Chief Prosecutor of the International Military Tribunal, United States Supreme Court Justice Robert Jackson, who said something in this very courtroom just twelve months ago which will, I sincerely believe, go down in the annals of civilised nations as the guiding principles by which all must behave. At that time, Justice Jackson, prosecuting the major war criminals Göring, Dönitz, Frank, Frick, and others said, *inter alia*:

> 'What makes this inquest significant is that these prisoners represent sinister influences that will lurk in the world long after their bodies have returned to dust. We will show them to be living symbols of racial hatreds, of terrorism and violence, and of the arrogance and cruelty of power. They are symbols of fierce nationalisms and of militarism, of intrigue and war—making which have embroiled Europe generation after generation, crushing its manhood, destroying its homes, and impoverishing its life. They have so identified themselves with the philosophies they conceived and with the forces they directed that any tenderness to them is a victory and an encouragement to all the evils which are attached to their names. Civilisation can afford no compromise with the social forces which would gain renewed strength if we deal ambiguously or indecisively with the men in whom those forces now precariously survive.

'Your Honour, I make no distinction here between the duty imposed upon your brother judges in the trials of the major war criminals, and Your Honour's need to judge this minor and pathetic war criminal Deutch. The magnitude of other Nazis' crimes might be different, but Deutch, like they, must be punished for his willing participation in crimes which were so repugnant as to leave the civilised world agasp, wondering how human beings could possibly behave like this towards other human beings.

'Your Honour, the defendant Wilhelm Deutch was part of a machine which tortured, enslaved, murdered, and behaved in a way not seen since before the era of Christ. He will try to convince you that he was a cog in the wheel of that machine, that the makers and the drivers of that machine have been punished, and that he should be allowed to live the rest of his life with the crimes, which they committed, resting on his conscience. That, Your Honour, is the punishment he believes he deserves. He will contend, Your Honour, that as a mere mechanic in the concentration camps, he was just following orders. That he took no part in the determination of those orders, but was merely the instrument of their directives.

'This defense has now become part of the parlance of the war which has gone before us. It's now being called the Nuremberg Defense. And it holds no truer today for a minor criminal like Wilhelm Deutch than it did a year ago for the monstrous war criminals who have been found guilty by your brother judges, and hanged for their bestial crimes. Crimes are crimes, and criminals are criminals. The contention of the prosecution will be that the major crimes could not have been committed without the willing participation of a nation of executioners.

'Your Honour, the prosecution will contend that it is just as important for you to punish this insignificant man for his complicity as it was for your brothers a year ago to send the Nazi leaders to whatever hell will be the final resting place for their evil flesh. Your finding of guilt of the mechanic, Wilhelm Deutch, will send a clear message to each and every German, to each and every citizen of each and every nation, that they are as responsible for the actions of their leaders as are the leaders themselves responsible for the crimes they commit; that while those in minor office might just be following orders, the nation which closes its eyes to the behaviour of its leaders is as responsible for their crimes as are the leaders responsible to their nation.'

William Sherman, the prosecutor cleared his throat. He had no idea of how many cases he'd prosecuted during his thirty-four-year career. But in each and every case, he found this the most exhilarating moment, the time when the entire court—judge, jury, defendant, spectators—hung on his every word to determine whether the finding would ultimately be guilty as charged, or innocence and freedom. But he felt no such charge of emotion right now. There was none of the adrenaline which normally coursed through his body when he stood in court for the first time to present a case.

He was tired. He'd been prosecuting these monsters for the better part of a year now. He'd interviewed living corpses to garner evidence, and been told the most heart-rending and incredible stories of human depravity and cruelty he'd ever heard. He spoken to ordinary foot-soldiers, men who had been bloodied in war and tempered by the furnace of battle, and he'd had to console them as they recounted their experiences of entering concentration camps like Ravensbrück and Sobibor and Dachau and Buchenwald; and the very nadir of evil, Auschwitz-Birkenau. He'd spent weeks disbelieving written depositions about the activity of the *Einsatzgruppen* and their mobile killing vans, until he saw the engineer's plans and read the first-person accounts of the participants.

He wanted to go home. Wanted to go back to Maine and breathe the air and swim in the rivers and creeks and see the colour of the leaves in fall and clear snow from his porch. He didn't want to be prosecuting such a man as Wilhelm Deutch, a mechanic, a functionary so minor as to be nothing more than a cipher in the alphabet of the Nazi bestiary. But he'd written the words he'd spoken carefully, after having discussed them with his staff. What he'd just told the judge was his honestly held opinion, and it was his role to ensure that every Nazi was punished for every infraction conducted during the currency of the war. Regardless of how trivial his crimes compared to those of Göring and Hitler and the real monsters, men like Deutch had committed evil. He was a slave master, and in the memory of all of the slaves who had dropped down dead from exhaustion, Deutch and all like him would be punished.

'May it please the court, I call my first witness . . .'

Allied Occupied Germany, 1946

From the memoirs of Joachim Gutman:

'It came as a complete surprise that my name was suddenly called. I was asleep in the barracks. I'd been back from the factory for only a matter of minutes, yet I was already in the deepest of deep sleeps. Indeed, I had to be roused by the Barracks Captain, pushed and shoved until I almost fell off my bunk.

'He screamed at me, 'Gutman, you filthy fucking Jew scum. The adjutant wants to see you. Off your fucking bed now.'

'I knew that something momentous was about to happen to me the moment the evil swine told me that I had to go before the camp adjutant. Me? A piece of filth, vermin, a skeleton, walking and talking and still living because of some manic determination not to succumb to the will of the beasts called Germans. Give in to exhaustion and it would mean your death and they would have won!

'I struggled to walk down the central aisle of the barracks. Nobody who hasn't been a slave labourer can ever begin to understand the exhaustion I felt at that moment. The only thing I wanted to do was to lie down and try to breathe. Yet I had to walk. Even when I slowed, he hit me in the back with his stick. Pitching me forward, nearly making me fall.

I hadn't even eaten yet. Not a thing since breakfast. The potato and beet broth was particularly evil that day, and I'd vomited it up in a gutter. Secretly. Without the guards seeing, for I would have been beaten and forced to clean it up with my bare hands. Some of my co-slaves could drink many litres of this thin and evil stuff, but I couldn't and that was why I was wasting away, why my hair was falling out, my skin flaking as if I had some sort of disease . . . Maybe I did. Who knows? So much dirt, so much disease. And wasn't I some vermin? Some bacterium . . . according to my lords and masters!

But how could I continue with such a hunger eating away at me, gnawing my very insides? What would I do if I had to stand around waiting for the adjutant—whoever he was—to see me. For one such as me, for a half man whose bones stretched his thin white skin to breaking point, minutes could equate to death. In the beginning of my stay in Sachsenhausen, fear had been my companion; but since the mechanic had gone from the camp, I was no longer afraid of death, only the daily, yawning ache of starvation. And the only thing which kept it at bay, letting me live to work for another day, was the watery and evil-tasting broth they called soup which kept me alive, stuff which in their heyday, my family would have thrown out in disgust as unfit for human consumption.

Most prisoners lasted only three months on that starvation diet. I had managed to remain alive for nearly nine months . . . long enough for a woman to bring new life into this evil world! Alive? An odd way to define my condition. I was closer to death than to life; yet in that demi-world between life and death, instincts somehow sharpen. Colours become more vivid, as though they are the stuff of living; sounds which we take for granted, such as the chirping of a bird or the mewing of a cat, take on a whole new meaning, a celebration of life; and smells translate into blessed memory. The wind changes, and the smell of fat cooking in the officers' mess becomes the memorial of a family feast or a barmitzvah or the joyous wedding of the girl next door. In death, we remember life.

The peasant kapo led me to the door of the hut and pushed me out so that I sprawled onto the ground at the feet of a sadistic SS Nazi guard, whose job it was to conduct me to the adjutant's office. I stood, and followed the guard who screamed in my ears, 'Up Jew scum.' Then he hit me, so that everyone around in the command area could see what a good guard he was. He screamed at me again, 'Pick up your feet, fucking Jew swine. Walk slowly and I'll kill you.'

Someone in a uniform of an officer looked in our direction. The guard hit me on the head with his stick. My eyes lost focus. I saw black and white. I pitched forward as if I were going to fall, but retained my balance. Somehow, my feet kept moving; every step was an agony. I had no energy to do more than try to walk to the gates and then into the command compound.

The guard had a dog which he threatened to set on me, barely restraining the German shepherd so that I could feel its hot, salivating breath on my hands as it tried to rip into my flesh. But the guard held it on the leash . . . as though fear of a dog could make a dead man walk.

We arrived at the office of the adjutant. I had never before been inside the camp headquarters. This was not a place for prisoners. We had often talked about it, this building on a hill at the edge of our camp, protected from us inmates by electrified barbed wire. What went on in here, we wondered? Was it at Monday morning meetings that some faceless Nazi executives picked up the phone to Hitler to get instructions on how many of us were to live, how many to be tortured, how many starved, who should work till he dropped, who would die? Like the opening of the solemn *Kol Nidre* Service of *Yom Kippur*, before Almighty God, Blessed Be He, closes the Book of Judgement for another year, the time when the Almighty One, decides who will prosper and who will decline, who will live and who will die . . . so were there godlike Nazis in some heavenly antechamber in this building deciding on our fate? Maybe now I would find out.

It was a squat, ugly building, part wood, part brick. There were guards standing smartly to attention outside. Oddly, as we walked up the stone staircase, I felt embarrassed. I felt as though I hadn't dressed properly, as though my clothes were inadequate for the occasion.

How strange that I should feel embarrassed about my appearance. After all, I looked like I did because of these men; yet I felt weak and foolish and ill-dressed in this most alien of environments.

The guard followed me to the top of the stairs. But a drama suddenly took place, something which could only have happened in

Teutonic Germany; for suddenly my guard met the eyes of one of the senior officers who appeared at the doorway of the building, and a curt nod of the officer's head dismissed the guard, who nodded back, turned, and hurried down the steps.

Odd; in my hell just beyond the barbed wire, this guard, and all those like him, were gods. I was his object; my life was at his disposal . . . yet here, on the other side of hell where heaven resides, he was shown by the dismissal of his superior officer to be nothing more than a functionary, a mere cipher in their system, as I was a cipher on the other side, in his world.

I followed the superior officer into the building, my wooden-clogged feet shuffling after the shiny black boots which clicked menacingly on the polished floor. What I noticed most was the activity; people shouting orders, dogs growling, the sounds of typewriters clattering on paper, feet walking hurriedly along corridors; there were people everywhere. But not like the people in the compound, or who crowded ten or twenty deep just to queue up for the gruel which masqueraded as food and where every man of two hundred in a room tried to find even a millimeter of space to call his own, and where we huddled in the dark taking shallow breaths just to stay alive, limbs twitching to scare off the rats; not crowded like in our straw beds, where we slept three to a bunk, and the feel of another person's warmth was a feeling of life . . . even though that person was a man.

No, these German Nazi people who ran the camp were efficient and groomed and wore clothes which didn't smell of the rain and dirt and the fetid, rotting straw in which we slept. The clothes these people wore smelled of cleanliness. Some of the men, I recognised. They were important people, dressed in immaculate black shining uniforms, who were in the parade ground in the evenings to count the inmates. These officers would be standing on trailers or wagons so they could look over the heads of the thousands of inmates and determine how many were still alive that night, and who during the day had perished from exhaustion or disease. There, on the parade ground, they looked like gods, tall and potent. Here, in their headquarters they looked like ordinary people, smaller than I thought. But they gave me contemptuous glances, repulsed by my rags and my smell, irritated that such a piece of vermin as me had infested their place of business, as though I was a bacillus. Didn't they realise that vermin such as me *were* their business?

The officer commanded me to sit on the bench and wait until I was called into the adjutant's office. I sat as I was commanded. The world around me was suddenly frantic. I felt as though I were in the centre of the activity, in the middle of a German maelstrom. Maybe it was my weakness, my lack of familiarity with my surroundings, but everybody seemed to be walking so fast, so purposefully . . . I was very frightened. People paced quickly passed me, beyond me, raced around the bench on which I sat. My head was light . . . that I remember clearly. Light from hunger, not happiness. I was terrified by all the business being conducted around me, by the speed with which the world was spinning.

And then I smelled it. An aroma from years past, from the time when I was growing up and was forbidden it. An aroma which started my mind reeling from the potential which it could afford me. The smell of richness, or normality. The smell of cleanliness and mornings . . .

What was the smell?

Coffee!

Not the ersatz rubbish made from acorns which we were given. This was real coffee, smelling like a ripe fruit, like a freshly mown field, conjuring up erotic and carnal thoughts I hadn't had since I became a prisoner. My eyes began to water and my throat constricted with the feelings of pleasure and pain. I blinked back the clouds of tears welling up in my eyes and searched the long corridor and reception area, and then I saw it. It was a table, set with a huge silver urn, surrounded by plates of biscuits and sandwiches and cakes. My mind raced back to one of the Sunday morning coffee parties my parents used to organise when entertaining the Jewish elite of Berlin; it was like being a guest in the palm-fringed conservatory of the Hotel Adlon at No. 1, Unter den Linden. I looked at the table in disbelief, and then I saw a couple of men deep in conversation coming down the corridor towards me, walking close towards it. Casually, almost as an afterthought, one of them reached down, and picked up a sandwich, which he started to eat as he listened to the other man, nodding as he stuffed the soft, fresh white bread into his mouth.

In the barracks, it was a cause for joy and celebration if we sometimes caught a dead rat. In the middle of the night, we would skin it, gut it, light a small fire of straw and wood shavings stolen from the factory, and roast the meat, tearing off strips as they charred and became edible. Others in the barracks would shuffle towards the fire, and beg for a bit of rat meat, even a bone to chew on, but whoever found the rat was the one who didn't go hungry for a couple of days.

And here, just a quarter of a kilometre away from thousands of people starving to death, was a table set with the food of the gods, where any casual visitor could simply pluck nectar while he passed, as though this table were a tree from the Garden of Eden, heavily laden with impossibly wonderful fruits. No fights, no threats, no frantic grabbing or punching, not rats' meat, nor the thin gruel and soup which was given to keep us alive so that we could work . . . Here was just fresh food always available. I was in heaven.

I felt myself standing. I didn't even think about the possibility of punishment. I began a painful walk to the table. I didn't see people looking at me, or hear someone barking an order for me to sit down. My ears were throbbing with the noisy sound of blood rushing through them. My stomach was making noises which deafened me to the threats; my eyes were dimly focussed on the cornucopia before me and they were blinded to the danger.

I remember staggering towards the table, too weak to run. The table and the food loomed nearer as I approached it. It was all so perfect, like a beautiful painting . . . fresh bread with lashings of yellow butter, seductive red jams and brown honey, delicate porcelain cups and saucers just waiting for someone to pour first milk, then tea from a silver teapot. Of course, it was all in my mind, because on the table were only bread and margarine and honey, but my eyes were seeing a picture of a time before I was sent to the camps, and I was fantasising in the world of memory.

And then I vaguely heard the sound of feet stomping towards me, and men growling like dogs and I remember stumbling before I reached the table and suddenly there was no table, only the wooden slats of the floor, and the sight of boots. On the floor, I could see the underside of the table. My head throbbed from where I'd been struck by a baton. But that was all I can remember because the throbbing stopped when I blacked out with an SS officer's boot hitting my head.

The next thing I knew, I was slumped on the carpet of the adjutant's office. All I heard was the noise of pounding in my head. Then, above the pounding, the words,

'What is your relationship with this mechanic?'

And then I knew I was dead. A memory of food. Of sitting on top of a boiler and smiling. Of breaking the law. Found out! Punishment. Death. Relief.

'Can't the fucking Jew understand German. I need to know what was the bond between this mechanic and this Jew.'

Somebody else spoke. Some other voice. 'As far as I know from the reports left by this Wilhelm Deutch person, this Jew Gutman is skilled at mechanics and he's needed in Auschwitz.'

'Absurd. Can't this mechanic Deutch find somebody else? Surely in the whole of Poland there's somebody who can turn dials and fiddle with machinery. Why send some Jew who's about to die all the way to Poland?'

'I don't know why you're arguing. The orders are quite specific. This Jew Gutman must have some special skills.'

A long, drawn-out silence. A rustling of papers. A curt, 'Very well. Send him by the next transport east.'

A click of heels. A *'Jawohl!'* And I knew I would live.

The Subsidiary Courtroom of the Palace of Justice
Nuremberg, Allied Occupied Germany
June, 1946

It was the second day of Wilhelm Deutch's trial, and three people had already given evidence. The previous day, under an almost respectful cross-examination by Theodore Broderick, a twenty-year-old woman, Rosl Lieber, told the court of how she had worked from dawn to dusk in the Daimler-Benz factory for over a year, making cables and lamps. She showed the court her scarred hands and the burns on the skin of her arms and shoulders from the hot machinery which she was forced to use with no safety equipment. The judge, who a month beforehand had stood in the gallery and listened to his brother judges trying and sentencing to hang the members of the death squads called *Einsatzgruppen* for crimes against humanity, was not unmoved . . . yet it couldn't be said that he was overly empathetic. The testimony of a slave labourer was hideous, especially a young woman starved and worked almost to the point of death, but it was not in the same league as evidence of the creation of a mobile gassing van which drove in the rear of the army to round up and murder Jews and Gypsies and others who had escaped death by gun or bomb. The evidence this young woman gave would have disgusted him if he'd been presiding in an American court, but he was almost ashamed to admit that it wasn't unduly discomforting when put into the context of this pantheon of evil.

'And did you see the defendant Deutch while you were working in the factory?' asked the prosecutor, William Sherman.

'Yes, many times. He would walk up and down and make sure that our lathes and the other equipment we used were in good working order. And when our equipment worked by using some hydraulics, he would regularly come around and check the gauges.'

'Did the defendant ever speak to you?'

'No. Never.'

'Did he acknowledge you, ask how you were feeling, offer to make the machine you were working on safer, test it to ensure that it was not dangerous?' asked the prosecutor.

'No. He treated me as if I was dirt. He sneered whenever he came near me and the others.'

'Did he ever attack you, mistreat you . . .'

'Your Honour, while I appreciate the difference between a military tribunal and a court of law, I believe that the rules concerning leading a witness should be obeyed,' said Broderick.

The judge didn't have time to respond because Sherman acknowledged the point and continued, 'Did he appear to be friendly with the guards, as though they were in some way . . .'

Again, Broderick jumped to his feet. 'Objection, Your Honour. The prosecutor cannot surely ask the witness what might or might not have been in the defendant's mind.'

The judge thought for a moment and then said, 'Mr. Prosecutor, I suggest you simply stick to the facts of the case, rather than wondering about the state of mind of the defendant at the time of these offences.'

After a dozen or more questions, the prosecutor ended his cross-examination. This was the first of ten witnesses he would call. Her testimony was the weakest, but he wanted to build a case so that surely, inexorably, the judge would see that slave masters were in the same league, albeit a notch or two down, as the mass murderers; that evil was a continuum and that no matter where one was placed along it, the actions were still evil and damnable and the perpetrators deserved the severest condemnation.

The other witnesses the prosecutor would call had worked directly for Deutch, and would testify that, while he hadn't been a monster in his personal treatment of them, he had participated in a slave labour program, and by association was as guilty as those guards who set dogs on Jews or beat them to death.

Broderick stood and politely said, 'Miss Lieber, it is not my intention to cause you any further distress by asking you to relive the horrors which you have already suffered. So I'll confine my questions to your observations of Mr. Deutch, and what actually was his standard of behaviour towards you and other workers in the slave labour factory in Auschwitz . . .'

An hour later, Broderick and his client were sitting opposite each other, the interviewing table between them.

'And so it starts . . .'

Broderick nodded thoughtfully. 'How do you feel, listening to what they're saying about you? Does it hurt?'

Deutch looked at the lawyer in amazement. 'You know, you still refuse to accept my version of the events of the war, don't you? Week after week, I've told you what amounts to the same thing, and yet you still look for a story which will satisfy you.'

'I don't understand.'

'Yes, you do. You understand perfectly well. You're waiting for contrition, for an apology. For me to burst into tears and rip off my clothes and try to hang myself. Then you can go home to your comfortable and safe lifestyle, and tell the world that you got the Nazi to see the error of his ways.'

Broderick was shocked. 'Not at all. I'm here as your lawyer, representing . . .'

'Rubbish! Look, Professor. I like you. I respect you. At first, I was very suspicious of you and this whole court procedure. I thought it was just a mockery of justice. But now I know I was wrong. Sure, I'll hang, but not because of this court. I'll hang because I was part of something which history will judge as monstrous. But that doesn't mean for one moment that I'm going to lie down and beg for my life. And nor does it mean that, at the time, in the middle of a war, I did the wrong thing.

You're not here to represent me. You're here because everything about me and Adolf Hitler and Hermann Göring is so alien to you, so utterly contrary to everything you've taught your students all your life, that you just had to come over to Germany and convert at least one German. You're like a Jehovah's Witness. You want to convert me to being sorry for what I did, and then you can die happy as one of the chosen ones. Am I right?'

He loathed admitting that his client—a mechanic and a Nazi who left school at fifteen—might have a better insight into his motivations than all the American lawyers and all the Allied justices with whom he had spent the past six months.

'No, that's not right. I'm here in order to ensure that even those who have committed the basest acts against humankind in a thousand years are afforded the benefits of Western justice.'

When the translator had finished his words, Deutch burst out laughing. 'Really. A thousand years? Why not since the time of Christ? Or the Egyptians? Tell me, Mr. Professor. Why do you think that the Nazis were any worse than the British in Africa? Or the Spanish in South America? Or the Turks when they invaded Europe? Or the Arabs when they conquered North Africa and Spain? They were all barbarians. We were merely following their example. Do you want me to tell you the stories of how the Mongol hordes raped and pillaged; heard the stories about how, after they'd raped a woman, they'd slit open her belly and sew in a live cat?'

Broderick winced in pain. 'Enough! Why are you trying to justify your behaviour?'

'Because we weren't the first, and we weren't the worst. But Western civilisation has caught up with us, and now we're to be made scapegoats for what all other nations have been doing throughout the ages.'

Broderick took out his handkerchief to wipe his forehead. In all his conversations with Deutch, they had both avoided discussion of Nazism; it was as though all the facts about the atrocities were known, and now the job was to establish that Deutch hadn't been as complicit as all the others. But now that the trial had started, and the lid had been removed from the festering jar, evil things were again forcing their way into the light of day. He bunched the handkerchief up in his fist and squeezed it hard.

'Mr. Deutch. You're an intelligent man. Do you seriously expect me to sit here and accept what you're saying? Of course there were evil deeds perpetrated by people in the past. I'm a student of history; I know perfectly well the barbarity which ordinary humanity has been forced to suffer in the name of nationalism, or tribalism, or religion, or whatever other philosophy drives madmen on. But how can you use the past to justify your actions today? Just because the Tartars and the Turks and the Spanish conquistadors were the epitome of evil, why does that justify building concentration camps?'

As if to prove his point, Deutch barely concealed his smile when he said, 'But surely you realise that Adolf Hitler learned about the benefits of concentration camps from the British and the Russians . . . your noble Allies. You say you're a student of history, Professor. Then read of the treatment of the Boers by the British in South Africa. Read of the treatment of the political prisoners in Russia. You've read the testimony which was given in the recent trials here, haven't you? They said that in 1922, Russia had twenty-three concentration camps. Millions and millions died in Siberia. We in Germany didn't start building our camps until the Allies had perfected them!'

Allied Occupied Germany, 1946

From the memoirs of Joachim Gutman:

My first view of Auschwitz was from the long cattle train to which we'd been driven by truck from Sachsenhausen. The journey started when the lorry deposited us in a railway siding in the middle of nowhere. There seemed to be no reason for us to be there. One minute, we were bouncing along in the back of the lorry, desperately trying to stand or to sit, anything to prevent our being thrown around like sacks, and the next moment, the canvas flaps of the lorry were thrown open, and we were ordered to step down on to the cinders of this railway siding. I looked around. There were no houses, no buildings. Just the junction of two long tracks, one seeming to come from the south and the other from the west. They met and blended into one, which disappeared as parallel lines pointing towards our certain death in the east . . . in Poland . . . in Auschwitz.

The wind howled like a banshee. It was all so cold and empty and desolate. There were no leaves on the trees, there was no grass in the empty brown fields. The dirty sludge, the remains of the snows of the previous week, was still in the hard-caked winter furrows in the fields. The wind bit into my thin pyjamas, opening the buttons, and touching my skin like a knife. For a moment, I yearned for the comfort of the hut in which, up until last night, I'd lived with a couple of hundred other men. How silly!

And then in the distance, there was a whistle. We all looked to the western track. We saw a small cloud of smoke, rising from the tiny train which was approaching us. Another blast of the whistle. As a child, I remembered, I'd once stood on the running board of my father's Mercedes as it waited at a level crossing for a train to arrive. I recall the thrill of seeing the smoke from the engine; then feeling the ground and the air vibrate as the massive train approached. I jumped down from the running board and ran to the gated level crossing. I climbed on to the wooden slats and screamed in fear and pleasure as the huge and overwhelming monster thundered past me. My mind spun with wonders . . . Where was it going . . . would I get to ride inside it one day . . . could I be in control of it when I grew up?

Now, I watched the train . . . Was it the same train, driven by the same engineer? . . . rumbling towards me, slowing when it saw us in order to pick up another contingent of Jews or Gypsies on their ride to the end of the track! But this time, there was no magic, no thrill, only the certainty of going to my death.

I was pushed and shoved into one of the back wagons along with three hundred others. We were so crammed, I could hardly raise my rib cage in order to breathe.

Someone asked why we'd been transported to the border of Germany and Poland by lorry instead of being taken to a station nearer to Sachsenhausen. Someone else from the other side of the carriage said, 'That's easy. This train's for first-class passengers only.' We all laughed. I looked through the slats of the wagon at the guard who was standing near the railway line, pointing his gun up at us. He was astonished that we were laughing. He knew and I knew what our fate would be. Maybe these other poor bastards didn't know, or wouldn't believe.

There must have been ten thousand people crammed like sardines on the sidings, all being pushed on board the train. They weren't talking to one another, they were just standing mutely or obeying orders, or staring into the void of their lives, because the SS guards were walking up and down the line with snarling salivating dogs, and because they were lost in their world of terror.

When the train had first arrived, I'd hung back as much as possible to try to be the last one on. When I was herded into the wagon, there was only room enough to stand by the door or by the slats of the wagon. Those of us like me who knew the ways of the Nazis were wise enough to keep to the outskirts of the wagon, even if it meant that our faces and mouths were flattened against the rough wood. At least then we had air. Those poor bastards who were in the middle of the wagon soon had no air to breathe. It only took a matter of half an hour before you could hear them whimpering, then coughing, until their breathing seemed to rattle.

It was the children for whom I felt most sorry. Sure, I could have given up my place next to one of the slits at the back and in the side of the wagon for a child. I could have gone to the inside. But chances are, in my condition of starvation and exhaustion, that I would have died within minutes. I needed everything I could to help me survive the journey.

Twenty hours, it took to get to Auschwitz. Twenty hours of standing in the fetid heat of a hundred people trapped in the space where once twenty cows had been herded and crowded together. Twenty hours of wanting to lie down, even to die, but having no room even to fall. Twenty of the worst hours of my life.

Of course, at the beginning of the journey, people spoke to one another. As the train pulled away from the lorries which had brought us to the border, when the guards were no longer a threat to our lives, people started to ask questions. These were the newcomers to Sachsenhausen, recent inmates about to be redeployed; hundreds and hundreds who were being resettled in the death camps of the east (yes! I knew they were death camps, even if these poor bastards didn't).

The questions were questions of despair. 'Where are we going?' 'What's going to happen to us?' 'Why are they doing this to me and my family? I'm a German citizen. I've never been a practising Jew. I've never even been to Synagogue.'

Nobody except me had answers, and I wasn't going to tell anybody. But they quickly guessed that we were heading to one of the concentration camps which everyone was now talking about, those in the east of the new and expanded Greater Germany. The war had been going on now for four years, and the whole of Germany was aware of what was happening to the Jews and others who were rounded up; everyone knew what the concentration camps were for; everyone knew of the smells of gas and burning flesh which arose in the east and in the camps in Germany and Austria. The difference between me and these people, these bodies who would be fresh meat for the camps, was that I'd experienced a Concentration Camp, whilst these poor bastards, freshly rounded up in Berlin, these people refused to believe what was happening. They knew of people who had been rounded up but never returned; but they thought they'd just been resettled. Whole districts which were once populated by Jews were emptied, and the Germans who had been bombed out of their homes were rehoused.

A man who was standing next to me, his body so close to mine that I could see into his very soul, started to ask me why I wasn't dressed in civilian clothes. Was I a political prisoner, a criminal? He looked at my striped uniform, filthy, torn, stinking, and fetid; I could see his nose turn up in disgust. Of course, he was no thing of beauty. He'd been a U-Boat, one of those Berliners who spent their lives living underground and travelling around on the transport system day and night to avoid being in any one place for too long to lessen the chance of being spotted by an SS informant.

This man was dishevelled, but he looked at me as though I were a thing of the gutter, and when he looked closely, he scrutinised my head and saw the lice crawling in my hair, and I could see he was revolted. I could have told him how I came down to this, but better for him to learn the cruel life of the Jew for himself.

Eventually we arrived in Auschwitz, and as the train came to a halt, and the doors of the cattle wagon were thrown open, I saw the full horror of my new life. There, above the gate were the words, 'Arbeit Macht Frei'—work makes you free. It was like the sign above Dante's Hell, 'Lasciate ogni speranza voi ch'entrate'—All hope abandon, ye who enter here.

Was it an obscene satire? A joke of the victor over the victim? Or was it a way of trying to inculcate into people a working habit which would enable them to accept with good grace and understand why they were being worked to death?

And then I saw the four lines of people. Fewer lines than in Sachsenhausen, but lines nonetheless. When I had first lined up in Sachsenhausen, I hadn't known what was about to greet me. Now I knew, even though the others clearly didn't. But these lines were somehow different. Instead of lines on racial or social or ethnic lines, it looked as if a decision had been made to differentiate people on a quite different basis altogether.

In one of the lines, which had been formed from the carriages which had arrived at the terminus first, it appeared that the elderly, or those who looked weak and sick, had been selected. In the second line were younger and stronger-looking women. In the next line were younger and stronger men; and in the last line, the shortest of all, young children had been forced together, along with dwarfs and midgets and others who looked hideous and odd. And then, when they turned around looking in fear for their parents, I realised that these children were twins. And it was then that I understood the purposes for which the people in the lines had been selected.

The first line of elderly and sick Jews and other socially undesirable people had been gathered together for extermination. Far in the distance, we could see evil-looking squat buildings, row upon row of barracks, and off to the left of them were tall chimneys from which were pouring continuous streams of grey-black smoke. Was I the only one to realise that this smoke was the last remains of some Jewish community, somewhere in Europe? The other lines of younger people were detailed for the slave labour establishments. The names of Krupp and I. G. Farben sprang immediately to mind, from what I'd been told in Sachsenhausen.

But what of the third line of people, the young twins and the deformed people? Even in Sachsenhausen, we'd heard rumours of Block 10, and the Angel of Death, Dr. Josef Mengele. These poor and tragic people had been selected for medical experiments from among those brought here to Auschwitz every year and who were deformed or twins or dwarves or homosexuals or with whom Nature had played a cruel game. So confident, so arrogant, were the Nazis, that the awful truth about the experiments was known far and wide throughout Germany, and it was the talk of the concentration camps.

We jumped—fell—down from our wagon, and were screamed at by a helmeted guard. Again, it was the snarling and salivating German shepherds which caused us the most fear, not the gun or the man who pointed it at us. As soon as they began to select us for the different lines, I knew that I was dead. In my condition, emaciated and obviously weak through the labour I had performed in the past nine months, barely able to struggle up from the ground to which I'd fallen getting off the train, I was certain that I would be sent to the line of elderly and sick people selected for immediate extinction as being of no use to the efficiency of the German war machine.

The guard with his rifle pushed men and women into a holding area. With the efficiency of a butcher, he steered old and frail people to another holding pen. He came across me, and was surprised that I was wearing the uniform of a concentration camp inmate.

'Where are you from?' he asked gruffly. I told him. He turned and called for his Lieutenant. Over to us walked a tall, thin, angular man with a shiny peaked cap and glistening black boots. I couldn't immediately make out the corps to which he belonged, until I saw the death's head on his lapel. He was SS.

He looked at me in disgust, his upper lip curling. 'You are an inmate of another camp?' I nodded. 'Which one?' I told him. 'Why are you here? This is not a train for collection of inmates. This is for a further batch of rounded up Jews from Germany.'

I tried to explain about Wilhelm Deutch, the mechanic I'd worked for at Sachsenhausen; about how he had asked for me to help him in the work he was doing. But my strength failed me. I fainted through the cold and the hunger, and I was suddenly lying on the floor at the feet of the surprised guard. I heard him restrain the dog, whose smell nauseated me because it was so close to my face . . . It was the smell of an animal about to attack its prey.

And then I heard a voice with which I was familiar. It came to me from somewhere in my dream. Somewhere distant.

'I sent for this man. He's an expert in hydraulics. I need him to help me operate the lifting equipment for the ovens. Help him up, please.'

Rough hands pulling me up from the ground. Filth on my face from falling so near to the railway track, where the feet of a million

Jews had jumped down in their innocence of what fate awaited them. The hands supported me under my armpits. I tried to open my eyes, but exhaustion overcame me. And then I felt my body being somehow shifted from two people, and being supported by one. It was the mechanic. I had been draped around his shoulders, as though I were a sack of grain.

'I'll take him. He is to come with me,' he told the officer.

'First he must be processed. Deloused. Recorded as having entered the camp.' It was a command, not a request.

'Very well, but can we do it quickly, please?' said the mechanic. 'I don't want to be here too long. This man has work to do immediately.'

Guttural comments I couldn't understand fully. I managed to open my eyes. My face was close to the mechanic's. He looked so happy, so hearty. His face was somehow fatter than I remembered. His breath smelled of sausages and cabbage.

He saw that I was conscious. I saw the look of surprise, then horror in his eyes. When our eyes met, I realised that he was on the verge of tears.

'My God,' he said softly to me, as though in soliloquy, 'what have those bastards done to you?'

CHAPTER SIX

Berlin, Germany, 1998

CHASCA BRODERICK FELT AN unaccustomed trepidation. Certainty had marked her life; rarely had she done something unless she was sure that it was the right thing to do. She'd think through the action, consider the consequences, and then embark on the exploit with confidence.

But the past few weeks had undermined her confidence in the decision to find Joachim Gutman and, when he proved too elusive, to seek out the remaining family of Wilhelm Deutch. In America, with its public records, its judicial system giving muscle to the freedom of information acts upon which a transparent society depended, she would have been much more confident. But Europe, and especially Germany, was foreign territory, and she frankly had no idea down which lane which to proceed, and whether the direction in which she was travelling was the right or the wrong one.

Now, standing in front of the plain door in the run-down apartment block, Chasca was insecure about her next actions, and particularly uncertain about whether she was in the right place and about to see the right man. Even though the Ministry of the Interior had appropriated many of the German records held by the Occupation Forces when the Allies handed over government to West Germany and left it to its own devices in 1949, and even though the Germans were scrupulous in their record keeping, it was still such a long shot.

Yes, she was confident that the ancient records were right, and yes, that she'd traced the latest address despite the fact that the man's family had moved three times since they settled in the home provided to them by the government in Berlin, according to the records kept of citizens just after the war . . . but still!

She hesitated before knocking on the door. And she didn't know why. This was the end result of her quest, so she should be full of confidence . . . and the official from the Berlin Department of Civilian Records had assured her that the man outside whose door she now stood in trepidation, must, by a process of elimination, be the Gottfried Deutch who was the grandson of the hanged Nazi war criminal Wilhelm Deutch.

Chasca lifted her hand to knock on the door, still feeling a profound level of uncertainty. What if a mistake had been made? How could she say to a man, 'Was your grandfather a war criminal?'

Maybe it was a family secret which had died when Deutch's neck was broken as he dropped through the platform into the unyielding grip of the noose in Nuremberg. Maybe the young man on the other side of the door, the grandson of the war criminal, had no idea about his grandfather; maybe his mother and father had told him that Wilhelm was a Jew, killed in the Holocaust, or a brave soldier whose body was still frozen in ice somewhere outside Stalingrad; maybe . . . maybe . . . What lies might he have been told to protect his innocence, or to hide the family shame?

There was only one way to find out. She knocked hesitantly on the door. Her heart was pounding more loudly than the noise her clenched fist made. She listened breathlessly for footsteps. Yet the door opened a few seconds later without any sound having come from within . . . a carpet in the hallway.

A young woman stood there, taller than Chasca, in her mid-twenties. An unattractive, heavy-set girl with brown hair pulled back severely. She wore a nose ring and her left ear was studded by metal in the way of the nonconformity of so many of the young.

'*Ja!*' she asked abruptly.

Chasca's knowledge of German at university had been good, and in the time she'd spent over the last year in Yugoslavia, her German had improved dramatically. It was the *lingua franca* of the French, German, Austrian, and Swiss lawyers with whom she worked in the war crimes commission.

She said, 'Good afternoon. My name is Chasca Broderick. I'm looking for Herr Gottfried Deutch.'

'Gottfried? What do you want with him?' she girl asked.

'Is he your father?'

The young woman burst into laughter. 'No, he's my elder brother. Who are you?'

Chasca explained, without saying anything about the testament of the Jewish man, Joachim Gutman.

She had no idea what the grandson of the hanged war criminal would look like. Having been sired from the genes of a man who was accused of being a Nazi murderer, Chasca had an underlying fear that the man who emerged, the grandson of Wilhelm Deutch, might be a skinhead, someone who had a swastika deep-etched into his brow; that he would be wearing a leather jacket with metal studs and boots with steel caps to kick Turkish migrants to death; or that he might be dressed like a member of the SS or the Gestapo, a black leather overcoat with a leather Homburg hat to hide his short-cropped blond hair. No, that was silly; this man was a modern German. If he had short hair, it would have been cut off in obedience to the commands of some fascist puppet-master who hated Jews and immigrants. Yes, she fantasised, the man who came to the door would be a skinhead, dressed very much like his younger sister. Chasca decided to turn and run. Why was she getting mixed up with skinheads and neo-Nazis and the evil of Hitler's grandchildren?

But when Gottfried Deutch came to the door to see what was happening, he was wearing a quizzical expression on his face, and Chasca could barely restrain her laughter, for the man who almost apologetically greeted her with a frown below his receding hairline looked just like a care-worn accountant. He stopped at his young sister's side and she closed the door in Chasca's face, refusing to allow her admission, while she explained to Gottfried what this girl wanted.

And Chasca just stood there, desperately trying to hear what sounds might be coming from inside the house. Now she regretted her silly fantasies. When the door opened once more, the man facing her could so easily have been a clerk in the housing department of a town hall, or a medical officer in a hospital admissions unit, or even a lawyer. Dressed in comfortable slacks and a short-sleeved shirt, he was tall and passingly handsome and ill at ease. The frown which creased his otherwise smooth face deepened in the silence which went between them.

'Yes?'

'Forgive me disturbing you, but are you Gottfried Deutch?'

'Yes. Who are you?'

Feeling less than comfortable standing outside in the hallway of the apartment block, Chasca introduced herself. She gave a brief definition of the journey that had led her to his front door, without any details of her knowledge of his grandfather's crimes. Instead she told him . . .

'My grandfather, Theodore Broderick, has just passed away. I have some papers which concern a member of your family. My grandfather was a lawyer in Germany just after the war, and I believe that he knew some members of your family. He's just died, and as I said, I was going through his papers and I came across mention of your family and some dealings which he had with them in 1946. I was wondering if I could discuss them with you for a few moments, so that you could just help me by filling in some of the details that are missing from his account . . .'

Gottfried looked at her suspiciously. She'd seen the look before, when she'd questioned people about their involvement in war crimes in Yugoslavia . . . but that couldn't be the case here.

'How can I help you? My grandfather died before I was born. And I never knew your grandfather,' he asked. 'I've never heard of him . . .'

'I know, but there are some aspects of your own family history in which my grandfather was involved, and it would help me enormously if you could give me about a half an hour, just to sort things out . . .'

Chasca fell silent. They looked at each other. She knew immediately that he hadn't believed her, but his face told her that there was enormous pain hidden within the family vaults, and he was terrified of revisiting that pain. But suddenly he moved, turning on his heels . . .

'Very well,' he snapped, 'wait here.' And he went back inside the house, shutting the door firmly in her face.

Chasca stared at the closed door in amazement at his rudeness. Now she seriously considered walking away. Indeed, from the moment she saw him, she wondered whether to forget the whole thing, whether to walk away and get on with her life. This man was so ordinary, so unexceptional. Why should she waste any more time on ordinary people?

She couldn't get over how rude and utterly discourteous he'd been in the way he'd slammed the door in her face. What a way to treat someone! She couldn't understand the hostility. First the younger sister, now the elder brother. Is this how Germans treat visitors? And why the hostility? After all, she'd said absolutely nothing about the real reason she was there, so they couldn't have a clue about the document, or the benefits it might bring.

A moment or two later, the door was suddenly pulled open, and Gottfried appeared in an overcoat. He slammed the door closed, making it obvious that she wouldn't be considered for entry into his domain.

'There's a bar on the corner,' he snapped aggressively. 'We'll go there.'

Again Chasca was stunned. She was an attractive woman, well dressed. Why shouldn't he just invite her into the house and get it over and done with? Why go to a bar? After all, she only wanted to hand over a copy of the testament written by Joachim Gutman so that

Gottfried's grandfather could rest in peace. Then she'd leave Germany and get on with her life.

He walked in front of her, and she bridled at his patronising behaviour. Suddenly Chasca bitterly regretted doing what she was doing. After all, it was one thing trying to find Gutman (or if he was dead, then his children or grandchildren) and tell him that his story had finally been heard . . . It was altogether another to tell the family of a German war criminal that . . . and then she stopped herself.

What was she thinking? The whole point of her quest was to resurrect the reputation of a man hanged for crimes he never committed. She bit her lip as she followed the grandson's silent form down the stone steps and out into the street. Indeed, as they emerged on to the busy road, crowded with pedestrians returning to their homes after a day's work, she had to walk faster than normal to catch him up.

She was amazed. It was almost as though this was an interview he'd been expecting, and his reaction was a response condition by years of anticipation.

'Herr Deutch, you're walking too fast . . .' she shouted, more in anger than reality.

He slowed down and allowed her to catch up. 'I'm sorry. The bar isn't much farther.'

'Are you angry with me for some reason?' she asked.

He turned and looked at her without slowing his pace. He said nothing.

She was getting cross. 'Would you rather I just went away? I mean, if this is causing you problems, which your behaviour indicates, then it would be easier for both of us if I returned home . . .'

Again, he said nothing. But as the bar came into sight, illuminated by an advertisement for German beer, he slowed and snapped at her, 'Every few years, I have this type of upset. I live in fear of this moment. Now it's arrived again. Good God, after half a century . . .'

But before she could ask him what he meant, he'd thrust open the door of the bar and stormed inside.

They sat at a table in the far corner. It was too early for the bar to be crowded. It was that moment in modern cities, the median division of labour, a sort of global interregnum for workers in which the day divided itself into two parts, time between the office workers returning home and revellers beginning the night's party. A waiter came over and took their orders.

'Well?' Gottfried Deutch asked testily, his avoidance of any pleasantries and formalities underpinning the contempt he already held for her mission.

Chasca fought to restrain her anger. 'Herr Deutch, what I told you just before was the truth. My grandfather was in Germany after the war, and he knew your grandfather.'

Deutch listened to her with increasing scepticism. Suddenly he interrupted.

'Tell me, why do you think I dragged you away from the house? Why do you think I didn't invite you inside?' It was a rhetorical question. 'My mother is in there. She is the daughter of the man you've come here to find more about. She is the one most hurt by your sort of questions. When my grandfather was hanged as a Nazi war criminal, my mother was seven years old. Do you think she's happy about this? Tell me, Miss American Woman, what do you know of the war? Have you any idea of how my mother has suffered for crimes which she didn't commit? How do you think it makes you feel to be branded for all your youth as the daughter of a monster?'

Chasca remained silent, suddenly worried about her own safety; this man was barely restraining his fury, and she was concerned that his anger might erupt at any moment and she'd get hurt.

'What are you? Anti-Defamation League? Jews for Torturing the Families of Nazis? Simon Wiesenthal Organisation? The International Society for Putting Everything to Rights Again? Well, who do you represent? What do you want from me and my family?'

'Herr Deutch. You've got it totally wrong. My grandfather, Theodore Broderick defended your grandfather Wilhelm Deutch. But there was no evidence which was presented in the trial which could have exonerated your grandfather. Some weeks ago, when my grandfather died, I went through his papers, and I found a testament, an incredible document written by a Jewish gentleman, a survivor of the concentration camps. It was too late to be presented as evidence in your grandfather's trial. It was obviously written when your grandfather had been hanged, which is the tragedy I've come here to try to remedy. Because if the information had come out in court, I very much doubt that your grandfather would have been hanged as a war criminal. Indeed, from reading the testament of this Jewish gentleman, I'm almost sure that your grandfather would have been found not guilty, and would have been treated as something of a hero by the Americans and the other Allies. I've come here to give you the document. I've come here to help you . . .'

But his response was totally different to what she expected. His anger didn't ebb away with her explanation.

'I don't want your help. I want to forget. Every few fucking years, someone comes to see us because my grandfather was hanged as a war criminal. First it was the Christadelphians who wanted to pray for his soul; then the Mormons; then the Jews and Christians for Understanding; then the fucking Allied Nations for Reconciliation; then the crazy Churches, then the Israeli academics; then the American academics; and lately it's been the fucking neo-Nazis who want to make the old bastard into some sort of hero of the new Fourth Reich . . .'.

Chasca took out the document written by Joachim Gutman. 'Please calm down. This testament tells of how your grandfather tried to save those around him when he was a mechanic at Auschwitz. He was a good man, a fine member of humanity. Are you hearing me? I'm telling you that your grandfather wasn't a war criminal, but was a good man . . .'

But Gottfried suddenly stood, raising his voice so that everyone in the bar stopped talking and looked at the couple in surprise.

'Keep your fucking testament. I don't want to know anything about Auschwitz and humanity. Leave me alone. I don't want anything to do with it. Go away from us. Forget it. Put it all behind you, for God's sake. And don't come near my mother or my family. We've been through enough. Just leave us alone.'

Allied Occupied Germany, 1946

From the memoirs of Joachim Gutman:

Humanity—assuming that there is any humanity left in the world now that the true nature of this war is revealed—will never forget the name Auschwitz. No, they'll never forget. But as time goes by, all that they'll remember is the name, not the reality of what the name means. Who remembers the carnage, the cruelty, the evil of the Romans and the revolt of the slaves under Spartacus? Who remembers the agony of the crucifixion? We remember Spartacus and his heroism because of the ballet and the books, but do we remember the suffering of six thousand of his followers, crucified by Crassus along the Appian Way?

Do we know the names of the countless Ottomans and Arabs who were killed by the English King, Richard? No, all we know are the glories of the Crusades and their remains, the castles and the chivalric Orders.

Why is it not recorded? How can humanity be so uncaring of the memories of the millions upon millions who have died in the name of nationalism or some philosophy or ideology? Why are we so callous? Is cruelty and barbarism so common to us human beings that we find these things so easy to absorb . . . and having absorbed them, we neutralise them, these abortions of history which cause so much misery to so many?

And will this apply to Auschwitz, to Birkenau, to Treblinka, to Belsen, and to the hundreds of other concentration and death camps which the Nazis set up to eliminate Jews from the face of the earth? Because one day . . . maybe tomorrow . . . maybe in a hundred years time, the realities of what happened here at Auschwitz will be called into question by those who need to deny, and then humankind will only remember the name. Because they'll never remember the suffering, nor believe the realities of what happened at Auschwitz. Never.

Nobody, in the fifty years that remain of this century, will be able to comprehend how human beings could behave with such a depth of hatred and barbarity. We remember the Crusades and the massacres of ancient peoples as stories, not as realities. Our mythologies and histories and folk-records are full of bloodthirsty, evil events which cause us no more concern than a momentary thought. Yet millions of people have died hideous deaths throughout history, and we have forgotten their pain.

Even we Jews are guilty of collective forgetfulness. To this day, we remember events which happened three thousand, five hundred years ago when the Jews were slaves in Egypt. We remember the cruel taskmasters, the way our backs were broken, the sweat of our brows mixing with the mud to make bricks to build monuments to the pride of a pharaoh. But does the reality of the enslavement of our forefathers make us shudder and cry and wail into the night? No, we spend two nights a year retelling the tale and drinking wine and eating food and congratulating ourselves on our good fortune.

Will some rabbi in the future, I wonder, consecrate the reality of Auschwitz into a prayer, and will future generations pray for the souls of the millions of innocents whom I saw being butchered in the world's largest and most evil abattoir?

We human beings will forget what happened at Auschwitz. We will allow time to pass by, and then some among us will say it never happened. They will say that we who suffered were mistaken.

But they will be wrong. For I saw things at Auschwitz which must never be forgotten. And I heard things which my mind will never shut out.

Music.

Yes, I heard music in Auschwitz which was played by an orchestra. Do you believe me, you in the future who are reading this, my testimony.

Everywhere in Auschwitz, there was music playing. The Jews or Gypsies who were able to play musical instruments were gathered together by the blockführers and given to the kapos who organised music. And these people made the musicians into an orchestra. One of the SS commandants at the camp had the idea that an orchestra would relax the inmates when they walked to their slavery, or when they were unloaded from the trains when they first came to the camp and were herded into Birkenau where they would be gassed and burned to ashes.

Three trains a day, each train with fifty to sixty carriages, in each carriage a hundred human beings squashed like sardines. Fifteen, twenty thousand Jewish men, women, and children a day had been scooped up from around Europe and were deposited in the murderous factories of Auschwitz in order to be used for the war machine, and then, when they were starving and exhausted and incapable of any further work, when they were so desperately in need of help and comfort and rest, they were discarded, like refuse in Birkenau, first burned, then the leftover dust was scattered into the eternity of the ground. And each of these trains pulled into Auschwitz to the tune of an orchestra playing swing music or tangos or popular ballads. The musicians were also inmates, dressed in their prison pajamas, but there was no look of joy on their faces as the music filled the air and tried to compete with the screams of people begging for water or air as the carriage doors were opened.

It happened to me when I was first brought to the camp, but I didn't hear the music, for I was too starved and exhausted, and the ringing in my ears drowned out all else. Nor did I see the devil's orchestra, for

I collapsed on the ground as I fell out of the carriage. Had it not been for the mechanic . . . but you already know that.

Of course, it was all a hideous shock from hell for the new inmates, those that hadn't been conditioned by the experience of Sachsenhausen or the other concentration camps whose names were now becoming familiar to us old hands, names which were whispered between us, like primitive people used to whisper secret curses on their worst enemies. No, these virgins, these fresh fodder from Berlin and Hamburg and other cities looked around them, trying to comprehend the enormity of what they'd fallen into.

First their hair was shorn from them as though they were sheep, then their clothing was taken until they were huddled and naked, then they were beaten for good measure, then their arms were tattooed with the latest sequential numbers, then they were given an identifying badge according to the barrel from which they'd been scraped . . . Jew, Communist, Criminal, Slav . . .

I think it was the tattooing which horrified them most. And what they didn't realise was that old hands like me would use the tattoos as a way of marking them out. The lower the number, the longer they'd been in camp, the less you could get away with . . . the higher the number, the more recently they'd come to the camp, which meant you could steal some of their clothing and rations, and they'd be too naïve to understand what was happening. Of course, it might lead to their death by starvation, or their death by beating if they had had some clothing stolen, but that was their lookout. And anyway, if they were beaten or starved to death, there were plenty more to take their place for the old hands. They soon got used to the routine, and new hands became old hands very quickly. If they didn't, they died! Simple as that. Law of the jungle.

By the time I'd been in Auschwitz for a week, I already knew the routine, but as it turned out, it was weeks before the mechanic was able to rescue me and requisition me for special hydraulic duty with him. So for the first month, this was my life. Four in the morning, the kapos, ordinary German criminals and utterly evil men, would enter the barracks, and bang drums or the sides of our bunks, and force us out of bed. *'Get up, fucking dogs. Out of bed or I'll kill you fucking Jew swine.'* *'Got your fucking shoes and fucking caps, Jew swine. I'll beat you to death if you can't find your shoes and caps'*. Men who lost or had their caps and shoes stolen often stole these same things in the night from others, because it was certain death to arrive at roll call without a cap or shoes. Yes, it meant that you were effectively killing someone by taking his cap and shoes, but like I said, if you didn't, you'd be killed . . . and anyway, someone had taken yours in the certain knowledge that you'd be killed. Life was so cheap, and yet most of us would do anything just to cling on. Even send one of our own to his certain death!

Then we would have to make our beds properly. It was called *'bettenbau.'* Somehow, we had to try to put a proper military shape into the shapeless straw mattress and fit the blanket over it in proper army style. The kapo would come over and beat us if it wasn't perfect. Many of us died with the beatings.

Then, we had to run to the sanitary unit to wash and piss (if there was anything inside you to piss out). It was always a race against the others to get to the sanitaries first, because there were only three or four, and there were hundreds and hundreds of inmates who wanted to wash.

After washing, the bells would ring, and you'd have to race to the central compound for breakfast. Stragglers were always beaten by the kapos, often beaten to death.

After we washed, we would go to breakfast, which was made up of beautifully salted fish and slices of cheeses and delicious meats and jams and honey, with lashings of buttered toast and eggs cooked in five different styles, and fresh fruit and treble cream. Yes! Of course I'm being sarcastic! Breakfast was horrible. It was always the same. Our stomachs revolted, but it kept us alive for the day. Well, most of us.

For breakfast, the kapos would hand out a quarter of a kilogram of bread and the thin, black crushed acorn coffee, and if you were incredibly lucky, a slice of meat or sausage and maybe some margarine. Most often, they'd deliberately aim the bread for the ground so that it fell into the mud. And they'd laugh at your efforts to reclaim what a dog would refuse. Or they'd trip you as you walked away, and all your food and drink would spill on the filthy ground, and they'd be nothing to eat until a thin vegetable-flavoured water at lunch.

But if you were lucky, you'd eat your breakfast, and some of the hunger in the pit of your stomach would be relieved for a while, at least. Of course, some people would save their bread until the evening because that was the last solid food they'd see for the whole of that day. The consequences of leaving your bread meant that you lived during the day on hope. Hunger was always there, but at least you had in your mind the joy of eating a hunk of bread at night, so that you'd be able to sleep four or five hours without waking from your bones creaking with starvation. So these people left their breakfast bread for the evening meal, but most were too hungry in the morning to think of anything but satisfying immediate needs. They didn't even care if they made it to the evening meal, so long as they staved off the starvation, the hunger in the very pit of the body.

And then, before we had the chance to finish our breakfast, we would hear another bell which would summon us for roll call. Everybody stands in line for the roll call. Even the dead. Even those who have been beaten to death by the kapos, or who have died in the night, or have been shot. Their bodies are carried out by men who had been their friends, and placed in the rows in which we, the still living, were standing as a reminder to us that *'Arbeit Macht Frei.'*

Roll call in the mornings didn't take all that long. The guards and the commandant were keen to get us off so that we would start work by six. Then, when the numbers had been counted, we could look forward to a day of murderous work. Of course, if the numbers, including the dead, didn't add up, then the whole process had to begin again, and that made the kapos very nervous and angry and particularly brutal, for if the numbers weren't precise, and the Germans insisted on precision, the kapos would be blamed and even punished. When the numbers of living and dead didn't tally, everyone was frightened, but usually the numbers were correct, and we'd be raced to the lines which were already forming and then on to our work duties.

Some days, especially when it was very cold and snowing or raining, we'd be forced to stand to attention for long periods. The striped pyjamas which we wore were made of the roughest material I'd ever known, and when they got wet, they weighed your already-weakened body down so that you could hardly stand. And the guards loved any poor Jew who didn't have the strength to stand to attention. If our bodies sagged for even a moment, a guard would come over and scream in our ears to, *'Stand to attention!'* God help us if we didn't, because it would be yet another excuse for the guard to beat us. But by strength of will, and hatred for the guards and the kapos, most of us somehow found the strength, and we ran off to our work details in our sodden uniforms. Some who were lucky developed colds and chills during the day, and died peacefully in their sleep at night.

Palace of Justice
Nuremberg, Allied Occupied Germany
June, 1946

The routine had become something of a game between guard and prisoner. Every morning, when the young American guard came to collect him for his court appearance, he would throw open the door and shout, 'Stand to attention'.

But Wilhelm Deutch was used to the Americans attempt to impose command on him and played along in the charade by ignoring the order. Instead, he finished writing, turned, and looked at the young man in his clean grey uniform, and stood, wishing him a cheery good morning.

These days, the guard who came for Deutch after breakfast and ablutions often found the prisoner sitting at his desk in his cell, writing. The desk had been placed in a corner at the request of his defense counsel, Theodore Broderick. As had a pad of paper and a pen. Deutch had requested these items after the trial began, saying that he needed them to write notes for himself to assist in his defense.

'You really think that this is a hanging court, don't you?' said Broderick.

The interpreter looked at him in concern. 'Sorry, sir, I don't know how to translate hanging court into German.'

Broderick gave an alternative to the expression.

'In a way, yes. I honestly believe that this show of justice is there to pacify the Western mind, to swell the breasts of the victors, to show the world and the future generations that every assistance was given to the Nazis before they were hanged. But it is, nonetheless, a court set up not to determine justice, but to punish the guilty.'

Broderick shook his head in disagreement. 'How can you say that? When the major war criminals were tried, the proceedings lasted for ten whole months. The judges heard masses of evidence. If the Allies had merely wanted vengeance, we'd have found them guilty within the first couple of days and hanged the lot of them. Don't forget that Schacht, Papen, and Fritzsche were acquitted.' As an afterthought, Broderick added, 'And remember that Dönitz, von Schirach, Speer, and Neurath were given prison sentences, and weren't hanged. No matter what you might think, these are not the actions of a judicial body set up for the sake of retribution, but in order to hand out proper justice and to avenge crimes committed by criminals.'

Deutch shrugged. 'Göring, Ribbentrop, Keitel, and nine others were sentenced to hang.'

'Of course they were,' Broderick shouted. These days, his philosophical mind and judicial temperament were sorely strained. The evidence being cross-examined was so horrific it was making him hate his client, and that caused him problems. An advocate had to be totally impartial, he used to warn his law graduate students; an advocate must suspend his own beliefs, his doubts, his prejudices, and think only of one thing . . . the story that his client had told him, and his responsibility to represent that story and his client properly and fairly. And what was he doing now, this great expert in jurisprudence and philosophy? He was losing his temper, that's what! And in front of his client, who was relying on him to save him from the gallows. But he couldn't restrain his temper. He was stretched to the limit.

Calming down, he said softly, 'These men who were hanged were mass murderers. They committed crimes against humanity. Crimes against peace . . .'

'How can any German have committed crimes against peace,' Deutch asked, 'when no such crime existed at the time? You've merely invented a crime, looked at what we've done, and said, *All right, now let's find them guilty of that* . . .' Is backdating an action and making it a crime the justice of fair-minded men?'

To the surprise of the translator, and to his client, the dam holding back Broderick's reservoir of patience broke, and he shouted, 'There are some crimes which are so evil that society hasn't even been able to give them a name; crimes which no lawmaker could have conceived possible in the repertoire of humankind. That's why we had to invent a name.'

The two men looked at each other in disgust and outright hostility.

Then, Broderick sighed and said softly, 'I'm here to defend you against charges which could see you hang. Now isn't the time to examine the right of the court to try you, nor to discuss the morality of the judicial system under which you've been arraigned. This court is legally constituted. Its decisions carry the full weight of the proper laws. Your concern is to determine how best to avoid the hangman's noose. And frankly, from the evidence which the prosecution has presented in the last two days, you'd better be more forthcoming, or the situation is grim.'

'What do you want me to say? That I didn't do the things which the witnesses say I did. I've told you until I'm blue in the face that I never committed crimes against humanity. I was a fucking mechanic,' Deutch shouted at his lawyer. 'I made the fucking place run. I was doing a job. No more, no less. I didn't kill anybody. I didn't torture anybody. Why am I here? I'll tell you why. Because I'm a German and you're an American. And you won the war, and now I'm your victim.'

'You were a Nazi. You were a vital part of the machinery of death. You did nothing to stop it,' Broderick shouted, his emotions carried downstream on a wave of hatred. He bit his lip immediately after he'd said it for forgetting that his job was to defend his client.

'When I was a Nazi, being a Nazi was an honour, it was a duty, it wasn't a crime. What are you and those like you doing to me? Backdating guilt? When you were at university in America, Mr. Defending Lawyer, were you a member of any clubs or societies? A rowing club, a political club? Something like that. Now, Mr. Defender, how would you feel if ten years later some court in another country told you that you'd committed a crime by being a member of that political club? Eh? How would you feel?'

'Rowing and political clubs in American universities weren't constituted to kill an entire race of people.'

Breathing heavily from the tensions of the past month, Deutch slowly calmed down. He nodded. 'Of course they weren't. And it might surprise you, but neither was the Nazi Party. Oh, I know what Göbbels' propaganda said. I know about the Führer's speeches. But that was the top layer. The cream. I was an ordinary German. Not to join the Nazi Party was a sign that you weren't a proper German. But nobody in Germany really believed what Hitler and the Nazi leaders were saying about the Jews and about the international conspiracies. We just wanted to feel proud of ourselves again. Okay, so there might or might not have been a Jewish conspiracy, but we were interested in effect, not cause. We wanted things to be better. So we listened to Hitler. We attended the rallies. Our hearts filled with pride as we saw the phalanxes of men shoulder to shoulder with their flags, and the spotlights forming cathedral spires in the night sky. Just a few years earlier, we'd been the joke of Europe; on our knees, our Deutschmark in ruins, family savings destroyed, the economy wrecked, millions of unemployed on the streets fed by soup kitchens, old, proud people suddenly destitute, their entire belongings in prams being pushed nowhere, children begging on street corners, young girls not twelve or thirteen selling their bodies so their parents could afford to buy food.

'And then Hitler came along with the Nazis and the SA and the SS and told us that it wasn't our fault; that other people were manipulating Germany and that we had to fight back. Who wouldn't have fought back? Who wouldn't have followed Hitler? And it worked. By God, it worked. 1934, '35, '36 . . . the Olympic Games . . . life was wonderful. We all had plenty of food and beer. The restaurants were overflowing. The theatres were full, the cabarets were mocking Adolf and the Nazis, and everyone thought it was fun. We all laughed. Nobody took things seriously until it was too late to do anything. I remember those years as though they were yesterday. Laughter. It was all fun and laughter.'

It was the first time that Deutch had opened up. In all their interviews, Deutch had done nothing other than answer questions, rarely, if ever, volunteering information. Now there was a chink in his armour. Broderick was keen for him to continue. It had happened before in Broderick's experience. When he had been a trial lawyer with a difficult and recalcitrant client, silent and uncooperative during the gathering of evidence, things suddenly changed the moment the trial started. The defendant would listen to the evidence, and suddenly get angry at the way he was presented by the prosecution at the start of the trial when the initial evidence was being presented. Then the defendant would rant and rave about how unfair were the allegations, and his side of the facts would flow like a river.

'And when did it go wrong for the Nazis?' asked Broderick gently.

'When the war started. We didn't invade Czechoslovakia. We weren't hostile. We were invited into the country by the Sudeten

Germans. They needed to be freed from the oppression of the Czech government. Millions of Germans in the Czech lands were living in oppression. They had to be freed.

'So Hitler marched over the border. The same in Poland. Straight across the border, as though there was no opposition. But then his successes went to his head, and he took on the West and Russia. Shall I tell you something? If he had just done what he said he was going to do, and taken those two countries, Czechoslovakia and Poland, we would have had all the living space we needed. We could have expanded Germany to the east and had land and resources and factories and everything. Today, we'd rival America as the powerhouse of the world. And if we'd just stopped there, we wouldn't have gone to war. Why, when we would have been probably the most powerful country in Europe; then in a few years, the most powerful in the world. Do you think England or America care about those Eastern Europeans? They viewed them the same as we did . . . subhumans. Slavs.'

Broderick started to take notes, but it didn't seem to bother Deutch. 'But why did you join the Nazi Party? You were a mechanic. You weren't needed in the Army. Not until much later in the war. Yet you joined in 1935.'

'I was swept up with pride. I wanted to be part of the movement. I loved Hitler with all my heart.'

'And now? Do you still love him now?'

'How can you love your executioner?' Deutch asked simply.

Allied Occupied Germany, 1946

From the memoirs of Joachim Gutman:

It's remarkable how quickly the human body can recover. The body, mark you, not the human mind. No! The human mind can be scarred for life.

My body recovered within weeks. Not on its own, of course. Only with the assistance of the mechanic. Had I been forced to try to survive on my own, after nine months in Sachsenhausen, and especially the first few weeks at Auschwitz, I would not be alive to write these words.

When I had been through the delousing process, when I had had what remained of my hair again shorn off, once more depriving me of my dignity and my humanity, when I was pushed and shoved and threatened by the guards, I was sent through the fences to the barracks compounds. I didn't see the mechanic for a couple of weeks. Four or five, I think. I later learned that despite the fact that he had requisitioned me from Sachsenhausen, the commandant of Auschwitz thought I should become familiarised with the routine of his concentration camp before I started to work in the special area of hydraulics. So for the first three or four weeks, I struggled to live in a state of uncertainty. But I was far better off than the other wretches with whom I was now living. For I had a modicum of hope. Somewhere in the back of my mind was the feeling that all this was for a purpose, that the mechanic had some sort of plan or policy in his mind and that somewhere I was to be a part of it. I was different from the other pathetic, lost souls with whom I shared the barracks. They perpetually looked numbed, as though they were sleepwalkers by the shores of Hades' River Lethe, all their hopes stripped away from them as their hair was shorn, and as the smell of burning Jews wafted into the camp from the chimneys of Birkenau, three kilometres down the railway line.

Although I had life-sustaining hope, I was still forced to live in the barracks with hundreds of others, and I suffered the evils which befell my brothers-in-hell. The rats, the lice, the overcrowding, the airlessness in the barracks at night, the eternal cold. A couple of blankets to protect the four or five men I slept with from the rawness of a Polish winter; it was in the depth of evening, with the wind howling through the slats and rattling the windows, with the guards patrolling and the dogs baying like wolves, with the searchlights sweeping the compound and blinding our eyes, used only to the heavy blackness of the night, that I truly appreciated human warmth.

If you'd told me as a twenty-year old whose hormones raced at the sheen of nylon stockings and the erotic aroma of perfumed breasts, that I'd ever welcome the warmth of a man lying pressed up next to me, I'd have hit you. But in the icy reaches of our lives in Auschwitz, any human warmth was comfort, and any comfort gave the spirit the power to live through the next day.

In the mornings, when it was still grey-black dawn, we'd endure hours-long roll calls. Just as we did in Sachsenhausen. The same monsters controlling our lives, just different faces in the uniforms and different places in the landscape of Nazism. But here in Auschwitz, certain things were different. Here they were far stricter. The commandant, Hoss, enjoyed keeping us standing around in the freezing wind far longer than my previous commandant. He enjoyed seeing the misery on our faces as we suffered the pain of cold rising from the lifeless and numbing ground into our feet and legs.

On this particular morning, the morning in which my life began to change, I was laying in my bunk, fast asleep, when suddenly there was a voice in the Barracks. A *kapo*? The *blockführer*? My name was called. 'Gutman? The Jew Gutman. Come here. Attention Gutman. Come here immediately.'

Others thought the voice was a death sentence and looked at me in sorrow as I woke with a start and struggled down from my bunk. But I knew that my fortune was about to change. I knew that it was a life sentence, not a death sentence. The mechanic had finally got his way, and now I was to work for him, and not with the other slaves. Did I feel guilty that I had been selected for special privileges? Not for a moment. The thought that I might have food and rest and the others in my barracks would still be slaving away didn't enter my mind for even a second.

In Sachsenhausen, in the beginning, I'd shared my good fortune with my co-sufferers because I felt guilt at feeling satisfyingly full while they were starving. But nine months of brutality in Sachsenhausen when the mechanic left, and then this latest month of savagery in Auschwitz, had knocked all the conscience out of me. To hell with my fellow men. They'd kill me if they could eat my flesh. So nothing would have made me share even a crust of stale bread with a starving man in my barracks. I was looking out for me. Only me. I had to survive, and if it meant that I had to steal a cap or shoes, or a sharp tool to save digging with bare hands, then I would do so willingly and without conscience. Even knowing absolutely that some other poor bastard would die for my selfishness. I rationalised that I was probably doing him a favour. He'd die quicker than the lingering life/death of slavery and savagery.

Are you disgusted with me? Does it horrify you to think that I, a Jew, would allow another Jew to die just so that I could live? Well, before you start saying what *you* would have done in my place, having noble thoughts about how you would have sacrificed your life for another, then understand one thing. The only thought which kept any of us going was the thought of revenge. Yes, revenge against our slave masters, against the guards, against the kapos and the dogs and the blockführers, and the Nazis and Hitler and all the rest of them. That's all we thought of. Living for the purpose of being witnesses. Of telling the world our stories. Of making people in other countries believe that this had happened to us, to living, breathing people. To husbands and wives and children and parents and grandparents. And the revenge we wanted was to strangle the kapos and the guards with our bare hands, to somehow have the strength to kill and maim those who were our tormentors. All I dreamed about was grasping a kapo by his windpipe with my strong, well-fed bare hands, and pulling it out. To see the look of horror in his face as his life ebbed away from him; to ensure that the last thing on this earth that he saw was my face, my eyes tearing into his soul, and saying to him, 'There's no heaven, but you're going down to the lowest reaches of hell, and you'll suffer for all eternity for what you did to me.'

But I stray. I'm being indulgent with my time, and your patience. I apologise. This is to be a record of my experiences in Auschwitz. So I will return to my tale.

When I began to work for the mechanic, my path diverged from the paths of those with whom I shared the barracks. Some were marched to the I. G. Farben factories to slave away; others to the Krupp factories. Me? I was marched to the mechanic's building to work morning till night with Wilhelm Deutch as we repaired the machinery which made the camp work. He knew he could only keep me for a matter of months while he was doing his work, and for some reason I'll never, ever fathom, he decided to help me live. Even to this day, now that I am able to think more clearly, and to record the events of my life in the camps, even to this day I can't understand why Deutch chose me to live. He must have worked with so many men and women. He could have chosen to kill any of us, to work us to death; or he could have equally well chosen to give any of us a helping hand and aided our survival. Maybe he did help others. Maybe there are many Joachim Gutmans living now in the ruins of Germany thanks to this man. I don't know. All I do know is that were it not for Wilhelm Deutch, I'd be dead, a corpse, part of the dust of Europe, one of the six million forgotten.

Early on, when I first began to work for him in Auschwitz, I did ask him why. Why me? Why not others? Why was he, a good German, performing this act of grace, this act of salvation?

We were working on repairs to the drainage system from the kitchen to the ditch outside when I asked him. The camp was fairly quiet. Most of the work detail had gone off to the factories and compounds which had been built by the German industrialists within the grounds of Auschwitz. It was approaching midday, and the first guard shift had gone off to have lunch, and the second shift were taking up their positions. Security was at its least observant. It was then that I casually asked him why he was helping me.

'Why?' he responded. He shrugged. 'I have helped others. Many others. You're just one of the many. But if I made a big song and dance about helping you prisoners, the guards and the SS would soon hear about it, and then my neck would be the first to be stretched. Just count yourself lucky, Gutman. I've chosen you, just like your God Yahweh chose your people. Don't fight it. Go along with it and keep your mouth shut from now until the end of time.'

I remember gulping, nervous of asking the question. But it had to be asked. I had to know the reason that this lone, brave German was trying to save my life. I had to understand the underlying reasons. So with some trepidation, I whispered, 'Are you a homosexual? Is it my body you want?'

He burst out laughing and then suddenly became very angry. 'Quiet, you fool. Don't you know what happens to homosexuals? Of course I'm not a queer. How could you even think such a thing? I have a wonderful wife and a beautiful daughter whom I love more than life itself. And when this damn war's over, and I can get on with my life, I'm going to have many more children, repopulate Germany for all the losses we've suffered. How could you even consider saying that about me? A queer? I've never had any interest in men.'

Then he looked at me, dressed in stripped prison clothes, filthy and emaciated, not yet benefiting from the additional food he managed to feed me when the guards weren't looking. 'And anyway, do you seriously think I'd be interested in a physical relationship with somebody like you—thin and scrawny and ridden with lice? And Jewish.'

He suddenly burst out laughing. It was then that I realised something which struck me with the force of a guard's rifle butt. This was the first occasion in all the time I'd known him that he'd ever referred to my religion. It came as a shock, as though this was a barrier between us. And then with an awful clarity and insight, I realised that it was . . . that this was precisely the barrier which separated Deutch from the other Nazis. They treated me as a thing. He treated me as a person.

'Then why are you helping me? Why are you taking such a risk by feeding me? Why?'

He stopped what he was doing. I was standing in the trench, digging it deeper; I supported myself on the shovel; if I'd taken a break like this in a factory, I'd have been shot to death or torn to pieces by a dog. He looked at me and smiled strangely. He shrugged and then continued tightening the bolts on a pipe. His silence frightened me.

Curiosity overcame my caution. 'You risked your life taking me from Sachsenhausen and bringing me here. And you're risking it again by feeding me. Is it something you want from me?'

'Carry on with your work, Gutman. If that trench isn't dug by nighttime, we'll both be shot.'

There would be no answer to the question that came to dominate my mind. It was the last time I ever asked him. For all intents and purposes, he was a good German. A good Nazi. I'd seen him with the guards, laughing and sharing cigarettes; even a beer outside their building. I'd seen him standing mutely by as Jews were shot or torn to pieces by dogs. I'd seen him walk away from some of the most hideous sights ever orchestrated by mankind.

Yet with me, and no doubt with the others before me, he was kind and understanding . . . as though I was the apprentice and he the master. But I wasn't the slave. As far as he was concerned, I was there to help him, and as though he was paying me wages, I deserved rest and consideration for a hard day's work.

Did we speak? Oh yes, all the time. We judged the moments to talk according to the patrols of the guards. As they neared, his tone would become aggressive. *'Pick that up, you stupid fool!' 'Don't do it that way, or I'll have you shot, you filthy pig.'*

And when the guard passed out of earshot, he would look at me in an almost apologetic way, and pick up the conversation again from where we'd left off.

He asked me about my life in Berlin, my friendships, my sexual experiences, my studies. It was as if he were trying to get inside my soul, my body. There were almost no areas of my life which were sacrosanct. *'Tell me about the feeling when you first made love to a girl?' 'What happened when you first went to the university . . . who did you meet . . . what were their names . . . what did their fathers do . . . ?'*

I answered fully. I kept nothing back. Nothing. It was as if he were my most intimate life-long friend, from whom I held back no secrets. Yet he was old enough to be my father, and he was of a far lower social class than that to which I'd been born, making our friendship impossible in the old world. I wouldn't even have noticed him in that world. The world from which I'd been ejected when the Nazis cleared the Jews out of Berlin.

And what did I learn of him? Nothing. Wife, daughter, where he lived in Berlin . . . that was all. I knew nothing of his life, his past, his likes and dislikes . . . not even if he'd fathered an illegitimate child or if he'd been a member of one of the many patriotic German clubs and societies, the *ringvereins*. In many ways I was scared to ask him questions. He was, after all, a Nazi, and he held my life in the palm of his hand. And my life could have been extinguished at his whim. While I was eager to please him by answering his questions, I was uncertain if a two-way traffic was allowed. Almost all I knew of him was what he'd volunteered. So I held my peace. And he seemed glad that I wasn't too inquisitive. In that way, I suppose, he was a surrogate father.

CHAPTER SEVEN

Berlin, Germany, 1998

CHASCA BRODERICK FUMED WITH indignation every time she thought about the way she'd been treated by Gottfried Deutch. How dare he throw back at her the work and effort and expense she'd gone to just to resurrect his precious grandfather's reputation? Who the hell did he think he was?

When he'd stormed out of the bar, leaving her all alone at the table and feeling the humiliation of the publicly jilted girlfriend, she'd forced herself to sit for half an hour staring at the other patrons, returning their knowing smiles, looking nonchalantly at her glass of lager, the photographs on the walls, the influx and egress of customers, and trying to ignore the occasional outburst of muffled laughter from couples on other tables, the women looking at her as though she were an overpriced whore.

When the time was right, when the music which filled the empty spaces in the rapidly filling bar was sufficiently loud to muffle the noise of her chair scraping against the floor, Chasca stood, straightened her dress and coat, and slowly walked away from the smoky and claustrophobic room, vowing never to return to it, nor to any other part of Berlin again.

It was still early when she hailed a taxi on the rain-slicked road, and so she returned to her hotel room in the Unter den Linden, had a quick snack in the coffee lounge, and then took herself to a performance of the Berlin Philharmonic playing Brahms. As she crawled into bed later that night, Chasca realised that for once, the genius of Brahms' seductive rhythms hadn't managed to soothe her ire, and she still bristled with embarrassment at Gottfried's treatment of her. The last thing she thought about as she closed her eyes and went to sleep was, '*Who the hell does he think he is?*'

Over breakfast, she bundled the copy of the testament into an envelope with a curt note on hotel letterhead saying, '*This belongs to you . . . a decent Jewish German gentleman wanted somebody to remember your grandfather kindly . . . Perhaps you should follow his example . . .*' and signed it. She gave it to the reception desk with instructions for it to be sent by courier. Then she went to the zoo.

When she returned in the late afternoon, she showered and took herself out to a restaurant. She was quite comfortable entering a café or bar or restaurant on her own and treating herself to a meal. Many women of her age, women in their late twenties and early thirties, felt uncomfortable doing something social without an accompanying man . . . but not Chasca, who enjoyed time with herself.

That evening should have been her last in Berlin, except that when she returned to her hotel, there was a message under her door. She ripped the envelope open and read the words:

'Thank you for sending me this document. I behaved very badly last night. I want to apologise. Please phone me on your return, so that I can make amends. There is much about my grandfather that I didn't know. I've only read a dozen or so pages of this Gutman's testament, but already I'm amazed. And delighted. But I don't know whether or not to show it to my mother. I don't want to reawaken awful memories. I'd rather find out if Mr. Gutman is

still alive. I need your advice. Please, please contact me. Again, I apologise for my rudeness, my stupidity.

Gottfried.'

She didn't know what to do. Emotionally, the document and Gottfried, and especially the mechanic, had receded into her past. Right now, they were on her back burner. But the note brought them very much to the fore again. Should she phone him and continue the search? Or should she pretend that she'd never seen the note and continue where her life had left off a very long month ago?

But above all else, she hated loose ends, and so she picked up the phone and dialed the number. It was as though he had been waiting by the phone all evening, just for her call. Without her introducing herself, he said, 'Chasca?'

'Yes.'

'Chasca, please forgive me. I was totally wrong in the way I behaved last night . . . I behaved like a stupid person. I'm really, really sorry.'

'So you said in your note.'

'I tried to explain that we never seem to be free of the sins of my grandfather, but this is different. What this man Gutman says about him . . . well, I don't know what to do. I need your help. I don't know whether or not to show it to my mother. She's not well, she's got high blood pressure, and is on pills. I'm scared that this thing, this document, might upset her. I need your help, your advice . . .'

His words were bursting out as if from a volcano.

'Can we meet?' he asked. 'I can come over to your hotel. I know where it is because it's on the letterhead. I know the building . . . It'll only take me half an hour to get there. Please. You can meet me downstairs in the coffee shop. In a half an hour, yes? Let's meet. I must get your advice . . . my mother . . . she's so frail . . . she needs to know.'

She didn't have time to agree or disagree; he'd hung up before she could say anything. But she worried about what would happen. She was a lawyer, and human emotions, especially those of the frail daughter of a hanged Nazi war criminal, were way beyond her experience.

Palace of Justice
Nuremberg, Allied Occupied Germany
June, 1946

Theodore Broderick was a worried man. He was concerned over the mood swings of his client. Other Nazi criminals had sat in varying stages of distress during the many Nuremberg trials listening to the evidence amassed against them; some had shown outright contempt for the proceedings; some had smiled and grinned with callous humour as the evidence of their crimes was paraded before the world; others had shown visible embarrassment that their crimes were no longer hidden but were exposed to the scrutiny of an unforgiving future; still others buried their heads or shielded their eyes as visual evidence of the bestiality of their colleagues was recounted in open court.

But Wilhelm Deutch sat alone in his dock, unsupported by others. Only a phalanx of tough-looking American guards stood behind him as the evidence was presented. He had no shoulders of comrades to support him, no other eyes to look into to answer the unspoken questions.

Some mornings, Deutch was positively jovial as he walked into court, nodding to the defense team, bowing his head curtly as the judge walked in and sat down. Other mornings, the armed guard almost had to carry him into the dock and support him under his arms to prevent him from falling.

Broderick had asked an Army psychiatrist to examine him, to determine whether he was capable of understanding the proceedings against him, and if so, to determine whether he was of a mind sufficiently sane to continue with the trial. The psychiatrist spent two hours examining Deutch, coming to the conclusion that, 'The bastard knows exactly what's happening to him, and hopefully will still be as sane as I am when the noose is tightened.' Hardly a medical judgement, but then the psychiatrist was more concerned with the minds of the Nazi's victims than the sanity of their torturers.

Broderick had taken to visiting Deutch in his cell, making unauthorised inspections to ensure that he was representing a man aware of what was happening to him. He invariably found his client at his small writing desk, penning notes on the trial, *aides memoires* to assist him in the following day's evidence, and generally jovial. He always offered his visitor a cup of coffee, but then, as part of the ritual humour, apologised when he suddenly remembered that he hadn't been to the grocers that day, and was right out of coffee, milk, and sugar.

And so, in the hope that Deutch would make it through to the end of the trial, Broderick continued from day to day, treading the delicate path between defending his client, and refusing to add to the palpable distress of witnesses who were giving evidence of Deutch's cruelty as a slave master. The major problems for Professor Broderick and his defense team came from the seventh and eight witnesses respectively which the prosecution called. The seventh was a man in his early thirties, who, despite a year of recuperation under the care of the Red Cross and the American miliary authorities, still looked cadaverous. He stood with the help of two walking sticks, even though in evidence he told the court that before the war, he'd been a keen football player.

'My name is Gerhardt Neimann. I am now thirty-two years of age. I was interned in the concentration camp at Dachau outside Munich in 1933 at the age of eighteen years for crimes against the state. My crimes were being Jewish.'

'And how long were you in Dachau?' asked William Sherman, the Prosecutor.

'Initially for three months. During that time, I was beaten and abused. And I was anally raped by two guards. I suffered from a torn anus and got gonorrhoea. It didn't heal properly because when I was released from the camp, Hitler was well in charge of Germany and things were already going very badly for Jews, and even Jewish doctors began to find it hard to get good medicine.' The young man answered the questions in such a matter-of-fact way that he made the ordeal he'd suffered even more onerous to bear for those listening.

'Before you tell the court when you were sent to Auschwitz, Mr. Neimann, perhaps you could briefly fill in the rest of your experiences under the growth of Nazism.'

'When I returned from Dachau, my parents and sisters and brothers decided to pack up and go to Palestine. But by the time we'd sold our business and our house, things were already getting incredibly dangerous. We couldn't walk in the streets without somebody pointing the finger at us and screaming out, 'Jew!' Friends and neighbours we'd lived with for fifty years turned their backs on us, refusing to help us in our time of need. People we'd done business with now refused to trade with us. Our reserves ran down; we were destitute. We thought things couldn't get any worse for us, but we didn't realise how much Hitler needed to pay for the growth of his armed forces.

'There were sudden new taxes on Jews who wanted to emigrate to Palestine. Having almost no money left, and unable to sell our property for anything like the price it was worth because our Aryan German neighbours knew they could take advantage of our situation, the only place we could move to as a family was Berlin, where we'd heard things were just a little bit better for Jews. And indeed they were. Göbbels was openly ridiculed in the streets, the SA were booed. There were local laws and ordinances forbidding the wearing of the SA uniform. Marches were banned. Berliners hated Hitler, which is why he made it his headquarters . . . to rub their noses in it.

'When we moved to Berlin, my father and mother began to see things from a new and more pleasant perspective. It seemed as though the rise of Hitler and the Nazis was a local phenomenon, that he was some southern bully boy and he and his kind were confined to Bavaria and the areas of the south of Germany, centered around Munich. Oh, we read about the electoral successes of the Nazi Party, but Berlin never voted for him . . . and that was good enough for us. So we made the decision not to emigrate, but to allow the German peasant people in the South to have their fill of Hitler and his crazy speeches and his insane rallies, and we knew that soon it would all settle down. We Jews had seen his type a dozen times before in the thousand years we'd been in Europe. Men like Hitler, all puffed up with hot air. They caused problems for us, then after a couple of years, their mania would die out and we Jews would just wait for the next anti-Semite to stand up and tell the people that we're the cause of all the problems of the world.'

The young man was starting to become distressed, so Sherman said, 'Why don't we take up your story when you're interned in Auschwitz? On what date were you sent there?'

'I don't know the exact date. You see, the Jews of Berlin weren't all rounded up until fairly late in the war. We were part of the final round-up which took place at the beginning of 1943. I'm sorry I can't be more accurate, but the days all seemed to blend into one another. We seemed to spend our days and nights desperately looking for somewhere to live. Because of the British bombers, many houses were destroyed, so all the Jews were moved out of their apartments so that they could be given over as accommodation for Aryan Germans, and there were always Jews on the streets with suitcases looking to rent anything, just for a roof over their heads.

'But then the Gestapo suddenly picked us up off the street and we were taken to concentration camps. I was taken to Auschwitz. I was separated from my parents. I've not seen them since. My sisters and I were taken to Leverzowstrasse Synagogue, and we were forced to sit in the freezing cold of the bombed-out building for three days before they put us on a train. I was separated from them in the train . . . in the cattle wagons . . . and I haven't seen them since. I think they were sent to another concentration camp, but I don't know.'

Gently the prosecutor asked, 'When did you first see the accused, Wilhelm Deutch?'

Neimann looked at Deutch for only the second time since he'd been in the witness box. His mouth seemed to grow thin with contempt. 'Because I was healthy, I was allocated to him because of the drainage work which needed to be done. There were three of us in the gang. We worked with inferior tools, and were worked without break from early morning till midday when he was forced to allow us to leave our work and go for some soup.'

'Forced? Could you tell the court what you mean by that.'

'I mean that he would have worked us all day and all night had he not been forced to allow us some small amount of time to eat. That man would have happily allowed us to drop dead from exhaustion. I worked in the factories and in the compound, but the work I did for that man was the worst of all, because he was relentless, he never let us rest even for a second.'

Theodore Broderick glanced over to his client, who sat there impassively, taking the occasional note, shaking his head while listening intently to the evidence. Broderick wondered what was going through his mind.

Counsel for the prosecution continued, 'What work did you do?'

'I dug. I used a pickaxe and a shovel. And when the wooden handle broke because we were digging into rock, he made me scoop up the rocks and stones with my bare hands.'

'What else?' asked William Sherman.

'One day, a friend of mine, someone whom I'd known in Berlin before the war, was digging near to a sewage pipe which led into the open ditches outside the wire of the compound. Deutch told him to be careful where he dug. My friend was careful, but he was exhausted. So tired, I . . . he . . . he was so exhausted he could hardly stand, let alone swing a pickaxe. But with every ounce of strength left in his body, he lifted the axe and brought it down; but it bounced sideways off a piece of rock, and the point entered the sewage pipe. It was nothing very bad. It could easily have been repaired by another length of pipe.

'But Deutch looked down into the hole and saw the excrement seeping out of the pipe, and went crazy. Insane. He screamed and shouted and pointed. He picked up a rock that was at his feet and threw it into the ditch we were working in. It hit my friend on his head, and he fell down into the hole which was slowly filling up with raw sewage. I was beside myself with terror. At least the guards were controlled in their fury. Deutch was . . . I don't even know the word. He was insane. He was screaming, *'Fucking Jew. I'll kill you for that, fucking Jew.'* And then he ran away. Disappeared. I tended to my friend's wound as best I could, and we started to climb out of the ditch. I got out first in order to help my friend, but then I saw what had happened. Deutch had run over to one of the guards and was pulling the man towards the trench. He was shouting hysterically. When the guard got here, I was already out of the ditch, but Deutch pointed to my friend who was staring up with a look of such fear on his face. I knew what was going to happen. The guard took out his machine-gun and shot my friend. He emptied a machine-gun into him. His body . . . sort of . . . well, it came apart. There were bits of his body not attached, if you see what I mean . . .'

The judge looked at the witness in astonishment, as did the prosecuting counsel and Theodore Broderick. It wasn't so much the language which the witness was using, as the utter, dead, emotionless way he was speaking. It was as though he was describing a shopping expedition. His total lack of emotions spoke more eloquently of the way in which the Nazis had destroyed the humanity of life than almost anything which Broderick had yet heard in his time in Germany.

Without noticing the astonishment of the court, as though he were refreshing his memory of some nondescript event, the witness continued, 'Deutch made me get back in the ditch and pull out the pieces of a man who I used to know.'

The court was in total silence. Broderick stole a glance at Deutch, who was still scribbling notes, like a forensic examiner. Softly, Sherman asked the witness, 'Do you have anything else you would like to add?'

Neimann thought for a moment and muttered a barely audible, 'Yes, an hour later, I was repairing the pipe, and Deutch was talking to me in a completely calm voice, chatting amiably about the unusually mild weather we were having for that time of the year. It was as if nothing had happened.'

The irony wasn't lost on the court. William. Sherman turned to Theodore Broderick, and said, 'Your witness.'

Theodore Broderick sat there for a long moment, agonising about his next move. Then he pushed his numbed body to its feet and said in a low and husky voice, 'I have no questions for this gentleman.'

His decision not to cross-examine the young man was more a question of respecting his suffering than of defending his client. But he judged he would do more harm to Deutch by trying to deny what the witness claimed to have seen with his own eyes. In the absence of contradictory evidence, it would be Deutch's word against that of the victim, and right now, that was a no-contest. At the start of the day, Broderick had asked Deutch what he knew of this witness, but his client said he couldn't remember him. They'd discussed the evidence which Neimann was going to give, and Deutch said he knew of no such incidents. Yet Deutch was scribbling away in the dock, writing some sort of rebuttal. But rebutting what? Evidence so damning against his character that, in the absence of contradiction of the facts, no mitigation was possible.

So Broderick determined that he would wait for the gale to blow over, in the hope that he could mute its effect by calming words when it came his turn to present a case.

It was the eighth witness, though, a young woman, who caused Theodore Broderick the greatest concern of this trial, and who probably did Wilhelm Deutch the most damage. So many witnesses during so many Nuremberg trials recounted tales of utter horror that their effects were at times numbing. The catalogue of mass evil was so damning that individual cases of base behaviour often failed to move the judges. But Hannelle Cohen told a story of a different order.

Broderick had read the transcript of her evidence, but the concrete words on paper denied the rawness of the emotion to which he was witness when Hannelle Cohen told her story in the courtroom. For a half hour, Hannelle, sobbing, grasping a handkerchief and sitting with her head bowed in shame, was led through her evidence by William Sherman, the prosecutor. She told of how she was selected for the brothel at Auschwitz by the guards. It was because of her breasts. They were still firm and full. Stripped naked, she had been forced to run past the guards and the camp doctors for an initial appraisal, prior to being shorn of her hair. She told the usual story of the various lines at the induction point into the camp, the left-hand columns of the sick or the elderly or the very young, and to the right-hand columns of stronger, younger people. Those who went to the left were never seen again; those to the right usually lasted between three and six months.

But Hannelle had always been an attractive young woman. In her home town, Bonn, she'd once been selected by a local newspaper as a 'face of Modern Germany youth,' one of a dozen young teenage girls who typified nationalism and beauty. Later in her life, as a captivating twenty-two-year-old just before the war started, she'd had a portfolio taken by a local photographer who'd tried to seduce her, saying she was one of the most exciting models he'd ever photographed.

And four years later, she was again selected, this time as a whore, the plaything of the guards in a concentration camp called Auschwitz. She told the court that as she ran naked past the jeering, cat-calling guards, she tried to think of the wonderful experiences of her life till then; but when she came to the end of the line, and the naked women were selected for the various barracks, a short and unshaven Polish camp guard stinking of the smell of the unwashed, grasped her firmly by the arm, and pulled her in his direction. 'You're lucky,' he had told her. 'You've been selected to be a *hure* by the *Lagerfürher*. Now all you have to do is to use your body, and you'll live like a fucking queen. Your days will be free, and you'll only work nights. Like all

Jew whores.' She told the court that never would she forget the guttural laugh as he said it.

In many ways, she said, her life came to an end at that moment. But there were a couple of things which made her existence somehow better than that of the other women who weren't selected to be whores, but were sent for slave labour. For example, she told the judge, she didn't have to wear the dreaded *Holzschube*, the wooden shoes which caused so much pain and damage to feet of the other inmates; nor did she have to become a '*Klauenmädchen*,' a woman who stole food from another prisoner to survive—stealing food was the greatest crime that one inmate could commit against another and was never ever forgiven. No, one of the advantages of working in the brothels was that they were well supplied with food. The guards and the favoured kapos didn't like skinny women. Like Christmas geese, they were fattened to make them more appetising.

The prosecutor asked her what were the conditions the women such as her had to endure while working in the brothels. And she told him. She spared him no details. She told him of the indolent days when she and the fifty other women would sit around in the brothel house, talking about their nightmare. And they would wait in increasing horror as the clock inexorably marched on towards evening, when the guards would return from their work details, and they would want to unwind with slave sluts. Then, when they heard the guards and the inmates returning, the women would go back to their cubicles in their rabbit warren, and wait for the door to be thrown upon. They had no choice. And they would have to service eight or ten men a night. Every night. Even on the Jewish Sabbath, and the Christian day of rest. Even when one of them, still occasionally menstruating, would be bleeding down her leg; even when one of them fell pregnant and before her forced abortion and subsequent sterilisation.

Sometimes, Hannelle said, she would be forced to entertain—yes, they used the metaphor, 'entertain'—SS guards as well as Ukrainians and Poles and others who were not in the SS. Others, such as the mechanic who was on trial; or lesbian guards; or kapos; or blockführers, or on occasions, even selected prisoners who had done special favours for the SS, or who had given information for which this was their reward.

How did Hannelle remember entertaining the mechanic in particular, out of all the hundreds of faceless, nameless men she'd been forced to have sex with? Perhaps, said William Sherman, she could look at the defendant and reassure herself that he was, indeed, the man who had caused her so much grief. The witness remained silent for some time, hardly having the strength to lift her eyes. She clutched a handkerchief in her hands, her knuckles white with anger. Slowly she lifted her head from staring into her lap, and looked across the gulf of the courtroom, across the void which separated them.

She gave an imperceptible nod. The prosecutor apologised for causing her additional grief and asked her, for the sake of the court record, to answer the question with a yes or a no.

She nodded again, as though incapable of saying the word. But then, looking at the prosecutor and the defense counsel, and the judge and the dozen or so other observers of her misery, she said softly, 'Yes. I know that man. I knew him many times. Like a farm animal, I serviced him.'

The words cut through the court. 'I remember when he first came to visit me. He selected me. He told me that he'd been to look at all the other girls in the brothel, all the other *hures*, but he decided that he wanted me. As though he was bestowing a favour on me.'

'Are you absolutely certain that it was the defendant Wilhelm Deutch who used your . . . services?' the prosecutor asked diffidently.

Gaining strength, she said, 'Oh yes. I know him. I will never forget him. You see, the others were brutes. Animals. They just used to get me to lie down, then take off their trousers and undergarments, and they'd force me to have sex with them. All kinds of sex.' She bit her lip and struggled to continue. 'Sex with all parts of me. Some of them liked to smack and hurt me. Some liked to see the look of terror in my face. But him,' she said, pointing to Deutch, 'he was different. He was truly terrifying. He was so horrible. In my nightmares, it's him I remember above all others.'

'Would you tell the court why?'

'The others just used me. I was an object to them. And as the months went by, I came to terms with the fact that I could live with being just an object, at least until the war was over, or until I died of a disease or the men grew tired of me and complained, and then I'd be thrown into the gas ovens, spent and exhausted.

'So to protect myself for as long as possible, I simply used the technique which the older women . . . those who had been there longer than me . . . used. I locked myself up in my mind and wouldn't let them through. All they were using was my body. But him,' she said, now looking at Deutch, her face twisted in hatred and repulsion, 'he knew what I was doing. He even told me so. He knew that when he was in the cubicle, and I was servicing him, giving him oral sex or other kinds of sex, he knew that I wasn't there; that only my body was there. And he didn't like it. He wanted to possess me. Totally. He wanted all of my attention, for me to know that when he was inside me, he was in complete control. So he used mind techniques to get inside my brain. He tried to unlock those parts of me which I didn't want to unlock if I was to remain sane. He wanted to get to know me. He pretended to want to understand me. To empathise with me. To assure me that he had a wife and a daughter and that he didn't normally do this sort of thing. But I knew that it was all a lie,' she said.

She was barely able to be heard in the court. Nobody, not even the judge, was willing to interrupt her story to ask her to speak up. She looked at the judge and realised that she'd lapsed into virtual silence. She took a sip from a glass of water and apologised to the court. The judge, Jonathan Parker, smiled at her and encouraged her to continue, if she was able. She said she was able to carry on, coughed, and then turned and faced Wilhelm Deutch.

Her face was a mask of confusion. At first, she frowned, then she screwed up her eyes in hatred . . . but then, slowly, a smile of superiority etched itself into her thin lips, because she realised that her nemesis, her hated German client from the master race, was now impotent, was now the one trapped in the cubicle, and she could expose his most private and shameful actions to the whole world, just as he had once been in control of her.

Hannelle continued. 'He understood exactly what I had to do to stay sane, and he was determined to add to my suffering by denying me the privacy of my mind. He was the most cruel and terrible of all the men I serviced.'

'And why,' asked the prosecutor, 'did you find this particularly difficult? Why did you find the defendant's behaviour worse than that of the men who beat and terrified you?'

Now, in her mind, she was back in the cubicles, Hannelle was thinking thoughts which had been buried for the year since she'd been liberated from Auschwitz by the Russians. Now, revisiting what she had become, she began to lose control. Sipping a glass of water, Hannelle fought back tears.

Softly she struggled to answer the question. 'Because the SS guards and the Ukrainians and those other men who used you . . . those men you could deal with. Those animals, you could shut out of your mind. With them, you only felt physical pain when they thrust their . . . their . . .' she couldn't bring herself to say the word '. . . you felt pain and fear. But you knew it would be over as soon as they'd finished their sex. As soon as they'd emptied themselves into you, you knew that the pain would stop, at least until the next man burst through your door. You somehow managed to close your mind to the fact that these were men. You thought of them as mindless machines. You became a machine yourself. It was the only way you could survive.

'But him,' she said, again lifting her arm and pointing to Deutch, her voice rising in fury, 'as I said, he was the worst of all. All the time he was with me, he was asking me about my life as a young woman. About my first kiss. About my parents. And he knew how much it hurt me. He knew it was killing me inside my mind. He kept on reminding me of times past, times with my family and with my friends. He made me realise what my life had come to in Auschwitz. And he enjoyed it so much, seeing the panic on my face as I remembered what my life had been; he enjoyed seeing the grief.

'I hated him more than any of the others, because he pretended to understand me. He used to get so excited when he was able to get inside my mind. To make me feel like a woman rather than a machine. He knew precisely what he was doing. The worst moments of my life in the camp were when he forced me to tell him about the times I'd been a pretty young girl in Bonn. About the young men I'd known. He said he wanted to understand the difference between the sunny, beautiful life that I'd led, and the life I was leading now, that of a whore in a filthy room in a concentration camp; a subhuman, a non-person. He loved the hurt in my eyes when I stopped being a machine for the guards and the Ukrainians, when he saw me become a woman. And when I felt like a woman, I realised what was happening to me, and I felt so . . .' She whispered the next word. The entire court strained to hear. The prosecutor asked her to repeat it.

Softly, she said, '. . . guilty.'

'Clearly the young man is lying about what I did or is unfortunately mistaken,' Wilhelm Deutch said to his defense counsel. 'I don't remember him working in a ditch. He's confused me with somebody else. I wasn't the only mechanic, you know. There were many others, and some of them were real bastards. You should have cross-examined him. But what I fail to understand is why you say that the evidence of the prostitute, Hannelle Cohen, is so damning? There was no evidence of my brutality. I never beat her. It's obvious that she simply misunderstood my intentions. You see, I tried to help her.'

'And that's what I'll be telling the court when I cross-examine her this afternoon. But you have to appreciate my problem. She's left an indelible mark in the mind of the judge. She's singled you out from all the hundreds of men she serviced because she claims that you hurt her more than the other brutes. It's not hard to unpick her evidence and cast doubt upon your motives for whatever conversation passed between you, but it's almost impossible to counteract the deep impression I could see she was making in the mind of the judge.'

'So why did you want to talk to me? What can I tell you?'

'I need to know whether you want me to cross-examine her, or whether we leave her evidence and move on to the next witness. Hannelle Cohen was their last minor witness before they bring on the big guns. I want to know whether you want me to put her through the mill again, and force her to confront the evidence you've given me about the reasons you wanted to know more about her, her private life before she became a prostitute. But I warn you again that it could react against us.'

Deutch shook his head as the translator finished Broderick's last words. 'How can you adequately explain your actions in time of war? Yes, I wanted to know about her private life, but not for the reasons she gave; not for reasons of cruelty. Only because I wanted her to know that one day her pain and suffering would be over and that she could return to the world before the war, to the music and the dancing and the sunshine that are the right of every young man and woman. But whether you ask her these questions is your decision, Mr. Defense Lawyer. That's why you're here. There's so very much you don't know, and will never understand about those days. You're in charge now, Professor Broderick. Thank God it's your decision, not mine.'

Allied Occupied Germany, June, 1946

From the memoirs of Joachim Gutman:

I'd never been into a brothel before. Not even as a teenager, when it was all the rage in Berlin amongst the Jewish kids. They'd tell their parents they were going around to a friend's house to study, and instead they'd steal a handful of Reichmarks from their fathers' wallets and go into the city centre with its lights and girls standing on corners wearing leather skirts and fishnet stockings, and find a woman for an hour or so.

The richer kids used to ignore these street woman because of the risks of pox, and instead go to brothels.

I never went. Not for any moral or ethical or religious reasons, but because I didn't need to go. When I was fifteen, I looked as though I was twenty, and it was easy for me to pick up girls in cafés or in clubs. I'd take them to parks in the summer and make love to them under the canopy of an oak tree; or in the winter, we'd find the apartment of a friend whose parents had gone away for the season, and we'd spend hours in the act of passion. We'd whisper silly words into each other's ears like *'I love you'* and *'marry me'*. But the love only lasted until the following morning, and then again the field would be lying fallow and I would find another girl with whom to plough a furrow.

Nor, I remember, did I ever have a real and true love. Oh, I liked the girls with whom I shared my body, but nobody ever haunted my nights or consumed the thoughts of my days. Each would be a conquest; none would prevent me, the warrior, from seeking another battle.

Before I could be swept up in the rhythms of a normal life ... finding a true and virtuous woman and marrying her ... I was swept by the Nazis into the dragnets which they used when fishing for Jews in Berlin. And I eventually landed in Auschwitz. It was there that I first went to a brothel.

I didn't want to go to the brothel, especially as the women there saw dozens of men a week ... Nazis ... and they were almost certainly diseased. But when I'd been working for the mechanic for four weeks, and we'd dug the trenches from the kitchen area, and done all the work which needed doing, he said to me that I deserved a reward. I hardly thought so. I wasn't losing weight like the others I lived with, and there were some suspicious looks in my direction every now and again. Nor was I exhausted at the end of the day like the others, walking cadavers who only just managed to struggle into bed. Yes, there were looks of surprise at the way I comported myself in the barracks. I had energy; I didn't have the emaciated, skeletal look of the starved. The suspicions began to grow.

Of course, there hadn't been sufficient time since arriving for the weight gain to really show . . . after all, I'd come to Auschwitz from nine months at Sachsenhausen, so the extra bread and meat he gave me was only keeping me able to do the work without starting to look like a skeleton.

But the mechanic insisted that I had a reward for all the hard work I'd done in the past four weeks, got the okay from the captain of the guard, and that night took me to the large wooden hut, called Building Number One. There were four fairly new buildings which had been erected. No. 1 was the brothel for the use of the SS, the guards, and privileged prisoners like me. No. 2 was the camp administration, where office staff and others in the so-called political department were housed; No. 3 was where they did the laundry; and No. 4 was a complete secret, though rumours abounded that it housed the infamous Block where Dr. Mengele and the others were said to carry out their experiments on human beings.

When I first entered the building which they used as a brothel, I was curious about the smell. It was the aroma of a hospital, the sort of smell which you experience in a ward . . . antiseptic . . . washed surfaces, cleanliness. It was alien to anything I'd smelled in many years . . . since my appendix operation when I was a nine-year-old. I didn't associate this smell with a brothel. For some reason, I thought that brothels smelled of perfume and sensuality. And nor was I concerned about getting the pox, even though I was certain that each of the whores inside was pox-ridden. Why? Because life had taken on a different meaning. On the outside you could plan your future; avoid sexual diseases because you wanted to marry a nice young woman, and you didn't want to infect her; there was something to look forward to; and you could take steps to defend yourself from what nature threw at you. But in the camps, there was no future; only the present. If you survived the day, you looked forward to sleep; if you survived the night and awoke the following morning, you thanked the Almighty for giving you another day. Did I think about the pox as I entered the brothel? Did I worry about its effects on my future? Of course I didn't. I looked forward to no future; all I lived for was the present!

There were steps up to the building. The door opened, and facing us was a small reception area, and then four or five corridors which led to a series of cubicles. It was as though we had entered a corporate headquarters and off the corridors were a whole series of tiny little offices, each with a door. Some of the doors were open, and I could detect movement. There were no signs on the door, but I assumed that those that were open contained prostitutes waiting for someone to enter, those that were closed contained prostitutes busy with a customer.

I think it was seeing the closed doors which made me fully realise that this was a brothel where slave women were used for their bodies. And I also remember my mind splitting in two. One side was saying, *'Well, isn't that what the Nazis have everybody else doing?'* The other side was saying, *'How can you be in a place where women are forced to act like animals?'*

Things which happen in wartime could never happen in peace time. It's not just the way we accept killing and death . . . it's the way we accept the loss of value of the human life. Our own, and others.

The mechanic led me to a door with which he seemed to be familiar. It was the fifth or sixth door in the left hand corridor. The door was wide open. He nudged me in the arm and said, 'Go in. Enjoy yourself. Don't worry.'

I entered the room. There was a bed, a wooden carpetless floor, a wooden cabinet beside the bed, a chair, and that was all. It was as though this was the cheapest room in the cheapest boarding house in some rural hamlet in the Black Forest. And on the bed was a woman.

I smiled at her. I didn't know what else to do. She was just sitting there, looking into her lap. She was wearing only a blue dressing gown. She had short, dark hair. For a moment I thought she was asleep, somehow in a sitting position, but then slowly she looked up at me. Except on the dead, I've never seen a face so devoid of expression. I was shocked to my very core. Her eyes were those of some extinct animal, as though once there had been light and laughter, but now the forces of nature had robbed her of existence. Never have I seen such dead eyes.

Her lips were frozen together in a thin line. I think I tried to smile, to show her some feeling of warmth and human empathy. But if she saw through those mortified eyes, then it failed to translate to her mouth, because she remained expressionless as she stood, and allowed the dressing gown to slip from her body, showing her nakedness.

I felt a shock, as though hot metal had pierced my body, as she stood before me, exposed but without any self-regard. Embarrassment was an emotion felt only by those who control their own destiny. Embarrassment had left this woman in her first few days in the brothel. She walked past me and closed the door. We were standing there, and she nodded at me to remove my clothes.

But my mind left her presence and flew out of the room, to a time five or six years beforehand, when I was still young in mind and strong in body; when Giselle had accompanied me to a weekend away at a friend's lakeside home. Giselle and I had been chaperoned, but we managed to elude her aunt and found ourselves alone in the boatshed. Without talk, without pleading, she removed my tie and shirt and trousers and undergarments, as she allowed me to remove her dress and silks and laces.

Giselle's perfume, the rustling of the silk she wore, the softness of her skin came back to me over the years with an intensity which took away my breath. I looked at this pathetic, naked creature, standing there with a look of hatred buried deep within her dead eyes. I looked down at myself as I struggled to undo the top button of my coarse, filthy striped prison pyjamas. I saw my hands, rutted and filthy with scabs and sores and ingrained dirt; I felt my hair, once strong and shining and lustrous with pomade, now as dead and lifeless as my present; I ran my hands over my face and for the first time in a year, felt how it had shrunk with starvation and how my beard struggled to grow. And I saw then how the Nazis had brought me low. And I fell on to this unnamed woman's bed and sobbed my eyes out.

For the first time since I'd entered the room, some life came into her eyes. As I sat there crying into my cupped hands, I felt her sit beside me. She knew I was a Jew, a prisoner. But she must have assumed that I was a traitor, earning the special privilege of entry to the brothel because I'd given the Nazis information against my people. So it must have come as a shock to her when I fell on her bed, weeping. I felt her gently take my hands away from my face, as though forcing me to look upon my own shame. And then she spoke for the first time.

'Why are you crying?' she asked simply. Though she was still young, her voice was deep, as though old with experience.

'I'm so ashamed,' I told her, though I wasn't sure she could understand my words though my sobs.

'Why?'

'Of what I've become.'

'And what have you become?' she asked me gently. Her voice, deep and soothing, was sweet to hear. But there was a gulf between us. She wasn't in sympathy with me; rather she was asking these questions as a doctor asks a sick patient.

'Look at me. Look at you. Is this how people should behave towards each other?'

'We're victims of this war. This is what happens to victims. What have you done that you've been brought in here?'

I looked at her eyes, and it was then that I saw some life had returned to them. They were dark, deep, Semitic eyes, the eyes of Naomi and Judith and Sarah and Rachael. The eyes of a woman who has seen the desert stars and known the torment of five thousand years of being different.

I told her about how I'd been in Sachsenhausen, and how the mechanic now working in Auschwitz had requisitioned me for special hydraulic work. That I'd been digging a ditch all on my own, and as a reward, the mechanic had offered me . . . I was about to say 'a prostitute,' but I couldn't use the word. So instead, I told her that the mechanic had offered me . . . 'you.' There was no sense of shock on her face, nor of betrayal, nor of hatred. Just acceptance.

'I've heard of this mechanic,' she told me. 'He comes in here sometimes. The girls say he's very good to them. That he's not violent, and he shows them respect. He even brings in food and sometimes tobacco and once, he brought in some chocolate.'

I felt her stroking my lice-ridden hair. She was actually touching me. I realised that I hadn't been touched by a woman in nearly two years. Her hands were gentle and probing, feeling the contours of my skull, moving down to the exposed cords at the back of my neck. Yet I could tell that it was a mechanical movement, devoid of emotion. Something which she'd been taught when she became a whore. Maybe something she'd used in the early days, thinking that her job was to bring pleasure, before she realised that all she had to be was an outlet for relief.

I moved her hand from my head. 'I'm sorry,' I told her. 'You don't understand. I'm here because he told me to be here. You're my reward. But I don't want a reward like this. All I want is food and rest. And to get away from here and to go back to my home and . . .' I began to sob again.

Her mood turned to condemnatory. 'Pull yourself together. That sort of thing leads to death. You know you mustn't show weakness in front of these bastards. Tell me, what's your name?'

I told her. I told her about my life in Berlin, and my about my parents and brother and sister. I told her about the work I'd done when I was first sent to camp.

While I was talking, there was the sound of feet marching outside the window. Then the noise of screamed commands, and wafting through the air, as though from a heavenly orchestra, the sound of swing music. Then we heard the sounds of boots climbing the steps of the brothel, and the laughter and coarse remarks of men walking down corridors. The prostitute—I had no idea of her name, even though she now knew something about me—visibly stiffened at the sounds from the outside world. Her mood changed, and she appeared to withdraw from me in body and in mind. Suddenly there was a bang at the door, a rough thump which shook the light fitting.

'Come on in there, you whore bitch. Hurry up. There's others waiting.' It was the accent of a Ukrainian guard, the voice of a sadist. They were all sadists, the Ukrainians.

The girl called out, 'I've only just started, go somewhere else.' She looked at me urgently and whispered, 'Shout out *go away!*'

I did. In my loudest and most commanding German. I heard the Ukrainian mumble and his boots disappearing down the corridor to find an open door.

Funny, in all my time in Auschwitz, my most insistent memory was of being able to shout a command . . . *'go away.'*

Palace of Justice
Nuremberg, Allied Occupied Germany
June, 1946

Theodore Broderick was about to give up on his Nazi client. Well-known for defending the defenseless, the impoverished, the mentally incompetent, as well as Negroes and Latins from South America and other members of the distressed minorities which made up the family of America, in his career as an advocate for people brought before court, he'd also come to the aid of people whom he would not even have bothered recognizing had he met them under other circumstances.

He'd defended white racists accused of murder of black people, and he'd felt disgust at their self-justification, but he'd reasoned that if he didn't defend them, then American justice was not for all; he'd defended wife-beaters and serial murderers and traitors and rich city businessmen who had made their wealth from the sweat and misery of others.

But in each and every case that he'd defended, the accused man had assisted him in his work as defense attorney. It might not have been at the beginning of the case, but somehow, sometime during the taking of evidence, or when the trial began and the evidence against the accused was being amassed, the wall of indifference broke down, and the defendant began to defend himself.

It had nearly happened with Wilhelm Deutch. A day or two earlier, the prisoner had been angry in self-justification. Broderick could sense it from his occasional snorts of contempt at the evidence which was being presented in court; even his body language, shifting on his chair, squaring his shoulders as witnesses were unveiling a litany of brutality during his time as a mechanic in the camp, gave expression to his pent-up rage at the way lies were being told and his character was being systematically degraded.

But then, by the end of the day in court, the wall was rebuilt, and again he was indifferent in his silence. Broderick was beginning to wish that he had respected Deutch's desire to be tried by the initial arraignment with the mechanics from the *Einstazgruppen*, for by now he'd be in the death cells, waiting for the ultimate penalty. This trial was a waste of time, resources, and energy when there was so much evil abroad, still unpunished.

Thinking back, it was the evidence of the pathetic Jewish prostitute that seemed to have turned him silent again. Broderick had looked deeply into the face of that poor woman, Hannelle, and then at the face of his client. They both appeared to be deeply hurt—she, because of her accounts of how she'd been forced to give her body to the animals—he because the prostitute had told everyone that he was as bad as them. It was strange. Broderick realised that he hadn't even begun to get underneath the skin of his client. If he had to draw a pen portrait of Deutch, he'd have to admit that all he could do was to show the crudest of features. Underneath, there'd be no humanity, no real man. He waited for the guard to bring his client into the interview room before the start of the day's evidence. And what a day it would be. This was when the prosecution would present evidence of the horrors of Birkenau, the death camp of Auschwitz.

The door to the interrogation room opened, and two guards entered, followed by Deutch. He was dressed in his usual grey shirt, blue-striped tie, and dark blue suit. He looked more like a clerk in an accountant's office than a man accused of being an important cog in the machinery of death. He looked—Broderick searched for the appropriate word, and as Deutch sat down, it occurred to him how best to describe his client—banal! Ordinary! Commonplace! He found it hard to mask his contempt. Broderick knew full well that he was breaking the cardinal rule of the advocate . . . he was believing the evidence against his client.

Broderick began to speak immediately when he saw Deutch shuffling the bundle of papers he'd brought with him into the interrogation room. 'My view is that the trial proper begins today. All the evidence so far . . . about your treatment of people and your alleged cooperation with the brutality of the Nazi guards when you were mending the machinery in the slave factories, about your treatment of the camp prostitutes . . . all of that was the prosecution painting a character for the judge to illustrate your base side, in preparation for laying the groundwork of your willing complicity in making the gas ovens work so that the Nazis could follow Hitler's orders.'

Deutch nodded in agreement. 'So it begins.'

'Is there anything you need to tell me? We've had a couple of surprises so far from what came up in evidence against you. The Neimann testimony . . . the young woman prostitute were very damaging.'

'Why so? All the camps worked people to death and had brothels. All the guards and commandants used the women there. I was given access because I was on the staff of the camp. What that woman told the court was that I hadn't beaten her, nor treated her brutally, nor demanded any abnormal sexual performances, as was all too often the case with the others. I could have told you stories of women, prostitutes, who were beaten to death during sex . . . not for crimes they'd committed, but as a part of the sadism which some of the guards enjoyed. They didn't need to be restrained, as they were in civilian life. In the camps, you could do whatever you wanted to a prostitute, no matter how base and immoral, and nobody would say a thing. Even if a woman was carried out dead, another would be sent in to replace her before the customer had even lost his erection, and the whole thing would start all over again. What did this witness, this Hannelle Cohen, say about me? What was the worst crime I committed? That I tried to befriend her. That I tried to get to know her.

'I was lonely. I was separated from my wife and daughter. I worked long, hard hours. There was a great deal of tension in the place. Allied bombers were flying over the area all the while. Air raid sirens. We didn't know whether they'd target the camps. There were rumours that the Jews in America were petitioning the British government to bomb the camps and put their fellow Jews out of their misery; and to prevent the camps from being used for the purpose of genocide. Whether or not that was true, I don't know. But it was a rumour, and in those days, our daily bread was rumour.

'I was always on edge, nervous, frightened. So naturally I went to the brothel to ease my bodily needs and to calm my mind. But I was never like the others. I had no need for lust or brutality. All I needed was a woman with a soft voice and comforting hands to remind me of my wife and the life from which I'd been separated.'

Broderick interrupted. 'That wasn't the way in which the witness described your visits to her.'

'I know what she said,' Deutch responded angrily. 'But again, you're listening to facts, to things said, in a cold and hostile courtroom. You have no understanding of how things were. Of how easy it was to be caught up in that fast-moving vehicle which was Nazism.'

He stood, his mood suddenly growing furious. Broderick noticed that his mood shifts were getting increasingly rapid and regular since the trial had begun, not an altogether unusual phenomenon.

But what was unusual was the anger which Deutch suddenly directed at his defense counsel. 'Why can't you understand, you stupid, arrogant American?' he shouted. 'Why can't you get it through your thick skull that I'm innocent? That I tried to help people like that woman, Hannelle; that there were many people given to me as slaves who I treated with kindness, with respect; that I fed and tried to keep alive. Why can't you understand that I'm not like the Nazis?'

Softly, Broderick said, 'Because what I understand isn't important. We're in a court of law, and we can't prove what you're saying. Because I've only got your word, and it's your word against a truckload of evidence showing that you were there, and you were a willing participant. I might believe you, Mr. Deutch, but I have to convince the judge, and he's a very sceptical man. A man who, for the past year, has been listening to some of the most horrific tales of bestiality in the litany of humankind's experience.

'Where's the evidence to prove the facts of which you're trying to convince me? Where are the people you helped? What acts of kindness did you show? You've given me nothing except words. Just a constantly repeated theme, a refrain, a chorus that you were forced to be there, that you were swept up, but that you didn't do what the others did. You keep telling me that you helped the slaves you were given, that you gave them food and sheltered them. But where are they? Why won't they come forward? I've had men out in the refugee camps and the Red Cross and the other agencies all asking for people who'll speak on your behalf, but not one person has come forward saying you helped him. Not one. Mr. Deutch, I'm trying desperately to present your side of things in the best possible way, but you've given me nothing to work with. Nothing.'

Wilhelm Deutch sat down and looked at his lawyer. 'Even if I did, nobody would believe me,' he said.

CHAPTER EIGHT

Allied Occupied Germany, June, 1946

From the memoirs of Joachim Gutman:

In Auschwitz, I was afraid of dying.

In Birkenau, I was afraid of living.

Even now, even a year and a half after I left that hell on earth, and no matter how long I live, nothing in my life will erase the smell of that place from my mind. Nothing will shut out the pictures which shimmer in the twilight of my days.

No matter how long I live, or what I might do with my life, nothing will ever help me understand what happened to me when I was given the job of tending to the gas ovens in Birkenau. One day, I'm digging trenches, fixing laundries, mending machinery, putting new wooden staves into shovels to replace ones which had broken–the sort of thing for which my parents once employed a disabled handyman called Heinz; next day, I'm a part of the machinery which kills human beings and burns their bodies to ash. Then I take the ash and sprinkle it on the vegetable gardens so that the dust and embers, the sole remnant of a thousand years of European Jewry, can help lettuces and cabbages grow to feed Nazi concentration camp guards.

If the change had been gradual, I might have been able to understand it. A week, even a month of occasional work in Birkenau to acclimatise, to get me used to the place, and things might have fitted together more gently in my mind. But one day I'm sitting in the open air on top of a roof, repairing the damaged and broken tar and pitch, gratefully sharing the forbidden fruits of Wilhelm Deutch's lunch, and the next, I'm one of the servants of Lucifer, stoking the fires of hell. From roof repairer over-viewing all around me like some Renaissance prince in his bell tower, I suddenly and inexplicably became a part of a team of Sonderkommandos whose life expectancy is no more than three or four months; and that's only if they don't go crazy within a month or so of joining because of the work they're forced to do.

Some of them did go crazy. These Sonderkommandos were often Jews, human beings! They'd push and shove and shovel their living fellow Jews into the gas chambers, and then when their souls flew up to whatever deity was overseeing this bit of handiwork and only agonised and contorted bodies were left behind, the Sonderkommandos would haul their co-religionists' bodies into the ovens for burning. So how could you stay normal when you're doing this sort of demonic work hour after hour, day after day, like some monstrous factory worker on an assembly line?

Yes, some did go mad, and, while still alive, numbed from reality, their colleagues, men with whom only hours before they'd been working, would help them strip off their clothes and assist them in walking towards the doors of the gas chambers. Then their colleagues would bid them farewell and they'd willing die along with all the other pathetic flotsam of Jewish humanity . . . unbelievable; utterly macabre.

But again, I'm racing on. I must be annoying you, reader, but I don't mean to. It's just that these events are not only momentous to me, but so defy my belief in what has happened to me and to the rest of the world, that my mind skips from one nightmare to another.

So let me start from the beginning and tell you how I was sent away from Wilhelm Deutch, the mechanic of Auschwitz, to become the Jew, the prisoner Gutman, one of the Sonderkommandos of Birkenau.

We had just finished putting pitch on the roof of the kitchen, which had sprung a leak after some rainwater froze inside some of the cracks in the old tar. It was a very cold day up there, especially for me in my prison pajamas; there was no protection from the icy wind, no building in whose lee I could shelter. But it wasn't all bad. From my vantage point on the roof, I could see almost all of the camp. You have no idea how big Auschwitz-Birkenau was. It stretched away for kilometres, as far as the eye could see. Barrack blocks arranged in precise Germanic lines like soldiers on a battlefield, utility huts, administration blocks, and kilometres of barbed wire and fencing, interspersed at regular intervals by guard towers. There were three separate fences made of different wires. The most notorious, of course, was the electrified fencing, against which more and more inmates threw themselves in their despair.

Up on the roof, I could see the layout of everything. But my eyes were invariably drawn to Birkenau, built just three miles away. Originally it was planned to be built within the compound of Auschwitz, but some high and mighty ruler from Berlin came and decreed that it would be built away from the camp . . . perhaps so as not to frighten the natives. Ha! As if the natives in the camp didn't see the trains and the crowds of old men and women and young boys and girls being torn away from their relatives and shuffled off to join the long, snaking queue going towards Birkenau. They went in, but no one, ever, came out again. A one-way ticket to extinction.

It was in Birkenau that the evil chimneys kept pumping out their black and grey smoke. Jewish bodies were being burned in increasing numbers as the German armies retreated under the Allied assault. Madness. Mania. Hitler was so desperate to destroy European Jewry, even when the officer corps realised that the war was lost, that he'd ordered increased numbers of roundups, increased gassings, increased burnings. Trains and trucks and precious fuel which must have been urgently needed for the war effort were diverted for Hitler's insane drive to achieve his Final Solution. The gas chambers and furnaces could hardly keep up; which was why my life suddenly changed course so badly. One minute, I was up on the roof mending old pitch, next minute...

As I was peeling back the pitch, I noticed that one of the commandants from the administration block was on the verandah, looking up at me. Now, I'm no thing of beauty, and this man was a tall, lean, muscular Aryan in an immaculate uniform, known for the sexual demands he made on recently arrived and attractive young women prisoners. Many times, he'd selected one out of a new intake, and she would disappear for a week before being tossed back into the cesspool of Auschwitz, shorn of her hair, and forced to live and die in the camp with the rest of the refuse.

So I knew that this particular officer wasn't looking at me for the beauty of my body. When a guard or an officer studies you, it's a sure sign of trouble to come. Why would they waste their time or their precious eyesight looking at human garbage, the bacteria of Europe as Hitler called us, when they could be doing other things for the war effort, like beating prisoners to death and thereby saving on rations? When for the third time I saw him looking up to the roof examining me as if I had horns growing out of my head, it was then that I knew something bad was going to happen to me.

I kept working harder than before, slapping the pitch on to the roof as though I was a demon. Come lunchtime, when Deutch sat on the end of the roof and whispered for me to sneak over and share in his lunch, I kindly declined, whispering that I thought I was under observation from one of the hierarchy. I climbed down the ladder and went to the food table where our watery soup was being doled out. Stupidly, I thought that this might save me. It didn't.

At the end of the day, the officer came over to the kitchen area where we were working and called Deutch to climb down the ladder to the ground. I say 'called.' The mechanic wasn't called, he was ordered. When this officer came close to us, I could tell that this was Hauptscharführer Habschin, the deputy commander in charge of organising labour in the camp. Not God, not as powerful or as evil as the man in charge of labour, a bastard called Hauptsturmführer Frauenfeld, a sadist and utterly evil man whom every inmate feared; no, this man wasn't God, just one of the important Archangels, a man who positively rejoiced in the act of persecution.

Deutch responded immediately. He went over to the Hauptscharführer and began to talk to him, casually at first, with what seemed like pleasantries. I watched in horror, my heart pounding, as first the Hauptscharführer looked up at me, and then Deutch, his back turned, also glanced over in my direction. Now the conversation changed. Deutch was arguing . . . not forcefully, but passionately. I could hear his raised voice, but not what he was saying over the other noises in the camp. Hauptscharführer Habschin shook his head, as if saying, 'My decision is final,' and strode away, leaving Deutch immobile, rooted to the spot. I saw him call after the Hauptscharführer, but the arrogant bastard just kept walking away. Deutch walked quickly to follow him, talking all the while, but the officer simply ignored the mechanic, whose body seemed to slump in defeat and acceptance of the inevitable.

Slowly, looking much older than moments earlier, he turned and walked back to the kitchen and climbed the ladder. I knew he was coming to give me news of my doom. I finished my soup, my hands shaking. As though walking to the gallows, I returned to the administration hut where I was repairing the pitch on the roof and climbed the ladder, all strength in my body completely gone. How I struggled up the ladder, I'll never know. But I eventually reached the top. I saw my benefactor sitting there, looking vaguely into the distance. He was straddling the roof, idly pulling up clumps of old pitch. But his face gave him away; he couldn't look at me. Every other day, he'd beamed a smile as I breasted the ladder or arrived at his work-site. Every day, he celebrated yet another day of beating the system, of getting the better of the guards and the administration. But now his face was like one of the losers of an important race, a man who had tried hard, yet stumbled at the last hurdle.

'The Hauptscharführer has decided that they're shorthanded in the Sonderkommando section of Birkenau, and as you look so strong and fit, he has selected you to make up the numbers. It appears that they had three suicides last night. And their numbers were down anyway because of last month's revolt.'

The mechanic glanced down at the roof, unable to look me in the eyes. 'I'm really sorry. I tried to dissuade him, but he had already decided. You start tomorrow morning.'

I could have argued. I could have told him that he needed me on the roof, that by now I was an expert at spreading pitch, and that I was useful in other areas as well, like mechanics and hydraulics . . . that it would take him weeks to train another inmate up to my skills . . . but the look on his face and the godlike demeanour of the Hauptscharführer were enough for me to realise that anything I might say would have no effect. And Deutch knew it too. When at last he looked at me, it was as though he was saying goodbye forever to a friend.

I returned to work silently and smiled at him. For the first time, I reached over and touched him on his hand, a gesture of friendship, of comradeship. 'I owe you my life,' I said gently.

'I feel I've let you down. As I've let all the others down when they were taken away from me,' he said.

I squeezed his arm. 'You've given me a reason to live.'

But he shook his head and whispered, 'All I've given you is a few months reprieve from the inevitable.'

I could be wrong, but I believe that there might have been tears in his eyes.

Then we continued to work, silently, until the end of the day. He didn't look at me again. I just thanked him for being a truly good man, climbed down, and joined the others in hell.

Tell me, my friend, the reader of this document, this testimony, do you have any idea of what a Sonderkommando did in Auschwitz? And in the other death camps that the world is just beginning to learn about? Can you for one moment imagine the living hell in which we worked?

But the question is, do I want to tell you? And if I did tell you, would you believe me, sitting in your comfortable chair and reading this memoir and thinking to yourself, *'My God, but Gutman had it tough in the war!'*

Maybe I should leave you thinking that Auschwitz was simply a place which wasn't very nice; a bit like a refuse dump, or a strict prison, and now that the war's over, it would be a good idea if we human beings never allowed such a place to exist again; maybe that's how I should allow you to read this memoir, thinking that it must have been pretty dirty and disease ridden; thinking that some people might have died there, and wasn't that a tragedy?

Yes, maybe I should allow you those thoughts. Why, after all, should I burden you with reality? I assume that you had nothing to do with the war, nor with the creation of Auschwitz-Birkenau.

But no! That's not what I intend to do. I said right at the beginning of this, my memoir, that *I, Joachim Gutman, am witness to unspeakable acts. Yet if I don't speak of them, who will? Who is left to act as witness? For if I don't bear witness, then they will have won, and that is something which I cannot permit.*

I said that right at the beginning of my memoirs—go back to the beginning and read what I said if you don't believe me—because nothing will stop me from telling you, and everybody else, what happened. For it is important both to me . . . and to you . . . that you are made aware of every evil which went on in the death camps so that these things can never—*never*—be repeated in the future of mankind. Oh, I know what they're now saying about the Germans; that they were all guilty. Well, they weren't. Many were! But there were also men like Deutch ... men who risked their lives for a Jew. But let me get back to my memories of those days ...

I became a Sonderkommando. We were the people who did all the inhuman, dirty work. Like I've said, on average we lasted about three months; then many of us would simply stop working. Just like that. We'd stop doing our assigned tasks. Maybe we went crazy with what we were doing. Maybe we lost touch with reality. Maybe we were so struck dumb by the inhuman surroundings that death would have been a holiday.

Whatever the reason, one moment we'd be working at pushing men and women and children to their deaths in the gas chambers, next moment we'd be pulling their twisted corpses out and sending the thousands of dead bodies, every day, by the elevators from hell, up to the retorts for burning. But then a look would come over our faces. Suddenly one of us would stop the struggle of trying to untangle arms and legs, locked in a macabre dance of death. We'd look up as we emptied the gas chambers of the latest batch of murdered Jews; then we'd smile at our colleagues; then we'd strip off our clothes and walk willingly, smiling, singing a song, into the gas chambers and the ovens to luxuriate in the peace and quiet and release of our death.

We couldn't go on anymore. We didn't want to live this life. Why? Because we'd seen the reality. We were part of the killing. We were part of the machinery. We were the cogs which made the deaths happen; the oil which allowed the engines of death to run smoothly. And there were so many people to kill. Did we feel pride in our special situation—the slightly better food, the slightly better sleeping accommodation? Does a man about to hang feel privileged and enjoy the taste of a steak when he's eating his last meal?

In the entire complex of Auschwitz-Birkenau, there were about a thousand Sonderkommando, divided up into different units. Each of the units was given special jobs to do. None of us was spared the very worst jobs; but the guards realised that we had to be rotated regularly, or we'd suicide too quickly, and that would cause disruption to their precious rosters, to the good order and the smooth running of the establishment. And God forbid anything at all should happen to disturb the production line!

Some of us had to meet new arrivals off the trains which arrived two or three a day. No, not to greet them and show them around like a tour guide. Our job was to climb into the carriages after the living had jumped down, and carry off the dead. They would usually be older people, grandmothers and grandfathers . . . or the young children, whose hands, now permanent claws, had gone cold with death, as though still trying to clasp the arms of their mother or a father who had been pulled screaming hysterically away by the guards.

Others of us Sonderkommandos had to stand on the ground where the train pulled up, and help the guards herd people into their correct lines . . . men to the right, women to the left. Then they'd go for a quick shuffle past the doctors, who would select those capable of working into one line, and direct the old and the young incapable of working into another . . . one which led straight to the crematoria. Our job was to ensure that there wasn't a riot. Not that the poor bastards knew what was happening. The orchestra was playing, and they were told that they were being sent to be cleaned up, and to be given a strong cup of coffee after the ordeal of the train journey. And we, the Sonderkommandos, were complicit in their deception. If we'd opened our mouths to warn them, we would have died beside them.

Others of us, on a rotating shift, would greet those about to be exterminated at the changing rooms. Sometimes we'd hand out towels and soap, to prevent what would undoubtedly have been mass panic and an affray if they thought they were going to die. But in the changing rooms, we had to help the elderly and the very young undress. Everything had to be done quickly, if the production line wasn't to be held up.

The extermination programme was under the control of the Political Department of the camp, and they were infinitely more ruthless in their determination to follow the Führer's orders than were the guards in the concentration camp proper. They were killing thousands a day, but that's something I'll come to later.

In the beginning, when I first started to undress the elderly and the young, I felt hideous, as though I was prying into someone's bedroom and watching them in their most intimate moments. There was nothing pleasant about doing it. They were smelly (not that I wasn't!) because they'd been travelling by train for upwards of two days without a break and had had no food, air or water. Their clothes were filthy from the journey, and because many had come out of the living hell of a ghetto, and were exhausted, it made the removal of their coats and dresses and jackets and undergarments incredibly difficult.

And of course, we were beaten mercilessly by members of the Political Department and their special guards, if our 'batch' wasn't ready right on time for the next stage of their journey into death. So, as these Jews were going to die within minutes anyway, why should we make their last moments on earth more pleasant and risk a beating and probable death ourselves? We, after all, were the living. So we pulled and tugged and tore their clothes off their backs. When they complained and cried in pain, we said that they'd be issued new and pretty clothes in a few moments after their shower, so why worry about their old things?

Eventually, they all shuffled out of the changing rooms, naked and embarrassed and exhausted, their skinny hands desperately trying to cover their intimate parts. The men looked horrified; the women looked down at the ground; the children were terrified. Only occasionally did a woman (never a man, mind you, always a woman) stand magnificently, knowing by instinct and deduction where she'd soon be going, and glare with utter contempt at the guards and the Sonderkommandos. She wouldn't hide her breasts; she'd stand solidly upright and say to them wordlessly, *'You can kill my body, but you and those like you will never ever kill my soul, which belongs to the Almighty.'*

Almost all of the others, though, left the changing rooms in tears, or in controlled hysteria. Many were jabbering in Yiddish because they were from Poland or somewhere in the east like the Ukraine. But I understood much of what they were saying. They were asking how their God could have allowed this to happen to them, questioning what was the purpose of living if they were to be stripped naked by men with guns and forced to parade around like animals in a zoo. By the time they'd reached the entry to the 'shower' rooms, the men and women were crying, weeping, terrified. In the beginning, when I first came there, everything left me bereft. I thought of my grandparents, my parents. But soon, I became hardened to it. All I wanted to do was live.

When the old people and the young children had left the changing room to walk to their gassing, we were then ordered to clear the clothes from the floor and make the changing room presentable for the next batch of inmates. And it . . . oh God, I'm so ashamed . . . it gave us precious minutes to do things with their clothes. We were the only ones who knew for sure where they would be going, what would be happening to them, and the certainty that they wouldn't be returning on their one-way journey to heaven.

On instructions from the guards, they had left all their clothes on the floor, so we Sonderkommandos quickly searched their pockets, where we'd often find scraps of food they'd managed to save from the journey. Stale bread crusts, mouldy, filthy meats, cheeses eaten almost to the rind, pickles . . . anything. And the moment we found it, we'd gobble it down, because any extra food was a gift from God.

These things were what we were forced to do to the Hungarians and the Russians and the Poles and the German Jews. However, I quickly learned not to consider them Jews . . . or even Hungarians or Germans or whatever. Nor even human beings. I could only think of them as things, objects . . . *Golems*. It was the only way I could survive without screaming. It was what I did so that I didn't go insane. I had to fix in my mind that these weren't people. I had to view them as lifeless, as mechanical, as automatons on their way to the efficiency of German industry's glorious destruction furnaces in order to be dismantled into their component parts and returned to the earth so that the new Germany could grow on fertile soil. I had become part of the machinery of destruction.

These people we were party to destroying, these in my eyes were anything but living, breathing humanity, because if I recognised their humanity, I would have committed suicide after the first day.

I knew something about the *Golem*, the soulless creature which legend has it was made from clay by Rabbi Judah Löw of Prague. I'd been to Czechoslovakia before the war on a visit with my father when he was advising the Czech government on some legal matters, and I'd visited the cemetery. I'd read the legend. So long as I didn't view these people as human beings, I could live with myself.

Don't dare criticise me, you reader, sitting there in your comfortable armchair, reading this. What I did, I had to do! It's called survival.

And now I have to tell you what I did when I was a Sonderkommando. And believe me, what I'm about to tell you isn't pleasant. Of course, much happens in war which is horrific. What happened in the Pacific with the Americans bombing those two Japanese cities isn't pleasant; but neither was the unprovoked attack on Pearl Harbour in Hawaii by the Japanese. What the Allies did by fire-bombing Dresden was an act of unspeakable barbarity; if the Allies had lost the war, would Churchill and Eisenhower have been lined up before the Nazi High Command and suffered their own Nuremberg trials for crimes against humanity for the bombing incineration of innocent civilians in Berlin and Hamburg and Dresden? Churchill and Eisenhower created their own, outdoor, death ovens. So who knows whether, if Germany had won the war, the Allies would have been brought to account? Justice and honours go to the victors.

But these things, these dive bombers and tanks and other equipment which murder civilians, are part of the currency of modern-day warfare. A nation attacks another nation, and people get killed. As did trustworthy citizens in the time of the Egyptians, the Romans, the Ottomans, and all other conquerors who rampaged through innocent communities in the name of a god or a national border, or an ideology.

All these things changed forever in 1942. Oh, there had been concentration camps in previous times. Dachau outside Munich, for instance, was first opened in 1933. And the British in South Africa and Russians in Siberia boasted of their obscene marshalling yards where they concentrated their enemies to immobilise and emasculate them.

But on January 20, 1942, everything changed. That was the date on which it was decided at the Wannsee conference in Berlin that we Jews were to be worked to death and those of us who couldn't be worked to death were to have 'special arrangements' made for us. Oh, please don't think that the Nazis suddenly woke up and decided on January 20 that it would be a nice idea to murder all the Jews. Hitler had given his first indication of his plan in *Mein Kampf*, but we Germans really understood his message when he addressed the Reichstag on January 30, 1939 and threatened us Jews with extermination if we didn't stop whatever it was he thought we were doing. I'll never forget his words. They sent shivers down my spine. *'Europe will not have peace until the Jewish question has been disposed of. Jewry must adapt itself to respectable, constructive work, as other peoples do, or it will sooner or later succumb to a crisis of unimaginable proportions.'*

It was only when I went to Birkenau, the Extermination Camp of Auschwitz, that I fully understood what Hitler meant by *'unimaginable proportions'*. And he was right, because what happened there defies the imagination. What I am about to tell you in these, my memoirs, will shock and sicken you. But you have to know. For if you know then at least one other person alive today will pass on the knowledge, and it stands a chance of being remembered. And this is especially important when, at some time in the future, people look back on what happened in the middle of the twentieth century and say, 'Of course it didn't happen. Nobody could have behaved like that!'

But it did happen! They did behave like that! And I was a part of it.

Firstly, let me tell you something. When I was forced to leave the mechanic, Deutch, I was taken over to Birkenau, and I could smell death hanging low over the buildings. They looked like some nineteenth-century factory complex, squat, red-brick buildings that could have been a hospital or a sanitarium or an ancient asylum, except for the central building which had huge chimneys billowing dark grey or black smoke. There were nine hundred of us Sonderkommandos, specially selected because we were strong and young and still had the inexorable will to live. The administration knew that we'd do anything to stay alive. They read it in our eyes.

In each of our groups—those work units rotated to do the various death tasks—there were about ten SS Sonderkommandos, who had been seconded from the killing squads, in charge the *Einsatzgruppen*. These *Einsatzgruppen* were a band of truly evil men, utterly devoid of conscience. They were 100 percent Nazis, the scum of Germany and the Ukraine. They enjoyed the activities which drove so many of us Jewish Sonderkommando slaves to suicide. They reveled in the piles of corpses, in the naked dead bodies of the old and the young. They got such a thrill of seeing the naked men and women and children pushed and shoved into the gas chambers, and then to the gas ovens for their bodies to be burned into cinders.

Of course, we Sonderkommandos lived separately from everyone else, because we were pariahs. Most of the Jews accepted that we had been forced into this work, but there was still an underlying hatred of us for what we were doing. There was an expectation that somehow, we Sonderkommandos, we who were chosen at random from the healthier inmates to do the ghastly work, should be noble and refuse to do this work; that instead, we should willingly go into the fires of the ovens rather than becoming a part of the machinery which was exterminating our race. But that assumes we would choose death over life. It wasn't until we became Sonderkommando that we understood that death was a more pleasant alternative to life.

More than anything, more than any other work I had to do, what I hated most was the rotation of my squad when it came to pushing the naked people into the gas chambers after they'd stripped off their clothes in the reception room. That, more than anything!

When the poor *yidden* had come out of the changing rooms, they were cold and terrified and naked and crying for help. The assurances of the other squad who had helped them strip naked meant nothing when they came out of the changing rooms and saw the halls into which they had to go. We parked a van, painted white with a large red cross on it, to prevent them panicking. Our Nazi masters thought that a Red Cross vehicle would calm their fears and prevent a riot, making it easier to get them into the gas ovens. The van was used to deliver the Zyklon-B to the gas chambers.

Zyklon-B. Now there's an interesting thing. We Germans, it turns out, had been using Zyklon-B since the 1920s for exterminating rodents and insects such as lice and cockroaches. Very effective it was, too. It's a compound called Hydrocyanic Acid, manufactured by two German companies, Tesch/Stabenow and Degesch after they bought the patent from I. G. Farben. The Nazis called the directors in one day and asked how it could be used on human beings. All too willing to cooperate, they removed the 'danger-odour'—used to warn human beings of the danger of being too close to it—and gave good advice on how much to use, and how quickly the air would clear under forced ventilation so that one load of bodies could be cleared out in preparation for the next load. Between them, these two companies supplied nearly three tons a month for use in the Final Solution. Oh, what patriotic Germans were these industrialists, these directors of good upright German companies. How proud the Führer must have been of them. Doing such good work for the Fatherland, and at the same time making a handsome profit from genocide.

What did we Sonderkommandos have to do? We ushered the naked Jews into the room where they were to be gassed. On top of the door was the word, *SHOWERS*. Many thought it was genuine, and only objected to the overcrowding, to bodies of men and women and children being too close together. But there were always some in the groups who you could tell didn't believe it. And then they would start to object, flailing their arms wildly and crying and appealing. Then we'd have to push and shove and force them, and beat them with sticks until every last one was inside the room, squashed like sardines, and we could close the door. Sometimes, before we could close the door, one of the children would slip through legs and escape. We'd catch the struggling naked child, and despite his screaming, we'd throw him or her on top of the crowd. Then we'd close and lock the door, and sit down to wait for the Zyklon-B to be administered.

This would happen when a doctor or a guard climbed a ladder and, wearing a gas mask, opened the tin and dropped the granules through the funnels in the roof. It would drop through what looked like shower-heads on the people down below. God knows what it felt like, but the moment the granules started to drop on to naked flesh, we could hear the screaming getting louder and louder until it reached a crescendo of panic, and then the crescendo slowly getting quieter and quieter until through the airtight door, all we could hear was the horrifying empti-ness of silence.

Yes, I think that was the most horrific part of the whole thing. They would be forced into the gas chamber screaming and yelling and complaining and begging. Then the volumes of their voices would suddenly drop as we closed the door . . . as though they were wait-ing for something awful and dreadful to happen. Then there'd be this rising sound of hysteria in fear and anger which wafted through the closed and locked doors of the airtight chamber as they realised the horror of their situation; that this wasn't a shower room at all, and that there were no spaces between the people for them to move, or for the water to cleanse and refresh them; that there would be no water dripping down from the showerheads. But despite the thick walls and the airtight nature of the chamber, we could hear their screams well enough as we sat outside on the benches, waiting for their death. We'd hear . . . and feel . . . the hammering of fists on the door and the walls in their utter terror of what was going to happen to them.

And then, as the funnels leading to the showerheads were unscrewed and the granules poured down, the screaming would become louder and louder, more and more hysterical. Through the portholes, we could see the men and women writhing in agony and terror, clawing at the walls and one another to get out. The look of terror on their faces was something which . . . well, it didn't take me long to learn to close my eyes and shut my ears.

But then the hideous phantasmic noises started quickly to go away. As they died, the volume of screams and shouts and agony grew softer and softer. And it was always the children whose voices I heard last. They were stronger than the adults. Their lungs worked better, their little hearts were stronger, they lived longer. Was that the hardest thing of all that I had to bear? To hear the screams of children who hadn't enjoyed the peace and quiet and privilege of a quick death?

After twenty minutes, when the ventilation system had removed almost all of the Zyklon-B, we put on our gas masks, opened the door, and were greeted by a sight which will never leave the memory of my eyes.

I can think of no image which will explain to you what it was that greeted the Sonderkommandos when they opened the door of the gas chamber and saw the plug of humanity blocking the entrance. Every image fails to pay homage to the reality, to the fact that these were human beings. What words can I use which don't sound banal? Human spaghetti? A nest of dead snakes, all arms and legs intertwined. You see, nothing which human language has dreamed up will enable me to describe the horror of the scene.

Peoples' faces had changed from human to demonic; limbs were weeping dark, thick, and rapidly congealing blood; arms and legs were gashed with gaping wounds where others had tried to claw their way out with their fingernails; imagine necks twisted almost completely around; imagine a mouth fixed open as someone dying tries to get a last breath of life-giving air; imagine . . . but what am I saying? Why am I saying this? You can't imagine it, can you! You had to be there.

We opened the doors of the gas chamber, and it was only our gas masks which prevented us smelling the terrible smells of human waste and gases which the ventilation system hadn't yet extracted. We began the task of pulling bodies out of the chamber to make it ready for the next batch of prisoners, already being herded into the changing rooms, being told that they would be given a cup of strong coffee after their shower in order to help them recover from the harsh train journey.

Sometimes the bodies were almost impossible to separate and would fill the entry to the gas chamber like some obscene naked human cork. Then we would have to pull them out in whichever way was possible, nearly tearing heads off shoulders and arms and legs off bodies. Our SS guards would force us to work harder, quicker. They'd beat us, even though they could see that we were straining every muscle to remove the tangle so that we could clean it up for the next batch.

And eventually the bodies would be cleared and loaded on to the elevators which took them upwards to the upper levels where there were retorts that were used for burning the bodies to ash. An efficient killing production line. In the final days of the war, however, they often took the bodies outdoors and piled them into ditches, where they'd burn on open fires; you see, the ovens couldn't keep up with the demand. After all, they were only machines!

When we'd loaded the bodies onto the elevators, we'd then go in and clean out the gas chamber. It had concrete walls and a concrete floor, and so wasn't all that hard to clean. We used buckets of water to get rid of the shit and the piss and blood as best we could, but time pressures always prevented us from doing a good job. We would be hurried out of the particular gas chamber in which we were working, and have to prepare ourselves yet again for forcing in another batch of Jewish Hungarians or Poles or Ukrainians into their chamber of death.

That was probably the worst job in the world. The job upstairs, in the retorts, the ovens, was not so bad. It was not dealing with the living, but with the dead (except where someone was still alive despite the Zyklon-B, and then we had to toss him alive and twitching into the ovens). And upstairs, you could actually be allowed a sense of humour. Yes! Oh, I know that sounds bizarre, but human bodies make strange noises when they're dead. Farting and creaking and blowing up with gases. I sometimes laughed. It was my escape mechanism.

And it was upstairs, in the people-burning section, where I again met my saviour, Wilhelm Deutch.

Palace of Justice
Nuremberg, Allied Occupied Germany
June, 1946

'Mr. Deutch, let me now come on to your transfer to Birkenau, to work on the ovens into which the recently killed Jews were placed to burn their bodies to ashes.'

Wilhelm Deutch nodded. It hadn't been a good day at the trial. More evidence from people whom Wilhelm had never before seen, or whose faces he couldn't remember; testimony about how he'd done evil things with the SS, how he'd stood by and allowed men and women to be shot; one witness even said that he'd lost his temper over something totally trivial and had deliberately thrown a huge sack of tools down into a ditch being dug in the ground near to the administration building, crushing to death a sick inmate who was working in there. Under cross-examination, the witness said he knew it was deliberate because Deutch had called over four SS guards and two kapos to allow them to watch. But Wilhelm Deutch told Broderick he couldn't even remember the incident; just as he couldn't remember killing the man about whom the other witness the previous day had given evidence. Broderick was stunned. 'Do you mean you can't remember whether or not you killed a man?'

'No,' he insisted to Broderick, when the lawyer insisted that he must remember the faces of some of these witnesses. 'It isn't that I can't remember, just that these things never happened. The witnesses are confusing me with another man.'

Now it was early evening, and the American lawyer was going over what would be the prosecution evidence for the following day, hoping that Deutch could give him some line of inquiry.

'When were you called over from your work as a mechanic in Auschwitz to work on the ovens in Birkenau?'

'In October, 1944. Just before they were closed down on orders of the High Command, when they knew that the Russian invasion was very serious and was driving the German Army back in full retreat from occupied lands. There were major problems with bottlenecks which were forming, and they wanted to process as many Jews as possible. The gas chambers were working very well, but the retorts . . . the ovens . . . which they used for burning the dead bodies couldn't keep up. They kept on breaking down. The other death camps, places like Belsen and Sobibor and Treblinka and Kulmhof and Majdanek, were having far fewer problems, although in fairness to the Auschwitz camp commanders, these other extermination camps weren't being sent nearly as many prisoners as were we.'

Despite a year or more of listening to the way in which genocide had been mechanised by the Germans, Theodore Broderick still found it nearly impossible to listen to this kind of an explanation without howling in disgust. But he retained his professional detachment.

'And what was the job which you were told to do?'

'I had to work out why the retorts weren't working properly, and how to fix them as a matter of great urgency. This meant that I had to consult with the engineers of the companies which had manufactured them. The engineers from the firm Topf and Sons were excellent. They really knew their job, but despite their skills, the ovens still kept on breaking down.'

'What was the reason given?' asked the lawyer. 'What was going wrong over there?'

Deutch thought for a moment. It was like a discussion between a student and a teacher—cold, clinical, precise.

'Well, in the early days of the war, when the Final Solution was no longer a theory but something which the High Command was going to put into practice, experiments had been carried out by various companies for the most efficient ways of getting rid of dead bodies. In theory the ovens worked well. But in reality, they suffered in their operation from the war itself. You see, proper fuel supplies like oil and petroleum spirits and even gas were very scarce towards the end of the war, and so we had to rely on coking coal to do the job. But the heat wasn't sufficient, so it was worked out by trial and error that the best combination to produce the greatest amount of heat and the greatest efficiency was to determine the combustibility rate of different body types. In the end, to reduce fuel consumption, they experimented with burning well-nourished corpses with emaciated ones. They burned three or four bodies at a time and monitored the results. They soon determined that the most economical and fuel-saving procedure was to burn the bodies of a well-nourished man with an emaciated woman, and vice versa, together with that of a child because in the experiments, it was found that when the bodies caught fire, the fat from the well-nourished dead man or woman would be sufficient to continue to burn the other corpses without any further coke being required.

'This, however, didn't translate to the large scale on which Birkenau operated. They thought it might be the selection process which the

Sonderkommandos were using, but my view was that the ovens were inefficient from when we started to use the different and poorer grades of fuel, and I was sent over to see what I could do.'

Deutch looked at his lawyer and wondered in surprise why his face had suddenly turned grey.

'I'm sorry. Is this distressing you? You wanted to know.'

Broderick urged him to continue.

'It was as early as 1943, a year before I arrived at Auschwitz, that the ovens were going wrong. They seemed to be falling apart. Crematorium Four failed totally only weeks after it had been installed, and Crematorium Five was shut down completely shortly thereafter. There were about fifty retorts altogether for burning bodies. It took about half an hour to burn the four bodies completely, so they worked it out that with all the crematoria and all the retorts working full time, they should be able to handle about twelve thousand dead bodies a day. And with more planned, the number was hoped to reach twenty-five thousand each and every day of the week. But there were major problems, and I was regularly told to go over and fix them. When I wasn't working in maintenance at Auschwitz, I'd be working on the furnaces at Birkenau. I did it for all the time I was at the concentration camps, on and off.'

The look of horror, of sickness, hadn't left Broderick's face. He'd sat through similar evidence in previous trials of arch-criminals, especially torturers and serial killers, but he'd never been quite so close to such complacency. The clinical nature of Deutch's evidence was threatening to make him gag. Deutch noticed the revulsion on his lawyer's face.

'Look, if I hadn't gone over there, I would have been shot. In those days, towards the end of the war, when the Nazis were desperately trying to make the Final Solution happen before the Allies took over Germany, things were mad. Crazy. And they were doing everything in their power to burn the evidence. We were all caught up in the drive to do what the Führer ordered us to do. End the Jewish conspiracy. Put an end to the Jews. What would you have had me do, Professor Broderick? Refuse to do their bidding? I didn't enjoy what I had to do. But I made life easier for those Sonderkommandos who worked for me. I gave them food and rest, more than they were getting before I arrived. I did what I could.

'But in the end, I was only obeying orders.'

CHAPTER NINE

Berlin, Germany, 1998

IT WAS A STRANGE partnership, the sort of relationship which happens on a holiday when the norms of everyday living overflow usual boundaries and constraints, and unusual friendships are formed in strange and exotic places.

For Chasca Broderick, the place was strange enough, but even on a holiday in an exotic island, she doubted she would have taken up with such an ordinary man. And every time she thought these kinds of thoughts, she checked herself for being elitist and snobbish.

But she *was* the granddaughter of a patrician American, a man hailed by presidents and judges as one of the great Americans of the twentieth century; and the man with whom she was forming a working relationship bordering on friendship *was* the grandson of a hanged Nazi war criminal, a mechanic, a man whose life would have been led in the anonymity inhabited by the commonplace had it not been for the advent of Adolf Hitler.

Yet suddenly and unexpectedly they were partners. Chasca had originally arrived in Germany with the intention of resurrecting the reputation of Deutch and gaining a judicial decision to reverse the finding of guilt for him, even though she could do nothing about the fact that they'd hanged a man they thought was a war criminal;

Gottfried had, since his birth, tried to put his grandfather's crimes behind him and lead as normal a life as possible, despite the presence of original sin coursing through his veins.

And now they were together in her hotel suite in Berlin, reading and re-reading the testimony of Joachim Gutman, trying to determine any hidden message, any obscure clue which might have been written into his aching account so that they could take their investigations further.

'Of course, there's really no need to go beyond what we have here,' Chasca said after they'd re-read the document a third time. 'To me, although this wouldn't be admissible in a court of law without much more forensic examination, this document should give comfort to you and your family. Perhaps we should leave it at this.'

But Gottfried shook his head. 'No, you don't understand. Since the war, as I told you last night in the bar, we've had whole legions of people and organisations making our lives hell, trying to make us come to terms with the fact that we've got this bad blood in us. We can't seem to put it behind us. My mother has had her life ruined because of my grandfather's trial. That's why it's so important that we find this man, Gutman, if he's still alive; why it's so important to get him to tell his story in public . . .'

He stood from the couch and began to pace the room. 'There's much you don't know, Chasca. Much you don't understand about what it's like to be a German today, with the whole world looking at you as if you're personally responsible for the concentration camps and the evil that our grandfathers did. Again, I'm so sorry for being rude to you last night, but I thought you were one of these young and innocent American evangelists who was going to offer me life after death or somehow make me atone for original sin, or try to convince me not to feel guilty for the crimes of my grandfather.

'But when I read the testimony, I knew that this was a way of changing my own life, and that of my mother. Yes, the main reason for trying to find out more is because of my mother. For all of her life, she's hidden the fact that her father was a Nazi criminal. She's pretended he died in the war, she's denied he was hanged when some journalist tried to do a story on the family, she'd actually run away when people came to our door and hide in a cupboard . . . she's tried to live it down, despite the fact that every decade or so, she's reminded of it by some event or people like you appearing out of nowhere. But times have changed. Germany isn't the same Germany as when we were growing up. Among some of us, there's now a new pride in what the army did during the war. There's a reason to be a German and not to be ashamed. We're no longer hiding our heads in humiliation for what we did to the Jews or to the rest of Europe. Of course, pride can go too far. Now there are gangs of skinheads roaming the streets beating up homosexuals and Turks and immigrants, just like the SA used to do in the 1920s and '30s; there's a whole neo-Nazi movement which is trying to resurrect the Third Reich. They're trying to rehabilitate Hitler and Himmler and Göring and Göbbels and the rest of them.'

Chasca stared at him in silence. She knew all about the neo-Nazi movement, and the revisionist historians like David Irving and Fred Zundel and the rest of the motley troupe of Hitler's apologists. But what did that have to do with Gottfried?

Chasca listened in apprehension, uncertain where he was going with this approach. But there was a story which was about to come out . . . of that, she was certain.

Diffidently, he avoided her eyes, speaking to the carpet as he paced the room, 'Even I, when I was younger . . . well, two years ago to be precise . . . I played around with German pride. I was fed up with everyone in the world saying that my nation was perpetually guilty. I was fed up with trying to live down the crimes of my grandfather. I just wanted to be able to hold my head up in pride and say to hell with the rest of the world.

'So I went along to meetings of a group which was composed of the sort of people I'm sure you'd hate. It was a group called the *Kammeraden* and was composed of such people as the sons of guards from the concentration camps and soldiers in the Wehrmacht or members of the Waffen SS, a few of the actual soldiers, or their sons and grandsons. Not just Germans, but Austrians as well.'

Tentatively he looked at her, as though he were admitting some heinous crime. 'I joined because I didn't see why I should be punished because of the crimes my grandfather committed. Yet I was punished. In school, in the Scouts, always somebody knew that my grandfather was a war criminal. And so I joined the *Kammeraden* and I went along to a few of their meetings. But it was horrible. It wasn't a self-help group of people like me. It was full of young Nazis and people who glorified the war and who were trying to relive the past or make the past into the future. Anyway, one day my mother was taking one of my jackets in for dry-cleaning and she found a leaflet I'd kept from one of the meetings. That was how she found out that I'd joined. I've never seen her so angry. She was shaking. She screamed at me. She's not a well woman, she's fairly weak, and yet she could have murdered me with her bare hands. I've never seen her so near to hysteria. She shouted, *'Isn't it enough I lost a father to these bastards, now I'm going to lose my son . . .'*

'I never went to another meeting . . .' He lapsed into an ashamed silence.

Chasca was stunned. 'Gottfried, why are you telling me this?'

He remained silent for many moments. Softly, he said, 'Because this document might turn out to be my salvation.'

Allied Occupied Germany, June, 1946

From the memoirs of Joachim Gutman:

It might sound odd to you that I call Wilhelm Deutch 'my saviour'. Saviour is a term used for a Messiah—a Christ or a Moses or a Muhammad. Was Deutch like these religious heroes? Was he like some chivalric knight in shining armour, come to save me from the Teutons who were threatening to put me to death?

No, of course not. He was an ordinary man. Prosaic, commonplace, and somewhat matter-of-fact. But how often do ordinary people do extraordinary things in exceptional circumstances? How often do we read tales about foot soldiers becoming heroes in the thick of a battle, or a mother plunging into a torrent of icy water to rescue her drowning child?

No, I'm not going to exaggerate what Deutch did. He used his powers of manipulation and persuasion to keep me alive. He didn't plunge into a whirlpool or race across a battlefield laden with mines to pluck my dying body from barbed wire. But he did put his own life in jeopardy in order to save me. And he did so not once, but on dozens and dozens of occasions. In many small ways. Oh, we recognise our heroes from one heroic act, but true heroes aren't just brave once, but are consistently brave in lots of little ways. That's why I consider Deutch not only a Messiah, but also a hero.

And as far as I know, he did the same for others as he did for me. But when I asked him, he'd never admit it. Possibly for fear of what he was doing being found out by the Germans; possibly because of modesty; I'll never know.

Let me start at the beginning. I'm always racing ahead, but I've said that before. I had been in the Sonderkommando unit for about three weeks. I've already told you that we lived separately from everybody else in the camp. The reason the guards made us live separately was so that our work would be a secret . . . so that nobody would know what was going on in Birkenau. Ha! As if every Jew and Gipsy and homosexual and Jehovah's Witness walking like an automaton in the compounds of Auschwitz didn't know precisely what happened to half the people on the trains which pulled in many times each day, people whom they never ever saw again. To their mothers and fathers and children. Where did they think these hundreds of thousands of people had disappeared to? What fools the Germans were for thinking that the death camps could be their little secret until the war had been won. And what then? When they were the master race and everybody knelt down before them? Did they think the world would thank them for getting rid of the Jews? Yes, they did!

But our masters thought they could keep the destruction of European Jewry an international secret, and so we Sonderkommandos were housed separately. Of course, that meant that we would never leave the camp alive. How could they afford for us to live and be witnesses?

Indeed, the Sonderkommandos knew this very well, and had revolted several days earlier. On October 7, 1944, something like four hundred Greek and Hungarian Sonderkommandos blew up Crematorium Four and attacked the SS guards with hand grenades they'd made themselves. They, like us, heard the low and welcome drones of the Allied bombers ruling the sky night after night. They, like us, smelt the acrid tang of high explosives and incendiary devices dropped from Allied bombers into the air of Europe. Some even thought that they could hear the distant boom of cannon coming from the East . . . from what could be an advancing Russian army.

And like us, these brave Sonderkommandos who revolted knew that if the war was coming to an end, their time on earth was limited; so they thought that they'd either escape to freedom by breaking through the walls and disappearing into the forests, or die like heroes in the attempt.

How did they get grenades? Well, a group of Jewish women who were slaves in the Union ammunition factory in Auschwitz smuggled out the gunpowder from their factory and gave it to the resistance group in the camp who worked in the clothing storehouse. These incredibly brave women and men then gave it to the Sonderkommandos.

Somehow the SS got to know of the escape plan, and that the Sonderkommandos were plotting an uprising, and decided that they would kill all the troublemakers. So they rounded up three hundred of them as a work detail, ostensibly to dig ditches outside the camp, but really to execute them. Well, the Sonderkommando instantly knew what was going on and began throwing stones and rocks at the SS and naturally refusing to go with them to the work detail. They shut themselves into the buildings surrounding Crematorium Four and blew up the charnel house with the stolen explosives. One hundred trucks filled with heavily armed SS men immediately arrived to put an end to their rebellion, but the Sonderkommando had stolen machine-guns from guards they'd killed and fought them off.

What did the SS do? When they saw that three of their number had been killed by the slaves, they released fifty German shepherd attack dogs, which tore men's throats out. The rest of Birkenau's Sonderkommando group, all seven hundred, then rose and revolted. By the end of the vicious day, not one was left alive.

It was because of their revolt that I was selected to be a Sonderkommando. We'd been told a lie. We'd been told that I was replacing some who had suicided. But in fact, the entire work troop had to be reconstituted. As if we wouldn't have found out eventually!

Three weeks of this living hell, and I was ready and eager to have my own throat ripped out by an attack dog. Anything would be preferable to what I was doing. A day as a Sonderkommando is a lifetime of normal work. Indeed, I was very seriously thinking of stripping off my own clothes, mixing myself in with a batch of inmates walking into the gas chambers, and ending the pain. After all, when we're naked, we're no longer Sonderkommandos or inmates, or even SS guards—when we're naked, we're human beings.

But my life changed, again, when I caught sight of Wilhelm Deutch. Had I not seen him at that moment, I know for certain that I would not be alive today to record this testimony. I know with absolute confidence that the next day, or the one after, I'd have stripped bare and gone to meet my God. Had I not seen Deutch!

I remember so clearly what I was doing. I was working the elevators, carrying dead bodies off the line, and sorting them out for the ovens in an obscenity of the arithmetic of death . . . nourished one, plus starving one, plus child, plus old person in one pile. Fat old woman, plus thin grandfather type, plus young woman who looks pregnant, plus baby—no, that pile can afford two babies if we can squeeze them in . . . and so it went on, as though we were working in a draper's shop sorting out bales of cloth while doing a stock-take.

My movements had become increasingly automatic, like those of a *golem*. I knew that I was jerky in my responses. I never smiled, I never frowned, I never complained. I just worked. Of course, that was what my body did . . . as to my mind, well, I did everything in my power to shut out the reality of what I was doing, but no matter how much I tried, reality always broke through, and I understood that these still-warm, lifeless things not moments ago had been terrified for their future, praying to a God who had abandoned them.

Wait! What I've told you is a lie. I determined that when I wrote this memoir, I wouldn't lie or exaggerate the truth, and I don't intend to now. So I'll tell you what went through my mind as I worked pushing dead bodies into the ovens . . . humour. Yes, I tried to think humorously. I looked at each body and tried to see different aspects of humour in the expression (*this one looks like Adolf Hitler dead drunk*); or the way the limbs were setting upon death (*this one looks like he's just been making love to a woman and her husband caught him in the act*); or their physical shape (*this one's so fat she looks like she's got rabbits in her backside*). Or maybe when men and women, maybe husband and wife, were locked in death in each other's arms (*they look like lovers, and her husband just walked into the bedroom at the moment of his climax, and then the husband raced to the gun cupboard before her lover could extract himself from her body, and now the husband has shot them both . . . Look, you can see the wound on her face, and where he's tried to scratch her eyes out*).

Does this disgust you? Talking about the dead that way? It disgusts me now, but it was the only possible way I could stop from going completely mad.

Another couple of days and I *would* have gone mad. Humour, even bad humour, isn't funny when it's repeated too often. And then I looked up and I saw Wilhelm Deutch. Thoughts of sitting in the sun on the roof, of digging a trench and talking to him about myself, of eating fresh bread and meats and eggs and pickled cabbages suddenly burst into my brain. I clearly remember feeling giddy, as though I were about to faint. Suddenly I was a young lad again, and I'd just caught a glimpse of a brassiere or the top of a woman's stocking, and my hormones were racing around my body and I felt giddy from the excitement. It was the same when I caught a glimpse of Deutch, my saviour. In death, I found life. I remember clearly feeling giddy at the sight of him, and starting to reel over. But fainting was punishable by beating, and probably death. Yet I couldn't stop myself from shaking.

At first, he didn't recognise me. It was a room full of the smoke of the ovens and dirt and the smells of freshly killed bodies; it stank of the combustion gases of the coke we used as fuel to burn the bodies, and at times, the air was almost impossible to breathe. And it was almost impossible to see through the Stygian gloom of the place.

Deutch looked at me. I was one of ten men working in the immediate area, and of course we were all wearing the same filthy, grime-encrusted prisoner pajamas. To an outsider, even to the guards, we were indistinguishable from one another. Every mark of identity had been stripped away from us by our work; our expressions, the set of our mouths, even the way we held ourselves. We had all become identical robots in the machine.

But when my eyes met those of Deutch, there was a spark of something; and the something made him look again, made him peer through the murk and try to identify where he'd met me before. And when recognition dawned on his face, it was as though he'd been felled by an axe. His jaw dropped, his body seemed to shrug in horror, and I could tell he wanted to run over to me and help me in my moment of need.

But he stayed where he was. He listened attentively as the captain of the guard explained what was going wrong with one of the ovens. But I knew he wasn't listening; I knew that out of the corner of his eye, he was looking at me, aching to reach out and comfort me.

Deutch was no fool. He'd been associated with the Nazis long enough to know that he had to save his own life in order to save mine. Yes, he had sufficient experience and knowledge of the way the Nazis would react to a sudden act of heroism to stop himself from reacting in that way. And in their present mood of frantic desperation, the mood of soldiers about to lose the war, Deutch's action of heroism would undoubtedly have led to his own death. So instead, when the captain bent over to point out something concerning the air flow of the ovens, Deutch used it as an opportunity to put his hand to his forehead as though to wipe it, and inconspicuously put his finger to his lips, telling me not to show any signs that we had recognised each other . . . that he knew me, knew I was there . . . that he would help me at some stage in the near future, as soon as he could. I stopped shaking. Suddenly my life turned around. Suddenly, I had been given hope again. Suddenly, I looked different from the other Sonderkommandos.

For a week, Wilhelm Deutch worked in my area among the dead (and sometimes living dead), trying to get the retorts to fire in proper order, trying to get them to work at their maximum capacity, trying to put life into death.

In the last days of the war, of course, the ovens were more of a backup to the alternative method devised by the Nazis for burning Jews. Months and months earlier, the Auschwitz Sonderkommandos had been forced to dig huge trenches outside the building. These trenches were used for when we burned the bodies in the open air. The ovens weren't burning all the Jews who were being gassed, and so the Nazis had to resort to more primitive methods of disposal than machines. Indeed, the open burning pits were far more efficient methods of burning human beings than were the expensive ovens. It made me wonder whether Hitler would demand back the money he'd paid to the manufacturers.

Working outside in the open air disposing of dead bodies was more pleasant than working in the ovens, but reality kept impinging itself on us, and suddenly—when we'd see a rabbit in the distance or a bird landing on a distant tree—we'd come face-to-face with nature, and we'd realise precisely what it was that we were doing.

And what we were forced to do was indescribable. In the bottom of the trench, we would put masses of wood, douse it with petrol, and throw the dead bodies on to a fire. The Nazis quickly learned that if runnels were dug downwards to collect the fat which ran off the smouldering bodies, it could be used to pour back on to the bodies, and make them burn hotter, better, cleaner.

Then when the hundreds of human beings were nothing more than white ash with the occasional bone still smouldering, we'd dig up the ash, take it to a collection point where it was thrown in the river, or used in the fields, and be ready for the next batch. We could do thousands of bodies in a single day by this method.

But, sticklers to a fault, the Germans wanted good value from the ovens they'd paid good money for, and so Herr Mechanical Engineer Wilhelm Deutch was set to work ensuring that they became operational.

Our eyes often met as he tightened his bolts and adjusted air flows and regulated temperature gauges and checked that the temperature of the coke at the top of the furnace wasn't too different from the temperature at the bottom and that the slag which fell from the burning coal didn't block up the airflow systems.

But while he was doing that, he'd find an excuse to do something near me and would whisper to me, *I'm doing something soon. Be strong.* Or, *'I've left some meat bread and margarine in an old satchel underneath that pile of rags over there. Be careful when you get it . . .'*

He gave me a reason to continue living. Even if it was only curiosity.

Allied Occupied Germany
Western Sector (American Army)
June, 1946

The Second International Conference of Allied Judicial Officers, held in one of the few hotels in Berlin which could still boast anything resembling a good dining room, had been meeting over the weekend. The war had been over for a year, and Allied soldiers were keen to return home. The Potsdam Conference told the citizens of defeated Germany that, *'It is the intention of the Allies that the German people be given the opportunity to prepare for the eventual reconstruction of their life on a democratic and peaceful basis',* and then proceeded to quarrel over the spoils of victory without thought of the needs of the German people. And it was becoming increasingly likely that Stalin would bring down some sort of barrier between the Eastern half of Berlin that Zukhov had captured, and the Western half of Berlin which was controlled by Britain and the United States, and complicate the fragile movement towards restructure.

Professor Theodore Broderick was included with twenty-five other judicial officers who had participated in the trials, which were now almost at an end in the city of Nuremberg. It was important to the victorious Allies that the trials were held in this particular ancient German city, where Hitler had orchestrated his triumphal rallies before the war.

Broderick had spent the weekend listening to politicians, city planners, military and financial experts explain the new landscape of Europe. Even general of the Army George C. Marshall, now the new US Secretary of State in Harry Truman's White House, had spoken to them. At the end of his speech, everybody in the conference hall was excited about his plan to rehabilitate the economies of seventeen western and southern European nations in order to create stable economic and democratic conditions and prevent them falling to the Communists.

But it was in the interludes between the sessions that Theodore enjoyed himself most. It was light relief from the indissoluble gloom of a war crimes trial.

And it was in these after-conference sessions that he met with his counterparts from England and France and Russia. On the Sunday evening, just before he was due to catch the transport back from Berlin to Nuremberg to begin the defense of his client, Wilhelm Deutch, Theodore accepted an invitation to dine with the Chief Liaison Officer for the American Forces of Occupation, Colonel Donald Gerherty. The two men knew each other slightly from other conferences. But Gerherty's influence had been profound in the early days of Theodore's working and social life in Nuremberg. When the American lawyer first arrived in Germany, Donald had sent him a package of information as well as some useful contacts which had made his stay more pleasant and enabled him to circumvent almost all of the red tape which caused so many problems for civilian workers in the allied military administration. It was good to get to know such a man as Gerherty.

Over martinis before their dinner, Gerherty asked about the defense strategy he was planning for Deutch. 'What sort of defense can I put up against the overwhelming weight of evidence against him? God knows I've tried to find witnesses who'll testify on his behalf, but it's like finding a needle in a haystack. Even if there was someone out there who knew him, why in heaven's name would they come forward and testify for him?

'He still claims he was only a cog in the machine. But past trials of major war criminals have found the entire hideous machine guilty, and being a cog isn't an excuse any more. D'you know what they're calling the *'I was only following orders'* excuse? The Nuremberg Defense. Funny, isn't it?'

Gerherty sipped his martini. He had huge, pudgy hands and stood at least a foot taller than Broderick. The conical martini glass, with its delicate glass needle of a stem, seemed ridiculously dainty in his fist. 'Do you think there's any justification in what he says, though? I mean, so many of these bastards weren't bastards to start with. They were just ordinary joes, then Hitler came along, swept them down into the sewers, and now in the sweet light of day, so many of them are saying, '*My God, what did we do?*'

'Bit late for that. Under similar circumstances, how many Americans would have put on a Nazi uniform and built concentration camps and joined a squad like the *Einsatzgruppen?*' asked Broderick.

Gerherty thought for a moment and said, 'How many American Indians are left in the old Wild West, Theo? Wasn't that as much of a genocide as what the Nazis did to the Jews? Aren't the reservations where we've got the remnants of the Red Indian nations just like concentration camps, only on a larger scale?'

The lawyer refused to acknowledged the point. 'Sure, that was a genocide, but it wasn't ever a government genocide. The army was uncontrolled and the individuals were at the forefront of civilisation, and sure, evil things happened. And yes, there was a genocide of the native Indian. Nobody's denying that. But here, things are altogether different . . . Here you have a nation state, a supposedly civilised nation state of philosophers and scientists and theologians and writers and artists, acting in complicity with a government whose official decree was to dehumanise one of its groups of citizens. And worse, here you have a government which legitimises the right of its citizens to kill a minority just because they're Jews. No, Donald, this genocide was nothing like the genocide of the Indians. This was altogether on a more evil scale . . . indeed, it was so bestial, it was off the scale of humanity.'

Donald Gerherty was grateful when the waiter arrived at the bar and showed them to their table. They ordered shrimp as an appetiser before they went on to order their main course. However, Gerherty wouldn't let Broderick's comment go unanswered.

'Theo, I accept what you were saying about the particular evil of Hitler. But when the war came to an end, and we could travel around the country, I was ordered by Allied Command to go around and photograph and film the evidence of what the Nazis had done. I was one of the first to enter the German concentration camps. Believe me, I've seen things which would turn your stomach and give you nightmares for the rest of your days. I've seen evil in the concentration camps which made me puke; the piles of clothes; the bodies; the gas chambers; the ovens, the mounds of humanity . . . or what once was humanity. I know as much as anybody about what the bastards did. I don't excuse it for one moment. But I'm still trying to come to grips with it. Before the war, I was a doctor. A psychiatrist . . .'

Broderick looked at him in surprise. Although he hadn't known Gerherty's profession before he enlisted, from his efficiency, contacts, and demeanour, he suspected that he was a business executive. Gerherty smiled; Broderick's was a common reaction.

He continued, 'That's one of the reasons I was so keen to get over here in the last days of the confrontation. We'd heard reports back in the States about what the Nazis had done, and like you, I had to come over and see for myself what can happen to a mature and sophisticated nation when it's in trouble, and hands over the reins of government to a demonic force. To try to understand what happened to a national psyche which lost its collective conscience and became a collective of beasts. To try to find answers to how an entire nation went nuts.'

'Yes! You're right. That's precisely the reason I'm here,' said Broderick. 'What happened between 1933 and 1945 was so incomprehensible to me, that as an ethicist and a jurist, I felt I had to be here in the midst of things and try to come to comprehend the reasons that the German people suddenly threw off all the trammels of civilisation. How a nation which can not only produce a Beethoven and a Bach, a Schiller and a Heine and a Thomas Mann, which can worship their geniuses as demigods and promote these great men to the rest of the world, can also go on to produce monsters like Hitler and his Nazis.'

Gerherty thought for a moment and then said, 'Ever heard of a psychiatric term called psychopathy?'

'Are you saying that the entire German people are psychopaths?'

'If you look at Nazism as a psychiatric, rather than as a social manifestation, then you'll get somewhere. You're concerning yourself with the ethics of the situation. But for ethics to come into play, you have to have sanity. A national attack of psychopathy could explain much more than we realise about what happened to the German people . . . that it wasn't a conscious act of deliberately following a monster like Hitler, but an unconscious illness which suddenly gripped the country.'

Broderick looked at him in amazement. 'You're talking about tens of millions of people suddenly falling ill at the same moment?'

'It's not so out of the ordinary as you'd think. Remember the Crusades. The whole of Britain and France and German went nuts, just on the say-so of a couple of bishops and the pope. And tens of thousands of formerly normal people tramped across Europe slaughtering whatever got in their way.

'It's what could have happened in Germany. Psychopathy is an unusual ailment. In individuals, it manifests itself in relatively unconflicted deceptiveness or duplicity and the characteristic absence of empathy, compassion, or remorse toward the victims of the psychopath's exploitative self-interest. I don't want to use too much psychiatric mumbo jumbo and jargon, but it really does explain a lot about what happened to the German people when they came under the spell a demagogue like Hitler.

'A psychopath can lie, cheat, steal, extort, exploit, or hurt another human being without normal compunction. But does that apply to an entire nation? I think in this case, it does. You see, one of the first things which Hitler did was to make the Jews, the homosexuals, the Communists, the Slavs, the infirm, and the insane into non-people. He dehumanised them. So suddenly, the German people weren't looking at Jewish or Slavic human beings . . . they were looking at non-people. At things. At objects. Just like the American frontiersman and the army portrayed the native American Indian as a nonperson . . . *The only good Injun's a dead Injun*' . . . as the saying goes. By officially, by governmentally, taking away the humanity from an entire group, you change the perspective of the majority to that group; you make it much easier to kill and harm and destroy that group. And once Adolf had dehumanised them, he enacted laws which denied them the protection of the state.

'Suddenly, the German people were faced with a minority group within their boundaries which was officially classed as subhuman, and who could not claim any privilege under any of the states laws. The government and the law said that you could do what the hell you liked to a Jew and get away with it. That, in my opinion, led to a national attack of psychopathy. Suddenly good German herrs and fraus and frauleins, well-meaning and professional teachers and doctors, lawyers and accountants, grocers and butchers and fishmongers, didn't have to apply the normal customary niceness to Jews and Slavs; didn't have to treat them in any way of respect. Suddenly, the base nature which is in all of us was allowed out, to take a holiday. And not only didn't they need to be nice to Jews any more, but they could do what the hell they wanted to them and get away with it.

'The question is, *did that make the entire German people, rather than individuals, into a nation of psychopaths?* That's what I'm trying to answer.'

The waiter placed a platter of shrimp between them. Broderick forked a couple up, but before he ate them, he said, 'What you're saying is very dangerous. We've been prosecuting these war criminals on the basis of individual responsibility. On the basis that they knew what they were doing, and that they were acting outside of the compass of internationally recognised norms of behaviour. Now you're saying that the entire nation is incapable of taking responsibility for its actions because it was suffering some sort of mass psychiatric attack. If what you're saying is right, then that makes the whole basis for the trials, even for the responsibility for these monstrous acts, beyond the power of the victors to mete out justice for crimes against humanity, and for the victims to seek revenge from the perpetrators. I find that impossible to accept.'

Gerherty nodded and ate his food. They dropped the subject, and talked pleasantries while they ate their shrimps, but there was an underlying mood that there was something much deeper, of far greater moment, yet to surface. By the time their steaks arrived, Theodore said, 'As a law professor, I can comprehend the parameters of good and bad, and the redemptive quality of punishment, and of the way in which the law is integral to civilisation. When I was attorney general for New York, I felt myself part of the apparatus for fighting crime. My city was founded on law and order which led to justice. I was the arm of the law and the police were the arm of order, but we were different sides of the same body, which was named justice.

'I came over here in order to defend people for whom I feel the most unutterable hatred because of what they did. But everybody needs access to defense counsel, so I put my personal feelings to one side. And now, I feel as though by association, I'm floating in the same cesspool as they inhabit. I feel I'm becoming corrupted by my affiliation with these monsters.'

'What can you do about it? Do you have any more cases after this Deutch character?'

Broderick shook his head. 'They want me to be part of a body which assists non-Nazi German jurists, men who played no part in the machinery of evil, in putting together a legal code for the future nation. But there are others just as competent. I think I've done enough here to last me a lifetime. Perhaps it's time I went home.'

'Have you learned what it was you came to learn?'

It was an odd question from someone with whom he'd never shared more than a few social occasions. He'd never before divulged to anyone in Germany that his real purpose in coming to the War Crimes Tribunal was for a personal journey into his soul.

'No,' Broderick said softly. 'I haven't learned much. I was hoping to understand evil, to see it in its true perspective, but all I can see is pathetic, ordinary, banal men who did extraordinary and utterly evil things.'

'Who are you talking about? The Nazis, the Russians, the Yanks, the Limeys, the French, the Poles who willingly cooperated with the Germans, the Ukrainians who worked alongside the SS in the camps . . . who?'

'Oh, I know that evil flourishes in wartime, and that all armies did evil things, but nobody sank to the level of bestiality to which these SS people sank. Nobody. Sure, you can play the angle of psychopathy for as long as you want, but for me, that doesn't explain how an entire nation supported a regime which performed the consummate evil which the Nazis inflicted on the weak and the defenseless. And I won't have you trying to blacken the name of the Allied forces by aligning their names with people like Himmler and Göring and the others.'

'Theo, I'm not trying to blacken anyone's name. Just trying to strike a pose of interventional neutrality. You've got to open your eyes to what others have done in this war, especially when Germany was collapsing, and the Reds were moving in.'

'Is this anti-Communist rhetoric I'm about to hear?' the lawyer quipped.

'This is fact, brother. Straight down the line, hard-core fact. The Russians did things when they were entering Berlin that make what the SS did look as innocent as a Sunday School picnic.'

'Oh, come on,' Broderick retorted. 'I've heard the stories. I know what went on. But . . .'

'But nothing. Tell me, where were you in May, '45? At home with your wife and kids? Teaching law? Driving your Packard to your country club? Spending the weekend in the Adirondacks?'

Broderick left the rhetorical question unanswered.

Geherty continued, 'I was in France, mopping up after the occupation, liaising with de Gaulle, arresting collaborators and members of the Vichy Government. Then we heard reports about what was going on here, in Berlin.'

Gerherty cut a cube of steak and put it into his mouth, hardly stopping the conversation. Broderick hated people who talked while eating, but remained quiet, knowing that he was no longer a dinner partner, but an audience.

'When the Reds arrived, they found a city pounded into rubble by American B-17s and the other massive bombers which dropped death from the skies on a city which was already defeated. But that didn't stop the Russians. Oh no, not them. They blasted their way to the centre of the city with tanks and guns and rockets. Sure, they encountered fierce resistance for every block they took, but the resistance came from old men and boys. Before they arrived, the Berliners were living in holes in the ground. Their apartment blocks had collapsed under the Allied bombardment like matchboxes. And under the rubble, tens of thousands of bodies were rotting and decomposing and stinking to high heaven. They were bloated or charred or torn apart by rats and dogs . . . and people who were still living were starving. There was typhoid and dysentery and tuberculosis and diphtheria . . . It was like something out of hell itself.

'And everybody was waiting for the Allies, they were even waiting for the hated Russians, because everybody was starving to death and there was no government in the city. Oh sure, when they arrived, the Soviets set up soup kitchens, but it was nowhere near enough. The Berliners even raided the zoo and butchered the animals, they were so hungry.

'But that wasn't a half of their problems. When the main Soviet army arrived, they busied themselves emptying the central banks of gold and money and credits; they even emptied the city of the treasure of Schliemann, the treasure of Helen of Troy, for God's sake. And they rounded up tens of thousands of German soldiers and carted them away to captivity in the Soviet Union. God knows if any of them are still alive. We certainly don't have any idea what happened to them. We and the Red Cross have asked the Russians, and we get no answers.'

Broderick started to interrupt, but Gerherty held up a fork with another lump of meat on it as a sign to allow him to continue unabated,

'In the streets, there were gangs of *trümmerfrauen*, rubble women, who spent morning till night picking up bricks from the mountains of rubble, in order to clean them of their mortar so they could be used to build brick houses.

'Like I said, the first wave of Russian soldiers were battle hardened and tough as they come. They were professional soldiers, and well disciplined. They obeyed orders and didn't break ranks.

'No, the problem wasn't with them; it was with the second wave. It was those animal bastards who caused all the problems, and their Russian commanders knew all about what these scum were doing. The second group were support soldiers, and many had been prisoners of the Germans, or in the siege of Stalingrad, or were criminals in Russia before the war and had been co-opted into the army when Stalin was desperate for more cannon fodder. Well, these lovely gentlemen came into Berlin looking for fun. They'd been brutalised by the Nazis, and they weren't going to forgive. They roamed the streets, just looking for a woman. Any woman, no matter what age. Every single woman in Berlin was available to them, regardless of how old she was or whether she was pretty. The only ones spared were women with children, because these Russians still had some humanity or upbringing or fear of God to consider mothers to be sacrosanct; oh, and they never bothered women in trousers, which the Russkies didn't like. They thought they were like men.

'But every other poor bitch was fair game. I'd go so far as to say that with a few exceptions, every woman who ventured out on the streets of Berlin was raped repeatedly every day. Some women hired out their babies to neighbours for protection if they had to go somewhere. Others used their husbands' or fathers' wardrobes. They'd wear trousers and jackets and even shirts and ties to make themselves look like men, or even transvestites.

'But that only saved a few of them, because when you live in rubble, it's not easy to change your outfit. So most women would be walking through the streets of Berlin, and they'd hear the command, *'Woman,* come here.' Then they knew they were going to be raped, right there in the streets. Pack raped, sometimes by as many as a dozen men. And the Russians would walk off laughing, and these poor women would be forced to get up and stagger away; and then there'd be the shout, 'Woman, come here,' and they knew that they were going to be raped again. I've heard reports from independent and authoritative sources that some women were raped ninety times in a single day, and then raped again and again the following day and the day after.'

Broderick realised that he'd stopped eating.

'Nothing,' said Gerherty, 'absolutely nothing seemed to be able to stop the barbarity. Nothing, that is, until Marshal Zhukov suddenly decided, for no apparent reason, that enough was enough. And then just as suddenly as it had started, it stopped. You know Theo, it's been two years since that happened, and German women are still committing suicide every day because they can no longer live with the shame.

'Sure, the SS did hideous things. But is it fair to identify the Germans as the only monsters in this war? Is it fair to single out one insignificant cog like this guy you're defending in Nuremberg from the massive machine which went crazy, and say that the cog is as guilty for doing what it's forced to do, as is the crazy machine for what it produces? When are we going to say, *'Enough is enough?'*"

Gerherty and Broderick finished the remains of their meal in silence.

**Allied Occupied Germany
June, 1946**

From the memoirs of Joachim Gutman:

When it came, it came with unexpected suddenness. I had been sleeping in our special barracks, reserved only for the Sonderkommando.

Often we didn't even go back to our barracks, but instead knew that we could only get a couple of hours of sleep in between the batches of new arrivals earmarked to die, and so instead of going across the compound of Birkenau to our quarters, we pulled together some coats and dresses that the now-dead Jews had stripped off, and used them for mattresses and blankets.

Can you imagine sleeping in a charnel house? We didn't dream, for how could nightmares have been any more frightening than the daytime visions which we saw. But sleep we did, fitfully and restlessly, breathing in the smoky atmosphere and the stench of old clothes.

And yes, we worked hard, and we needed our sleep, or we'd have been beaten, and we'd have been the ones gassed and burnt. So we slept and in the morning we rose and stripped off the clothes from soon-to-be dead men and woman and children, and we forced them into the gas chambers and pushed their bodies into the ovens . . . and that was what we did to survive.

I was sleeping in the barracks when I heard my name being called. I didn't respond at first, because I didn't realise that the name belonged to me. It was so long since someone had referred to me as anything by 'you' or 'hey, Jew', or 'fucking Yid' that when the guard called out the name 'Joachim Gutman' it simply didn't register on my brain that he was talking about me.

Someone thumped me in the ribs. The man next to me, a Pole, was even more taciturn and uncommunicative than I had become. He almost never even looked at me . . . or at anybody. He just seemed to stare at the ground and perform his tasks. Never seemed to show any feelings, any emotions. I'd seen them like that before. They were the first to commit suicide.

I awoke with a start and listened to the guard. 'Gutman!' he shouted again. And then I remembered that it was my name and I realised he was talking about me.

When I'd been a student at school, if the teacher had called my name, 'Gutman!' I'd have been mortified. I knew I was in trouble and would stand reluctantly in order to follow him to the principal's office for punishment.

But this place wasn't school. And when you were about to be punished, they didn't call you by name. They simply took out a truncheon and beat you or clubbed you with the butts of their rifles. It was all so anonymous.

So I knew when I stood that this would be to my advantage. I struggled over the other still-sleeping forms and followed the guard out of our barracks. There was a motorcycle and sidecar waiting there, its exhaust making clouds in the freezing early-morning air. There was no point in asking where I was being taken, or complaining, or even being frightened. If I was going to my death, then I was travelling in style; if I was going to be tortured and bludgeoned, then I would be rested by the time I arrived. Either way, a feeling of peace overcame me.

I struggled into the sidecar and shifted my matchstick legs until they were comfortable. On top of the sidecar was a machine-gun, although it was obvious that it wasn't engaged. I suppose that given sufficient time, I could have reengaged it and killed a few Nazis; I could have gone out in a burst of glory. But to do that, I'd have had to have the enthusiasm, and anyway, I didn't have the strength to be a hero.

But despite my braggadocio, it was all fanciful. The moment the guard saw me fiddling with it, he would have brought his massive hand down on my skull and killed me. And now wasn't the time for me to die. I was travelling by motorcycle. And I was intensely curious about where I was being taken.

It's odd that, having been among the dead and the almost dead for three weeks now, the fear of death was no longer any part of my being. It had been expunged, eliminated, driven out by the demons which circled my head every waking moment of the day. Being a Sonderkommando, the only thing which I had to cling on to, the only thing which differentiated me from the dead who I threw into the furnaces, was my sanity. In the workplace of the damned, my death would have been the sanest result of my life. So as the guard and I rode off in his motorcycle towards the gates of Birkenau, and then out into Auschwitz, I knew that I was leaving death behind.

CHAPTER TEN

Allied Occupied Germany, 1946

From the memoirs of Joachim Gutman:

It was as though I was taking part in one of those Hollywood movies. As though this wasn't me, or my life, but I'd become part of a dream. Suddenly I wasn't part of the reality around me; suddenly neither death nor the darkness of the rooms where I burned corpses, nor the awful perpetual stench of the gas chambers, were any longer a part of my existence.

No, this was altogether a performance of my inner mind, a play put on by my imagination to make me happy just before I died. Even though I pinched myself and bit the inside of my cheek to anchor me in reality, my mind wouldn't accept that where I was, and what was happening, was my existence. Suddenly I was playing the part of an actor who's forgotten his lines and wanders through the set, trying to work out what's going on. Surreal is the only thing that I can call it. Suddenly my life was lived in one of the paintings which Hitler and Himmler said were the corruptions of the Western decadent mind . . . paintings by Degas and Renoir. I felt as though I was float-ing in a dream. As though the colours were muted and gentle, flimsy green and blue and yellow pastels; as though the landscape was that of gently flowing rivers whose banks were given cooling shade from the warm sun by the cascading leaves of willow trees.

I could smell again; smell the fragrant air of the countryside. I could see again, the sharp edges of buildings and the distant outlines of the poplar trees. I could taste again, the saltiness of the sweat of my lips, the erotic flavour of the turnip and beets in the soup I was given. It was as if a protective angel had come to earth, touched me with his finger, and transported me into the arms of God.

Where was I? Was the war at an end? Was I once again in the bosom of my loving family, and had the past six years been just been a nightmare from which I was slowly waking? Was I sleeping in my comfortable bed in my bedroom in my house in Berlin, having woken up in sweat and confusion from the middle of some hideous and terrifying psychotic episode?

No, it was none of these things. But I suddenly found myself away from the gas chambers and the ovens and the hell of Birkenau, and back in the safety, the protection, the ease of Auschwitz. Back where people were still living, where occasionally they still smiled, where there were still expressions on faces instead of the look of living death which we Sonderkommandos wore as part of our uniform.

I think back now and still cannot believe it. Sachsenhausen had been the worst place I'd every encountered when I was there; but it was a virtual paradise until I came to Auschwitz. Could there ever have been a hell more obscene, more painful, than Auschwitz? Could humankind in its most evil and bestial nightmare have invented a place more hideous than Auschwitz? Yet when I was released from being a Sonderkommando in Birkenau just three kilometres down the railway line, on returning to Auschwitz, it seemed like a heaven on earth. I could see its beauty, the freshness of the air, the cleanliness of the barracks, the delightful precision of the barbed wire fences which surrounded it. I actually walked around Auschwitz smiling. People thought I was crazy. How can one smile in Auschwitz? Well, when you've survived Birkenau, then yes, you can smile, even in Auschwitz.

I was working beyond the perimeter of the prison's fence, within the compound of the guards and the administration. I was now ensconced in the head office, pretending to be a highly qualified bookkeeper. I was doctoring the figures of what Auschwitz had been all about.

Instead of killing human beings, I was killing history. I was murdering truth.

So how had I escaped the landscape of death? How had I been chosen to become a clerk in the employ of the Greater German Government? How could I have been plucked from the maw of Hell and allowed to enter the gates to Paradise?

What happened was simply this. When I was chauffeur-driven in a motorcycle out of Birkenau, we roared down the road to Auschwitz. I remember the cold, clear air against my face. It felt glorious, erotic, elegant after the coke-laden noxious atmosphere of the ovens. When the motorcyclist guard circumnavigated the compound and drew up outside the steps of one of the blocks, I stepped cautiously out of the sidecar and found myself weaving giddily in front of the central administration building. I knew it was where the commandant and his assistants worked, because I'd been inside the administrative building of my former concentration camp at Sachsenhausen, and I knew the look and the feel of a place which administered the reality of genocide. Guards standing like sentries at the entryway; men in middle-ranking uniforms running up stairs clutching sheaves of papers; and occasionally a primly dressed woman secretary or typist who walked down a corridor, who looked at me with a sneer on her face as though I were sullying her environment.

Perhaps it was these women whom I found most amazing. I'd known such women who were the clerical workers for my father and his fellow judges in the days before the war, plump and officious *fraus* who organised the legal system; and here were their sisters, more plump *fraus* who administered the system of death and destruction. It didn't matter what their job . . . these women would have been as efficient and purposeful running a charity as running a killing machine.

To them, the nature of the place and what was done there was incidental, compared with the necessity to do the paperwork accurately, to make sure that everything was just so, and to ensure that the management could get on with its work.

But I digress. I'm getting to the end of my story, and I'm beginning to smell the seductions of freedom. So I shall continue where I left off.

The motorcycle guard had deposited me at the foot of the stairs which led up to the main entryway of the large administrative building, ordering me to climb the steps and ask the guard for the office of Hauptsturmführer Erich Frauenfeld.

Again, as happened to me in Sachsenhausen, I noticed how filthy I was. My prisoner pajamas were covered in the grime of death. There were blood and mucus and excrement stains all over me from where humanity had leaked its insides in the throes of dying. In Birkenau, I didn't notice any of it. It blended in with the filth of my environment. But here, amidst the clean uniforms and the sparkling walls and the shining floors, I quickly noticed myself. I felt ashamed. Again! When would I stop feeling guilty for what these monsters did to me?

Guards in the Administration Block seemed to know of my arrival. I mumbled, 'Hauptsturmführer Frauenfeld?' and they just pointed to a door along a corridor. What struck me most forcefully was that I was left on my own to wander down the corridor. For the past year of my concentration, I was guarded, pushed, shoved, threatened, never ever alone even for a second . . . always within the immediate control of an SS man or a slavemaster or a *Blockführer*. Yet suddenly I was at liberty, with no one by my side. Suddenly I was free to wander.

I knocked diffidently on the door. A command to enter was barked out. I opened the door, and sitting behind a large wooden desk, full of reports and papers and open books, was the man who dealt out work to the Auschwitz inmates, their slavemaster, the Mephistopheles of Auschwitz. It was Frauenfeld who often stood on a mobile dais—the back of a flatbed truck—and took morning parade, determining those who would work and in which of the many factories within and around

Auschwitz they would do their work. But he didn't simply give out work; he was also keeping his eyes on those who were so exhausted that even though they stood up straight, and tried to look as if capable of a twelve-hour day, were so exhausted that a light wind would fell them. These, he would order to remain where they were; these we wouldn't see again; these were the men and women sent to Birkenau.

Frauenfeld was a large, square-set man of middle age. He sat comfortably behind his desk, as though in his den at home, looking at me in curiosity as I struggled with the weight of the door. It was a very large desk, and his arms only reached halfway across; and the desk lamp was like something out of one of the fashionable shops on the main streets of Berlin, delicate and flimsy with a cord which you pulled to turn it on. It seemed ridiculous, so out of place in comparison with its surroundings. More on his desk . . . photographs of him in his shiny uniform with other uniformed men wearing heavy medals on their breasts. Yet none of a woman or children . . . only him in the various stages of his career.

I remember he was wearing half-moon glasses, staring at me in curiosity. He could have been my favourite uncle, except that he was dressed in the death-black uniform of an SS officer. And sitting opposite him, smiling at me in encouragement, was the Messiah. There, ensconced in a chair opposite Hauptsturmführer Frauenfeld was my saviour, Wilhelm Deutch.

'Stand in front of my desk,' the Hauptsturmführer ordered. I did as I was commanded. 'Herr Mechanical Engineer Deutch informs me that while you were working for him on the roof of the kitchen, you informed him that you were an expert in bookkeeping. That you were the chief accountant for a large Jewish firm of jewellers. Is that correct?'

I looked at Wilhelm Deutch. His face was impassive because the Hauptsturmführer was observing both of our reactions; but in his eyes, he was begging me to play along with the charade. I nodded. I remained wordless. Morally it was better than lying. Morals? Ha!

'What type of work did you do there?' asked the Hauptsturmführer.

I cleared my throat and tried to remember what the clerks in my father's old law practice used to do, though I was little more than a child when they used to do it. 'Sir, I used to keep the records of income and expenditure, of debits and credits, of stock and sales, of prices and international dealings.'

I began to warm to the deception as a wave of relief swept over Deutch's face. 'I occasionally had to visit stock markets in other countries and I also bought and sold precious stones and metals. Sometimes we had additional stocks which we'd bought at good prices and . . .'

'Enough!' he ordered. 'I don't want to know everything about your life. Come. Sit,' he said, standing and bringing over a chair. I felt my mouth drop in surprise. An SS officer being hospitable to me. Unheard of. But I sat.

'Gutman. I know from Herr Deutch that you're not a fool. You're a highly educated man. So it won't come as a surprise to you that Germany is doing badly in this damn war. The Russians are within smelling distance, and despite brave resistance by the Wehrmacht, we're being overwhelmed. We have plans for Auschwitz-Birkenau, but what I'm more concerned about is myself. I'm talking to you like this, Gutman, because Herr Deutch assures me that you can be trusted, and that I can be open with you; that you've learned the bitter realities of what happens to men who betray secrets.

'Be aware that what I am about to discuss with you must be known only amongst the three of us. Remember, Gutman, that I'm the one holding the gun.'

Quite suddenly I felt faint. It occurred to me that Deutch might have told the Hauptsturmführer about our secrets, about the meat and bread and margarine; but then I realised that the secrets he was talking about were those of the Hauptsturmführer and not mine. So I sat and listened.

'Do you understand what I'm saying, Gutman? I'm trying to save my life, and if you breathe one word of this conversation outside of this office, I'll blow your head off.'

I continued to stare mutely at him.

'Well!' he demanded.

I had no idea what he wanted me to say.

Softly, Wilhelm Deutch spoke for the first time. 'Joachim, the Hauptsturmführer wants your assurance that your work for him will remain absolutely secret and confidential. Being the commandant in charge of work rosters, he has the power to employ you in a private capacity, working for himself. He is commanding you to keep any activities you undertake here on his behalf strictly private and confidential, and that you tell no one on pain of death. Do you understand?'

Again, I remained silent. The changes were too rapid, too great.

'Is he a moron?' snapped the Hauptsturmführer, looking at the mechanic as though he'd introduced some contagious disease into the office. 'Why doesn't he answer?'

Wilhelm turned to the SS officer and said cautiously, 'The Hauptsturmführer is aware that Gutman has been working as a Sonderkommando in Birkenau. That's where I found him again. I think he's in shock. The sudden change, his removal from that place . . .'

The Hauptsturmführer stood and went over to the credenza in his office, where he poured me a cup of coffee. It came in a porcelain cup with a saucer. I'd not held such a thing in nearly four years. It felt so light, so delicate. And then the aroma of the coffee struck my senses, and my eyes opened wide. It was like being kissed by a young and pretty girl. With trembling hands, I sipped a bit of the coffee. It was bitter, far bitterer than I ever remembered. But it had taste. For years, I'd eaten starvation rations without any taste at all; vegetables in soup which had been so boiled that there was nothing but mush; bread which was so stale that you had to dip it in hot liquid for it to bend. Nothing I had tasted in years tasted good. But then I drank the coffee, and it felt as though my mouth and senses would explode. The coffee tasted like all the good things of a past and forgotten life, like a blessed memory of childhood. It seemed to fill my mouth with comfort, with hope, with a future.

I felt tears welling inside me; tears of joy and relief. Even if I died at this minute, even if the Hauptsturmführer took out his gun and killed me, this moment was worth living for. I had taste in my mouth again, the taste of real coffee. I quickly swallowed my sudden eruption of joy, and sipped at the coffee again. My mind seemed to explode open, clear and precise for the first time in years. In a controlled voice, though I'm sure my voice was trembling, I said, 'I understand precisely what the Herr Hauptsturmführer requires of me. He wishes me to do some book-work for him. It would be my pleasure. And I apologise for my diffidence, Herr Hauptsturmführer, but the shock of leaving Birkenau and suddenly finding myself . . . but then the Herr Mechanical Engineer Deutch has already explained that.'

I giggled like a girl. The two other men looked at each other and nodded. Deutch was the next to speak. 'Joachim, as you will appreciate, and as the Herr Hauptsturmführer has said, the Russians will be here shortly. Now, it's no secret that the commandant will destroy the buildings and level the site. He is planning to march the inmates back to Germany. But ultimately, the winners of this war will look at the events in Auschwitz over the past four years and try to blame certain people for what happened. It is no surprise to you, I'm sure, that some loyal Germans will be called to account. What the Herr Hauptsturmführer is concerned about is that many people will be blamed for certain events which happened in this war. His desire is that he is not one of those who will be called to account. After all, his job was only to allocate work rosters. He was nothing more than a functionary, a man obeying orders which came to him from high above, no matter how exalted his rank. All the Herr Hauptsturmführer was doing was following the instructions which originated in Berlin.'

I remember having to hide my look of incredulity. After all, I was in the middle of the spider's web, and only his desk separated his gun from my head. I was good at masking my emotions; and it was important he should think me a willing ally.

Deutch continued, 'I have no problems about my own behaviour. I was merely the mechanic, the fixer. But because the Herr Hauptsturmführer was in charge of labour details, of allocating men and women to the factories, and also, along with the medical staff, was a part of the selection process as to who could work and who should be sent straight to Birkenau, it's important to him that he has a set of figures which reflects that he wasn't to blame for the excesses of the command structure of this place. Is what I'm saying to you making sense?'

By now, I was beginning to recover. The coffee which had started to open my mind was now activating my brain properly for the first time since I'd been incarcerated. My spirits were slowly lifting. Life was coming back into my being. The past was suddenly put into perspective. It was still a nightmare, but one with which I would deal at the appropriate time! I felt a fury rising in my very being, a hatred of the Herr Hauptsturmführer and everyone like him. But that hatred would lead to my immediate extinction, and so it was vital for me to remain calm and act the part of the willing clerk in the madness of his life, as the man who would account for his salvation.

So for the time being, I quickly made a bargain with myself that what had happened to me in Sachsenhausen and Auschwitz and Birkenau was suddenly behind me and I would think about it in my own time . . . that I was now more in charge of myself than at any time since I'd been in Berlin.

Now, I had to think only of my future; now I was a part of the escape plans of the Third Reich. I felt like bursting out laughing. One minute, I'd been a voyager in hell, having spent the previous three weeks killing and burning tens of thousands of my fellow human beings; the next minute I was consulting to the architect of humankind's misery about how best he could escape his punishment and my retribution. And in my mouth was the sweetest taste I'd ever known, the taste of coffee.

'I understand precisely what the Hauptsturmführer requires to be done. Now specifically, what do you want me to do?'

But it wasn't quite that simple. Because something in my manner told the Hauptsturmführer to be wary. 'Why are you so willing to do this, Gutman? I'm a Nazi, you're a Jew. In a few weeks, if you're not killed, you stand a chance of being rescued by the Russians or the Americans.'

I could see a look of concern in Deutch's eyes. But I suddenly had the answer. Slowly, like a fox, I said to him, 'Sir. When the commandant blows up the gas chambers and the ovens and destroys Birkenau and Auschwitz, he's going to bury a thousand Jews. If I'm working hard to save your backside, I won't be one of those buried.'

I will never forget the look of incredulity on Deutch's face. He thought I'd gone too far. That I'd just signed my own death warrant, and possibly his. But it was a risk I had to take. He looked at Frauenfeld, eyes wide in fear. But the Hauptsturmführer burst out laughing, roaring his approval to the ceiling.

'Why can't all Jews be like this one? Then we wouldn't have had to kill them all.'

And we all laughed!

A wave of relief seemed to sweep over Frauenfeld's body. It seemed to relax. The Hauptsturmführer said, 'You'll be given a new set of books to construct. Naturally we'll destroy the real books. All the records will go up in smoke when the Russians are a couple of days away.

'By then, the camp will be largely empty, so there won't be much for the Russians to find. The crematoria and the burning pits will be covered over. We'll mask the truth. But an explanation needs to be constructed, and that's what you'll do for me.'

As an afterthought, he continued, 'Maybe there'll be some sick inmates who stay behind and who can't be disposed of before the Russians get here. Those who can't go on the commandant's march will probably be left behind. It's a shame we can't dispose of them and burn their bodies, but there simply isn't time to hide the evidence. They'll be the witnesses who will speak against us.

But without records, the stories these witnesses tell will never be believed. So I need my own records. I need to show that I was generous in my selections; that I was only following orders when I gave out work details to inmates. That I was never one of the selection party who sent people off to the gas chambers. I need records showing that I was just a clerk in an office, that I was a functionary. I expect to be tried as a war criminal. Certainly Churchill and Roosevelt have recently spoken about vengeance for our so-called atrocities. We've heard reports from our people in Switzerland that there's even talk of a tribunal being set up. But I expect to be given no more than a token sentence, compared to the real criminals, Hitler and Himmler and Göbbels. They will surely hang when the Americans and the Russians seek vengeance. Me? I'll probably serve a year or two in prison and then return to the bosom of my family.' He sipped another mouthful of coffee cup; so did I. It was like old work colleagues sharing reminiscences about how things are in business. Absurd!

I was rapidly gaining in confidence now. He was treating me like a human being. I had something which he desperately needed. I wasn't going to sell it easily.

'Why don't you just escape?' I asked, as though I were his best friend, discussing where to go on a Saturday night.

'Many of the lower ranks are taking the identity of dead inmates, and pretending to be Jews or Poles or Hungarians. These lower ranks consist of the guards and those who have assisted us like the Ukrainians and the Poles. I know that some officers have been scratching around the mountain of clothing and taking yellow stars off dead inmates' shirts. They intend to slip out when nobody's looking and blend into the crowds of refugees escaping the Russian advance. But these officers are stupid. They're not being realistic. They're too well fed. They'll stick out like sore thumbs. And frankly, any interrogator asking about something Jewish, and they'll hang themselves.

'I could try to do that, but those of us who were in the command structure are too well recognised. No. I have only two options. One is to escape to South Africa or South America where there are friends waiting to help us; I've decided against that, because the risks involved of crossing Europe to get to Trieste and then contacting the Brotherhood in order to catch a boat are massive; and I stand too great a chance of detection.

'So I have decided to clear my name, and surrender when the camp is taken. I intend to present myself to the Americans and the British as a decent German soldier who performed his allocated tasks in a humane and compassionate way, in line with the demands of the Geneva Convention. Even the Russians will accept that, if I tell them that I'm willing to take my punishment like an officer. So, in this way, the Russian High Command or the British and the Americans will have to respect me as a serving officer, and accord me my rights under the Articles of War as drawn up in the very Geneva Convention which I served so faithfully. As I said, I expect to serve a small amount of time in a military prison, as befits a man of my rank. There'll be no shame involved of my having been in prison when I return to normal life; it's not as if I will be a criminal. And then I'll get on with the life I led before I joined the SS; or maybe I'll try something different . . . use the skills I've gained in administration.' He looked up towards the ceiling, contemplating the excitement which life offered him once the war was over.

It occurred to me that Hitler had refused to sign the Geneva Convention, but I managed to hold my peace. He wasn't in a mood to listen to logic. And I wasn't interested in dealing with the truth, only my survival. Thanks to Wilhelm Deutch, my saviour yet again, I had been rescued from the jaws of the abyss and landed in the Elysian Fields.

'So, Herr Hauptsturmführer, you wish me to create a complete set of books which will record your having given out working duties, but also tended the sick, given old men and women time to recover, and . . . and what else?'

Hauptsturmführer Frauenfeld nodded. He bent down and opened the bottom drawer of his large desk. He extracted a big leather-covered book, about the size of a large bible, and handed it over to me. 'This is an unused record book. I will set you up in an office at the top of this building. I will give you four or five different pens, with different kinds of ink. You will begin in October 1942 when I was first posted here, and start to make out the records. I will also supply you with another book, not dissimilar to this, but which represents the true events of what happened here. You may copy this book into the new one, altering the record to distance me from the realities of what I was ordered to do. I've already worked out how you will do it, and I have written the following page as a pro-forma. You will use this,' he said, handing a page of paper over to me which he had just taken from underneath a large sheet of blotting paper on his desk, 'and you will make an accurate record of my innocence during the past three years.'

I took hold of the paper he'd given to me. It was a series of columns. In the first was a name; in the second an age; the third was the sex of the inmate; and in the fourth, words like *'fit for work, allocated to factory.'* Another said, *'unfit and recommended rest in sanitarium,'* or *'unfit for heavy working detail, so ordered to do light duties in kitchens'* or again, *'too old and frail for work, so ordered to assist gardeners.'*

I remembered that my father once had to sit in judgment on a certain matter, and came home complaining to my mother that the defendant had told a farrago of lies. I never understood the meaning of the word until reading the Hauptsturmführer's list.

'I will do whatever the Herr Hauptsturmführer demands. But,' I said with increasing confidence, because I was now a party to the conspiracy, 'what guarantees do I have that when I've finished the book, you won't dispose of me? I will be one of the few who knows the truth about you.'

The Hauptsturmführer smiled. 'You have no guarantees. But one thing I do guarantee. If you refuse, or don't do it immediately, or don't do it properly, I'll put a gun to your head and kill you.'

I looked at Wilhelm Deutch. He had turned quite pale.

And then the Hauptsturmführer relented, for he knew that he needed my assistance as much as I needed his protection. 'Put it this way, Gutman, when the Russians come and I hand over the books, I need you to verify that they're true. If you tell them that you falsified them, then you'll die as a conspirator, just as quickly as will I. So it's in both of our interests to remain in each other's good books, so to speak.'

He raised his head to the ceiling and burst out laughing. So did I. So did my saviour.

I began work immediately that morning. I was given the large, blank leather-bound book which the Hauptsturmführer had shown me earlier in his office to carry upstairs to the attic, as well four different kinds of ink and five different pens. I was also told to make my writing differ on each page, so that the book looked as though it had been written by different amanuenses.

When I was ensconced in my attic, looking out of the window and over the compound of Auschwitz camp where I had first been placed on being transferred from Sachsenhausen, I saw thousands of people. I could also again see the layout of the camp, something which I'd only ever properly understood when I was on the roof laying new pitch. I refreshed my memory of the layout, soon to be destroyed as the Russians came within view, if Hauptsturmführer Frauenfeld was to be believed. And with the loss of how many additional lives of how many faceless Jews?

There were dozens of long wooden barracks in a row, but what continued to amazed me was the barbed and electrified outer perimeter. Of course, I'd seen it many times before . . . Indeed, it was impossible to miss when you were on parade. And from the sentry posts, brilliant floodlights illuminated the compound at night as they swung from one barbed and electrified side of the compound to the centre and then back again.

But until that day on the roof, I'd only ever seen the barbed and electrified wire fences from the inside, as an inmate. Now, again, I was above it all, safe in an attic, far from the danger of the parade ground, from the nightmare of being an inmate.

What struck me was the orderliness of it all. The long, straight, deliberate row of barbed wire fencing, then electrified fencing, then barbed wire fencing again. It had been planned meticulously. As had the barracks. They were like gigantic rows of vegetables, planted in a garden by some Lord of the Universe.

I was standing, staring out of the high attic window at those below me in the camp compound, men and women who were walking and talking softly and slowly, when the door burst open.

Hauptsturmführer Frauenfeld stood there, looking frightening but somehow magnificent. I had this vision of a South American spider from deep in the Amazon jungle, dangerous but arresting. He snapped at me, 'This door will be locked from now on. I am the only one with a key. I've told those who might come up here that you're doing special work for me, and that you're not to be disturbed. You will speak to nobody. You will answer the door to nobody. I will come up here with food and water during the day. I will release you at night and send you back to the barracks. But remember that you are forbidden to say a word of what you're doing. If I find out you've told anybody, then not only will you die immediately, but I'll kill everybody else who knows. Now, during the day, you will copy out these . . .'

He said it so matter-of-factly that its full impact didn't hit me until long after he'd gone. He knew no evil, that man. For he was evil itself.

Hauptsturmführer Frauenfeld passed over two large leather-bound folders, the same as the one now on my desk; however, these had the look of books that had been written in. I opened one of them and studied the pages. The book had been completed during June of the year 1942. It recorded hundreds, possibly thousands of names of men, women, and children. I guessed that all of them were now dead, or on their way to death. And it was then that I realised the full impact of the disaster which had befallen the Jewish race.

'You will copy the names from these books, into this book,' he said pointing to my blank ledger which would soon be filled with his far-rago of lies—I was getting used to my father's phrase—which would be his passport to a short prison sentence, and then a normal rehabili-tated life. Perhaps he was even contemplating being thanked by the Allies for saving so many of the elderly and the infirm. Perhaps he was anticipating a humanitarian medal.

'Are there any questions?' he asked. I shook my head. 'Good. Now remember one thing, Gutman. You are here to save my life. Yours might be saved if you cooperate. I've selected you on the recommen-dation of the mechanic. But I owe neither him, nor you, anything. You are nothing to me. Dirt under my fingernails. I'll kill you without giv-ing it a moment's thought if you even for a solitary second give me the slightest concern. Out there,' he said, pointing in the direction of the Auschwitz inmates' camp, 'are ten thousand Jews and others who I can use for this task. Work hard, produce a month of facts and figures a day, and you'll live. Slacken off, even for one moment, and I'll kill you immediately.'

And with that, he turned and walked out of the room. I opened the book and began the work of transcription instantaneously.

'Walter Grossman. 44. Healthy. Work in factory.'
'Ita Grossman. 79. Frail. Gardening duties.'
'Hanelle Grossman. 40. Healthy. Work in factory.'
'Samuel Heinfarben. 22. Healthy. Construction duties.'
'Rosl Bender. 71. Frail, possibly sick. Sanitarium.'
'Nachum Goldfarben. 56. Crippled. Hospital.'

And so it went on for the next four hours. I managed to put down over eight hundred names in these first few hours of work. I was becoming skilled at using different hands, different pens, different inks. Even I would have found it hard to tell that this was just a far-rago . . . if you'll excuse me again using my father's expression.

By now I was becoming light-headed and lighthearted. I was starving, having had almost nothing since the previous night except for a cup of coffee. And then, when I was thinking of how I could communicate to the Herr Hauptsturmführer and get something to eat, I nearly jumped out of my skin, because outside the window, four stories up, was the beaming face of the mechanic.

He tapped on the window and mouthed the words, 'Open up.'

I did, and he climbed in, remarkably nimble for a man of his age.

'Well, I told you I'd save you, didn't I?' he said, as though he were a proud father boasting of an achievement to his favourite son. 'So, what do you think of these conditions, eh? Bit better than that hell-hole over there.' He nodded towards Birkenau three kilometres away. I looked and saw dark smoke pouring out of the central chimney. I thought to myself, *'Oh good, they've managed to get the ovens to work . . .'* and then I realised with a horrible shock, and with great anger, just what it was that I was saying.

'What a job. Eh, isn't this better than down there?' he said, nodding through the window at the scenes of horror in Auschwitz, scenes which were so familiar to us all. I remained silent. 'Well, aren't you going to say anything, Joachim?'

He was waiting for praise. But somehow, I felt no gratitude. Oh, I knew he'd saved my life. I knew if I'd stayed in Birkenau, that by today, or tomorrow, I'd have been stripped of my uniform by the guards, and pushed naked and uncomplaining into the gas chambers with another contingent. That's what they did when they saw that look of deadness in your eyes and you became useless to them as a Sonderkommando. Then your former colleagues and workmates, men you'd been working with only hours before, had to pull your dead body from the chambers and burn you. But even though I knew for certain what my fate would have been, somehow I couldn't feel gratitude towards him.

'What is it you want from me?' I asked.

The look on his face was one of surprise. 'What are you talking about? I want nothing. I'm trying to save your life.'

'Why?'

'Why? Because I'm your friend.' He began to get angry. 'Look, if you don't like what I've done for you, I can send you back to the ovens. Is that what you want? Or would you rather say, *'Thank you, Wilhelm'*, and realise how lucky you are.'

But I wouldn't give in. When you stare at death and then suddenly are given the freedom of your life, death no longer seems as frightening. 'Why are you doing all this for me? You're a German, I'm a Jew.'

'Because I like you. Because we worked together and enjoyed ourself. Because we tricked the Nazis and beat them at their own game. Don't you understand, I'm helping you because you're my friend. Why can't you understand that? I've helped many people during this war. People like you, Joachim. It just so happens that I'm helping you save your life when the war is coming to an end. Just luck, I guess.'

But he looked offended, as though I'd insulted him. In embarrassment, he continued, 'You're nothing special, you know. Over the years I've been working in these camps, I've helped many Jewish prisoners just like you to survive. I've shared food with them, helped them rest, helped them avoid punishment. I didn't have to, you know. I just did it because I knew that what we Germans were doing was wrong. I did my bit. The least you could do is to say 'thank you.''

And then I knew that deep down, he was a really good man. That he'd risked his life to help me. That, in true friendship, he wanted nothing from me, other than recognition of the fact that he'd risked his life to help me. Nothing. And suddenly, I felt so deeply ashamed. Ashamed of my treatment of him, of my lack of gratitude, of my selfishness in seeking ulterior motives. I walked across the small room and threw my arms around him, kissing him on both cheeks. He hugged me back. He was not a Nazi. He never would be, or could be. Well, maybe in his body because he was forced into it by what happened to his Germany. But Wilhelm Deutch could never in his mind be a Nazi. And under other circumstances, had life continued and Hitler hadn't arisen, he and I could have been good friends. He had saved my life. I wondered how many others he had saved by his kindnesses.

We separated and smiled at each other. 'There's only a couple of weeks to go before this damn thing ends. Then we'll be prisoners of the Russians or the Americans. I'll be in a stripped uniform, and you'll be free. Now there's a turn of events,' he said.

'Why will you be arrested? ' I asked.

'Because I'm part of Germany. And Germany will be on trial for what Hitler did. Hitler and the rest will be hanged for their crimes; but it's Germany which will suffer for ever more for creating places like Auschwitz.'

That was a year and a half ago. I never realised how perceptive the mechanic was until now.

**Palace of Justice
Nuremberg, Allied Occupied Germany
June, 1946**

'Yes, Professor Broderick.'

Theodore Broderick stood slowly. It was the mark of a man who was part of, but who would not be hurried by, the judicial process. It was his method of telling judge and onlookers that he, and he alone at this pivotal moment in the currency of the trial, was totally in charge. When he was on his feet, all eyes in the courtroom staring at his every movement, he straightened the volumes of notes resting on the advocates' table, and cleared his throat.

'Your Honour, I am about to begin the defense of my client, Wilhelm Deutch. I am about to call him to the witness stand. In many ways, this is an unusual act in itself, because the defense normally calls the accused person last, after it's called its own witnesses to prove the innocence of its client, and also to rebut the prosecution witnesses' evidence, and build a case for itself in the minds of the judge and jury. The arrival of the defendant is the *denouement*, the moment when the defense opens its arms to the courtroom and says, *'Here, ladies and gentlemen, is the answer you've all been waiting for.'*

'Unfortunately, Your Honour, I can only call Wilhelm Deutch, because I have no other witnesses.

'Your Honour will be aware that I moved for the truncation of Deutch's previous trial when he sat in this very dock, surrounded by men of the killing squads, the infamous *Einsatzgruppen*, accused of crimes against humanity. I was the defender of some of those men, Deutch included, and it was so very obvious to me that we were doing Deutch an injustice. For those other men, his co-accused, who had worked in the gas chambers and the death ovens of the concentration camps like Sobibor and Maidanek and Treblinka . . . and Auschwitz, where Deutch was posted, were active participants in the industri-alised process of mass murder. They were the guards who worked the Sonderkommandos, who supervised the genocide of a race, the burn-ing of the bodies, the tortures and the inhumanities. And these men, whom your brother judges found guilty and sentenced to be hanged, were part of the SS; they were killers without conscience; they were men who were profoundly and irredeemably evil.

'For Wilhelm Deutch to be in the same room as them, let alone the same dock, accused of the same crimes, was to me a travesty of the justice which is the very foundation of our civilisation. He was in the dock because witnesses testified that he was a mechanic who worked in the Birkenau death ovens, tweaking their dials and adjusting their performances. And so he was deemed guilty by association. But when the defense came to examine the true nature of the prosecution's case, it became obvious that he was being accused of complicity, of being in the same place as the crimes, but that there was no evidence that he had ever committed crimes against humanity.

'I demanded that he be allowed a separate trial. However, in the month and a half since that previous trial ended and those dastardly and irredeemable men have had justice brought down upon their heads, I have done everything in my power to find a witness who will speak on his behalf. Of course, Your Honour knows the extraordinary problems of finding anybody in particular in Germany, let alone a witness to my client's actions, even to this day, over a year after the end of hostilities. The Red Cross and dozens of other agencies are trying to deal with the greatest humanitarian and refugee crisis in the history of the world. Millions and millions of people are still adrift, trying to find sanctuary, trying to find family and relatives and friends.

'So finding anybody who will speak for Deutch was always a long shot. However, Deutch's trial has been broadcast widely, and yet nobody has come forward to speak on his behalf.'

The judge shifted uncomfortably. 'What are you trying to tell me, Dr. Broderick? That you can't carry on?'

'Not at all, Your Honour. What I'm trying to say is that I have only one witness . . . and that witness seems determined to hang himself.'

Shocked, the judge said, 'I beg your pardon?'

'Judge, I would have made application to treat my own client as a hostile witness, had there been leeway granted by the constitution of this Military Tribunal. He has failed to cooperate with the defense, he's failed to provide any evidence which I might be able to use on his behalf. He's merely railed against the unfairness of the prosecution's case as it applies to him, saying he didn't commit the crimes of which the witnesses have accused him, and yet when I ask for chapter and verse, all he'll say is that he's going to hang anyway, that there's no justice in this court, and so why bother.'

Judge Jonathan Parker looked at Deutch and waited for the interpreter to finish the translation so that the defendant could clearly understand what he was about to say. 'Mr. Deutch, do you really believe that you are here for rough justice? That I've already decided to hang you?'

Several moments later, Deutch finished listening to the voice in his earphones, stood, and said, 'Yes.'

'Are you aware of the numbers of men that I and my fellow judges have acquitted at these trials, because on evidence, we couldn't find the case of crimes against the peace or crimes against humanity proven to our satisfaction?'

Deutch nodded.

'Yet you still believe that my task is not to judge you fairly, but instead that I'm going to sentence you to hang?'

Deutch simply shrugged his shoulders, annoying the judge

'This might be a ploy by you, Mr. Deutch, to convince me that you want another attorney; or that I should mitigate in your favour. You might think that you can waste this court's precious time and patience. But it's not going to work. You have the privilege of one of America's very finest advocates defending you. If you chose not to cooperate with him, that's your decision. Dr. Broderick, I will take into account that you have difficulties in defending your client, and I will not hold it against him that nobody has come forward to speak on his behalf. But now, I would like you, please, to continue with your defense.'

'Your Honour, might I deal with my client as a hostile witness?'

'Professor Broderick, you may deal with your client in any manner you see fit. Continue.'

He had been examining his witness for only a few moments before the change became noticeable. But the difference in the way Deutch slowly opened out, like a flower welcoming the morning sun, was visible only to Broderick. Indeed, it was clever, subtle, and perhaps designed to make the American lawyer look a fool in front of his peers. For the time being, Broderick decided to go along with whatever it was that Deutch was doing.

'And for what reason did you join the Nazi Party in 1936?'

'Because everybody did. It was patriotic, nationalistic. I was a good German. Married, three children. I was urged to join by my colleagues in I. G. Farben. Had I not joined, I would have been thought less of. Today it seems sinister, but ten years ago, with the economy booming and Hitler as our Messiah come to Earth, it was the right thing to do. The only thing to do.'

'Weren't you concerned about the statements which Adolf Hitler and Joseph Göbbels were making in regard to the Jews? The obscene libels, the threats to their safety? Did you have no regard for the activities of the SA and the SS towards the Jewish people, the beatings, the humiliations, the depiction of Jews and Slavs and Gipsies as subhumans in those vile propaganda sheets, Der Angriff and Der Stürmer?'

Deutch thought for a moment. 'Honestly, I didn't let it affect me back then. I thought it was just the politicians talking to get votes.'

He looked across to where the judge was sitting. 'You see, we'd been through hell and back with hyperinflation, with people eating from soup kitchens in the streets, with Wall Street crashing and American banks calling in massive loans which we couldn't repay, and our German industrial companies laying off millions of workers. In 1914, my parents could buy a bottle of milk for a mark. In 1923, that same bottle of milk cost them 726 billion marks. So what about their meagre savings in the bank? What about their future, their security? They'd just been through the Great Patriotic War. Now, after they'd lost two sons and brothers and uncles in the trenches, instead of facing a life of serenity, they were facing a lifetime of hardship. After the war, they were totally ruined, with not enough money to buy bread. Is it any wonder that they looked around for someone to blame?

'So when Adolf Hitler said, *Why should we suffer because of what's going on in other parts of the world? Why should we be victims? It's not our fault, it's the Jews'* to me, and to the rest of Germany, it all made perfectly good sense. Sure, I didn't like the fact that he was blaming Jews. I worked with Jews in I. G. Farben. We had Jewish neighbours. My kids played with Jewish kids. But Adolf was our leader, and he convinced us that our problems were caused by Jews.' Deutch shrugged. 'I was only a mechanic. He was the Reichführer. Who was I to argue? I assumed that he knew. Anyway, I trusted him.'

Broderick adjusted the sheaf of notes, playing for time. He'd begun his examination as though Deutch was a prosecution witness, but the German had been cooperative and positively effusive with the openness of his answers to the lawyer's questions. He was playing a game, but Broderick wasn't sure which one.

It was time to deal with how he came to be in Auschwitz. And what it was that he did there.

CHAPTER ELEVEN

Berlin, Germany, 1998

FOR TWO DAYS, CHASCA Broderick and Gottfried Deutch had worked the phones. She'd asked for, and managed to have installed, a separate phone in her hotel suite, so that Gottfried could make his phone calls from one room, while she hit the phones in another. They phoned the Simon Wiesenthal Centre in Vienna and Los Angeles, the Centre for the Justice for Victims of the Holocaust in Munich, the Red Cross in Switzerland and dozens and dozens of other centres which had rescued European Jewry or assisted in the retribution of justice against Nazi criminals at the end of the war.

Each conversation they began invariably started with them saying, '*Yes, I know it's an awfully long time ago . . . yes, I'm sure your records are all archived . . . yes, of course I'm willing to come in to your offices . . .*' but they became skillful in extracting maximum value out of each phone call so that they easily eliminated those which they knew would be useless.

They took regular breaks from their work, leaving the suite and enjoying each other's company in the coffee shop attached to the hotel, or in one of the numerous restaurants which abounded in the Unter den Linden, Berlin's most famous street and the one so hated by the out-of-towner Adolf Hitler, that he deliberately ordered the cutting down all of the Linden trees to widen the road for parades, earning him the eternal enmity of pre-war Berliners.

In the beginning of their intense working relationship, Chasca had been curious about Gottfried and had asked him many personal questions. No matter how closely they worked together, she couldn't find anything about him which was attractive. He was . . . she hated herself for thinking it . . . so ordinary.

He'd answered her questions courteously, without magnifying his standing to appear as something which he simply wasn't. Gottfried was a high-school drop-out and worked for the Berlin Postal service in the job of keeping records of new developments and upgrading the city's delivery network. When he told her about his life, living at home, working for the post office, Chasca tried to sound enthusiastic, telling him that it must be interesting; he smiled and said, '*Yes, fascinating . . .*'

He'd taken a week's holiday without pay in order to trace his grandfather's records, and from the number of dead ends they'd encountered, it looked as though that unpaid week was money down the drain. Chasca had offered to make up the money he'd lost from her own bank account, for it was money she could easily afford, but Gottfried refused outright, saying it was his duty to his mother to try to exonerate his grandfather.

Over lunch they discussed what to do with the paucity of information they'd been able to scrape together, none of which illuminated any real facts about the elusive Joachim Gutman or further details about Wilhelm Deutch's role, except for his having been hanged as a war criminal.

'It's not unusual that there's no trace of Gutman,' said Gottfried. 'Most of the Jews who survived the war left Europe and went as far away as possible. Thousands and thousands to South America, North America, Canada, Australia, even New Zealand. They just wanted to be as far from the concentration camps as a ship or a plane would take them. And when they got there, they changed their names to blend in and began a new life. Perhaps we're wrong to be searching in Europe . . . maybe we should approach the Australian Embassy or America or somewhere.'

Chasca finished her green salad while she listened to him. He was a good and decent man, she now knew, even if he was mundane; yes, decent, despite his earlier flirtation with the rump of German fascism. How easy it was to get caught up in something so utterly evil when you have nothing to fall back on, and when you think that these people are speaking on your behalf. And he'd been of enormous help in assisting her in her efforts to trace the elusive Gutman. It would have been so easy for him to take the testament at face value and leave it at that. But he'd decided to search beyond the words, and try to find out more about his grandfather through the eyes of someone whom he'd helped.

Yes, she thought, Gottfried was right. Finding him was more difficult than finding a needle in the proverbial haystack. Joachim Gutman must have been one of the millions of European refugees who wandered the crater-ridden roads and byways of Europe immediately after the war, pushing their entire lives in front of them in their pathetic wheelbarrows or children's prams, not so much going anywhere, as getting far away from . . .

She dabbed the French dressing from the corners of her mouth, and said, 'Well, we've done the best we can. A week isn't a long while, but my gut reaction is that if he was going to be found, we would have found some trace of him by now.'

And then he stunned her. 'Would you like to come to my home tonight and meet my mother? I've discussed what we're doing, and she said that she'd like to read the testament of this man Gutman.'

Chasca smiled at him and reached over to hold his hand. 'Yes, I'd love to,' she replied.

'Good. Then maybe we can fill her in with the missing details about precisely what it was that my grandfather did in the camps. All her life, she's lived with the fact that her own father was a monster . . . but Gutman's testament shows quite the opposite. And maybe we can pick up some of my grandfather's life from when the war ended and before he was hanged.'

Palace of Justice
Nuremberg, Allied Occupied Germany
June, 1946

'What did your work involve,' asked Professor Broderick.

'I was a mechanic. When I worked for I. G. Farben, I was in maintenance. I took a number of courses in hydraulics at the Berlin Polytechnik, and assisted the Chief Engineer in the siting of hydraulic systems for the factories. It was when the Chief Engineer, Herr Dr. Martin Schur, was called up and was seconded and began to work for the war effort in 1938 that I was appointed Chief Mechanic, and was responsible for all the hydraulic and mechanical work of the factory.'

'And when were you posted to Auschwitz?'

'Posted? I wasn't posted! You post people in the armed forces. I was a civilian. A request was made to the management of I. G. Farben to send someone to Poland where urgent and skilled maintenance work needed to be done. I was selected and went there in 1943.'

'Why weren't you drafted into the army? A man of your skills would, I'd have thought, been essential to the war effort.'

'On the contrary, sir. I suffer quite badly from asthma, and so was rejected in the 1941 call-up. And furthermore, the work I was doing for the I. G. Farben group of factories was considered essential to the war effort.'

'Tell me about Auschwitz. What was your most vivid impression when you first arrived?' asked the lawyer.

Deutch thought for a moment and nodded to himself, deep in thought, as though oblivious of the presence of prosecutors and judges and armed American guards. 'The filth. The desolation. The complete absence of anything human.'

His answer surprised Broderick. 'Could you elaborate, Mr. Deutch?'

'Everything seemed so mechanical. People were walking around like robots, dressed in striped prison clothes. I remember arriving at the end of October, and it was bitterly cold. There was a vicious wind blowing from the northeast. Even though I was wearing jumpers and a thick overcoat when I stepped out of the lorry with the SS men, the wind went right through me. I shivered inside. Yet on the other side of the barbed wire, I could see hundreds of prisoners in these thin striped pyjamas and these ridiculous striped caps, just walking around slowly, mechanically. Some of them were wearing yellow stars. I knew these were the Jews. Some were wearing triangles of other colours, with the letters on them signifying their country of origin; or their crime against the fatherland. The crime of being a homosexual, or of being a Jehovah's Witness, or something else which didn't happen to please the Führer.

'Even the guards were mechanical. They shoved and shouted and bullied, but there seemed to be no life in their eyes, as though by dealing with death every day, they had somehow become a part of it.'

The lawyer interrupted, 'Did you know it was a death camp before you went there?'

'Of course I knew. Everyone in Germany knew. You can't keep genocide, the killing of millions and millions of people, a secret. Oh, they tried. They said that the Jews were being resettled, they were being shifted to the east, and an entire nation was being created which would have armed borders so that the Jews couldn't get out and infect the rest of Europe. But we knew.'

'And did you object to being sent there? Did you object and fight against the decision to second you when you knew Auschwitz was being used to kill people?'

He took a sip of water and adjusted his headphones, using the time the translator took to help him think through his answers. 'What would have been the point of objecting, Dr. Broderick? I would have been shot, and another mechanic would have been pressed into the work.'

257

'Tell me what you did at Auschwitz . . . and at Sachsenhausen when you were sent there to find the fault and repair the machinery.'

'Just that. I repaired machinery. Kitchen equipment, roofs, leaking drains, and at times I even managed to practice my specialty, hydraulics . . . whatever needed doing, I did.'

'And while you were repairing this machinery, did you use slave labour?'

'Yes.'

'Did you abuse that slave labour?'

'No. Quite the contrary.'

'But we've heard from people who were employed directly by you that you were harsh and brutal and beat them. We've also heard testimony from one witness . . .' He glanced down at his notes. 'Marinus Flockmann, that he was in the factory where you were working when one of the slaves appointed to you caused you some minor irritation. According to Mr. Flockmann, he answered you back, or failed to do something immediately enough for your satisfaction. Mr. Flockmann swore on oath that when this happened to his bunkmate, you complained to a guard. You said that this slave you had been given was, according to his, Flockmann's, testimony, accused by you of being lazy. That man was beaten to death right at your feet by the SS guard. Mr. Flockmann says that you showed no reaction. You had the body removed, and you continued with your work, demanding out loud that another slave be brought immediately. We've also heard evidence that you have personally killed men by dropping heavy tools on their heads just because they caused some minor infraction which displeased you. Would you comment on that, please?'

'Would you believe anything I said in my defense?' Deutch said quietly.

The judge looked at him harshly. 'Just answer counsel's question. Please don't ask questions yourself.'

Deutch thought for a moment. 'The short answer is no. As to the murders, I never committed them. Dropping tools on men's heads? I'm not capable of that level of brutality. I couldn't and didn't do it. I'm sure the witnesses thought I did it, but I swear before God that they have me confused with some other man. Understand, sir, that there were many repair men, many mechanics, many slaves over many years. How could the witness identify me with certainty?

'As to the other events, well, I'm sure that the event of causing that labourer's death actually happened in front of Mr. Flockmann, but it wasn't done by me. As I've told you, there were many supervisors of slave labour in the factories and the concentration camp. I'm sure he thought it was me, but it was another man. Maybe another mechanic or guard or supervisor. Look, there was unbelievable brutality and cruelty in those days. Hitler had a pool of a hundred million slaves from the East. Why should the SS care if they worked a man or a woman to death? There were a hundred million more to replace them. Why feed them, when they were expendable?

'But I could never do that to another human being. I swear before God that Flockmann and the others who have testified against me in the past few days are mistaken. Genuine in their belief, but mistaken. The things they said were not done by me.'

He took a sip of water, looking around the court. 'I never, ever treated any of the prisoners who were given to me badly. I gave them food, comfort. I eased their suffering as best as I could. Of course, I was severely constrained in how much I could assist these poor wretches. After all, the SS guards with their attack dogs were looking at everything that was going on. They knew how hard a slave should be working. And if a slave wasn't working hard enough under my direction, then I would be blamed and punished by the commandant. But all in all, I believe I can honestly say that I treated people well. Under very difficult circumstances.'

Broderick also glanced up, but not around the court. He looked surreptitiously at the judge to see if the impassioned plea was believed, but the judge's face masked his feelings. So he continued, 'I want to come on now to your work in Birkenau. The reason why you were originally arraigned and put on trial with the men from the Einsatzgruppen. Is it true that you worked on the death chambers and the ovens?'

'Yes. I was ordered to.'

'And could you have objected?'

'Yes, but you must remember that it was late in 1944. September, I think. The ovens in Auschwitz II, Birkenau, were closed down shortly thereafter. The SS were instructed to burn as much as the evidence as was possible. All stops were pulled out to dispose of the Jews before the Russians advanced too far to hide and bury their crimes. By the end of November, it was deemed too late to burn or hide the evidence, and some of the ovens were ordered to be destroyed. Auschwitz was liberated by the Russians on January 27, 1945.

'But in the weeks leading up to the evacuation, there was madness in the camp. Utter chaos. Everyone was desperate to cover his tracks. And that meant, as I've said, getting the ovens to work properly. They kept on breaking down. They were needed to dispose of bodies. In desperation, nearing the end of the year, I can't remember when, but it could have been in late October or November, the SS seconded me to do the work and ensure that they were efficient.'

Professor Broderick was reading his notes as his witness was giving evidence. But when Deutch gave such calculating information about the mass destruction of human beings, even when the war was lost, the American suddenly forgot who and where he was and snapped, 'How could you have agreed even to set foot in such a hellhole when you must have known it was all over? Surely, for God's sake, something deep within you must have revolted and prevented you from walking on the same earth as that charnel house. If there was an ounce of decency, of humanity, in you, surely something inside you would have screamed out that you couldn't do it.'

The judge looked at Broderick in astonishment. Such an emotional question from a defense lawyer? He assumed that Broderick was trying to rile his witness as some sort of defense trick. But it didn't work because Deutch was impassive in his answer.

'Either I obeyed, or I would have been shot. Either I lived and worked in hell, or I would have been killed and sent to hell. So would my wife and daughter. As the war came to an end, the SS became increasingly insane in their actions. They were taking retribution on the families of deserters, shooting them on footpaths, or hanging them from lampposts or arresting them and murdering them in SS headquarters. We all knew what those madmen were doing. We were told it by the Wehrmacht, who were terrified of them . . . possibly more terrified of the SS than of the Russians and the Americans. So what choice was there for me, Professor Broderick? What choice for other ordinary Germans caught up in this nightmare?'

He waited for an answer. Deutch looked around the silent courtroom.

'Well, Professor? What choice did I have?' he asked quietly.

Allied Occupied Germany, June, 1946

From the memoirs of Joachim Gutman:

'Of course, it's easy to determine precisely when a war has ended when you have the certainty and perspective of history. We can look back and say with confidence, *'It ended at such and such a time, on such and such a day as a result of such and such an event.'*

But when you're in the middle of it, when you're a foot soldier on a battlefield, and a commander calls out, *'Cease firing'*, you're waiting hours, sometimes days, for information. *'Is it really the end? What do we do now? Can we go home?'*

In Auschwitz, we knew the end was coming, but we didn't know when. Or where. Or how. Or whether we'd be left alive in the frenzy of the Germans. Frenzy? Oh yes. In those last days, the normally efficient and precise Germans were visibly going to pieces. Screaming, shouting, barking, pushing, shoving . . . not against us; not because we were Jews or anything; but because they were in a terrible panic. They had to cover up their crimes. They had to destroy any evidence which might lead the Russians to suspect what the buildings at Auschwitz . . . and worse, Birkenau . . . were really used for.

Of course, if the guards and the administration were in a panic as the Allied planes filled the sky like huge cockroaches, or the wind blew from the East and carried with it the sound of cannon fire, then we inmates were in a state of euphoria. Our emotions were almost insuppressible. Sure, we knew that we were likely to die at any moment. We weren't stupid. We knew that we were witnesses to horrible crimes which the Nazis had committed. But we couldn't suppress our thrill at what was happening.

There was exultation in the barracks every night. Whispered conversations underneath blankets, guesses, debates . . . but along with the joy came hideous insecurity. Many of us felt not the excitement of winning a competition, or the bubbling ferment of children about to go on holiday, but a fear of the unknown.

For those of us who truly knew the minds of the Nazis, our excitement was much more realistic. *'Will they shoot us all before the Russians arrive? They'll have to bury the evidence . . . does that include us? Where will they take us? Who's heard of this forced march back to Germany? Can you walk that far without dying?'*

Because of my work for Hauptsturmführer Frauenfeld, I had a vague idea of what was going to happen. I'd been his amanuensis now for three days, and he seemed delighted with my work. He'd even confessed to me what the Commandant of Auschwitz was preparing to do. But he'd sworn me to secrecy, and I had no qualms about keeping his information a secret. What, after all, did I owe these other Jews? If I played my cards right, I could avoid being shot, or locked in a building which the SS were going to blow to smithereens, or being force-marched back to Germany. The Hauptsturmführer told me that he needed a witness, a Jewish prisoner witness, somebody who had worked with him over a period of years and seen the humanitarian side of his nature. He told me it was important for him to be able to prove to the Russians that he hadn't participated in the brutality of what the other SS men had done. And because he brought me good food and coffee and treated me kindly, there was no reason why he shouldn't choose me as his witness.

While he stood over me with a gun to my head, it was in my interest to nod and tell him that I'd be delighted to act as the Hauptsturmführer's referee. That, should there be a trial, I'd happily stand as a witness on his behalf. I don't think he believed me, but it suited us both to live the fiction.

And in the meantime, the frenetic activity of the headquarters where I turned up for work every morning became more and more chaotic. As I've said, the whole scene was so unusual for the Germans. Normally, they had things ordered down to the last detail. They were always so precise. Now, while they were running down corridors instead of walking; while they were burning records in braziers out in the open; while they were screaming orders at one another as well as at us, I simply sat in splendid isolation from all the mayhem in my comfortable attic room, hastily concocting lies in a book which I knew, in the end, would count for nothing. Ah well, it was all my part in the war effort!

I saw the mechanic many times during each day. He was now working without supervision. Nobody was interested in repairs any more, nor in how well things worked, nor even in keeping things going. If things fell apart, there were far more important things to worry about than fixing them. So he spent his days up on the roof of the administration building doing this and doing that, while far below him, the world devolved into chaos.

But he often used to swing on his hoist down from the gables and on to the sill of my window, tapping on the pane for me to open up. In some ways, his increasingly regular visits were dangerous for me, not because I didn't enjoy his company, but because he was holding me up. Increasingly, the Hauptsturmführer would come upstairs to the attic at unpredictable times in order to check on how my work was progressing.

It was during these two weeks of working on the ledger that I really got to know the mechanic. For the first time, he opened up to me, telling me about why he entered the Nazi party, why he stood on the pavements and cheered as the bully boys marched past, why he went to the rallies and stood on his seat at the end of Hitler's speeches, arms upraised, screaming out '*Sieg Heil*' at the top of his voice. For some reason, he seemed more relaxed as the war was ending than he'd ever been while I knew him.

In Sachsenhausen, he was guarded and diffident; in Auschwitz he was cautious and somewhat secretive; in Birkenau, he was a co-conspirator in setting me free, but because of the circumstances, I wasn't able to notice his mood. But now, chatting amiably to me in my eyrie, talking to me about his background and his family, he didn't seem to be nearly as nervous as the other Germans were of the spectre of the Russians, who were now approaching rapidly, if the rumours we heard were true.

'Of course I'm not frightened. Oh, sure, I might be killed in some battle. Civilians are always killed in battle. But we've all been living with death for the past six years. I'd be upset not seeing my wife and daughter after all this time being separated, but I've become very fatalistic since the war started, and I suppose I'm ready to accept my fate.'

'But your work here? Aren't you worried?' I said.

He seemed genuinely surprised. 'Worried about what?'

'You were part of a concentration camp. The Russians and the Americans are going to be looking for those Germans who were guilty of horrible crimes. Aren't you worried that you'll be swept up by what happens when the war finally ends? The Allies won't just pack up and go home, you know. There'll be hell to pay. Germany's going to be in real trouble when Hitler surrenders.'

'Why should I be worried, Joachim? I'm a mechanic. All I did was fix machinery. I did nothing like what the SS did. I'm not even a soldier. I never even held a gun. No! The British and the Americans and the Russians aren't interested in mechanics or plumbers or factory workers. They're interested in Hitler and Göbbels and Göring and Himmler. It's them who should be shitting themselves right now, wondering how the hell to escape or what to tell the enemy.'

'Do you think they'll live to be prosecuted?' I asked. 'In the barracks, there are wild rumours about how Germany is now in a stranglehold, how the Americans and the Russians are fighting to reach Berlin first.'

He was amazed. Horrified! 'How do you hear all these rumours? You're prisoners, for God's sake. Where do you get this information?'

I remember smiling. I could trust this man now. We were friends. He continued to bring me food and drink. So I told him. 'We have a radio. One of the men stole it from the factory a year ago. For some reason, nobody missed it, and then they must have forgotten about it. One of the inmates was a radio mechanic before the war, and he's been able somehow to tune it so that we can pick up the radio frequencies that the Allies use. At night, we lie under the blankets and listen to American Armed Forces Radio and this new programme called Voice of America, and sometimes we listen to the British Forces Overseas programmes from the BBC and we hear about how the German army is in total disarray, and how the Allies are making giant strides across Europe. Those who speak English and Russian translate it for us.'

Wilhelm nodded. He hadn't heard such news. He didn't know that the Allies had breached the borders of Germany. He told me that he harboured the vague hope that the Wehrmacht would pull back behind the 1939 borders, and the Allies would then be satisfied and pack up and go home. That somehow we could hand back Poland and Czechoslovakia and France and all the other countries we'd conquered, and retreat to where it all began. He had no idea that his homeland was being occupied and destroyed.

His manner suddenly became still, as though a part of him had been silenced. Softly he said, 'Last month, I sent my wife and daughter

Christmas cards. It's now the beginning of January. I've tried to get through by phone, but the commandant won't allow us to make personal phone calls. He says that the telephone lines are urgently needed for communications with the Front. Every day, I've been waiting and waiting for some word of my family. Now you tell me that . . .'

I stood and walked over to him. He'd helped me so much. Now I was perhaps able to help him. 'You mustn't worry,' I said. 'The Allies aren't like the SS. They'll never harm civilians.' He looked at me and attempted a smile. 'And that goes for you too,' I told him. 'You won't be in trouble when the war ends. You're only a mechanic. I will tell the Allies what a good man you are. I will be your witness.'

I knew the war was coming to an end when the air started to smell differently. The chimneys of Birkenau had not been pouring out grey and black smoke for some time. Not for a month or more. It took me some time to realise it, but it meant that they weren't burning Jews anymore. That must be a good . . . or a bad . . . sign. For while they were burning Jews, I might still live; now there's a sublime irony; when they stopped burning Jews, they might blow up and level the camp and bury all the Jews inside. Then use bulldozers to cover all of the human evidence with soil, and pretend to the Russians that it was only a hill and there were nothing underneath. How many future generations of Poles would run and play and scamper over the hill of Auschwitz without realising the misery buried beneath their feet? And would they care if they did know?

But the other way in which the air smelled different was with the acrid odour of cordite. I could almost smell the vapour of a bullet or a shell in the air. And when the wind was in the right direction, I could swear that far in the distance, I could hear a distant rumble, like a train on railway tracks, still kilometres away from the station, but getting nearer and nearer.

It wasn't only the smells, of course, which told me that my war would be finished within a week or so. I also noticed that there were fewer and fewer guards. During the night, increasing numbers of our brave and valiant SS slave masters took off their vaunted uniforms which had once sent cold ice through my veins, and stole the trousers and jackets and shirts and shoes from the mountains collected from dead Jews which were contained in the storerooms. Then these fearless SS men, these heroes who once terrified us with their truncheons and rifles and killed anyone they didn't like, found a time when the guard was changing and security was lax, and walked unnoticed out of the gates, leaving their identities and crimes far behind.

Of course, as soon as the commandant realised what was going on, he caught two of the SS defectors, put them on public trial, and had them shot in the open, in public, as deserters. You would have thought that would have resulted in a howl of pleasure and revenge from the Jewish inmates on the other side of the barbed wire. But no. All they did was look and then wander away.

I, myself, was shocked to the core. Oh, I'd seen death often enough. More death than any human being should have been allowed to see in a thousand lifetimes. But what stayed in my mind was the sight of the expressions on the Germans' faces. They were SS men. They were brutal and evil. No question about that. But there was a look of complete surprise as their colleagues raised their rifles and, on command of the officer, shot and killed them. It was a look which said, *'How can you, Germans and colleagues, possibly kill us? What have we done wrong?'*

Was that the expression which the Jews wore when we Sonderkommandos were forcing them to undress before gassing them? I can't remember. My eyes now are blind to all the memories of those gas chambers. One day it will return, but not now. I can still recall events, things which happened. Yes, these I can see in my mind's eye. But I can't for the life of me remember faces. There were whole seas of faces of old and young people, children, babies . . . dark-skinned people, and fair skinned; people with scars and beards and blue eyes and brown eyes. Attractive people, elegant people, terrified people. But I can't remember their faces, God help me.

But I do clearly remember the events which ended my stay at Auschwitz. And I remember feeling such a sense of self-righteousness at the fear in the faces of the staff of that damned place. They were terrified of the Russian advance, of the loss of the war, of being found out, and also of their commandant. But despite the vigour with which the Commandant of Auschwitz tried to keep his men's minds on their jobs, and insist upon their continuing loyalty to the crumbling Reich, the decision to evacuate the camp was put into effect. Every able-bodied Jewish man and woman . . . *able-bodied? Now there's a thought which would put a smile on your face, if only you could have seen what they looked like* . . . was to be force-marched back to Germany. Think about that, for a minute. From Auschwitz to Berlin. From the South of Poland they had to cross the Sudeten Mountains into Czechoslovakia, then north to Germany. What? Five hundred kilometres? In the cold dead of winter. When they were starving and diseased and desperately exhausted. Reports I've read since the war ended say that from all the camps and the ghettos, seven hundred thousand Jews were force-marched out of the east and away from the oncoming Russian Army. And before those poor bastards had finished, a third had died on the way, from starvation, exhaustion, and, most of all, a desire to die.

Me? Oh, I was safe in my attic, with my two good German friends. One was there to save his skin, using me as an accomplice. The other . . . well, he was a genuine friend.

Hauptsturmführer Frauenfeld was spending more and more time with me. And I played right into his hands, his willing accomplice. Because I knew with complete confidence that if he suspected for one moment that I might double-cross him, he'd have put a bullet into my head. He continued to bring me up coffee and sandwiches for my lunch. He told me what was going on outside.

He said to me, 'So, Gutman, not much longer before you're a free man. Today, they're emptying the camp of all prisoners who can walk and are well enough to go back to Germany. Those who are too ill will be kept here. As for me, I'll stay and wait for the Russians. No point in my leaving. I'm too well known. An hour down the road, and I'll be turned in. So I've decided to do the honourable thing, and stay and explain to the Russians precisely what my part was in this camp, and what the others did. And frankly, Gutman, it'll be good to have this war over and done with, eh? Oh, I expect they'll put me into some Allied prison for a couple of months and then I'll return to Germany and resume my life. You know, with my experience running this place, I could get a career in administration. Somewhere with a large staff. Maybe allocating work for a large German company. Maybe they'd even be a place for you, you know, Gutman. I've seen the way you've been working these last weeks. Don't think I'm not impressed. I could do you a good turn when this madness is over . . .'

I smiled and rapidly changed the subject. Why should I participate in his insanity? Anyway, I wanted to know more about him so that when the Russians arrived, I would be in a good position to tell them what this madman had been up to.

'Tell me about your war, Herr Hauptsturmführer,' I asked. 'Why did you sign up for the SS?'

He looked at me strangely, but there was an innocence in my eyes, an innocent look which I'd learned to cultivate since I'd been in his service. This look had saved my life, prevented him from suspecting my real motives, and stopped his inclination to distrust and disbelieve me and put a bullet in my head. It now encouraged him to open up. There was nothing else for him to do. He wasn't busy. The work he'd been so skilled in doing, the allocation of tasks to the inmates, selecting who would do which slave labour, who would die immediately in the gas ovens, who would work till they died, that was over now. There was no more work to be done. There was nobody left for him to allocate to slave labour jobs. No factories, no tasks left in the camp . . . nothing.

It was bizarre. While his commandant was going crazy blowing up the gas chambers and the killing rooms and destroying the evidence of the morgues and the dissection rooms and laboratories used by

Mengele and the other German doctors for their fiendish experiments on living human beings; whilst his commandant was busily blowing up the fuel storerooms and the elevators which took the Jewish carcasses up to the ovens and the triple muffle furnaces built by Topf and Sons, and the retorts ... while all this was going on, I was taking genteel coffee and chatting about the old days with one of his senior officers who was actively planning his surrender to the Russians and his subsequent post-war career. A man who knew he would be turned in by some, torn to pieces by others; whose salvation lay in convincing the Russian victors that he'd been some sort of camp hero. Amazing things happen in wartime!

He ignored the sounds of hysteria wafting in through the attic window, and answered my question. 'I was unemployed in 1930. Destitute. Thrown out of work with the Wall Street crash and the inflation. I worked in a factory making chocolates. I was talked of as being an up and coming young process worker, and the floor manager mentioned that if I keep up my work patterns, I might become a foreman. But then the Jews tried to take over the finances of the world by causing Wall Street to crash, and suddenly the factory closed down and my life became very difficult.

'I remember wandering the streets and noticing the other young men who were unemployed. We met together, but we were always cold and hungry. Then Ernst Röhm started to put together an army of civilians. He fed us, clothed us, sheltered us, and gave us purpose. He trained us, inspired us, led us, told us who our enemies were, and he made us feel good about being Germans. That was the SA. We grew to the biggest civilian army in the history of the world. Six million men. We were invincible. But when Röhm insisted that the SA take over many of the duties of the Army, that was the end. Hitler was terrified that Röhm would equal him in stature. The last thing the Führer wanted was an equal and opposite power source.

'So in 1934, Hitler had Röhm murdered, and the SA was amalgamated into the SS. We couldn't believe it. We in the SA were six million tough young men. The SS numbered about a hundred thousand. You'd think that with our beloved leader Röhm shot like a dog, we would have risen up and taken over the government in our anger. But no. Somehow, the genius of Hitler made us realise that he was our leader, not Röhm. And that's how I became an SS officer.'

I looked at him, wondering whether to ask the next question. I had my life to lose, but for once, an SS man had more to lose than me. 'Tell me, Hauptsturmführer, why do you hate Jews?'

He looked at me strangely. And then it was as though he suddenly remembered something. He stood, said menacingly, 'Never forget, Gutman, that even though we might lose this war, we will have lost because the nation has been stabbed in the back, once again, by the Jews; and at least for the next couple of weeks, I'm holding a gun,' and stormed out of the room.

I knew I had made a serious error of judgment. I'd overstepped the mark. I'd risked my life for an arrogant question. I was suddenly terrified. It wasn't until my real friend, Wilhelm Deutch, entered the room through the door . . . yes, there was hardly anyone around in the administration centre any more, so nothing prevented Wilhelm from walking around the building and using the door . . . that my mind was put at ease.

I told him what I'd said to Hauptsturmführer Frauenfeld. I waited for the mechanic's anger at my indiscretion, my impulsiveness. But he shrugged, smiled, and said, 'Good for you. About time those Nazi bastards were told a thing or two. Anyway, I've just been into his office, and he congratulated me on introducing you to him. He says you've done marvellously. You've almost completed two whole books, and they're full of evidence to prove he saved Jews' lives. He's really pleased.'

I remember feeling an intense moment of relief. I appreciated the irony of being so close to freedom, and yet to being shot and killed just as victory was mine. I remembered the stories about the young men killed on the battlefields of the Great Patriotic War, just minutes before the final ceasefire. How their families must have grieved for their special misfortune.

'I've come here to say good-bye,' Wilhelm said to me. I shook my head in incomprehension.

'I have to return to Germany immediately, or I might be captured by the Russians and sent to Siberia,' he said. 'Your Hauptsturmführer is living in cuckoo land if he thinks that these damn books are going to save him from the executioner's noose. He'll hang, along with all the other Nazi concentration camp commanders. And many of the SS guards. But I don't for one minute think that I or anyone can talk sense to the Russians. I know them. They're madmen. And Stalin's the worst of them all. So I'm afraid that this is the last time I'll be seeing you. I can't be captured, or they'll definitely send me to Siberia.'

'Siberia? Why would they send you there?' I asked him.

'That's what they're doing, it seems. Whenever they capture a brigade of our boys, they send them behind the enemy lines, and they're not heard of again.'

I panicked. I couldn't lose him. He was my saviour. I had to try to save him. 'Look,' I said, 'put on a dead prisoner's uniform. Take his identity. I'll swear you're a Jew, that you were a prisoner. That we were bunkmates in the barracks. I'll tell them you were taken prisoner with me. You'll be fine in my protection. I promise you.'

At first, he looked at me like a father looks at his favourite child. But then the corners of his eyes wrinkled in that familiar smile of his. 'Dear boy. How could I possibly pass for a Jew?' He thumped his stomach. 'Do I look starved like those poor bastards on the other side of the fence? And I haven't been circumcised. I still have all my equipment, though God knows I haven't used it in months.'

He shook his head. 'No, I have to escape. I must go to Berlin right now and try to find my wife and daughter. The Reich can't protect them anymore, and so I have to. Today is January 17. The talk is that the Russians will be here within two weeks. Maybe even ten days. Our defense is crumbling.'

'Take me with you,' I pleaded. 'I don't want you to leave me here. You've saved my life on so many occasions. You fed me, gave me rest. You saved me from the gas chambers. You can't just go!'

I thought I could see tears in his eyes. 'If I take you, you'll be shot by the SS, or by the Wehrmacht; or maybe by the Allies for associating with me. I'm filth now, in the eyes of the world. But you're not. You're going to be a hero of the world. You're a Jew, and you've survived what the Third Reich tried to do to you. I'm a German. From now on, I have to avoid being shot. We have to separate. Go our own ways. We'll meet up again, my dear friend. Of that you can be sure. The mechanic will never be far from your thoughts.'

He walked across the small room and threw his arms around me. There was more of me to hug this time. The bread and coffee had stopped me from losing weight.

Without another word, he disappeared from the room. From my life. Will I ever see him again? He was a good man. Not a great man, but a good and decent man. In the midst of a sea of misery and evil, he was an island of calm and goodness. He never told me how many other lives he had managed to save. Many, perhaps? Or a few? But the one thing of which I am absolutely certain is that had it not been for the bravery and kindness of Wilhelm Deutch, the mechanic of Auschwitz, I, Joachim Gutman, would not be writing my memoirs. I would be one of the millions and millions of nameless, forgotten Jews, who are now the dust of Europe.

CHAPTER TWELVE

Palace of Justice
Nuremberg, Allied Occupied Germany
June, 1946

No one, not prosecution, not defense, not Wilhelm Deutch, not the occasional citizen who wandered into the public gallery, no one had any idea of the judgment that Justice Jonathan Parker was about to deliver.

The prosecution had presented their case over six searing days of testimony; the defense, devoid of witnesses, called only the man accused of crimes to offer any sort of rebuttal, any defense to the allegations of the witnesses. The defense had made great play of the fact that the real criminals of the Nazi era had either been tried and found guilty, tried and acquitted, or had managed to escape to freedom through an SS organisation of old boys known as ODESSA, along what were now being called the Rat Lines. These men, Mengele among them, were probably in South America or South Africa, a whole world away from their crimes.

And the judge had listened carefully to what the prosecution and the defense had to say. During the summations of both prosecution and defense, Jonathan Parker had taken notes of various points which William Sherman and Theodore Broderick had made. He seemed to be taking more notes in Broderick's submission, which the American considered a good sign. The judge especially paid attention when Broderick spent much time explaining that human behaviour was neither absolute nor consistent, and must be viewed for judgment within the context of when the action happened, and not in retrospect; that while allowing for the amorality of the Nazis, ordinary Germans like his client were living in a different environment from any which they'd previously known, and hence must not be judged too harshly by the standards which apply in humane societies.

The judge occasionally nodded and interrupted, asking a question which often related to some ethical issue. Matters of individual as opposed to collective responsibility; matters concerning the nature of the guilt of the individual in a society where the rule of law no longer applied; matters concerning the nature of good and evil.

Broderick had answered them as though he was in a master's degree seminar with his graduate students. He quoted the great Greek philosophers, the Bible, the words of ethicists from ages past . . . even the Constitution of the United States as a model of human rights. Best of all, he expounded at length from Jean-Jacques Rousseau's *Social Contract* about the responsibility of a society to its members.

But at the end of the trial, it was anyone's guess. William Sherman for the prosecution had concerns, because even though the witnesses had given compelling evidence of direct involvement in men's deaths, only a few had identified Deutch directly with brutality and inhuman punishments. He'd have liked a couple more witnesses, but they were so hard to come by. Oh, there were thousands of witnesses to the hideousness of the Nazis, but few people could be found who had been in direct contact with the accused. He was, after all, such a small fish in such a big and malevolent pond. However, as a prosecutor, he put on the mask of confidence to colleagues and the defense that what he'd presented was enough of a case to convince the judge.

Professor Broderick thought that the defense needed a greater amount of the weight of corroboration. Hopefully, with only a comparative handful of witnesses pointing a finger directly at his client and saying they'd seen him being inhuman and a murderer, the judge might err on the side of caution. So many witnesses were sick and frail at the time of the incidents. Their minds might not have been all there. Or they might have come to court intent on wreaking revenge against an innocent, anyone with a German name who had been in the concentration camps. Certainly, Broderick was confident enough to think that on balance of probabilities, Deutch might get off . . . or at worst, the judge might bring down a finding of guilty with a sentence which would be more of a slap on the wrist, a couple of years in prison.

The judge, on the other hand, had looked at the impassive face of the prisoner Wilhelm Deutch and determined, with the lack of witnesses willing or able to come forward and speak on his behalf, that his crimes not only were proven, but that, as world attention focussed itself elsewhere, some strong and potent statement had to be made that crimes like these, crimes committed by ordinary Germans against humanity, crimes committed in concert with a government which was out of control, these crimes must not go unpunished.

He had listened carefully to Professor Broderick. He enjoyed listening to the Bostonian's elegant mind clarify issues of great moment. But these discussions belonged in tutorial rooms in universities, or in gracefully furnished eighteenth-century salons. What he, as judge, had to do was deal with men and women who had acted in a way never previously seen in the long history of humanity. Ordinary Germans and Ukrainians and Poles and Latvians, who had turned their ancient and evil prejudices against Jews into murderous and uncontrollable rage. He as judge had to determine whether a man like Deutch was capable of continuing to live in society; and whether society should continue to be exposed to one such as him; one who at a whim ordered the brutal death of a pitiful man; one who delighted in torture, in slavery, in being the master of his universe.

Judge Jonathan Parker entered the courtroom in his most formal suit and gown. He sat. He looked at the counsel for the defense, and then the counsel for the prosecution. He had dined with them, played tennis with them, laughed with them. Both were elegant, intelligent, cultured men. Neither seemed to have been overly diminished by their cohabitation with evil. So for them, just as much as for the world's newspapers, just as much for the defendant, Wilhelm Deutch, he would remind everyone of what precisely they were in Nuremberg to do. As he sat down, a Solomon come to judgment, so did the court.

'The defendant will rise,' the Clerk of the Court ordered. The military guard had remained standing, but either in ignorance or confusion, Deutch had sat down at the same time as counsel. Deutch immediately stood as the two guards reached over and assisted him to stand.

'It is my duty to deliver a verdict in the case of Accession Number: AX-00452-C1947; the trial of Wilhelm Augustus Deutch conducted under the auspices of the International Military Tribunal. But before I do, I think it apposite to remind the court of why, precisely, the International Military Tribunal was established in August 1945 by the governments of the citizens of Britain, France, America, and the Soviet Union, meeting in London. These allied powers signed the agreement which created these courts at Nuremberg, and which set ground rules for the trial.

'I can put it no better than the closing summation used by the distinguished Chief Prosecutor, Robert Jackson, who said,

> 'The war crimes and the crimes against humanity of the Nazi criminals here today cannot be said to have been unplanned, isolated, or spontaneous offences. Aside from our undeniable evidence of their plotting, it is sufficient to ask whether six million people could be separated from the population of several nations on the basis of their blood and birth, could be destroyed and their bodies disposed of, except that the operation fitted into the general scheme of government. Could the enslavement of five millions of labourers, their impressment into service, their transportation to

Germany, their allocation to work where they would be most use-ful, their maintenance, if slow starvation can be called mainte-nance, and their guarding have been accomplished if it did not fit into the common plan? Could hundreds of concentration camps located throughout Germany, built to accommodate hundreds of thousands of victims, and each requiring labour and materials for construction, manpower to operate and supervise, and close gearing into the economy, could such efforts have been expended under German autocracy if they had not suited the plan? Has the Teutonic passion for organisation suddenly become famous for its toleration of nonconforming activity? Each part of the plan fitted into every other. The slave-labour program meshed with the needs of industry and agriculture, and these in turn synchronised with the military machine. The elaborate propaganda apparatus geared with the program to dominate the people and incite them to a war their sons would have to fight. The armament industries were fed by the concentration camps. The concentration camps were fed by the Gestapo. The Gestapo was fed by the spy system of the Nazi Party. Nothing was permitted under the Nazi iron rule that was not in accordance with the program. Everything of consequence that took place in this regimented society was but a manifestation of a premeditated and unfolding purpose to secure the Nazi State a place in the sun by casting all others into darkness.'

The judge took off his reading glasses and looked at the defendant. 'Wilhelm Deutch. You have claimed all along that you were a cog in the machinery of the State of Germany. You have claimed that you were acting under orders. Your counsel, Professor Broderick, has been at pains to explain, in the absence of witnesses to support your claims that you'd helped slaves and inmates survive the Nazi death merchants, that you weren't the monster to which nine people have testified under oath. Yet despite widespread public interest in this trial, not one single human being has come forward to speak on your behalf. I will give you the benefit of the doubt, and not invest too much capital in the fact that no one has come forward to speak for you. I will ignore that as a mark against your character. But the evidence of the witnesses arrayed against you cannot be ignored.

'Were it but one or two or three people only who claimed you had been brutal, violent, murderous, and evil in your treatment of slave labour, then I would have erred on the side of caution. Were it but a handful who said that you'd worked in the hideous charnel house of Auschwitz II, Birkenau, fixing the gas chambers and the death ovens so that the Nazi crimes could continue unabated, then I would have given you the benefit of the doubt. But you sought neither to rebut the evidence of your work as a mechanic in Birkenau, nor did you seek to excuse yourself. You said that you had to do it because you were ordered to. You said that if not you, then another would have done it. And you and perhaps your wife and young daughter in Germany would have suffered certain death as a result of your refusal.

'But I find it impossible to believe you, Mr. Deutch. Indeed, I would go so far as to say that your entire testimony was a patchwork of lies, distortions, and self-serving fantasy. You were more than a mechanic, a cog in the awful machinery of death. You, and all the mechanics like you, did more than just fix broken equipment. You, and all the other noncombatant Germans who cooperated and assisted Adolf Hitler's Third Reich, played an active role in the industrialisation and mechanization of a process designed to kill off an entire race of people.

'You were one of the gears that drove the machine of death forward; you were the oil which made it work. Had you and millions of others refused to participate in the Nazi machine, had stopped it going forward to run like a train out of control, crushing all before it, then, Mr. Deutch, there would have been no war. Tens of millions of men, women, and children would still be alive today. Entire Jewish communities in Poland, Hungary, Russia, the Ukraine, Czechoslovakia,

Rumania, Latvia, Estonia, and countless other places would still be flourishing today. A thousand years of culture, of learning, of history, would still be alive, celebrating its past, flourishing in the present, and investing itself in its own future, had you and millions like you refused to do as you were told. Mohandas Gandhi in India is currently giving the world a lesson in humility and peaceful non-cooperation. It's a pity, Deutch, that you and those like you, aren't learning the lessons of that simple and great man.

'It was because of ordinary and inconsequential men like you, Wilhelm Deutch, that the *Einsatzgruppen*, the specialised Nazi killing squads, had the machinery, the power, the ability, and the resources to do their hideous work. It was because of men like you that Nazism was able to flourish, that Hitler had so many willing hands to do his evil work!'

Justice Jonathan Parker realised that he was close to shouting in his disgust at the man who stood in the dock before him. The judge cleared his throat and pronounced the words which everyone now knew with absolute certainty were about to be delivered.

'Wilhelm Augustus Deutch. By the power vested in me by the International Military Tribunal, I hereby sentence you to be hanged by the neck until you are dead. The sentence will be carried out at a time to be determined by the Control Council and Military Government of Germany.'

The judge stood. The court stood. The judge started to leave the court-room. Everyone turned and looked at him, but Wilhelm didn't notice their reaction. He was holding the earphones close to his ears, listening intently, still waiting for the words of the translator to reveal his fate.

'I'm deeply sorry,' Theodore Broderick said.

Wilhelm shrugged. 'I knew it. You knew it. In these last few days of my life, I feel I've been privileged to have known you. You're a good man, Theodore. I may call you Theodore, may I?'

Broderick sat at the desk. The guard was outside the cell door. They were no longer entitled to use the interview room, as the case had just been tried and concluded. Now he and his client, with the translator, had to meet in Deutch's cell.

'What will you do now? Go back to your wife and children in America?'

'No. I intend to apply for clemency. Unfortunately because of the way in which the rules of the London Charter have been set down establishing the International Military Tribunal, there's no right to appeal and no court to which you can appeal. So in the past, defendants have asked the Control Council of Germany—the Allied occupation government—to reduce or change their sentences. Most of those who were found guilty did seek clemency from the Control Council. That's what I intend to do tomorrow.'

'And what happened to their appeals?'

'They weren't successful,' he said softly. 'But it's an avenue which might produce results in our case. You see, the judge's sentence can be questioned, not on the basis of the evidence, but because of the points I've been making in terms of collective guilt . . .'

'I don't want you to appeal.'

Broderick fell silent.

'Instead, I want you to make me a promise.' Deutch looked at his reaction when the translation had finished. It was impassive. 'I don't want to be remembered by the world as a war criminal; as one like Hitler and Göring and Himmler. I'm a mechanic, not a mass murderer.'

'What do you want me to promise?' Broderick asked.

'Firstly, promise that you'll do everything in your power to keep this promise. I assure you, it will harm nobody. It isn't breaking the law, or any code of judicial conduct. But I want you to promise that you'll try your very hardest to obey my last request of you.'

Broderick was inclined to deny the request without knowing what it was. But the statement was made in such earnestness that the American bent his head and whispered softly, 'I promise to do whatever I can.'

The German nodded. 'Good!' He stood and went to the small wooden foot locker underneath his bed. He slid it out, opened it, and took out a sheaf of handwritten papers.

Berlin, Germany, 1998

Gottfried's mother took the sheaf of photocopies. The original, the handwritten records of Joachim Gutman's life in the concentration camps of Nazi Germany, were in the records of Yad VaShem in Jerusalem where they would be examined by historians for any insight they might give into the greatest crime of the entire history of humanity. And she'd left them there also because of a promise that the Director of Yad VaShem had given to Chasca that he would look sympathetically to making some sort of addendum to the literature of the Nuremberg Trials to the effect that recent evidence showed that Wilhelm Deutch, hanged for war crimes, had not been as bad a person as was originally believed.

Gottfried's mother was a slight woman, frail with age although only in her midsixties, and had obviously made an attempt to look neat and attractive for her important American visitor.

'This is the document?' Annelise asked her son Gottfried. He nodded. 'This is the testament of the Jewish survivor?' She looked upon it as though it was holy writ, a sacrament from a godly place.

Again, he nodded. Chasca smiled in anticipation of the joy that the testament would bring to a prematurely aged woman, whose entire life had been clouded by the grave miscarriage of justice.

Annelise took the sheaf of papers and fondled them as though she were holding a new granddaughter. Her face beamed a smile. 'May God Almighty bless this man for telling the truth about my father,' she said and clutched them to her bosom. Tears were welling up in her eyes, but she felt no embarrassment. Indeed, she turned to Chasca, and said, 'And you, young lady, who have worked so hard to find the truth about a man you never knew, your rewards will come in heaven.'

Chasca reached out and touched Annelise's cheek. The German lady turned and carried the document lovingly over to the table so that she could sit down and read the words which, despite the half century, would clarify before her eyes the image she, as a young girl, had of her father's true and genuine nature, a father she had only known up to the age of seven before a rope broke his neck, and before the nightmares began.

But as she sat and began to read the writing on the front page, then as she turned over to several more pages inside, a frown seemed to crease her brow. She looked up at her son, then at Chasca. She adjusted the pair of reading glasses she had put on and turned several more of the handwritten pages. She reached down and opened her handbag, taking out her purse. Within her purse, she extracted a photograph of her father, Wilhelm Deutch, and turned it round to study the writing on the back. Annelise looked from the handwritten testament of the Jew Gutman, to the words on the back of the photograph, words which Wilhelm Deutch had written to his young daughter Annelise, when she and her distraught mother had visited him just a few days before he'd taken that final walk down the steel corridor of the prison to be hanged for crimes against humanity . . .

After she'd compared the handwriting of the Jew to that of her father, she looked up at Chasca, and said softly, 'I don't understand.'

Prisoners' Cells beneath the Palace of Justice
Nuremberg, Allied Occupied Germany
June, 1946

Lovingly, Wilhelm Deutch carried the sheaf of handwritten papers over to where Broderick was standing and placed it on the table. 'I want you to get this published. After I'm dead, I want you to take it to reputable publishers and beg, even pay for them, to publish my memoirs. This is how I want the world to remember me.'

Broderick glanced down at the sheaf. He knew enough German to translate the title.

The Memoirs of Joachim Gutman.
  A Jew in Germany during the Time
  Of Adolf Hitler.
  A Story of Concentration and
  Death Camps.
  And how a single good German saved my life

'I don't understand,' he said. 'Who is this Joachim Gutman?'

'This,' said Deutch softly, 'is the way I want the world to know me. There's truth in here. Truth which hasn't yet been told. You ask who is this Gutman fellow. He's my mouthpiece, if you like. He's the person who should have given evidence on my behalf . . . if he was a real person. There's so much distortion, so many lies about what we ordinary Germans did during the war. Today, it's fashionable to hate us because we're on the losing side, but in half a century or more, people will look back on this war and see it very differently. They'll see what we Nazis were really trying to do. To purify our continent, to rid our bloodstream of the rubbish which is clogging up our arteries. The Jews and the Poles and the rest of those races. And when the hatred subsides, then people will write the truth about what happened here. They'll write about why we had to build the camps and what really happened in them.'

Broderick looked at him in astonishment, and Deutch continued, 'Okay, so right now we're monsters, but in the future, we'll be looked upon as a peoples' army of loyal Germans who were fighting for our country. This,' said Deutch, pointing triumphantly to the sheaf of papers, 'this will redress the balance a bit. Show the world we aren't all lunatics and killers.'

Broderick continued to stare at him, remaining silent as the magnitude of Deutch's deception began to sink in.

'Okay,' said the German, 'so there is no Gutman. But only you and I know this. Millions of Jews have been killed. What's one amongst millions? They'll never be able to trace somebody called Gutman. And in fifty years time, who will give a damn? Germany has to come out of this nightmare with some pride, doesn't it?

'This was written by me during the trial with great care and attention to detail. When I'm hanged, it will act as my memorial. It's how I wish to be remembered. It's the way Germany must be remembered. And you, Theodore, must remember your own promise to get this book published, so that I'll be remembered properly and respected by future generations.'

And he pushed the papers across the table into the open hands of Theodore Broderick.

END NOTE

DURING HIS TRIAL IN Israel for his involvement in the Holocaust and his crimes against the Jewish People, Adolf Eichmann wrote a long and detailed exposition of his side of events concerning his involvement with the Nazi Party during the Second World War.

After he was hanged, the Israeli Government made the decision that they would keep the diary secret from the public as its veracity was impossible to determine. Only a handful of bona fide historians and Holocaust scholars were ever allowed access to it. But the main reason it was kept secret was because of the fear of the Israeli Government that, like *Mein Kampf*, the diary of Eichmann, one of the architects of the Holocaust, would be used as a bible by neo-Nazis.

It was only released into the public domain when the Government of Israel decided to give it to the Defense Counsel acting on behalf of Professor Deborah Lipstadt of Emory University in Atlanta, Georgia, and author of the book *Denying the Holocaust*. Lipstadt was defending a libel action brought against her by David Irving, a notorious Holocaust revisionist. The trial was held in the High Court of Justice, Queens Bench Division in London, and for weeks the veracity of the Holocaust was again questioned, Irving claiming that it never happened. The judge, Mr. Justice Grey, found Irving to be a liar and a pro-Nazi polemicist rather than an honest historian, and that he had deliberately falsified facts in his own research.